ONE IRIDESCENT NIGHT

A CINDERELLA RETELLING

THE IRIDESCENT SERIES

BOOK ONE

BRIANNE WIK

ONE IRIDESCENT NIGHT
A Cinderella Retelling

Copyright © 2021 by Brianne Wik.

ISBN: 978-1-955430-01-2 (Ebook)
ISBN: 978-1-955430-00-5 (Paperback)

Editor: Cassidy Clarke - www.cassidyclarkewriting.com
Cover Design: Art by Karri - www.artbykarri.com

To be kept up to date about new releases,
please visit www.BrianneWik.com and sign up for her newsletter.

First Edition: June 2021

Printed in the United States of America

AUTHOR'S NOTE

This book contains scenes of domestic abuse and PTSD. I have done my best to handle these elements sensitively, but if these issues could be considered triggering for you, please take note. This book is recommended for ages 16+.

To my Mom.

May we never stop dreaming.

CHAPTER 1

Evelyn

I knocked as quietly as possible.

Secretly, I hoped he wouldn't answer, but it still needed to be done.

Gathering up my courage, I managed to project my voice just enough to scrape out the word, "Father?"

On the other side of the door, I heard an exasperated sigh and the shuffling of papers. Then his deep, displeased voice reverberated through the wooden fibers: "Open the door, Evelyn."

Even through the door, his muffled voice had the power to make my bones wilt.

Carefully opening the door, I tried to soften the creaking of old hinges scraping against one another, but the slow movement only seemed to aggravate them further.

Father sat at his large wooden desk, facing the door. Morning light poured through the window, brightening the right side of his face and making the normally invisible dust in the air glimmer.

"What do you want?" Father grumbled. He didn't even look up from his ledger.

I hated this room. I hated that it always smelled of stale alcohol and musty paper. I hated the scant bookshelves lining the wall and the slowly rotting chair that faced his desk. I hated the wooden floorboards that I had too often seen up close. I hated the dingy pale yellow walls that reminded me of Mother. She had wanted to make it the brightest and most welcoming room in the whole house. I hated the mess and dust that proved, without a doubt, Father had given up on that a long time ago.

Stay calm. This is a legitimate request. He'll understand.

. . . he won't.

I opened the door a little wider. "I'm headed into town, and—"

Don't stutter. Say your words plainly. Speak with confidence. Father's past words echoed in my head.

"—I'd like to ask for some new fabric, please."

My eyes darted down, taking in my dirty threadbare dress as I rubbed my forefinger and thumb over the worn brown cloth. Father still hadn't looked up.

"My dress is worn through and starting to tatter. Would you—" I nervously cleared my throat and then spoke as quickly as possible. "*May* I have a little extra money to take to the market today? I only need a few yards of fabric to make a new dress."

Still no response.

"I will sew the dress myself," I rambled on, my nerves getting the best of me. "No need for a seamstress. But I do believe it's about time that this old one is replaced." I chanced a peek to see if he was paying attention, waving a hand down my rotting dress as though putting it on display. "Wouldn't you agree?"

My hands twitched, and I clenched my fingers tightly to still them. I had a bad habit of picking at my nails when I was nervous, which was just about always, so they often got peeled too close to the quick, which made my nail beds bleed and ache.

Today's anxiety was my own fault. I had chosen to come here today, I had chosen to ask Father for new fabric, I had chosen to risk it. But every time I saw him, some part of me hoped today would be different. That he would somehow wake up and see me again. That someday he would come back to me.

He shifted his weight in the chair, and the energy in the room plummeted, like a cold snap stealing away the warmth of the sun. My heart started pounding, dampness gathering in my palms. Father's dark eyes lifted to focus on mine, and a few strands of his deep brown, greying hair swept in front of his wrinkled eyes. But he didn't reach up to fix them; instead, he wore a blank, apathetic expression. My stomach dropped low, a lump of fear forming in my throat.

I knew what was coming. I always knew.

He leaned back and steepled his fingers in front of his face. "You came in here to ask me for *more* money?" His voice was quiet, calculated, tense. "Do you know what I'm working on right now, Evelyn?"

I shook my head.

His eyes narrowed, and my heart dropped to my toes. "I'm working on the financial books."

He leaned forward again and looked back down at his ledger. He picked up his feathered quill, dipped it in the ink pot next to him, and slowly crossed out a few lines on the page in front of him. One. At. A. Time.

This was the hardest part. The waiting. The anticipation. I picked unconsciously at my nail beds until I felt the quick give way, and a rush of moisture flowed under my fingertips. Almost reveling in the self-inflicted sting, I quickly pinched my fingers together to staunch the blood flow, waiting for Father to speak again.

He exhaled a long, agitated huff of air through his nose. "I know you have no mind for business or how I'm able to provide for this family, but you're old enough to understand that your selfishness will never be rewarded."

I cringed, staring at a deep groove in the floor. My pulse matched the one in my finger, a frantic beat pounding in my ears. My sternum felt too tight, smothering my breath, bowing my shoulders. I tried my best to keep a blank face; Father never liked it when I got too emotional.

"I have debts to repay, a ship in need of repairs, a crew to reimburse, a family to feed, a home that's falling apart, a wife to please—" He paused and shuddered slightly, almost imperceptibly, at those words. "And *you* come in here asking me for *more* money than what is needed to put food on our table." His finger pointed hard at the desk. "You have one job, Evelyn. One, and that is to take care of this household."

I felt like I was drowning. I wished I could say something, anything to defend myself. But all I could feel was the lump of fear in my throat.

He rubbed a hand over his face before muttering, "Perhaps it's time for another lesson on selfish behavior."

I flinched when his hands suddenly slammed against the desk as he stood up. Cooly, he pointed a finger down in front of him. "Come here, Evelyn." His voice held that unnatural calm quality to it that always came before one of his 'lessons.'

My blood thickened in my veins, making my heart work harder to keep me alive. My feet ached to run, but every muscle was locked in place. The front door was close enough that I could have tried to make a run for it, but I knew that would only make it worse for me in the end.

When I didn't move, he repeated himself through gritted teeth: "I said. Come. Here."

My Father was no longer a patient man. Maybe he never had been. Maybe my entire idyllic childhood had been nothing more than a daydream. But I knew that wasn't *entirely* true. I had seen good moments from him, back when he was my Papa, but it seemed the good part of him had died with Mama. The man before me now just happened to wear the same face. A face I'd once thought handsome now twisted my insides in fear.

Closing my eyes, I slowly assessed where my feet were supposed to be and mentally willed them to shuffle forward. This was the hardest part; he never physically forced me to take my punishments. He had just trained me that well to obey him. Because when I didn't, it was always so much worse.

Standing before him at the side of his desk, my face heated with shame.

"Good girl. Now turn around and bend over."

I tried to stop my body's instantaneous reaction, but it didn't work. The trembling curled out from my stomach, reaching down my legs first, then up my arms. I bent over and clenched my fists to my chest.

Don't cry. It'll be over soon.

I blinked back the stinging assault of tears and clenched my fists even tighter.

Father's voice made my body stutter as he quietly leaned in and whispered, "Learn your lesson, Evelyn. You are not allowed to ask for things." He gave my backside a warning swat that jolted my body forward, almost toppling me over. "Whatever I provide for you is good enough. Is that clear?"

I nodded my head carefully, unable to find my voice.

"Stop trembling, Evelyn."

The minute he said it, my traitorous body only shook harder.

He gripped one of my shoulders as he towered over me, maneuvering my body where he wanted me. "Lift your skirts."

I slowly unraveled my clenched fists from my chest and reached for the bottom hems of my skirt and petticoat. His hold tightened as I struggled to raise the fabric over my hips. All that was between my backside and the brisk air was the thin overused fabric of my drawers.

As soon as I gripped the handfuls of fabric to the sides of my hips, I felt his hold on my shoulder tighten further as he used the other hand to swat my vulnerable backside. That was the only place he ever left marks or bruises; it was easier to cover up *and* ignore, because no one ever saw that area of me. *All fathers discipline their children this way*, he used to say, and it was true. If anyone ever suspected him of truly hurting me, it would be such an easy thing to explain away.

The first blow never felt like much, but it was always startling nonetheless, making my body jump. This hit was nothing like the warning swat prior. With his grip on my shoulder, I barely moved forward, my flesh absorbing the strength of the hit instead.

Don't cry.

"I said, *stop trembling,*" he seethed through gritted teeth.

The impact of the second hit stunned me enough to stop my shaking, only long enough for my body to catch up to what was happening and start trembling again, this time even more violently. Each hit rocked my whole body forward, one after the other. On the fifth hit I choked back the sob that lodged itself in my throat. Silent tears ran down my cheeks, and I gripped my skirts even harder, my knuckles whitening.

After five more hits, he released my shoulder and sat back down in his office chair, looking winded, dusting off his hands like they were dirty. I stayed right where I was, afraid to move until I was given permission to, grateful that my knees still hadn't given out on me. On the occasions that I collapsed, he often forced me back to my feet and started over.

"Did you learn your lesson?" Father's quiet question broke through the thick silence in the room.

"Yes, sir." I answered weakly, relief washing over me like cold water at the height of summer. It was over.

He laid his hand gently on my back. "You know I hate doing this to you. But you need to learn." I nodded silently, still bent over, my back muscles burning from the position. "Straighten yourself up. You're dismissed."

I instantly released my tight fists and let my skirts fall back down towards the floor as I slowly righted myself, wincing from the pain.

Father was already sitting back behind his desk, staring at his papers again.

"Go straight to town and pick up the items on your list. Nothing else." He raised his head and looked me over once, grimacing a little. "I'll see if Camilla can lend you an old gown of hers. The one you're wearing does look a little worse for the wear." He waved his hand at me in dismissal, looked back down at his ledger. "I expect you back here in time to help Cook prepare dinner."

Without saying another word I rushed out the door, carefully latching it shut behind me. My chest heaved up and down as I tried to catch my breath. Swiping my fingertips under my eyes, hoping to remove any evidence of my tears before anyone saw me, I tried to hurry away from Father's office and toward the front door. My backside muscles ached already, making it difficult to move quickly. I grabbed my discarded satchel and raced outside as quickly as I could.

CHAPTER 2

Evelyn

My body ached with every limping step, bruises already beginning to form. The slower pace annoyed me. Market day was the one day I got to see my friend Becca, and the longer it took for me to arrive, the less time I would have to spend with her.

Friend.

A wave of emotions threatened to overtake me. Becca was a dear friend, but a very recent one. Unlike my first best friend, from my life *before*, and the only person I missed as much as Mama . . . *Liam.*

I hadn't seen him since that last day. The day the king took him from me. The day we had our first kiss. The day he promised he'd come back . . .

The day he'd lied.

Before me, the worn dirt path became more and more crowded. It was three miles to the town of Hoddleston. This was the only major town before you reached the palace, so it was often busy. The palace itself had a small population that surrounded it, but that was mostly for those employed by the palace and their families.

Liam lives on the palace grounds now.

I shook my head, trying to rid myself of the clinging Liam cobwebs.

It had never done me any good to dwell on him, and it wasn't helping today either. For so many years I'd hoped and prayed that I would see him again. But it was long past time to give that up. Liam had never come back, and I didn't suppose he ever would.

Looking up toward the sun, I saw it was already past its highest point, moving far too quickly toward the west. Just as I'd feared, my slow pace had cut my time severely short. I tried to increase my gait, but my backside protested in response.

Gritting my teeth, I steeled my mind. *Work through the pain. Imagine it's not even there.* A small amount of relief trickled into my muscles and bones, easing my stiffness. Real or not, I would take it.

The sounds and sights of the town came into focus. The uneven cobbled streets, the shops all lined up in a row, the town square with the fountain in the middle, the people talking, laughing, haggling. Breathing deep, I relished the comforting scent of freshly baked bread, the smoking hot coals from the blacksmith, the sweet earthy smell of horses and hay, and of course the passing sour note of refuse and manure. All together, it smelled like Hoddleston, the only place I felt any sense of freedom these days.

"Evy!" Becca came barreling toward me, her curly black hair bouncing like a halo around her head, tawny brown skin gleaming in the sun. Every time I saw her, I was struck by just how pretty she was. A bright smile lit her face, making her look warm and inviting.

She swept me up into a big bear hug, both of us giggling as we embraced each other. Then she stepped back and briefly pinched my cheeks between her palms, beaming back at me. "I've been waiting all day for you to show your face! Where have you been?"

"Something came up at home that took longer than expected." I saw her grimace out of the corner of my eye, and I knew she knew. Dropping my eyes to the ground, I murmured, "I'm really behind today, so I can't visit like normal."

I did my best to move around her, but she placed her hands on her hips and planted herself in front of me. Pinching her eyebrows together, she said, "Oh no you don't."

I avoided her gaze. "Becca…"

She grabbed my chin with one hand, turning me from side to side, inspecting my face. "You've been crying. What did your old man do to you? Or was it the Evil Queen this time?"

Sometimes I hated how perceptive she was. "It's nothing, Becca, I promise." I grabbed her hand, placed a brief kiss on it, and gently moved it back to her side. "I'd really rather not talk about it today."

Becca immediately melted, her eyes and jaw softening. She embraced me again, whispering into my ear, "I'm here for you, you know. You could leave that awful family and come live with me and mine. My parents would welcome you with open arms. You know that, right?"

I gave her a small smile. "I know, Becca. Thank you."

This wasn't the first time she had offered this to me, but every time she did, I felt a surge of bitterness. I wished I still had *my* family. I wished my mother had never died, and Liam had never left, and Father hadn't lost himself. I wished it was as simple as choosing to leave, but it wasn't.

"It's really not so bad," I added, in what I hoped was a convincing voice. "Plus, I'd never impose on your family."

Becca's voice dropped, low and serious. "You would *never* be imposing, Ev."

I cleared my throat, waving my hand in dismissal. "It doesn't matter anyway. In just a few months I'll be eighteen, and I'll go off to find my own job. A few more months is nothing." Fidgeting with my satchel, I looked over her shoulder to the nearest produce cart. "Now, I *need* to hurry and get back to work." I gave her a little wink and walked around the fountain to my first destination.

Becca waited a short beat before linking her arm in mine as she walked with me through the first few shops, telling me the sordid details of her most recent tryst. I couldn't help but smile, relieved to lose myself in something other than painful memories.

"Hey, Ev?"

I looked over to see Becca's eyes probing my own. Worry lines creased her face.

"Hmm?" I tried to brighten my face, but I knew it was a fruitless endeavor. She almost always knew when it wasn't genuine.

"You're not alone."

Becca said this to me often. It both eased my burden and made my heart ache something fierce. I hugged her arm tighter to me and leaned my head into hers for a moment.

She gave my arm a little squeeze. "Let's divide and conquer. What else is on your list?" She grabbed the list from my satchel and scanned the items, pointing toward the last half. "I'll gather these and meet you back here."

I gave her a grateful nod. "Thank you, Becca."

We split up, and I went straight for the fresh produce in front of me. Mama had taught me how to know if something was ready to harvest from the garden, and how to pick the choicest fruits. When she married Papa, she told him her only desire was to have enough space for gardening. Her small garden turned the whole estate into a thriving farm, with abundant crop fields, esteemed stables, and a sizable portion of livestock that grazed in our meadows. Mama started teaching me how to care for the estate as soon as I was able to walk. She would run my hands over the fruits and vegetables, telling me to close my eyes and listen for when they were ready to be plucked.

"Are you alright, miss?"

I blanched and opened my eyes, looking up to see the cart owner staring at me with both curiosity and a hint of worry. His eyes darted to my hand, and I looked down to see I was clutching a cabbage rather posessively.

"Oh! Forgive me, sir. Apparently I would like to add this one to my bundle." I gave him a sheepish smile, and he chuckled.

"Whatever you need, miss. We've got the best crop in the whole town." He winked, and I smiled politely. A familiar sadness resurfaced with his words. Not long ago, it was *my* family who used to provide the town and the palace with the best crops from our estate.

Before I could get lost in my thoughts again, I gathered up everything else I needed and paid the man, walking away quickly.

Out of the corner of my eye, I saw soft, colorful fabrics rustling in the breeze. I could almost feel the cottony fibers caressing my skin. It had been so long since I'd worn fresh fabrics.

Father's hard face flashed before my eyes, effectively dousing my musings like an ice-cold dip in freezing water. I stumbled away from the fabrics, the memory of pain and humiliation driving me away—

Sharp, hot pain exploded through my face as I smacked straight into an unforgiving metal wall. My satchel dropped from my hands, dumping the contents out onto the busy street.

Stunned, I tried to catch my bearings again, but my fuzzy eyes wouldn't blink clear. Panic jolting through my body, I dropped to my knees and started groping wildly to find my satchel before it was trampled. Father would never forgive me for ruining our purchases.

I shook my head, trying to blink the fuzziness away. *What did I just run into?*

A man's body knelt in front of me, helping me gather my market items and place them back in the satchel. "In a hurry, miss?"

"I'm s-so sorry!" I stammered, staring at his armored uniform. *A palace guard. Oh, no.*

Blinking rapidly to clear my vision as my gaze traveled up, I was met with the deepest, warmest, most handsome eyes I had ever seen. He stared back at me, smiling, eyes gleaming, and achingly . . . familiar.

I stopped breathing.

CHAPTER 3

Liam

The sun was roasting me alive in my armor, sweat pooling in the small of my back and stinging my eyes as I scanned the town square for any potential threats . . . and for *her*.

Nothing.

This town was docile, much like I remembered from my childhood. At least my aching haunches were grateful for the respite from traveling. The constant chafing of horse and saddle was always uncomfortable, especially when wearing armor.

Even out here, I could hear the prince talking inside the bakery, likely shaking hands with the baker and his family with his usual charm. I was grateful this was the last leg of his goodwill tour. Visiting all the prosperous towns in the kingdom had taken its toll on all the men, the prince included. The king had asked him to spread the crown's goodwill for the kingdom, but we all knew the truth: he was trying to show the prince had kingly potential and wasn't just some wild and debauched boy who happened to own a crown. He'd made quite the name for himself through his various . . . exploits.

"You're wound up tighter than normal today, boss." Rafe sidled up next to me. He looked like the consummate guard, except for his laughing brown eyes and wide smile that made it nearly impossible to not grin back at him. A knowing smirk formed on his lips just before he opened his big mouth. "Maybe a little preoccupied with wondering if *she's* here today? Hmm?"

"I'm just tired," I said, blatantly ignoring his jab. "All of us are."

"Yeah, but not all of us are hoping to catch a glimpse of our *dream girl*." He paused and shifted on his feet, giving the crowd a once-over of his own, his eyes snagging on a pretty blonde in the distance. "On second thought, I take that back."

I couldn't help the snort that escaped, doing my best to control the laugh bubbling up.

"Maybe we can help you watch for her, yeah?" He raised an eyebrow, ogling a young woman walking past. "Why don't you tell us what she looks like. Or better yet, we could all start yelling *Evelyn* and see who responds."

"Don't you dare. Need I remind you, you're still on duty, Soldier."

He clicked his heels together and puffed out his chest in a mocking way. I glared at him out of the corner of my eye, but didn't reprimand him.

My men knew this was my hometown. They also knew it was where Evelyn lived, and I guessed they were hoping to see me fall all over myself if she turned up. What great entertainment it would be for them to watch their captain crumble at the sight of a lady. *And I probably would.*

It had been so long since I'd seen her. What did she look like now? Would she be angry with me? Did she have a beau? How would her family feel about me now? Would she still be the same? Did she still think of me?

A fresh wave of guilt threatened to overwhelm me. I had promised her I would return, and now here I was, barely a few miles from her home, and I *still* didn't have the courage to seek her out.

Thankfully, I was pulled out of my reverie when I heard the prince's voice. "It was a pleasure to meet you all. Thank you for these lovely loaves of bread. My men and I will be sure to enjoy every last morsel."

The prince backed out of the doorway, flashed one last obnoxiously bright smile to the baker and his family before he stepped over the threshold and promptly handed the basket of loaves to me. I then handed it off Rafe, my second in command, who handed it off to his third, John. We were so used to our system, it was second nature now. Everyone wanted to give the prince a gift, which kept us all well fed and taken care of in each town. John took the loaves out of sight as the prince's smile faded. He slumped, letting out a long sigh, rubbing his hands over his face.

"I'm exhausted, Liam. How many more towns to visit?"

I patted him on the back. "This is our last stop, Your Highness. Only a few more shops to visit here in the square, and then we'll head straight back to the palace."

Prince Ryker gave me a small nod, taking in a bracing breath before plastering on a brand-new smile and turning to enter the butcher shop next door. I posted myself beside the door, keeping guard while I listened to the prince introduce himself, followed by gasps and cries I assumed came from the wife and daughter of the butcher. The prince had that effect on most women, *all ages*. I couldn't help but chortle slightly under my breath, which I then covered up by clearing my throat. The edge of a smirk still clung to my lips.

Rafe nudged me with his elbow as a couple of pretty girls walked by, batting their lashes and smiling coyly our way. He nodded to them, his eyes giving them an obvious once-over. They both giggled profusely and scurried away to wherever they were headed.

"I'm going to assume neither of them were your Evelyn. Although, it would be rather fun to see her fancy *me* more than you at first sight." He rubbed his hands together in anticipation. "Now I *really* hope she walks by so we can see who she fancies first."

I stiffened at the thought.

"Easy there, old man," he laughed, slapping me on the back. "Obviously, she would fancy the Prince before any of us. Like every other girl." He winked playfully, and I gave him my best sideways glare again. The thought of her favoring someone else, especially Ryker, made my insides twist painfully.

Rafe sighed, pulling my imagination back from the precipice. "A day off can't come too soon. I've missed having a little female companionship . . . you know what I mean?" Rafe waggled his eyebrows as his eyes followed after the girls, both of them still giggling and shooting furtive glances over their shoulders.

I rolled my eyes. "I'm sure you've had enough female companionship to last a lifetime."

He snorted. "True." Then he flashed his brightest, full-teeth smile at another set of ladies walking by, one of them ripe with child. They both blushed and tittered at each other, offering him a second look as they passed.

"Shameless," I scolded him.

"Some of us aren't holding out for Miss Perfect, Liam. You know, you might lose that stick up your—"

"Rafe . . ."

"I'm just sayin'. Instead of idolizing Miss-So-Wonderful-I-Can't-Even-Look-At-Another-Woman, you could be enjoying yourself plenty of times over." Rafe nodded his head at a beautiful woman standing by the fountain, letting out a low whistle. "Now *she's* something. Just look at what you're missing out on, man."

Before I could reply, the dark-haired girl at the fountain suddenly jumped up, waving her hands, eagerness brightening her face. "Evy!"

All the breath was knocked out of my lungs by the sound of that name. Rafe met my eyes, his own blown wide.

I frantically scanned the crowd, searching for a hint, for *anything* I recognized. *Where is she? Come on, where is she?*

A flicker of chestnut hair. The faintest hint of a familiar laugh floating across the square.

There.

Even if I couldn't see her face, I knew it was her. I would know that girl anywhere, even after all this time.

I stood there, glued in place as the girl at the fountain laughed, throwing her arms around Evelyn, talking animatedly with her. I could feel my hands tremble with anticipation. But as they started to walk off into the crowd, I panicked.

I can't lose her.

I turned to Rafe, who was still staring at me, his mouth hanging open. "Rafe, I need you to stand guard a moment. The prince's next stop is the tailor across the street. I'll meet you there."

He gave me a once-over as a broad smile slowly widened on his face. "Sure thing, Captain. Go get her." He waved his hand in a lazy salute and took up his position in front of the butcher's shop, motioning for John to join him.

I stumbled forward, dazed and lightheaded. A new kind of heat was smoldering under my skin, like I might burst from the anticipation alone. My heart hammered in my chest and my feet felt weighed down, like the ground was trying to swallow me up.

Moving toward the crowd past the fountain, I searched every head, looking for that perfect shade of chestnut. *What if she doesn't recognize me? Will she even remember me?*

Even at a young age, she was easily the most beautiful girl in the room at any given time. Her infectious and unbridled joy made everyone love her just moments after meeting her. Even the other boys who'd worked at the estate with me had done everything they could to be noticed by her, but she'd never paid them any mind, because it was *my* company she'd preferred.

All too quickly, I was flooded with memories of picnics in the fields with her and her mother. Dinners with her family after everyone else had gone home. Lying in the grass and staring up at the clouds with her, finding all sorts of characters floating around in the sky. She always claimed she could see everything I saw; even when I tried to trick her by making them up, she would still somehow find a cloud structure that would come awfully close. I remembered holding her hand. Running with her. Laughing with her.

Kissing her.

Our first and last kiss, the day I left. The day I promised I'd return. The day I lied.

I'd already been a sweaty mess, but now I felt clammy and dizzy, my head spinning with the ambush of memories, the doubts swirling in my brain, and the crowd of people moving slowly through the square on either side of me. I kept turning my head from side to side, sweeping the crowd with my eyes, but I still couldn't find her again.

"Oh!"

A young woman collided into my armored chest, dropping to her knees before I could catch her. I looked down to see her shaking her head, trying to gather the contents from her bag littering the street in front of us.

I knelt in front of her, reaching out to help her, afraid to touch her, but I couldn't help smiling. "In a hurry, miss?"

"I'm s-so sorry!" She shook her head again, disoriented, blinking rapidly. Sunlight danced off of her perfect chestnut hair, her olive skin. Slowly, her dark lashes fluttered up.

Big eyes; bright, like a sunlit forest.

My brain melted into a giant puddle as her eyes widened a fraction, her mouth opening to form a surprised O. *Does she recognize me?*

She stared and stared, her chest heaving up and down as she tried to catch her breath. I held mine.

"I beg your pardon, sir. I wasn't looking where I was going." She clumsily reached for the items still lying between us.

I reached for several vegetables, cradling them in my arms until I could place them safely in her satchel. I couldn't stop staring at her, willing her to know me. To see me. To say something, *anything.*

Evy was somehow even more beautiful as a young woman than she had been as a girl. Her plump baby face had slimmed down, revealing her high cheekbones and thin pink lips. She blushed as she caught me staring, a creamy rose color blooming across her face. I couldn't help but smile then.

I shook my head, chuckling breathlessly. Holding out my arms, I motioned downward with my head. "Here. You'll need these too."

She opened up the satchel just enough for me to drop the items in. I gently took her hand and helped her back up to her feet.

"Thank you," she said, glancing down at my hand, still wrapped around hers. I couldn't let go. Not yet, maybe not ever again. We took each other in, and the overwhelming notion to pull her into my arms and squeeze her so tight that we melded together almost overtook me. The look on her face was unsure, unsteady in her evaluation of me. Her eyes met mine again, and I couldn't look away. I wanted her attention for as long as I could get it.

I felt her inspecting my face, taking in every angle, every scar, every shadow, and lastly, my hair. Her gaze latched onto that annoying little piece that always fell in front of my eyes. It was then that I saw true recognition glimmer in her eyes.

"Liam? Is that . . . is it you?" Her voice was quiet, breathy, unsure.

Relief flooded my body. She knew me. She still knew me.

"Hi, Evy." I grinned crookedly, bowing my head slightly.

She shook her head again, like she couldn't believe what she was seeing. "What . . . how . . . why are you here? Have you come back?" Her bright, hopeful eyes bored into mine, willing me to say yes, and my heart sank.

I hadn't come back. Not really. I hadn't come here for her today, and I wouldn't even be here at all if it hadn't been for the king sending Ryker on this tour.

I cleared my throat, feeling another drip of sweat slink all the way down my spine. "I'm captain of the prince's guard now. He's been on a goodwill tour throughout the kingdom. This is our last stop."

Her eyes sank. Really, her whole body did. In an instant, I witnessed what I had been so afraid to see all these years: her disappointment in me.

"Wait, you two know each other?"

I looked over to see the pretty girl from the fountain still there, standing with a hand on her hip, eyeing me with a skeptical look.

Evy blinked a few times, a brief shadow of pain glazing over her eyes, and my chest tightened. She looked over at the girl as if just now realizing we weren't alone, and her cheeks grew rosy again.

"Yes, once upon a time." The sadness in those four words almost brought me to my knees right then and there, begging for her forgiveness.

"Becca, this is Li . . . *Captain* Liam." The formality of that introduction stung, but what else had I expected?

"Just Liam is fine," I croaked, nodding my head to the girl. "It's a pleasure to meet you, Miss Becca."

"Captain Liam used to work at the Estate." She let go of my hand and clutched her satchel, pulling it closer to her. "We grew up together."

Becca's head bounced between me and Evy several times until Evy looked back at me, offering a timid smile that looked entirely too forced. "Such a prestigious job, Liam! It's wonderful to hear you're doing so well. I'm happy for you. You look well—are you? Well, I mean."

She grimaced at her own rambling words, and I couldn't help but huff a little laugh through my nose. To see Evy flustered like this was strange, unfamiliar. The girl I'd known before was always so confident, fearless with her questions and curiosity. The girl before me now looked ready to curl up in a ball and hide.

Becca laughed. "I don't think I've ever seen you this tongue-tied, Evy."

Evy's eyes widened as she looked over at Becca. She shook her head, pursing her lips while turning a deeper shade of pink.

Becca giggled. "Well, it was nice to meet you, Captain Liam. I'm sure Evy will tell me *all* about you when I see her again later?" Becca's eyebrow raised as she stared at Evy, making her words less of a request and more of a demand. I liked her already. But it didn't seem that Becca knew a thing about me, even though they seemed to be close friends. *Has Evy never talked about me?*

I dipped my head to Becca again. "Pleased to make your acquaintance, Miss Becca."

Becca gave Evy a quick hug, handed her a few more items for her satchel, then retreated back into the crowd of people. Evy stood before me, still gripping her arm awkwardly. I wanted to help ease her nerves, but I wasn't sure if she was mad at me, or if she simply considered me a stranger now. I'd thought of her every day since I left and talked about her all the time, but maybe she hadn't done the same.

I cleared my throat again, struggling to find my voice as I looked at her. "To answer your earlier question . . . yes, I am quite well." I smiled at her carefully, desperately trying to put her at ease. "I actually really love my job. I'm lucky to have been promoted to this position. It's been my honor to serve the prince." I offered a small bow for a dramatic effect, then brought my fist up across my chest in salute.

Her eyes widened, and I instantly regretted the formal pose. "Not that . . . I mean, it's not—"

A big, bright smile bloomed on Evy's lips, silencing my stammering. My heart swelled so fast at the sight that I thought it might explode.

"Of course you would take to being a protector. It makes perfect sense. That's what you always were for me." Finally letting go of her arm, she took a brief step back, tilting her head while looking me over. "You know, you look . . . so tall!" She reached her hand up into the sky as if to demonstrate, then paused, tilting her head the other direction. "It's strange to see you looking like a man." Her eyes grew wide again, and she covered her mouth with her hand, stifling an embarrassed giggle. "I mean, that's not what I meant. I just mean that for some reason I always expected to see you as a little boy coming back to our gate. I mean, I knew you were always a few years older than me, but I never truly imagined you growing . . . up." She gestured her hand high again. "I just couldn't picture it, I guess." She took a step forward, moving in closer to me, staring into my eyes again. "I wasn't sure if it was really you or if I was just making stuff up in my head again."

My heart stuttered, then soared. She'd imagined me? Tried to picture what I would look like now? Surely that meant she'd missed me, right?

This was the Evy I knew, the Evy with a sparkle in her eye and a playful grin on her face. The Evy I grew up with and loved for so many years.

Suddenly, her eyes darted behind me. They blew wide open as she hastily bowed forward into a curtsy.

"What's this, then?" Ryker's familiar voice came from behind me. "My Captain of the Guard leaves his post to come *flirt* with a pretty girl?" The prince passed a mischievous look over to me, mouthing, "*Finally.*"

His bejeweled hand beckoned her to rise. "Come, girl, you must tell me how you possess such charm as to lure my captain away from his duty to protect me."

Evy rose up, but kept her head bowed to the prince. "Forgive me, Your Highness, I'm afraid I ran smack into him. I wasn't looking where I was going . . ."

The prince raised his eyebrows at me in question.

I stifled a laugh with a fake cough. "Your Highness, I used to work for this lovely lady's family estate before I joined your service. We . . . spent our childhood together." I gestured to her and raised my eyebrows at him, hoping he'd catch my hint.

The prince looked puzzled for a moment longer, then understanding dawned. For years he had heard me gush about Evelyn, and though he always claimed she must be some mythical creature, he knew she was the reason I didn't truly entertain other women's affections. Much to his and Rafe's dismay.

"May I present to you, Lady Evelyn Coulter."

"Ah!" Recognition lit up his face. "Lady Evelyn, it's lovely to meet you. Liam speaks of you often." He gently reached for her free hand and gave it a chaste kiss before releasing her and giving me a knowing smirk. Evelyn's cheeks turned bright pink. "Liam, it seems this young woman has experienced quite the tumble today. I think it best you escort her home. We'll head back to the palace now, but I trust you know your way?"

Deciding to join in his theatrics, I bowed in an ostentatious manner. "Certainly, Your Highness. It would be my honor to escort Lady Evelyn back home."

Evelyn waved her hands in protest, a panicky laugh breaking from her lips. "No, oh please. I'm quite alright. I would hate to inconvenience either of you. I promise, I'll be just fine." She quickly turned to me and bowed her head. "It's been lovely running into you again, Captain Liam." Then she curtsied to the prince. "And thank you, Your Highness. It was an honor to meet you." Briskly turning around, she kept her chin tucked in tight and attempted to duck through the crowd.

"No, I absolutely insist." Ryker's voice rang out above the crowd, causing Evy and everyone else to freeze. "Captain Liam, you are hereby ordered to walk the lady home." Ryker flashed his brightest smile at her as she slowly turned back around. "And it was a pleasure to meet you too, Lady Evelyn." He gave her a respectful nod, then turned to the guards, ordering them back to the palace.

All around us, a crowd had gathered. Evelyn took in our audience, blushing furiously. The prince certainly knew how to make a scene.

Rafe walked my horse over to me, a devilish gleam in his eye. He gave me another nudge with his elbow, flashing a wink and a broad grin. Grabbing the reins, I rolled my eyes at him and turned back, only to see Evelyn making another hasty retreat through the crowd. I couldn't help but think she was trying to lose me.

Not this time, Evy.

CHAPTER 4

Evelyn

"Evy! Wait!"

A little yelp escaped my throat when a hand gently latched onto my arm, pulling me back through the crowd. Back toward him. A sweet zing of energy thrilled through my body as I looked up into Liam's deep eyes.

The magnetic pull was still there, an invisible force that always guided me to be near him. Even with the heat and the odor of unwashed bodies surrounding us, he still smelled like sweet grass and musky cedarwood. Like home. I wanted to bury myself in his arms and never let him go again.

I'd always loved Liam. He was three years older than me, but from the moment we first met, when he asked to wear one of my esteemed wildflower crowns in front of all the other boys without a hint of shame . . . I was smitten.

Standing tall before me now, with his broad shoulders and filled-out arms . . . he had always been taller than me, but now it felt different. He felt grander. What used to be a scrawny, scrappy, lanky boy was now a strapping, broad, attractive man. There was a new intensity to his thoughtful gaze, a confidence in his steps, and a magnetism that rolled off him, commanding people's attention.

It was then that I realized I had no idea what my face was doing. Shock had rendered it numb. I was certain that I was gaping like a fish out of water again, and my cheeks heated at the thought.

He reached over and carefully took the satchel from my clenched fist, tying it to his saddle. Then he looked back at me and smiled. The shy smile, the one that was all lips with a pronounced dimple. *At least he hasn't grown out of that.*

"I can't disobey orders, you know." He winked at me.

My face grew hotter, and his smile only widened. This whole constantly-blushing thing was going to make it look like I had been burned by the sun. Still, I couldn't help gawking at him until I remembered the last time I saw him, and then Mama dying, and everything that had happened since then. My eyes dropped to the ground, and I let out a pained breath. He was here now, but all these years . . . he'd left me. He hadn't come back like he'd promised.

For years I had hoped, even prayed, but he never showed. I used to dream of him riding up on a horse and whisking me away in the night. Saving me from my own misery.

Those were the nights I cried the hardest, waking in the morning with dark circles under my eyes.

I chanced another look at his face. His brow was etched with worry. I cleared my throat, trying to find my voice again. "I'd given up hope that I would ever see you again."

His face fell, and I silently kicked myself for saying it out loud. This is why it would've been better if he'd just left me alone. Even today, I needed to remind myself he hadn't been there to see me; he was there for his job. I wouldn't have even *seen* him if I hadn't smacked into him.

Turning away, I walked briskly out of the town, making my way toward the estate. My stomach sank, my shoulders starting to cave in. I clutched my arm to my side, pulling everything inward. He was going to see what I'd become. Maybe he already could. He would see what had become of the estate, and then I would lose him all over again.

"Evy, wait. I . . ."

"It's okay, Liam," I cut him off. "You don't have to say anything.

What's past is past. You're following your orders to walk me home. Let's just let it be that."

He tugged gently at my arm again, turning me to face him. "Evy, that's not what's happening here."

I took in a deep long breath, trying to gather my nerves. "It is truly good to see you, Liam. But I really should go home alone. It's . . . it's better that way."

His brow furrowed. "What do you mean, it's better that way?"

I shook my head. "Nothing. Just . . . it's been so long since we've seen each other, you know? We don't even know each other anymore."

I flashed back to the moment I last saw him, when I overheard the news that he was leaving. He chased after me as I fled, my tears falling without end. His arms wrapped around me from behind, stopping me from going further. His heart raced as he held me while my body shook with sobs.

His mother had told him the night before that he was called up to join the royal guard. He had no choice but to go, no matter how much he wanted to stay.

When I turned to look at him, to say goodbye, he kissed me. It was our first kiss. Our sloppy, tearful, soggy first kiss. But I loved it. I loved him. And he promised to return. He told me he would love me forever, that he would always come back for me.

Hot, heavy tears stung my eyes. I couldn't look up at him; it still hurt too much, even after all this time.

Reaching down to grab my hand, Liam quietly said, "Evy, I would know you anywhere."

His half-smirk made my stomach swoop, stirring a fluttery kind of nausea deep in my core. My nerves started to build up again as we kept walking, our hands still clasped together. I didn't think he had any intention of letting mine go, and I didn't have the strength to pull away.

I closed my eyes to breathe through the sob threatening to climb up my throat.

After a long pause, I looked back down at my shoes, the shoes Becca's father made me a year ago after my old ones had grown too small and worn. Gathering my courage, I softly whispered the question that I'd been asking for years now—only this time, I got to actually ask *him*, not just the imagined version of him that I pictured so often.

"How come you never came back?"

His body stiffened. Regret hung heavy in his voice when he said, "I'm so sorry, Evy. I wanted to." His hand tightened around mine. "I *really* wanted to. I've missed you every day. I . . . it sounds so foolish saying it out loud." He made a kind of choking sound before he murmured, "I was afraid."

I wasn't certain, but I thought I heard him swear under his breath. Tears gathered in his eyes, threatening to spill over at any moment. I stopped, my own tears finally falling at the sight of his. He stopped with me, turning his face away like he was trying to hide, but I gently turned his head toward mine.

"Year after year I made up excuses," he rasped, "and then it just started to feel too late, like I'd missed my opportunity. I convinced myself you'd forgotten me, or were angry beyond measure, or had met and fallen in love with someone else." His chin dropped to his chest as a tear finally snaked down his cheek.

I brought my free hand up to wipe it away. "I can understand that, Liam. But I want you to know I never forgot you, and I missed you terribly."

His eyes refilled with tears again. "And I wasn't there."

"No. You weren't. But I understand being afraid."

He brought my hand up to his lips and kissed my knuckles. "Not a day goes by . . ."

He faltered, and I couldn't help but smile sadly. "Nor for me."

His somber eyes searched mine. "You felt betrayed by me, though."

It wasn't a question. How did he still know how to read me so well? I closed my eyes tight and dropped my head, nodding. "Yes." I didn't want to lie to him.

He pulled me in for a bear hug, just like the one that still lingered on my skin even seven years later. It felt just as warm, just as safe, maybe a bit less forgiving because of his armor . . . but I leaned into his strength, relief softening my nerves, like a tense muscle relaxing. I wanted to cry all over again, but with happy tears this time. For the first time since Mama died, I remembered what *home* felt like.

We both reluctantly released each other. "It's never too late, you know," I said. His shy smile and dimple made another appearance, which made me smile even brighter in return.

We started to walk again, his horse obediently following behind us. He took up my hand again, giving it another little squeeze before intertwining our fingers. It seemed like he needed to keep holding it, like he was trying to remind himself I was really there. Or at least, that was how it felt to me. I gave his hand a little squeeze in return.

He cleared his throat before breaking our silence again. "So, tell me what you've been up to these past few years we've been apart. How's your mother?"

The dread instantly filled me all over again. A hollowness in my chest opened back up, like ripping a half-healed wound back open. I must've made some kind of sound, because Liam stopped again, turning me toward him. "Evy, what's happened?"

I let out a burdened and choppy sigh. "Mama died, Liam. About two months after you left. She caught some kind of fever."

He ran a hand over his face, disbelief and pain clearly etched into his features. "What? Evy, I—how could I not—I'm so sorry. I . . . I should've been there." He shoved his hands through his hair, clasping them above his head.

"It was sudden, but Papa and I at least got to say goodbye. She passed away peacefully, I . . . I think she knew it was her time." I paused, giving him time to process the pain I'd had seven years to sift through. "She loved you, Liam. She would never fault you for not being there."

I pictured Mama lying so still in her bed. I remembered holding her hand as her eyes slowly closed, that small, peaceful smile on her face. And I remembered . . . a second pair of bright green eyes. Someone holding my other hand. A soft iridescent glow.

Liam made an agonized sound that snapped me out of the memory.

This strangely emotional reunion with Liam made me feel both uneasy and soothed. I always tried to only ever release my emotions in private, and though Liam had always been an affectionate person, he'd never truly been emotional with me growing up. It felt like we were both getting a moment to open up. To simply be . . . us.

The sun was starting to dip into the horizon, and instant panic washed over me. I was going to be late. Really late. And Father was already in a mood today. "I need to get home, Liam."

I wished I could give him the time he needed to process this new grief I'd dropped on him, but I couldn't risk waiting any longer. My heart was starting to pick up speed, like it was trying to urge my body into action.

Liam jogged slightly to catch back up to me. "I'm so sorry, Evy. I would've come back if I'd known. I never would've left you to mourn alone." His eyes closed briefly and he squeezed his eyebrows together, creating deep, anguished rivets in his forehead. His voice cracked. "I should've been there for you."

"It's okay, Liam. Mama knew you loved her. She would be so incredibly proud to see you now." I pulled him along with me, my heart picking up from a canter to a gallop. "I'm so sorry, but I really must get home soon. Father will be ang—" I stopped myself. "He doesn't like it when I'm not home."

He nodded like he understood. "Understandable. Now that I know it's just you two, I would be worried about you too." He picked up his pace to match mine.

I smiled sadly at the sentiment. I didn't want to lie to him, but I also didn't want to ruin whatever nice image he still had of me and my father. Because as soon as we reached the estate, all that would change again.

CHAPTER 5

Liam

"So, Mr. Captain of Prince Ryker's Royal Guard. . . tell me more about this rise in position. It seems like a much happier story, and I'd rather appreciate an opportunity to celebrate your accomplishments."

Her eyes looked up at me, glowing with pride. I had waited so many years to see that look on her face, and it was *almost* worth it. But facing her hurt straight on had almost ripped me in half.

I had done that. I had brought that pain to her eyes.

Beyond the pride, there was something new in her, something heavy and hard behind her eyes. She wore her sadness like a shield. Where was her boundless joy? Her playful spirit? I pictured the girl I used to know: a girl with loose chestnut curls bouncing up and down in the fields, a bright smile consuming her whole face as she handed out flower crowns to anyone and everyone she could find, laughing loudly as we sprawled side by side in the grass and I pointed out ridiculous and impossible shapes in the clouds.

My sweet Evy from so long ago had changed, and I didn't know why. *Was it her mother's death? Was it seeing me again?*

Her brow furrowed, her lips pursing slightly. "Why are you

looking at me like that?"

I was nervous, so nervous. I still loved her, and I was so afraid I would scare her away, or that I'd already waited too long. Had I missed my chance?

"Are you . . ." I stammered, tugging a bit at the edge of my collar. "Are you glad to see me again, Evy?" *Pull yourself together, man.*

Her eyes widened. "What? Liam, of course I'm glad to see you! Today has been a wonderful surprise." Yet even as she reassured me, her hand twitched in mine like she wanted to let go—probably to draw her opposite arm in, like I'd already seen her do a couple times.

I cleared my throat. "Then perhaps, maybe after today, I could call on you again?"

That deep sadness swept through her eyes again, but she blinked it away and whispered, "I would like that very much."

I blew out a relieved huff of air and grasped her hand tighter. Perplexing woman. I felt so out of my element already, like I was thirteen again instead of nearly twenty-one.

Evy's shoulders tensed, her jaw ticking as we rounded the bend in the road. Before I could try to discern where that had come from, a wave of disorientation washed over me, like time had just turned back eight years. The familiar estate of my youth, with its multiple chimneys and dormer windows, peeked out through the now-overgrown bushes. It had always felt more like home than the small apartment I shared with my mother back then.

I turned to Evy excitedly, but she was as rigid as a statue, eyeing her home like a spooked deer watching for a hunter. Her chest shuddered and her steps faltered. But we had only leisurely walked here—she shouldn't have been so winded.

The large estate's intricate iron gate loomed before us with dead vines twisted around the bars. I paused just inside the gate, surveying the grounds I used to work tirelessly to maintain: the familiar pebbled courtyard we used to run through with Cook on our tails after we stole a sweet treat from the kitchen, the wide fields in the back where we planted enough crops to feed two entire towns, the smaller garden off to the side that Evy's mother, Clara, personally cared for, the stables that housed the prized horses . . . run-down, dead, rotting. All of it.

What happened here?

There were no people bustling about the estate, no lively chatter or cheerful laughter. There was an eerie hopelessness that seemed to settle into every greyed branch and wilted plant.

As we neared the house, the front door flew open, and adrenaline flooded my veins at the *crash* it made against the wall. A severe-looking woman stood in its frame, already sneering.

Who is she?

"Evelyn, *my dear.*" One side of her mouth tilted up to the side, like she had made some hilarious secret joke.

I inwardly cringed at the bitter tone of her voice. Her features were honed and tapered on her alabaster skin, unmarked by blemish or freckle: it looked as though she never allowed her skin a speck of sunlight. Her hair was thick and dark and pulled up into harsh, tight curls, with a straight edge of hair along her forehead cutting a sharp frame around her face. Her lips were bright red, her eyes painted dark and mysterious. She was . . . beautifully ostentatious.

"Where have you been, *darling*? Your father and I were starting to worry. He expected you back well over an hour ago. You know what happens when you disobey."

Evy flinched and dropped my hand like it had bit her, which made the woman smile smugly. Her steely gaze raked me up and down as she raised one perfectly-tailored eyebrow in question. "And who's this you've brought home with you today? A royal guard? I would imagine he was bringing you home after you got yourself into some trouble, but I think this surprise visit may be for another reason entirely, hmm?"

I looked down at Evy, expecting an introduction, but she looked petrified in place. Her breaths were coming in fast and perspiration bubbled on her brow.

"Forgive me, madam. I am Captain Liam of Prince Ryker's Royal Guard, at your service." I offered her a slight nod of regard. "I am simply escorting Lady Evelyn home after she took a tumble at the market today." I wanted to wink at Evy, but she wouldn't look up at me. Her whole body seemed to be caving in on itself.

The woman's eyebrows shot up in surprise, and her eyes darted from me to Evy. "*Lady* Evelyn, is it?" A sardonic half-smile grew on her lips, and she turned her attention back to me. "It's a pleasure to make your acquaintance, Captain Liam. I am Lady Katerina Coulter. Welcome to my home." She gestured toward the door. "Would you like to come in?"

My brows furrowed. Evy hadn't mentioned Katerina. "I would. Thank you, madam."

Placing my hand gently on the middle of Evy's back, I led us both up to the front of the house, tied my horse off, and grabbed Evy's satchel before following Katerina inside.

Upon walking in, I was caught up in memories of shared breakfasts with Evy and her family in the little breakfast nook and running up and down the stairs that led to the basement kitchen where Cook made all kinds of delicious treats.

Katerina immediately stepped up to me and slipped her arm into mine, leading me away from Evy as she said in a mock whisper, "Don't tell me my young stepdaughter has been showcasing her wanton behavior again. I do apologize if she misled you, or if you caught her in the act, heaven forbid. Either way, you are a true gentleman for bringing her home to us."

Every muscle in my body went taut. I couldn't believe she'd say or even suggest such a thing about Evy. *It couldn't possibly be true.* I did my best to remain stoic, silent.

Katerina tsk'd, almost playfully. "It's been hard, you see. Ever since her mother died, she's acted out in ways we couldn't have foreseen. Her poor father has tried everything to get her to behave like a proper young lady, but she just can't seem to behave herself."

Evy cringed, the center of her forehead knotting at Katerina's words. The sight made me long to reach out to her, to ease her burden, whatever it was. This woman was clearly trying to bait her, and it seemed to be working.

I briefly cleared my throat to bring the attention back to me before speaking. "Lady Coulter, perhaps I should have introduced myself more thoroughly. I am an old childhood friend of Evelyn's. I actually used to work here at the estate with the late Lady Clara Coulter. Evelyn and I grew up together."

Katerina looked over at Evy in surprise. "An old friend, you say? How remarkable. I didn't think Evelyn had any friends."

Another jab. By the barely-visible reaction from Evy, I could tell this kind of verbal assault happened often.

"Yes, Madam. Evy and I haven't seen each other in many years, and I'd like to call on her again sometime soon so that I may properly catch up with her." Katerina visibly bristled, but before she could spit another thinly-veiled insult, I added, "Is Lord Coulter home? I would very much like to speak with him."

Hiding her further surprise, she replied, "Yes, of course. He's in his office, I'd be happy to show you." Then she turned her head to face Evy. "And you . . . you know what to do now that you're home." She smirked. "Say *goodbye* to the captain, Evelyn."

Evy blinked back tears and offered me a grateful smile. "Thank you for walking me home. It was so good to see you, Liam. Goodbye."

I held out the satchel to her, and she hugged it close to her body before turning to walk down the stairs toward the kitchen.

I was missing something. I couldn't shake the feeling that Evy was in danger, and the danger seemed to be lurking in this home.

CHAPTER 6

Liam

"Right this way, Captain Liam." Lady Coulter gestured down the familiar hall to Lord Coulter's study. She tapped lightly on the door. "Frank, dear, you have a visitor."

I heard the sound of papers being stacked together and some light cursing before heavy footsteps walked to the door, swinging it open angrily.

"Yes?" Frank paused to stare at me, taking in my uniform and then my face. He opened the door even wider and gestured for me to enter. "Please, do come in." He looked to Lady Coulter. "Katerina, have some tea prepared and brought to us." She quickly nodded her head and left, closing the door behind her.

Lord Coulter eyed me carefully, looking slightly puzzled. "Forgive me, sir, have we met before? You look familiar, but I'm afraid I can't quite . . ."

"Captain Liam of Prince Ryker's Royal Guard." I gave a respectful nod. "But I used to work here on the estate when I was a boy."

Recognition lit up his face. "Liam? Yes, of course. Liam, my boy! It's good to see you. Please sit. No wonder I didn't recognize you, you have certainly changed from the young skinny lad who used to run around the gardens." He gave me a good hearty slap on the back and motioned for me to sit while he rounded the desk to sit on the other side. "To what do I owe the pleasure of this visit?"

Relief washed through me. At least some things were the same. It was good to see Lord Coulter was still himself despite all that had happened. "It's good to see you too, sir. It's been so long since I've had the chance to visit." Taking my seat, I continued, "While in town today, I had the delightful surprise of running into Evelyn." I smiled at my own private joke. "So I offered to walk her home, of course."

A dark emotion swam across his eyes, but before I could tell what it was, he cleared his expression and smiled again. "Well, like I said, it's wonderful to see you again—"

"My lord, forgive me for not coming sooner. I only just today learned about the death of Lady Clara. Evy filled me in on the years I've missed. Allow me to offer my deepest condolences."

His posture went rigid, and his face hardened. A tingle of uncertainty ran down my spine. He took a moment to compose himself before he quietly replied, "Thank you, Liam. It's been a long time, but her passing still weighs heavily on my soul."

I nodded in understanding, lost in my own memories of Evy's mother. "She was an incredible woman. I looked to her much like my own mother." Lord Coulter's face was stricken. "I'm grateful you have Evelyn to always remember her by. Seeing her now, all grown up, I'm blown away by how much she looks like Clara. She's the spitting image."

The lines around Lord Coulter's eyes tensed as he glared across the desk at me, the unexpected sharpness made me fidget awkwardly in my seat. Normally I wouldn't let any man intimidate me, but I wasn't here as Captain of the Guard. I was here to ask permission from the father of the girl I loved to call on her again. I needed to make my intentions clearly known, as was proper.

"Why do I get the feeling that you're not just here to catch up, Liam? Have you something else on your mind to discuss with me?"

The way he asked felt more like a threat than a genuine question. It made the comments Katerina had made about Evy's promiscuous nature flood back in my head. *Is her father used to having to turn down men seeking his approval?*

I cleared my throat, feeling far more nervous than I originally anticipated. "Well, sir, I . . . I'd really like—"

A swift knock on the door immediately interrupted my ramblings. Lord Coulter turned to the door and bellowed, "Come in!"

A striking young woman, about the same age as Evy, walked in. She smiled coyly at me. She was practically the spitting image of Katerina, except her dark hair was shorter. Cropped in that same straight line just above her brows, the rest of her hair fell straight and loose, hanging around her shoulders. Her movements were languid and alluring. I could just see Rafe in my mind now, his eyes popping out of their sockets at the sight of her. Her deep burgundy dress was revealing, but not too much, just enough to make you wonder . . .

"Captain Liam, this is my daughter, Lady Camilla."

He has another daughter?

"A pleasure to meet you, captain. May I pour you some tea?" Her voice was like rich honey, deeper than I expected it would be. Sensuality poured out of her, and I felt immediately flustered. Unfortunately for me, I acted the same way every time the boys brought me to a brothel. I still had yet to actually step foot inside one.

I willed my voice to stay calm and collected. "Yes, thank you, that would be lovely."

As she leaned down to pour my tea I caught her eyes. They were midnight-dark, cunning and sharp, standing out starkly against her translucent skin. Her face was all angles except for her soft, red, voluminous lips. I had to admit, those were the kind of lips men often fantasized about indulging in. There was nothing plain about her; she would easily stand out in a crowd, and yet, she was almost the exact opposite of Evy in every way. Pale skin to Evy's warm tones, straight short dark hair to Evy's long soft chestnut waves, deep and unreadable eyes to Evy's bright and expressive gaze. Evy was like summer sunbeams gleaming through a forest. Lady Camilla was moonlight reflecting on water at night. It made me realize that Lord Coulter had chosen his new wife to be the exact and complete opposite of Evy's mother, Clara. *Curious.*

She brushed her arm against mine, and my muscles instinctively tensed as she poured my tea. I glanced back over at Lord Coulter, who seemed thrilled with her performance.

And that was when I realized what was happening. The standard routine. Lords and Ladies loved throwing their daughters at me. I was the next best thing to Prince Ryker; or, if their hopes were *really* high, they assumed I was their ticket *in* with the Prince.

I smiled politely, thanking her as she moved on to pour some tea for Lord Coulter. But the familiar bitterness was creeping in. To think that even Lord Coulter saw fit to try and use me in this way made my hackles rise. Luckily for him, I did have a vested interest in his daughter. Just not the one parading about at present.

I took a sip of tea, hoping to calm my rising indignation before speaking. "Lord Coulter, as much as I do love getting to see you and visit the estate after so many years away, you were right that I have more on my mind. Seeing Lady Evelyn today . . . I must admit, I'd like to see much more of her. Would you permit me to call on her again, a bit more formally?"

Asking for the father's permission was always step one in the courting ritual of the kingdom, and though I had no idea if anyone else was currently courting Evy, I had to make sure I became one of her suitors before she gave her heart away to some schlub who didn't deserve her.

Both Camilla and Lord Coulter visibly stiffened at my request, gaping at me.

Lord Coulter took a sip of his tea and I saw his eyes narrow. "Hmm. I do remember Evelyn could indeed be quite charming."

Why is he speaking of her in the past tense? My brows furrowed, and that niggling sensation of danger came back.

There was an awkward silence that followed. Camilla was looking at Lord Coulter expectantly while he looked at me, and I did my best to remain calm at the odd and increasingly uncomfortable dynamic in the room. Taking another sip of my tea, I waited for his answer, hoping they didn't see my hand quiver.

He steepled his fingers in front of his mouth, tapping a few times. "I'm afraid I can't allow you to call on Evelyn again. She's been . . . a bit of a problem lately." He paused to look out the window. "I need to rectify the situation before I can allow any young men to call on her more formally. I do hope you understand."

I don't.

My eyes narrowed, and I opened my mouth to give him my retort, but he spoke before I had the chance. "However, my daughter Camilla is available, if you'd like to call on her. That would be acceptable and could easily be arranged any time."

And there it was. The clear push. But why push Camilla when I had clear interest in his other daughter? Why did it matter to him? He knew our history. He saw our bond growing up.

I didn't dare look at Camilla for fear that I may give her false encouragement. She was simply a pawn in this game. A seemingly willing one, sure, but it wasn't her that made my spine tingle in resentment and my stomach tighten with fury. Something was off. Something didn't feel right. I was trained to notice when things felt wrong, when people were lying. Being able to catch things both seen and unseen was an integral part of becoming an effective protector of the kingdom. But I hadn't figured out what was setting me on edge here, beyond the obvious intention to use me for the increase of their status.

I set down my cup of tea, leaning closer to the desk. I fixed Lord Coulter with a shrewd stare. "And may I inquire as to what Lady Evelyn's offenses are that make her so ineligible for gentleman callers?"

I spoke with my most formal captain tone, the one that promised a reckoning was on its way. The one that usually made criminals prefer to confess right away rather than face the consequences of lying and being proven dishonest.

His eyes widened at first, then turned cold as he leaned back in his chair and interlaced his fingers over his chest. Poor Camilla sat there awkwardly, watching the two of us in our power struggle. When Lord Coulter spoke again, it was not nearly as jovial as when I first arrived. I hadn't known him as a man, only a boy who looked up to him, but this didn't come across as new behavior. This was learned, taught, maybe even fundamental.

"I'm afraid, captain, that you may *not* inquire on such a personal topic." He leaned forward again, his voice abnormally quiet. "Evelyn is *my* daughter, *my* property, and I will deal with her however *I* see fit."

He slapped his hands on the desk, loudly propelling himself up, smiling widely even as I flinched at the sound. "Liam, it was so good to see you. Congratulations on your prestigious role. As much as we missed you, it seems you leaving this estate was the best thing after all."

A not-so-subtle hint that I'd overstayed my welcome.

Perhaps I had never truly known Lord Coulter. Perhaps now, later in life, he was finally showing his true colors.

I took my time standing as he rounded the desk, holding out his hand to shake my own. "I appreciate the visit Captain Liam, and I thank you for bringing *my* Evelyn home to me. Camilla will see you out now."

One last emphasis to drive his point home. And it was true: according to the law, children were considered property of their parents until they turned eighteen. Women in general were given even fewer rights, and King Penvarden had never felt the need to change that, though Ryker and I agreed it was a very antiquated and frustrating state of affairs.

"Of course, sir." I offered a stiff nod of my head, collecting my bearings before I turned to walk out the door.

Camilla smoothly linked her arm with mine as we exited the office. The door shut forcefully behind us, another clear gesture of how Lord Coulter truly felt about my visit. She leaned in close, whispering, "Don't mind him. He's currently in the middle of figuring out a new trade deal. It's been quite taxing on him."

I grunted in response, unable to say anything more.

She smiled slightly and gave my bicep a small but obvious squeeze. I inwardly cringed. Normally I would make my position bluntly clear, but this was Evy's stepsister, and I didn't want to make waves with her family. If I wanted to be one of them one day, I was going to have to be more careful. We walked out the front door toward my horse, who was munching on some of the overgrown foliage at the side of the house.

Camilla cleared her throat briefly before inquiring, "I hate to be impertinent, but I must ask. Why are you wanting to call on Evelyn?"

"Evy and I are old childhood friends. We grew up together right here on this property. Spent all our time together. She's now blossomed into an incredibly beautiful woman, and I couldn't imagine *not* wanting to call on her." I paused for a beat, smiling subtly to myself before I decided to be brutally honest. "From the first moment I saw her, she has always held my heart."

Hopefully that would destroy any hopes Camilla may have had of wooing me to her side. Before reaching my horse, I felt Camilla pulling me back, slowing my speed. I almost groaned in annoyance, but I choked it back down.

"Ah. How charming. It makes sense though. The poor dear still hasn't grown out of her pretty childlike looks yet. She catches the eye of many a man looking to . . . take advantage of that innocence. I'm afraid Father is rather overprotective of her." She tittered unhappily. "I tell her all the time that once she loses that innocence, there will be nothing for men to flock to anymore."

The message was clear. Evy was still a maiden, if only just, and many men wanted the opportunity to change that. It fit the same message Katerina gave me when I first arrived, but it didn't fit the Evy I knew.

The whole family dynamic made me curious and frustrated. Evy had looked terrified to be back here, and I was beginning to understand why.

Removing myself from Camilla's grasp, I mounted my horse and settled in. "Would you give Evelyn a message from me?"

She lifted an eyebrow in question. "What kind of message?"

"Tell her that I *will* see her again, and soon. It's a promise."

Her lips pursed for a moment before she gave me a slow nod. "Of course. I'll take the message directly to her."

"Thank you." I dipped my head in acknowledgement. "It was a pleasure meeting you, Camilla."

She dipped her head in a soft bow of respect. "The pleasure has been all mine, Captain Liam." She smiled again at me, like she was holding some sort of secret, before walking back toward the front door.

I gave one last glance at the crumbling estate, searching for one last glance of Evy, before riding out of the courtyard and back toward the palace.

I *would* see her again. And I would save her from whatever was happening here.

CHAPTER 7

Ryker

"What do you mean I *must* pick a bride at the Summer Ball? Don't you realize how ridiculous that sounds?" I ran my hands through my hair in frustration, then readjusted the various rings on each finger. How could he be so shortsighted?

"The kingdom looks at you as a spoiled, wild, immature child sowing your *oats* wherever you please. They call you 'The Rogue Prince,' Your Highness. Finding a bride will make you appear more . . . settled."

I glared at Apep, Father's advisor. He looked practically the same age as me, though none of us were deceived; he'd been my father's advisor for over twenty years. His face simply didn't gather lines like it should. But even so, his slithering voice grated on me. Not only did he always sound like a self-righteous know-it-all, but he attacked every consonant like they were somehow going to escape him.

I raised my eyebrows accusingly at him before Father chimed in. "Perhaps *must* is a strong word. I would, however, very much *like* you to take this seriously. To truly consider a woman for marriage. I was young once too, Ryker, but a new woman every *week*? I need you to try . . ." Father brushed his hand over his face, heaving a pained sigh.

"If your mother was here, she would know what to say." He shook his head. "It's time to prepare you to become king, Ryker."

"And you think having a wife will magically make me a better king?" Heated anger rose up my neck.

He turned from me to face the window overlooking the nearest town, bowing his head again. "I *know* you are capable of much more, and I *think* having a wife will at least give the impression to the people that you're taking your role more seriously. They need to feel confident that you'll be ready to take over the kingdom once I am gone."

Apep chimed back in. "A woman has historically had a settling effect on the people, Your Highness."

Women *had* always had a settling effect on me. I almost smirked at the thought of the pretty little blonde who'd settled me plenty last night. "And how would you know, Apep?"

That man hadn't even been seen with a woman in . . . well, ever.

I shifted uncomfortably, my frustration rising as Father continued staring out the window without a word. He had been given the chance to wait on love, to find it in his own time. Didn't I deserve the same chance? Before he found Mother, he'd been plenty *active* himself. How could he think less of *me* for it?

Apep stood perfectly unfazed, as usual, his hands clasped behind his back. His large black robes ruffled at every slight breeze.

Father turned and looked me dead in the eye. I watched the thoughts churn in his eyes for a long moment before he finally spoke. "Apep? Give me a moment alone with my son, please. I'll see you at dinner."

"Of course, Your Majesty." Apep bowed annoyingly low, then did the same to me. "Your Highness."

I acknowledged his deference begrudgingly, but when he left the room, I breathed out a relieved sigh. "I really don't know why you keep him around."

Father ignored that complaint. Instead, he muttered, "There's more at stake here than you know. Timelines have changed, Ryker. The kingdom needs to know their prince is trustworthy." He crossed the room and sank into a lush chair near his fireplace, rubbing his temple. "Reports from the lords say you did well on your goodwill tour. It seems the people loved getting to see their prince among them."

And I had loved getting to know quite a few of them more intimately. But of course, *that* would never be in his reports. My men weren't the kiss and tell kind. When I kissed, they didn't tell.

Gritting my teeth, I tried to reel in my annoyance. "Thank you, Father. But if the goodwill tour went so well, and the people have already seen me as something more than a *rogue*, why are you harping on this wife business?"

He paused, his brow pinching, uncertainty gleaming in his eyes. "Like Apep said, a woman—"

I cut him off, waving my hand irritably. "A woman has a reassuring influence, yes, I heard. But what does that have to do with anything right *now*? What do they need to be *reassured* of?"

Father's face fell. "I . . . I've been meaning to tell you something, Ryker. It's very difficult for me to . . ."

He trailed off, and a sharp suspicious unease stabbed low in my stomach. "Father?"

"You've already lost your mother. And I don't want to . . ." He trailed off again, his voice cracking before he regained his composure. "It's sooner than I wanted. The weight of the kingdom shouldn't have to fall on your shoulders so young." His tone turned to muttering again, and I only picked up every few words: "Only twenty . . . too young . . . so much time lost."

I raised my hands in frustration. "Is this your way of telling me you need me to be more present at meetings and start taking over more responsibilities? If that's the case, I will gladly do it. But I am *not* ready to take on a wife. I haven't even met a girl I want to be around for longer than a night, and—"

"My health is declining, Ryker." Father's words were solemn, sudden.

My heart stopped. I raised my head to look at him. "What do you mean, declining? I thought you were getting better. Y-you told me you were getting better. The doctors said—"

"There *was* improvement." Urgency sharpened his voice once more. "The doctors thought I was recovering, but just before the tour, I took a turn. They tell me it's worse than it was before. Getting worse every day."

My own desperation rose up in my voice, shock numbing me from head to toe. "You've known *that long?* You should have kept me home! Do the doctors know what it is?"

Father wouldn't even look at me now. I tried to breathe, tried to stay calm, but my emotions were fraying at the edges. I clenched my hands into fists to hide their shaking.

He didn't respond for a long time, staring at the flames instead of me. Finally, I knelt down in front of him, reaching for his hands. "Father. Talk to me."

His eyes were glassy as he looked up at me. There was a helpless sheen to them that I recognized, that I *hated.* The last time he looked like this was when Mother died.

I could tell then that he was afraid to leave me. I felt it. For all his bluster about brides, his fear wasn't for the kingdom, it was for me losing him. Coping with grief had never been my strong suit.

Gripping his hand, I remembered the night Mother died. How the grief had blinded and overwhelmed me. How badly I'd needed to forget, to distract, to find *anything* that would take the edge off that pain. That was the night I first lifted a woman's skirts and lost myself in her. I didn't remember much, only vague flashes of mouths and heat and skin against the cold wall of a back alleyway. I never even knew her name.

Liam was the one who found me there, swathes of skirt encircling me. I wasn't able to remember how I got there, or how I had found her. But I did remember thanking her, and her soft kiss on my cheek after she wiped away tears from my eyes with her dainty thumbs. I hadn't even realized I had been crying.

Liam helped me walk back to the palace, his hand on my shoulder the whole way. He hadn't said a word, just pulled me into a tight hug before we reached the main doors. We never spoke about that night, but somehow he'd understood without words. He'd been there for me every day since.

My eyes stung at the memory, and the back of my throat swelled up tight at the thought of losing Father. I wasn't ready. I couldn't do it again. I couldn't lose him—not yet, not *now.* Where was Liam when I needed him?

My eyes must've looked stricken, because Father's face crumpled in pain. "Oh, my boy."

It was all he said before tears spilled down his cheeks, and he reached out, wrapping his arms around my shoulders. He collapsed to his knees beside me, and before I knew it, tears of my own were falling. Tucking my head into his shoulder, I wrapped my arms around him even tighter.

His whispered words in my ear were full of longing and regret. "I never wanted it to be like this for you. I wanted to see you live a long and happy life before you had to take the throne." His hand reached out to cup my face, and I leaned into it, the cold metal from his royal signet ring nearly stinging against my hot face. He gently wiped at the tears.

"If I have to leave you sooner than I was expecting, I want to set you up for success. I want to make sure you are as ready as you can be, and, selfishly . . ." He chuckled sadly. "I want to see you happy and settled with someone. I know it's not fair to rush you, but I . . . I don't want to miss that, Ryker."

I looked up and saw him. Really saw him, with the dark bruises under his eyes, the new lines on his brow, the silver hairs outlining his sandy mane. He looked thinner than normal, paler even. His hands tremored as he held my face.

How had I missed this? I was only gone a few weeks. Had he really worsened this much in such a short span of time? Or had I been so caught up in my own world that I hadn't even seen my own father deteriorating right before my eyes? Somehow the latter felt the most honest, and my chest squeezed tight with guilt.

"Now, you see why this is urgent to me?" The lines on his forehead wrinkled with worry. "It's not because I think little of you. Never that. I was once a young man too, you know. I . . . ." The corner of his mouth tilted up slightly. "Well, let's just say I was much like you. Only, I never had competition like you do."

I puffed out my chest, raised an eyebrow, and let out a harsh, tearful laugh. "What do you mean, competition?"

He winked at me, then looked over my shoulder. "Liam! Son, I see you at the door. Come in, please."

At the sound of his name, Liam's face popped around the corner, looking a little sheepish. It was clear he'd been quietly waiting outside, not wanting to interrupt us. He must've just arrived back at the palace.

Immediately, though my heart was still in splinters, the ache eased somewhat at the sight of Liam. Things were always just a bit better when Liam was there.

"The two of you have broken many hearts, I can already tell." His eyes gleamed at Liam this time, but there was a new sadness behind them that felt foreign to me.

Liam bowed. "Forgive me, Your Majesty. I didn't want to intrude."

"Nonsense, son. You were doing your job, watching Ryker." Father's face turned serious as he stared at Liam. "Ryker is going to need you now more than ever. I'm not sure how much you overheard—" Father paused to catch his breath, a slight grimace crossing his face. "I'm dying, Liam."

Hearing the words made my throat catch, my stomach churning with panic.

"The healers aren't sure how much longer I have," Father continued, "but it's clear that I've been getting worse lately. Headaches, blackouts, nausea . . ."

I swallowed the burning anger, the panic, trying to control my tone. "How have you kept this from me for so long?"

He shrugged helplessly. "I didn't want you to worry. It's one of the reasons I sent you away on the tour."

Liam knelt next to me in front of Father, his right arm crossing his chest. "Your Majesty, you know that I will guard Ryker with my life."

"I know, but he will need more than a guard. He will need a true friend . . . a brother." Father's voice caught as he looked back and forth between us, unsaid words crowding in his eyes. "Someone he can trust above all others." After a beat longer than was comfortable, he shook his head, focusing his eyes solely on me. "Remember, Ryker, there are many who can defend you, but very few you can truly trust. A king must choose those he trusts with great care and keep them close at all times."

Father pulled both Liam and I into his embrace. "You two were destined to help one another. Trust each other. I love you."

A wrenching sob filled the air, and I was startled to realize it had burst from my own chest.

Liam's hand braced my shoulder, a warm and familiar weight, and

I closed my eyes, leaning into the support of the man who had always felt more like family to me than a guard. Even when I lost everyone else dear to me, I would still have him.

CHAPTER 8

Evelyn

"What were you thinking?" Father bellowed, throwing his fists in the air. "You stupid, selfish girl!"

"The only good thing that came out of this whole debacle was that Camilla got to have a nice moment with the captain. He is quite the handsome man, you know, and it doesn't hurt that he's connected to the prince either," Katerina chimed in, her nose turned in the air as she glared down at me.

Liam hadn't known this would happen, but I had. I should've tried harder to get away from him. I should've convinced him to go back to the palace and leave me be.

But it had been too nice to see him, too wonderful to be held by him again, too comforting to hear his voice.

"I don't care who he is," Father growled, entirely missing the fact that Katerina had been trying to provoke *me* with her comment, not him.

His fists slammed against the kitchen table, causing all the food I had just chopped to scatter on the floor. The scent of what had been Cook's delicious roux was already beginning to fester and scald as it simmered unattended on the stove. My breath was coming in short spurts, my stomach heaving at the acrid scent of burned fat.

He lifted his head to look me directly in the eye, then prowled around the table, grabbing my arm and forcing me to stand in front of him.

"I told you *not* to dawdle. I told you specifically to be back here in time for dinner. Did you heed either of my commands?" His voice was venomous.

My chin quivered uncontrollably and my mouth opened and closed several times before I weakly stuttered out, "Yes, Father. I-I was b-b-back here, I *was* back here in time for dinner. I d-didn't dawdle, I promise. I d-d-didn't expect to s-see Liam there t-today, it all just—it all just happened so *fast*."

The deep, dark dread was starting to take over. My body shook relentlessly, and my blood grew thick and heavy in my veins. Every movement felt sluggish.

"I also told you *no men*," he hissed. "And what do you do? You bring one *home* with you. A man from the past, no less." His voice waffled between yelling and mumbling to himself.

"You and I both know him, Father. It was—it was just Liam! Even *you* loved Liam back then."

My eyes widened, and I quickly shut my mouth. I had just made my biggest mistake. *Rule number one, don't bring up the past. Rule number two, don't bring up Father's shortcomings, ever.* A looming feeling of dread grew in my stomach.

I knew what was coming next.

Father's eyes narrowed. I felt like I was beginning to drown in fast breaths. My stomach wrestled with the meager contents I'd eaten at breakfast, and I tried in vain to pull away from him, but his grip on my arm tightened with bruising force.

A false calm stole over him, his voice low and quiet. "You don't get to talk back to me, Evelyn." A threat in and of itself. "Look at me." A demand.

I couldn't look at him directly, so I focused on a freckle just above his eye. It was so hard to see his face contorted with rage and disgust like this. *He loved me once. Maybe he loves me still. Maybe he won't do anything. Maybe it is all my fault.*

"Katerina, bring me my switch."

I recoiled from his grasp as fear surged through me, and I started to thrash in his hold. He hadn't used the switch on me in a long time, but the last time had left scars.

I didn't do anything wrong.

"No, Father. Please. What did I do that was so wrong?" He held me firmly in place as I writhed and whimpered. "The prince insisted Liam walk me home. I had no choice! Please, Papa!"

Katerina sneered as she stepped up next to my Father, holding the switch in her hand. But at the word *prince*, she and Father both froze. "What do you mean the *prince* insisted?" she demanded.

Another mistake. Father and Katerina, especially Katerina, were so desperate to be back in the king's good graces again. Any mention of the prince caused a stir in this household.

"The prince, he was—he was there, in town. He saw Liam talking to me and came over." Katerina's eyes narrowed further, but I rushed to say, "I didn't hardly s-speak to him, not to him, I promise. He just, just gave Liam the order to see me h-home and that—that was it! That's all that happened. I promise. I tried to stop him, I even tried to run away and lose him in the crowd. But he couldn't—I mean, he couldn't disobey the prince." My attention switched from Katerina's scowl to Father's grimace. "Please, Father. There's n-nothing I could've done. I—I hastened home as quickly as I could, I swear—*please!*"

Even I cringed at the shrill desperation leaking into my voice. The fear was taking over, and I hated how pathetic and weak I sounded. Tears streamed down my face in earnest now, my whole body trembling uncontrollably. Father's bruising grip didn't lessen on my arm, and my stomach kept trying to revolt.

"You met the prince? Talked to him yourself?" I blocked my face with my other arm as Katerina swung the switch at me wildly. It stung my forearm, but she had next to no strength herself. All she ever did was sit around all day pretending to read. She never made progress on her books, only switched out which one she pretended to be in the middle of.

"I didn't really meet him! I just curtsied and called him Your Highness. That's it, that's all!" I choked down the bile rising in my throat. At least I had stopped stuttering.

"He thought enough of you to ask his own *captain* to personally walk you home." She dug her well-manicured nails into the flesh of my chin. In her signature high-pitched screech, which made even my father visibly cringe, she started yelling. "*You* didn't deserve to meet the prince. You are nothing. Nothing! Do you hear me—"

My stomach lurched one last time, stronger than before, and there was nothing I could do to stop it.

Whatever contents I had been fighting to keep inside my stomach were now sliding down Katerina's front. Everyone stopped breathing. My cheeks flamed in mortification. I'd never done something like that before. It was like my body was rebelling against this harsh injustice in the only way it could. A small victory that filled me with new fear.

What will they do to me now?

Father turned away from Katerina in disgust as she shrieked in horror, a deafening scream that made everyone else in the room cover their ears. Snatching the switch out of her grasp, Father whipped me around so fast I was instantly disoriented as he shoved me against the stone wall at the back of the kitchen.

"Lift your skirts, pull down your drawers, then place your hands on the wall." His voice was like a hot knife being shoved into my chest.

My body shook uncontrollably as black spots covered my vision. *Breathe.* I couldn't. *Breathe.* "Father, please. Don't do this. Please—"

"Do as I say. Now! Or I'll add to the number of switches. Do not test me any further, girl."

I kept my eyes closed as my nerves dove deeper and deeper into my stomach. Embarrassment heated my body as I pictured Camilla hovering by the kitchen entry, Cook next to the stove, and Katerina standing behind Father, still coated in my bile. I wasn't a girl anymore, so this punishment held even more shame for me than it used to. Though, I was certain that was part of his intention.

"Lord Coulter, please don't do this. Can't you see Miss Evelyn is ill?" Cook. Sweet, gentle Cook was pleading with Father. Doing her best to defend me. He would likely fire her on the spot, or worse, just for speaking out like this. I shook my head at her, willing her to stay silent. She didn't deserve to be punished for my mistake.

"You dare tell me how to handle my own daughter?" Father's voice was soft, threatening.

Cook held a butcher's knife in her hands, staring at him defiantly. She'd been in the middle of butchering the meat for tonight's dinner, but I imagined by the look on her face that she was picturing butchering him instead. It was a dark thought, but it strangely bolstered my courage.

To distract Father from Cook, I numbly pulled down my drawers and lifted my skirts, exposing my naked and vulnerable flesh to the open air. Bracing my hands against the wall, I felt the stain of shame tinge my skin.

Hushed apprehension thickened the air. No sounds of boiling water, or chopping vegetables, or sizzling meats. No one spoke, or even shifted in their clothing. It was like the air around me held its breath.

Thwap!

The first hit startled me so much that I cried out immediately.

Thwap!

The second hit felt like fire seeping into my skin.

Thwap!

The third hit registered as a deep, searing sting. I bit my lip to keep from crying out again, but the fourth made my knees start to buckle.

Bracing my body for the fifth hit, I retreated into my mind, imagining that there was a shield between me and the pain of the next strike. I squeezed my eyes shut so tightly that a glimpse of shimmering light flashed behind my eyelids.

I kept bracing for the next hit . . . but it never came. I turned my head slightly to see my Father swing at me with all his might, his face raging red and simmering with sweat.

But I didn't feel it. My body didn't rock forward, my skin didn't sting. I heard the hit, but never felt the impact.

Frustrated at my lack of reaction, Father tried again. And again. And again.

Still nothing.

Relief flooded my veins. Whatever was happening to block this out, I hoped it kept working.

I heard him take in a ragged, incensed breath as he geared up to hit me even harder. A laugh bubbled up from inside me, feeling grateful at this sudden turn of events, but I refused to let it free. Instead, I flinched as I watched him release the hit, and then . . . excruciating pain.

A guttural groan escaped my lips.

Satisfied that he had finally broken through, he threw several more hits in quick succession that landed haphazardly all over my body, his grand finale. A startling scream wrenched from my lungs, and I tasted coppery blood in my mouth. My skin felt splintered open, and my knees buckled, leaving me a boneless puddle on the stone floor. My head rested half on the ground and half on the cold stone wall.

I closed my eyes, willing the rolling pain to somehow disappear once more as my father knelt beside me. His shockingly gentle touch turned my head to face him.

"I don't relish giving you these lessons, but you need to understand that they are necessary." His eyes were suddenly full of concern, and he looked almost remorseful, but he couldn't hide the strange exhilaration that such torments brought him. I believed he secretly loved the adrenaline of punishing me, since most days he walked around like a corpse, numb to the world around him. His eyes were usually dull and lifeless, but not now. Now, they were alight and alive.

"You are my daughter. I can't have you disobeying me or acting out like a spoiled child." He sighed, wiping a tear from my face with his thumb as he cradled my cheek in his hand. "Your mother spoiled you. She made you selfish and disrespectful. And now I have to right those wrongs. Just like my father did for me."

He didn't want to right wrongs, and neither had his father before him. This was about control. I knew it deep in my core. Katerina and Camilla were easy to control; they fit in with the societal norms. Mama and I never had. That was what had drawn him to her originally, but Mama was also the reason his father had disowned him verbally. The late Lord Coulter never put it in writing, though, so when he passed the Coulter fortune still fell to Father. But I knew he carried those scars still. Mama told me once that Papa had scars I couldn't see. I didn't understand then, but I did now.

He stood up and dusted off his knees, looking down at me. "Get up and head straight to bed. You'll be given no dinner tonight." With that he turned to Cook. "Clean this mess up. You'll be given more time to prepare dinner this evening, since Evelyn won't be assisting you."

Cook's eyes smoldered as she glared at him, never once looking away until he was out of the room. Katerina scuttled out behind him, whining about her ruined dress and her need for a bath. Camilla and Cook moved toward me cautiously.

I couldn't move. I just wanted to close my eyes and stay right there against the cool wall. Maybe they would let me.

I heard them both move closer to me, but Camilla reached me first. She shook her head, addressing Cook firmly. "You have a job to do, Cook. I'll take care of Evelyn tonight."

Cook looked down at me. Her soft, wide eyes were wrinkled with sorrow. Cook had too sweet a heart to work in this cruel place. She wasn't meant to see things like this. My heart broke that she'd had to bear witness tonight. Her curly grey hair framed her plump cheeks perfectly as she dipped toward me. "Miss Evelyn? Are you . . ."

Looking up at her, I grimaced, but nodded my head.

Both her and Camilla reached out their hands to help me up off the stone floor. I gave Cook a reassuring squeeze, doing my best to ease her worries before letting go.

"Come on now, lazy girl, I'll help you to your room." Camilla's tone held no bite as she dipped down and drew my arm over her shoulders. We started to walk, but I clumsily tripped over my trapped ankles. I'd forgotten about my drawers. I tried to reach down to grab them, an involuntary cry of pain burst out as my skin stretched and stung with the movement.

Camilla dropped down to her knees. "You won't want to put these back on quite yet anyway. Lean against me and step out of them." She carefully slipped them over each raised foot, then stood back up, pulling my arm around her shoulders again. "Let's get you upstairs now." She turned to Cook. "You'd better get started on cleaning up this mess and making dinner before Frank comes back in here."

It was both a warning and a threat, and Cook hesitated at first. But at a look from me, she hopped back into work.

That was how I'd come to see Camilla in our adult years. She was a double-edged sword, both a warning and a threat.

With my rubbery legs, we took it step by step. My body still trembled, and red-hot throbs of pain radiated from my backside, causing me to wince more than once.

Camilla's kindness surprised me. She was usually all hard edges, but I was one of the lucky few she'd ever shown her softer side to. It was still rare, and it had happened more often back when we were kids, but we hadn't spent much time together these past few years. Not once boys became more interesting and I became competition.

CHAPTER 9

Evelyn

Inside my bed chamber, Camilla instructed me to strip out of my gown and lie face-down on the bed. I obeyed silently, a wave of sheer exhaustion washing over me. I heard Camilla walk back into the room with a sloshing bowl of fresh water in her arms as my eyelids began to sink shut. A cool cloth gently dabbed my burning flesh, and I settled into the refreshing relief, grateful for Camilla's assistance.

"I saw the skin open up on those last few hits. Luckily, there's not much blood. But you do have some pretty angry welts back here." Her voice was calm, restrained, but there was something simmering beneath it.

We stayed quiet for a moment, the soft movement of water lapping the sides of the bowl the only sound in the room. Camilla finally broke the silence once more, her words hushed. "I, ah . . . I never realized how bad it was."

"How bad what was?" I whispered.

"Frank's . . ." She hesitated. "Frank's punishments."

I didn't know what to say. I supposed no one had ever really *seen* it happen—they just knew it *did* happen.

"You knew about my other scars," I whispered.

She paused, breathing carefully before murmuring, "Yes. I just didn't—"

"You mean it was harder to *watch* it happen."

Another long pause. The water stopped sloshing.

"I'm sorry, Evy." Camilla's voice was so quiet.

I remained silent. There wasn't really anything I could say. It had been like this since they'd moved in. Not that it was Camilla's fault, but that didn't make it any easier not to blame her.

She cleared her throat awkwardly, taking on a haughty tone, one so like her mother's that it took work not to flinch. "If you would just do as you're told . . ."

Irritation brought a little fire back to my voice. "Tell me how I *don't* obey, Camilla."

"They're always saying how disobedient you are. How destructive you are to this family."

"I know what they say." I couldn't help the defeated tone of my voice. "Have you ever seen me do anything to prove them right?"

By the controlled sound of her breathing, I could tell she was deep in thought. She lowered her voice, leaning closer to speak into my ear. "Have you ever thought of running away? Making a new life for yourself?"

It wasn't said with guile, but the question still stung. "Maybe I should."

"Why haven't you?"

I shrugged my shoulders as best I could. "I turn eighteen in three months. I can leave then."

She didn't reply. Instead, she grabbed a bottle of oil, gently pouring it onto my skin and massaging it into the stinging welts. With a deep sigh, she changed the subject. "Well, at least you had one good thing happen today, meeting the prince. Tell me about him. Is he even half as handsome as his captain?"

My body tensed. I hated the idea of Camilla fancying Liam. I felt like a petulant child yelling *"Mine!"* while yanking on Liam's arm to snatch him back from her. "The prince is . . . very handsome." Camilla sighed wistfully, and I snorted at her. "And, trust me, he knows it."

She chortled. "Are you calling the prince *arrogant?*"

I laughed at that. "Just your type."

She lightly flicked my shoulder. "I do like my men confident. A little arrogance just makes them all the more charming."

"You mean makes them all the more *annoying*. You just want someone as pretty as you are, so you can be the envy of everyone else."

Camilla laughed outright at my teasing. It had been a long time since we'd laughed together. It was nice to have this moment with her, even if it was painful.

"I do like all eyes to be on me."

"Well, *that's* an understatement," I said, twisting a bit to give her an awkwardly exaggerated wink.

She chuckled, but her mouth was pursed in a contemplative knot. "Perhaps if I had met the prince today, he would've been quickly swayed by my charms." She dipped the cloth back in the water, and I noticed it had turned a deep shade of pink. *I must be bleeding more than she let on.* "Unlike a certain captain I met today." She raised an eyebrow at me. "It seems he only has eyes for one specific girl. Didn't even give me the time of day." She looked into my eyes at that moment, offering the faintest hint of an encouraging smile.

I grinned at her. "Is that right?"

She hummed noncommittally and got off the bed, grabbing the dirty bowl of water and setting it on the side table before drying her hands with a fresh rag. "Well, there's nothing more I can do for you right now. You'll need to let your wounds breathe for a while so they can heal properly." She grabbed a blanket from the corner of my bed, gently draping it over me before she turned to leave. Pausing at the door, she asked, "So, what is it between you and the Captain, anyway?"

I shrugged as best I could from my flat position on the bed. "There's nothing between us. We haven't seen each other in over seven years. But as children, he was my best friend. My, um..." I hesitated, unsure how much I was willing to give her. "My first love."

She studied my eyes for a long moment, as though she was trying to decide or decipher something, then finally said, "Well, I'm glad you got the chance to see him again."

"Me too. Thank you, Camilla."

She nodded her head and left the room, gently latching the door behind her. My thoughts only had a second to swirl before the exhaustion finally took over, but the last vision I saw was of Liam's handsome face.

I couldn't help but smile.

CHAPTER 10

After our talk with the king, Ryker and I wordlessly walked back to our rooms. I should have said something, anything to comfort him, but nothing seemed right. He didn't appear to mind the silence, anyway; he merely kept pace beside me, his brows drawn low over his eyes, darkness drowning out their usual mischievous light.

Instead of entering through the main doors to his suite, we entered through my adjoined room. The minute I shut the door, Ryker immediately flopped face-down on my bed with a deep groan. His honey-colored hair, though cut shorter than mine, still splayed out haphazardly on the mattress. That was rare for him. He liked being all put together with his ornate clothes, his rings, all the other shiny baubles he attached to his daily attire. No one would ever mistake him as *not* the prince, except for maybe right now, if they saw him splayed out like a butterfly tacked to a collector's wall.

I quietly moved across the room and started to strip out of my sweaty armor. Luckily the odor was smothered by the soft, smoky scent of my already-lit fireplace. After leaving the Coulter Estate, I came straight back to find Ryker with his father. This was the first chance I'd gotten to peel the wretchedly-heavy metal off my tired body, and I desperately needed a bath.

Turning around, I was surprised to see Ryker sitting up now, leaning against my headboard. His eyebrows were raised, his bloodshot blue eyes boring into mine. "So, tell me. How did it go with Evelyn, brother?"

I looked at him skeptically. "You can't possibly want to talk about *that* right now."

He shrugged. "It's quite possibly the best topic at the moment, and the one with the highest probability of a happy ending. So yes, I daresay that's *exactly* what I want to talk about right now."

I rolled my eyes with a quiet scoff. "I'm not so sure about that."

He sat up straighter, looking even more eager to hear the story.

It was my turn to shrug. "It was wonderful to see her again, but it was, well . . . it was a bit disconcerting."

He gave me a disparaging look, crossing his ankle over his opposite leg and interlocking his arms across his chest. "*Disconcerting*? Liam. That is by far the *worst* possible word to describe a clandestine meeting with the love of your life." He threw his arms up in the air. "After all these years of being apart, all you can manage is *disconcerting*? Explain. Now."

Ever the spoiled prince. I chuckled softly and shook my head as I freed myself from the last of my armor. "At first I was just happy to catch up with her, but . . . it seems her life hasn't been without its sorrows." I tried not to linger on the memory of Evy's face when she had explained her mother's death. The way Frank had put me in my place. His conniving new wife and flirtatious new daughter.

Ryker silently waited for me to continue.

"Her mother passed not long after I was called to guard duty. That woman was like a second mother to me, and I didn't even know she was gone." A lump formed in my throat, and I did my best to swallow it.

Ryker's tone turned somber. "I'm sorry, Liam."

"No, I'm sorry. I know this isn't what you want to talk about."

He looked away, his mouth twisting downward. "It's okay. I understand that kind of shock."

We both quieted at the weight of the uncomfortable truth hanging in the air between us. The truth we were refusing to acknowledge for now.

"But even so . . . she's even more beautiful than I remember." I smiled slightly at the memory of her smile, her laugh.

"See, that's wonderful! There's nothing disconcerting about that! You walked a beautiful girl that you adore all the way home. The two of you, by yourselves . . . all *alone*." He wiggled his eyebrows at me, a sly grin creeping up his lips. "I mean, really, brother, if you don't know how this whole wooing thing works, I'd be happy to jump in and show your girl how it's done."

I shot him a glare, and he just sat back further, smiling smugly as he pulled his arms back behind his head.

"Of course I know how to woo a woman, but it's different with her." I sighed and finished hanging up my armor before walking back over to the bed, collapsing on the edge, dropping my head into my hands. "We had a lot of catching up to do, of course, and holding her in my arms again . . . there's never been another feeling like it, Ryker."

"Now you're speaking my language. Get to the good stuff." Ryker waggled his eyebrows at me.

I shoved his legs. "No, it wasn't like that. We cried—"

He groaned in mock disappointment. "See? I knew you didn't know how to do this whole wooing thing. Crying is not usually on the menu, brother. Unless it's in the throes of—"

"Will you stop?" I interrupted quickly, my face flushing hotter than the fire flickering in the hearth. "It wasn't like that. It was just . . . it was wonderful to see her again, but it was hard, too. She was so different than I remember her."

"Well, it has been seven years."

I glared at him sidelong. "Yes, I know that. That's not what I mean. She seemed afraid."

"Afraid?"

I nodded. "More nervous. Unsure of herself."

He scowled slightly. "She wasn't afraid of *you*, was she?"

I shook my head. "No. I don't think so. It wasn't really like that. But her father seems to have remarried, and meeting her new family, I'm starting to wonder . . . she just looked so run-down and tired. Her dress was worn through and ratted, and she had smudges on her face. Not that I mind, but she should—"

"Liam," Ryker interrupted, looking me over carefully before continuing. "You know as well as I do that's just how peasants look. Life is harder on them. It's not fair to judge her on that. Don't tell me that I've spoiled you too much, now." There was a glint in his eye. I knew he was trying to make me feel better, but it didn't help.

"She's not a peasant, though, Ryk. She's a lady. Her father is a nobleman of the court. When she was a girl, she was doted on. Spoiled, even. But when I saw her today . . ." I shook my head and looked down at my hands.

Ryker leaned in, frowning as he read my expression. "What happened?"

"They *berated* her. They said outrageous things about her character. And maybe she is like that now, but I don't see how it's possible. The girl I used to know was the same as the girl I saw today, but the light in her eyes is just *gone*. You know what I mean? Their estate was in shambles, and her father and new stepmother . . ." I tried to ease the headache I could feel building in the back of my skull by massaging my temples. "Her father seemed changed, too. Or maybe I just never saw it before. All those rumors we've heard about their family finally started making sense to me. I never believed them until I saw him today."

His face was wrinkled with concern. "Who's her father?"

"Lord Coulter."

Ryker sneered. "Lord Coulter? The one who's barely hanging on to his lordship?" He tsked. "I'm surprised he's even hung on this long, to be honest. The Court has already tossed him aside as a lost cause. I don't think he's even *been* to court in years."

I glanced at him out of the corner of my eye. "He seemed desperate, but not nearly as much as his new wife." I rolled my eyes just picturing her. "She made it abundantly clear that she was really only interested in my connection to you."

He scoffed. "Then they don't know you at all."

I brushed my hands through my hair again, a sense of loss weighing my shoulders down. "I can't wrap my mind around any of it. I just . . . I have this sinking feeling something is really wrong. She was so sad, but it wasn't just grief, it was more. I can't explain it. I don't even know if . . . it broke my heart, Ryk."

I avoided his eyes, even though I could feel them burning a hole through my skull. I wasn't used to being the emotional one out of the two of us.

"Liam. Look at me."

I grimaced, but obeyed. His hands were carefully placed in his lap, and he looked deep in thought as he studied me. "What happened with her father?"

"I asked him if I could call on her again. He knew me as a boy, he knew how close I was with Evelyn, but he refused me." I stood up and started pacing, anger shooting prickling energy through my legs. "He said Evelyn's been acting up. That he needed to *rectify the situation,* whatever that means. He condescended to me, tried to intimidate me . . . if he'd been here at the palace, he wouldn't have dared speak to me the way he did. But there, he didn't fear me at all. He even had the audacity to throw his new daughter at me instead. Blatantly." I gave him a pointed look. "You know how I hate that."

"Yes, I do, though I'll never quite understand why." He was a hairsbreadth away from smirking, but he had enough restraint to hold it back.

I, on the other hand . . . restraint was the last thing on my mind. "He acted like his daughters were interchangeable. As though one could easily replace the other in any man's eyes. The whole experience was alarming." I shivered slightly remembering the seductive touches, the looks, the glimpses of skin while Frank sat there watching.

Ryker looked perplexed. "How unbearable was this stepdaughter?"

I shook my head. "She wasn't, not really. I think she was just performing her part. The whole conversation was clearly staged, from beginning to end. I don't even know if she actually cared to flirt with me at all. The alarming part was how throwing herself at a man was the obvious expectation of her." I couldn't stop picturing Frank Coulter's smug face when he shook my hand and saw me to the door. Like he had somehow won a battle I hadn't even known I was fighting. "I didn't even recognize him. He was so cold and closed off. And now I can't shake this awful feeling . . ."

Ryker nodded his understanding. "All right, all right. Disconcerting is the word for it, then." He scratched under his chin, absently worrying his lip with his teeth. "So now for the most important question: is this stepdaughter still available? Father did mention I should be looking for a bride—"

I guffawed, and he grinned like he'd won a victory of his own. "Only you would think *that* the most important question. Well, you and probably Rafe."

"That man does have good taste."

I laughed and stopped pacing. "Honestly, if she didn't have the family she does, I would say she could be a great match for you. She was quite--" I cleared my throat awkwardly, "--alluring."

Ryker rubbed his hands together in fake anticipation and smiled lasciviously.

I lowered myself back on the edge of the bed, rubbing my eyes, suddenly exhausted. "I missed her so much, Ryk. She was *right there*. I don't know what I'll do if her father won't let me see her again." I looked down at my hands, the weight of helplessness and frustration curling them into fists.

Ryker nodded slowly as his brows caved inward and he absently massaged his jaw. "A predicament indeed."

I chuckled under my breath. "What are you scheming up over there?"

He raised an eyebrow at me. "Who says I'm scheming?"

"Your face."

We both laughed.

"Obviously, without proof of wrongdoing, there's nothing we can do to remove Evelyn from her father's home." Before I could protest, he raised a finger at me. "However, we could make it so that you could see her again, and soon." A glint of glee flashed in his eyes. "Maybe then you'll get the chance to really talk to her, yes? Find out what's going on? Maybe slip in a marriage proposal . . . that would certainly get her out from under her father's thumb."

My breath caught. *Marriage? To Evy?*

I'd always dreamt about it, but could it *actually* happen? For some reason, it still felt like some mad, far-off dream. *Would she even consider me after I broke her trust?* "I'm not sure about all that, but it's obvious you've got an idea, so let's hear it."

Ryker sat up further, dropping one leg off the side of the bed and bending the other to lean in conspiratorially. "As you know, I'm hosting the annual Summer Ball for the nobles of the court and their families, plus a few visiting dignitaries." He waved his hand in the air nonchalantly, several of his audacious rings reflecting in the glow of the fireplace.

I raised my eyebrow at him. "Yes, I recall. I've only been working on your security detail for weeks now."

He waved his hand at me. "Yes, yes, I know you *know* about the ball, but what you don't know is that an invitation to Lord Coulter went conveniently *missing*." He side-eyed me. "However . . . given the right expenditure of resources, I can't see why that 'lost invitation' couldn't be tracked down and delivered to a special lady's family."

Dumbfounded, I stared at him, marveling at his artful mind. My heart swelled at the thought of Evelyn all dressed up and standing before me once more, her big green eyes expectant, her mouth opened slightly in invitation . . .

A cunning smile spread across his face. "Everyone knows I'm currently looking for a bride." I opened my mouth to contradict him—that fact was supposed to remain a secret—but he waved his hand at me again. "No lectures, Liam. Gossip travels quickly whether I aid it or not. The point is, even if Lord Coulter's been trying to hide the wondrous Evelyn Coulter behind closed doors, a man as desperate for status as he is won't be able to resist the prospect of one of his girls possibly marrying the prince." He leaned back again, arms open, eyebrows raised, perfectly pleased with himself. "What do you think?"

"I think this is why I stick to sword fighting and avoid palace politics. It's brilliant." I slapped his knee and stood up. He flashed me his best princely smile, preening at his own cleverness, which just made me laugh harder. "Well, don't just sit there reveling in your own genius. You've got an invitation to write."

He laughed as I pulled him up off my bed and pushed him toward his bedchamber door. He dug his heels into the ground and turned to face me, placing his hands on my shoulders as he looked into my eyes. We were almost the same height, but I was just a hair or two taller. "Together we'll save your fair maiden, Liam. And who knows, perhaps after the ball, we'll have you married off by the end of the month, and you can take a little time off to thoroughly enjoy your marital spoils." He looked back at the door adjoining our rooms.

"Although you *will* have to move out of this room. I, for one, am *all* for bedchamber sports, but I don't want to listen to whatever sounds *you* make enjoying the game. Your fair maiden, however . . ." He shot me a lecherous grin.

I shoved him through the door to his own chamber as he barked out a laugh. "And on that note, you can officially *get out of my room.*"

I was certain my face had turned every shade of beet red. Just picturing Evy with me, in that way, here in my room, on my bed . . . my stomach tightened. I shut the door leading to Ryker's room and collapsed back on my bed, a broad smile plastered to my face.

I was going to see her again. This time, I would get to keep my promise.

CHAPTER 11

Evelyn

The next morning, it took five minutes to pry my eyelids open. I hadn't moved from the position Camilla had left me in, lying on my stomach, my face half-buried in my pillow. Streams of early morning light filtered through the small dormer window, stinging my still-puffy eyes. I tried to carefully twist my body so I could get out of bed, but the movement made my wounds scream in agony, like they were splitting back open again. A choked gasp of pain caught in my throat, but I pushed on, slowly getting to my feet.

My drawers and dress were draped over the wooden chair in the corner. I gingerly moved toward the garments, my skin tightening and protesting every new movement, but I didn't have time to lay around feeling sorry for myself. That would only get me punished again.

I didn't bother to check the damage in the nearby mirror. In my experience, seeing it only made everything hurt worse. Not that I really ever looked in the mirror these days anyway. I barely recognized the person looking back at me when I did. She was wasting away, bit by bit, more and more every day.

What had happened to my girlish, plump face? My filled-out

stomach? When had my eyes become dull and lifeless? I was a stranger in my own skin. When people complimented my looks, it felt like they were secretly making fun of me. There was nothing beautiful about me anymore. I was skin and bone and broken.

Skipping lunch and dinner yesterday was already taking its toll. My stomach had stopped growling several years ago, but today it hurt worse than usual. I had learned this kind of pain meant it was shrinking again, which meant I desperately needed to get something to eat.

Sighing heavily, I carefully inched down the stairs to the main level of the house, then down the next small flight from the dining nook to the kitchen so I could help Cook with breakfast.

Cook startled as I entered the kitchen, throwing her hands up and abandoning the sausage that was cooking in her skillet. "Miss Evelyn!" She ran to pull me into a tight embrace, choking on a sob. "How do you feel today? Are you okay? What can I get you? Sit down and let me feed you." She pulled away just enough to cup my face in her hands, her teary eyes and worried brow taking me in.

I gave her the whisper of a smile. "I'm better than I expected. But I'm so sorry I left you alone to clean everything up by yourself last night."

She tsked, tapping my nose with her finger. "That's not for you to worry about. I can manage the kitchen just fine without you. Now, let me feed you and get some tea started. I can handle breakfast myself this morning." She winked and walked back to the stove, putting the kettle on.

I eyed her sadly, moving to gather the plates for her. "You know it doesn't work like that." I walked them over to the kitchen table.

The memory of my father's fists pounding the wood made my lungs seize up. I squeezed my eyes shut, trying to breathe.

Cook was suddenly next to me, taking the serving plates gently out of my hands and placing them on the table. "You should let me serve them today. You need rest and nourishment." Her eyes glazed over, and she blinked back tears before whispering, "Would that I could take you from here." She pulled me into another all-encompassing hug, her tears soaking into my shoulder.

"Oh, please, Cook. Please don't be sad. I'm okay. Everything will be okay."

"I should be saying that to you." She released me and swiped her apron under her eyes.

"Let me deal with breakfast. I mean it. You stay here and eat yours in peace."

I shook my head. "We both know that will just make them angry. I can do it."

Cook eyed me for a long moment, her lips pinched in concern. I could tell by the red rims around her eyes that she was ready to cry again, but she moved back to the stove and started loading up the plates with food.

The serving bell rang loud and obnoxious through the kitchen, and I took my cue to load the pitchers onto my second serving tray. My skin ached and burned, but I gritted my teeth as I struggled up the short flight of stairs to the dining nook.

As soon as their faces came into view, my stomach tightened in fear. I put on my best pleasant face and willed my body to perform normally, as if I were in no pain at all. There weren't many ways to get back at them, but refusing to let them see me hurt was one I could manage.

"Good morning, everyone. I trust you all slept well." Without looking anyone in the eye, I set the pitchers down and arranged them in the middle of the table. "I'll be right back with your breakfast."

Moving as swiftly as possible back down the stairs, I grabbed the heavy tray of food, wincing as the weight settled into my already-shaky arms. At the top of the stairs, I made the mistake of meeting Katerina's delighted leer.

"We don't have all day, girl," she called out. Then she turned to my father. "That girl is getting lazier by the day."

Father looked back at her with a bored stare before returning his attention to his correspondences. He read them every morning during breakfast. My theory was that he read them to avoid talking to Katerina. The thought almost made me smile. Maybe Katerina was his own personal punishment, albeit a self-inflicted one. I set everyone's plates in front of them before going back around to fill their cups.

"You look a little worse for the wear today, Evelyn. Did something keep you up last night?" Katerina smiled cruelly.

"I slept quite well, ma'am, thank you for asking," I replied sweetly. And then I imagined pouring the entire pitcher of juice all over her head.

Father startled me when he snatched the pitcher away from my hands before I could pour his juice, setting it on the table in front of him. He stared up at me intently, clutching my hands in his. For a brief moment, the look in his eyes was almost like seeing my old papa again, the slightest flicker of kindness in his eyes nearly broke my heart in half. In that moment, I realized how much I truly missed him. How I longed for any moment of care he gave me, even these fleeting glances. But then the all too familiar dark shadow crept across his face, and his expression soured again.

"As part of your punishment for yesterday's debacle, you are only allowed one meal today. I know you didn't have dinner last night, so be sure to choose wisely today." He dropped my hands and looked back down at his plate, cracking his boiled egg open with his spoon. "I'll take water today, no juice."

It shocked me enough that I paused for a moment too long. I came to when Katerina snapped her fingers at me. "See what I mean, Frank? What did I tell you? Lazy. This kind of behavior is truly unacceptable. We wouldn't allow it from any *other* servant."

I grabbed the pitcher of water, my cheeks flushing red as I poured his water.

Any other servant.

After breakfast was finished, everyone went about their various activities for the day. Camilla would go to the sitting room across the hall, and Katerina would follow close behind her with whichever book she would pretend to read today. Father would go to his office.

I dutifully cleaned up their plates and cups, grateful to do my chores in relative peace. But before I could even finish clearing the dining table, I heard Camilla gasp. When I turned, I found her bent over, peeking out the window. "What in the . . . Mother! Come look! There's a royal horseman approaching."

Liam? My heart beat faster in anticipation.

Katerina rushed over to look out the window with her, both women straining their necks to spy whatever they could without being caught.

Katerina pinched Camilla's arms, shaking her slightly. "Looks like you made a good impression on the prince's captain."

All the air rushed back out of my lungs. Of course. After meeting Camilla, he wouldn't be back here for me.

Katerina sighed dramatically, draping herself over her daughter. "Oh, Camilla! I always knew you would come in handy one day."

I quietly snorted, rolling my eyes. *At least she's generous with her backhanded remarks.*

Camilla ignored the comment, shrugging her off. "It looks like a messenger of some kind. I can't fully make out the emblem on the horse yet, but it is most definitely royal."

Katerina grabbed Camilla away from the window, pinching her cheeks to add color, then pinching her own. "Act natural, darling."

"Mother, I am acting natural! Stop pinching my cheeks, that hurts!"

A knock at the door.

Katerina shot me a withering glare. "Well? Go answer it!"

I set down the plates, wiping my hands on my apron, and tried to smooth back my hair as best I could before opening the door.

"Good day, miss." The messenger hastily bowed his head. "I have a personal invitation from the prince for Lord Coulter." He handed me the invitation just as my father walked out of his study, probably wondering what all the racket was about.

I gave a polite curtsy, taking the invitation. "Thank you, sir. I'll make sure he receives it."

The messenger tipped his hat. "Good day, miss." He returned quickly to his horse, riding back out of the gate.

Katerina rushed over and snatched the invitation from my hand before I had even closed the door. "Frank! Get over here and open this message at once!"

Father sauntered over slowly, giving Katerina a patronizing smile before taking the letter from her hands and opening it painstakingly carefully. I smiled in spite of myself. *He finds joy in the most peculiar things.*

As he began reading silently, Katerina shrieked in his face. "Read it *out loud*, Frank!"

He chuckled, clearing his throat. "Lord Franklin Coulter, you are hereby cordially invited to attend the King's Summer Ball at the palace on the nineteenth day of the seventh month in the one hundred and twenty-seventh year of our King Amaury Penvarden. It is required that you bring your family and all eligible daughters in attendance with you."

There was a pregnant pause of silence before the explosion of excitement that came from Katerina and Camilla. Screams and jumps and kisses on Father's cheeks, chaos utterly erupting from them. Father simply looked bewildered, but when his eyes looked up to meet mine, he smiled for a moment before shrugging his shoulders as he embraced the excited women. It was strange, almost like he was seeing someone else instead of me, but I still relished another private moment with him.

Camilla surprised me by grabbing my arms and twirling me in a circle. "Aren't you excited, Evelyn?"

"We need to go to town immediately and get you a new dress. The ball is only seven days away! It's horrible that they should be so disorganized as to send us such a late invitation, but we cannot ignore His Royal Majesty's invite due to his lack of decorum, now can we?" Katerina was already fussing with Camilla's dress, her hair, her face. "We've got some work to do before you'll be ready for the prince."

Father slowly eased himself down into a chair, rubbing the back of his neck. Katerina looked over to him, practically scolding him with her eyes. "Frank darling, you'll have to pay more, of course, for us to get two new gowns in such a short amount of time. But it will be worth it when the prince chooses *your* very own daughter as the next queen!"

He bowed his head and let out a deep groan.

"Now don't you start that moaning and groaning routine again, this is important, Frank! Your own daughter could be—"

"That means I get to go as well?"

I wanted to swallow the words back down almost as soon as they were out. I hardly even knew where they came from, but the anger inside me was boiling. I knew she wasn't referring to me, but that's who I was. His *own* daughter, his only blood relation left.

The room fell uncomfortably silent.

Katerina looked over at me, incensed. Camilla looked aghast. Father hadn't raised his head yet.

It was Katerina who first broke the silence. Speaking in such low tones I could hardly hear her, she growled out, "What on earth makes you think *you'll* be going?"

My eyes fell to where my father sat, desperate for a way to reach him, to remind him that I was his daughter too. Hadn't we just shared a moment?

"Father, the invitation says for you to bring *every* eligible daughter," I reminded him, leveling a glare of my own Katerina's way. "I'd like to go."

She scoffed, looking incredulously at Father while Camilla's face turned ashen.

I began to scramble, thinking that somehow I was losing the battle before it had even truly begun. "I'm happy to make my own dress." He still hadn't raised his head to look at me. "I will still finish all my chores. The house will want for nothing in my absence. What would I even do here alone while all of you attend the ball?" I took a deep breath and exhaled quickly, exasperated. "Why would you *not* include me?"

He looked up at me then. I saw a gathering darkness collect in his eyes. He strangely looked like he was about to cry. But when he glanced over at Katerina, she shook her head in response. He quickly blinked away the shadows, and his face turned stony again.

Quietly, he replied, "It said every *eligible* daughter, Evelyn."

"But I *am* eligible, Father, I—"

"No. You're not. Eligible means desirable, a good match, a suitable partner for marriage. But you are . . ." He paused, looking to Katerina again.

Katerina snarled, "You are none of those things, *girl*."

I couldn't tell what face I was making, but I could tell it pleased her, because a horrible sardonic smile stretched across her face. "You are *nothing*. A forgotten girl, a housemaid, and a servant. You are nothing compared to my Camilla. What could you possibly offer that Camilla couldn't provide twice over?" She paused, making a show of surveying me up and down. "You're barely worth the added expense, and you know Frank is already struggling to pay for our gowns as it is. Why would we *ever* bring you? Our little house mouse?" She looked over at Frank. "Perhaps now you'll agree that it's time we send her away to serve a different household. We could easily get a different housemaid, you know. One that knows her place."

The words hit me just as painfully as the switch had my flesh last night. My face fell a mile, but I swallowed down the urge to cry. I wouldn't give her the satisfaction today.

Father looked down at his hands, collapsing back into the chair. Katerina's lips were moving, but I couldn't hear a word. The pity disappeared from Camilla's eyes, hardening as she looked at me. The softness she had shown me last night was completely gone now. I put a hand to my head, trying to decipher my thoughts. I couldn't tell if it was because of hunger, my bruised body, or the realization that my father had been entertaining the idea of giving me away, but my mind was whirling.

Anger boiled beneath my skin, and glowing light caught in the corners of my eyes as my breaths came in fast and short. I wanted to punch and scream and kick and destroy. But I knew if I acted out, I would only get hurt worse.

Katerina turned away from me and started to fuss with Camilla once more. Father got up and abruptly walked out of the room. And in an instant, I was invisible again.

I slowly made my way out the front door, stumbling to the side of the courtyard before my knees gave out in the dead grass. Sharp pain flashed up my spine, and I saw nothing but black as my mind whirled with one question.

Why?

CHAPTER 12

Evelyn

My lashes fluttered open for the second time today, my mouth tasting desperately dry and chalky. It took an extra moment for me to realize there was a cool cloth on my forehead and a cup of water to my lips.

"Here, drink, Little Miss."

I recognized the soft tone of Jimmy's reassuring voice and the sweet, comforting scent of fresh hay. We were surrounded by the warm musk of a stable and . . . soup? Blinking my eyes a few more times, I saw the insides of a stable stall. Cook quickly approached with what looked like a big bowl of soup and a steaming cup of hot tea.

As I gathered my bearings, I rubbed my eyes groggily. "What happened?"

Jimmy's wrinkled and weathered face hovered over me as he pressed the cup back to my lips. "Here, drink some more, Miss Evelyn." I tried to scoot up, but he stayed my hands. "None of that now, miss. I found you out in the garden. Cook and I guess that between not eating and working in spite of your . . . injuries, your body seemed inclined to give itself a break." He gave me a crooked smile that crinkled the corner of his grey eyes even further. "Long story short, you fainted."

I remembered feeling dizzy and overwhelmed. But there was also a sense of some kind of shooting pain, a draining of energy deep inside me that seemed unrelated to my recent injuries.

I blinked rapidly, trying to focus on the sweet people in front of me. "I'm so sorry I worried you two." I put my hand on my head, still feeling a bit woozy.

"How do you feel now?" Jimmy's face was creased with worry, and his short gray hair was all messy, like he'd been running his hands through it. "Cook's brought you some soup and tea. Do you feel ready to have some?"

I nodded as he helped me sit upright, leaning me against the back of the stall. I placed my hands on the fresh hay beneath me. "Does the hay feel okay? I thought it might be easier for you to sit on."

My face flamed with embarrassment, and I scrunched my nose a little before I nodded. "Thank you, Jimmy. It's perfect."

A big, contagious smile brightened up his whole face, and he leaned over to kiss me on the forehead. Cook scooted forward and handed me the tea. "Sip slowly now, Miss Evelyn, it's still quite warm."

I took a big sip and was rewarded with a spicy ginger taste, sweetened with some honey and lemon, that helped calm my queasy stomach. "Thank you, Cook, this tastes amazing." I took another sip before continuing. "I'm so sorry to be such a burden on you both."

Cook looked down and away, turning from me quickly, her face all red and blotchy. I could tell she was trying to cover up her tears as she leaned down to stir the small pot of soup she had brought out with her.

Jimmy's throat bobbed as he swallowed. "Cook told me about what happened last night . . . and this morning."

I sipped my tea again, letting the spicy ginger flavor settle on my tongue. "How long have I been out?"

"Just a few hours."

Panic blew my eyes wide open. "A few *hours*?" I tried to scramble off the ground.

"Don't you dare move, missy!" Cook turned back around, bringing the soup over to me. "You need to eat something, or we'll have a repeat incident on our hands." Jimmy gently took the tea out of my hands and set it on the ground next to me.

"I'm . . ." My voice faltered, and I looked away again, twisting my fingers together. "I'm just so sorry."

Cook placed the bowl of soup in my lap and propped my chin up with her knuckle, looking me directly in the eyes. "You are no burden, Miss Evelyn. Not now, not ever. We love you. Let us help you." Her gaze glassed over again, but this time she didn't turn away as a few tears spilled down her face. "I was so worried when I heard the commotion in the breakfast nook. I-I couldn't just let them . . ."

I knew what she was trying to say, even if the words weren't coming. I gave her hand an understanding squeeze.

Jimmy chimed in then, looking back and forth between us. "Cook's right. We love you, Little Miss." He leaned forward to kiss my forehead again. "And you are *never* a burden. In fact, we wish you'd let us help you more."

I forced a smile as I picked up the spoon Cook handed me. It was then I realized just how famished I was. Cook was right; I really needed to eat something before I passed out again. In between bites, I asked, "Have the others noticed me missing yet?"

Cook shook her head. "Not yet. They're still caught up in their own nonsense. The ladies left for the market to buy new dresses, and your father locked himself in his study, per usual." Her irreverent tone made me want to giggle.

I sighed in relief and nodded, grateful for a moment to rest and be cared for. I slowly enjoyed my warm soup, sipping on my tea while Jimmy and Cook argued over who had worked here the longest, whether I had inherited my mother's eyes, whether my wit would have outdone my mother's. A warm, happy sensation blossomed inside my chest. Moments like this were incredibly rare, and I thought the love in my heart might just bubble over.

The stable slowly quieted as I slurped my soup, and Jimmy's face sombered. He sucked in a long, tortured breath, and my chest tightened with concern.

"You know that if we could take you away from here, we would." His voice was a husky whisper, every word struggling to get out. Cook's head bobbed up and down in agreement.

I dipped my chin, looking down at my soup bowl. "I know you both would. And I wish the same for you. I feel guilty every day that you stay for me."

Cook's face turned a blotchy red again, and she shook her head at me. "There's nowhere else we'd rather be than helping to care for you, Miss Evelyn. We made that decision a long time ago, and neither of us have ever regretted it."

"I know." My voice was barely a whisper, and Cook gently knelt down to take my empty bowl away, sure to refill it. Jimmy handed me my spicy tea to replace it.

His fingers tapped anxiously on his pulled-up knees. His greying hair, grey eyes, and wrinkled face were worn from hard days in the sun doing manual labor. I loved the look of his tanned, leathery skin. It reminded me that we could take a beating and keep going without losing who we were. Jimmy, no matter what happened, always had the best attitude. He treated every living being with kindness and respect. After taking care of horses all his life, he had a healthy dose of patience that was more than admirable.

"You have no reason to feel guilty, Little Miss. We stay because we love you." He paused thoughtfully. "Did you know I struck your father once?"

"What? *No!* Why on earth?" Jimmy was too kind to even kill a fly. I'd never even heard him raise his voice before.

"It was right after the first time he took the switch to you a few years ago. I—I lost it. I charged right into his study and knocked him out of his seat."

I gasped, looking over at Cook, who didn't seem the least bit surprised at his confession.

"I really tried, Evy . . . I tried to make him stop, to see reason." His voice choked as his chin dipped to his chest.

Dread burrowed into my stomach. "How are you still . . . what did he do?"

Jimmy looked down between his knees. "He threatened to do worse. He threatened both you and Cook. He said if I ever attacked him again, he'd send both me and Cook to the stocks, and find someone new to replace us." Silent tears ran down his face. "We couldn't leave you. It wasn't worth the risk to leave you all alone here."

Cook laid a soft hand on Jimmy's shoulder, and I could see the weight of worry in the lines on her face. It seemed the last seven years had taken its toll on everyone. "Jimmy and I tried to come up with a plan to leave with you, but we knew that Frank would hunt us down, and then you'd be left with no one to care for you."

My eyes darted between the two of them. "I would never want you to risk yourselves in that way."

"And we never wanted to risk you." Jimmy's voice was hard and brittle.

Cook smiled softly. "When you leave, we will be with you, Miss Evelyn. For as long as you'll have us."

I pulled them both into a hug. Jimmy opened up his arms to embrace me, and Cook knelt down, her arms wrapping around the both of us.

Tears pulled at the back of my throat. "I love you both so much."

Jimmy pulled back, gruffly saying, "We love you too, Little Miss," before planting a kiss on my temple.

Cook stood and finished refilling my bowl of soup. "One bowl of soup is not enough to sustain you. Let's see how many you can eat." She winked as she set the fresh bowl in front of me.

I giggled. "You guys are spoiling me."

Both their eyes grew a little sad. Jimmy tucked a piece of hair behind my ear, "No, Evelyn. We're just taking care of you."

I sobered up at that thought. "Jimmy?"

"Yes, Little Miss?" His gaze twinkled as he looked at me with all the love and care in the world. I had wished many times over that Jimmy had been my father instead of Frank, but instead he had been like my adopted uncle, which was sometimes even better.

I hesitated on the question I was about to ask, not wanting to take that twinkle from his eye. He noticed my hesitation. "What's going on in that beautiful brain of yours? You can always ask me anything."

"Why did Father change?"

Both sets of eyes widened, hardened, then softened at the edges. I'd never really asked—I'd never really wanted to know, not enough to push. But today . . . today felt different, and I wondered if they knew more than I did.

Cook swallowed and dropped her chin, but Jimmy kept strong eye contact with me.

"You know, your Father and I used to be close." I nodded,

remembering how often they had spent time together. "When your mother was alive, I would've called him a friend rather than an employer. But I—" Jimmy shook his head mournfully. "There were signs that he maybe wasn't always as he seemed. I never really paid it much mind. Not until after your mother got sick."

I remembered the day they'd rushed Mama into her room. Papa had stopped me from following and sent me away to wait in a different room. No one came for hours and hours. That was the first night my trembling started. I sat on the bed and held my knees close, rocking quietly, listening to people rush back and forth in the hall.

Cook was the one who finally came to check on me. She'd looked surprised to see I was there, but she made me stay. They didn't know what Mama had, and they wanted to keep me in a clean room. She brought me soup and tea that night, too. But Papa never came.

Jimmy paused to swallow, like he was nervous. "I didn't realize your father tended towards cruelty. Every once in a while I saw it in the way he treated the horses, or the stableboys. But I always treated those instances like bad days, not the standard. He had always been well-liked at court. A very amiable man, popular even, especially once he started courting Clara." A small smile brushed the edges of his lips. "That's the man you knew before. He was better with your mother. Happier. She had a calming effect on him."

Mama seemed to have a calming effect on everyone and everything around her. Even the plants themselves seemed soothed by her presence, even when they were traumatized by the cold or erratic weather. Mama always told me plants were living creatures too, creatures that needed love and support just as much as any other being.

When I was much younger, I'd always imagined she was made of magic. I remembered seeing faint colors whispering off her fingertips, but Father would only tell me I had been imagining things, that magic wasn't real. Mama would just titter at us both and change the subject. But I always believed, even if it wasn't *real* magic, that she had been magical anyway.

Jimmy continued, "The minute your mother fell ill, your father changed. He became desperate to save her, and he never seemed to recover after her death. It was like it broke him open, but what poured out was the crueler side of him. The better part of him died with her."

He paused for a long moment, his eyes staring at a spot on the hay-covered ground. "I don't know where your father's cruel streak came from, but I know that I saw it long before now. I just didn't realize it could be so bad, or that he would ever act against you. I just never imagined . . ." He shook his head again, disgust distorting his agreeable features. "I wish I could tell you more, but sometimes we're not given an answer to these hard questions. But you need to know it was never because of *you*. Do you understand this?"

A sharp intake of breath scraped through my nose, and I nodded with wide eyes at his intense expression.

"You have done nothing wrong. You have done *nothing* to deserve the treatment you've had to endure." His voice cracked, his eyes squeezing shut.

Cook shifted her weight to kneel beside me, rubbing my shoulder. "I've known cruel men before, and they don't always start out that way. Jimmy is right. There's not always an explanation for their behavior." She gave my shoulder a little squeeze as Jimmy took her other hand, supporting her silently. "The most important thing you need to know is that it is not because of *you*. He made his decisions. He gave in to his cruelty, and that's on *him*."

I took in a deep breath and nodded again, squeezing her hand back. Jimmy's tale seemed to stir old memories from the littered floor of my mind . . . being left alone in that guest room when Mama got sick. My father hitting a stableboy once when he didn't know I was there. He'd even yelled at the household staff on occasion. But Jimmy was right. Everyone had loved him. Lords and ladies from all over the kingdom used to come visit the estate, just to see Mama and Papa. I remembered lots of laughter and parties. It was hard to reconcile those glittering memories with the harsh ones. *Did Mama see it? Did she know?*

Cook plucked the freshly-emptied bowl from my hands, offering more, which I had to decline. My stomach already felt uncomfortably stretched, full of much more food than it was used to.

Between this stolen moment and Liam's sudden reappearance, I was starting to remember what life was supposed to be like. A renewed spark ignited somewhere deep inside me.

Maybe it was from the love and encouragement I had just received, or maybe my confidence was simply growing, but I decided right then and there that I was going to go to the ball. Father and Katerina couldn't stop me. I had a right to attend, same as everyone else.

This delicious rebellion tasted especially sweet in my mind as I mulled over a plan to make it happen.

I could tell Cook and Jimmy relished this time together just as much as I did. It was such a rare opportunity for the three of us, and we were all in better spirits by the time we heard the sound of horse hooves approaching the estate again. Cook and I gathered up the empty dishes, giving Jimmy kisses on the cheek before we scurried back to the kitchen.

Just before dinner, while everyone was getting settled at the table, I snuck up into Father and Katerina's bedchamber and found my mother's old trunk. He had never let Katerina move it out of the room, much to her chagrin. I smiled to myself when my hands touched the silky soft fabric on top. At the end of this week, I would be dancing with Liam in this dress. My heart flipped giddily at the thought. Clutching the delicate fibers close to my heart, I darted back to my room to hide the evidence.

CHAPTER 13

Evelyn

"Where. Is. My. *Necklace*?" Katerina squawked.

The night of the Summer Ball had arrived, and the whole household was in a tizzy. Katerina and Camilla started getting ready four hours before it was time to leave. Father made sure the carriage was cleaned and sparkling for the family to arrive in. He spent the day with Jimmy yesterday touching it up with paints and polish. Everything almost felt like it used to when I was a little girl, and there was a strange comfort in the hustle and bustle of the day.

Camilla looked over at me and rolled her eyes. "It's right here, Mother. You left it sitting on your settee earlier." She grabbed the necklace and walked it over to Katerina while I stifled a giggle.

Katerina turned and clasped her hands over Camilla's, trapping the necklace between them. "You are our only hope, Camilla. Do you hear me?" Her voice morphed into a desperate whisper. "It's up to you to do what I couldn't."

My stomach turned over. It'd been obvious to me from the start that Katerina had taken advantage of my Father's vulnerable state when they met. For him to have wed again only three months after my mother died had felt sudden to everyone. It was obvious that she had preyed upon his wealth after the passing of her first husband, who had left her indebted and destitute. Knowing her habits, I was starting to wonder if she had sent him to an early grave, and left *herself* indebted and destitute.

My father *was* a wealthy man when they first met. However, she turned him away from running the estate to running an overseas trade instead. They'd lost most of his money from that change, and they've been struggling to recover it ever since. Never once had she recognized that it was *her* fault that we were the poor outcasts of court society now. I'd come to learn that Katerina was *never* to blame, not for anything.

Katerina snapped her fingers at me, breaking me out of my reverie. "Are you listening, girl? Come over here and brush my hair. I want it shiny and soft tonight."

I gave her my best withering glare as I walked over to her vanity and grabbed her hairbrush. Camilla gave me a small wink in the mirror and moved out of Katerina's room to finish getting ready in her own.

I took a deep breath to calm myself and started the brush at the top of her head, working my way down. Toward the bottom I caught the brush on some snagged hair. Before I could work out the tangles, she whipped around and slapped my hand.

"You stupid girl! Do you not even know how to brush hair?" She snatched the hairbrush from my hand. "You start at the ends and work your way up so that you never have to hit a snag." She paused, waiting to make sure I understood. I tried to take the hairbrush back from her, but she kept it out of my reach, glaring at me expectantly.

I barely held back a sigh. "Yes, ma'am."

Satisfied, she handed the brush back to me, and I begrudgingly brushed it her way until her hair was as smooth as silk and ready to be pinned.

"Evelyn! Could you tie up the back of my corset, please?" Camilla called out from her bedroom. Katerina gave me a nod of dismissal as she took over pinning up her own hair.

When I entered, Camilla was already clinging to her bedpost for support, waiting patiently for my help. She grunted and gasped while I laced her up, but didn't complain beyond that. Who knew how she planned to breathe throughout the night; as tight as she asked me to tie it, I was certain no breath would be able to get in or out.

She paused to admire herself in the mirror. Her breasts were pushed up so high they acted like a built-in shelf just beneath her neck. She reached in to adjust, raising them up even higher. One wrong move, and she'd be showing far more than the average lady tonight.

"Perfect." She bent over and shook herself a little, testing the movement. "Hopefully the prince is a breast man." She gave herself a coy smile and winked at me through the mirror.

I laughed outright. "Well, if he's not, I'm sure plenty of other gentlemen in attendance will notice and help bring it to his attention." I twisted her hips back and forth, giving her an extra shake. "See? Your breasts will be dancing right along with you tonight, so you'll always have a dance partner." I smiled at her in the mirror, and she laughed with me.

Next I helped her into her extensive petticoats and tied it all off before slipping her stunning gown over her shoulders. She'd chosen deep scarlet silk with black lace detailing and small cap sleeves. It perfectly complimented her alabaster skin and dark, rich hair. She looked like a ruby come to life, and my breath caught for a moment. "You are a vision, Camilla."

She turned and grabbed my hands, giving me a kiss on the cheek, a rare moment of affection from her. "Thank you, Evy. I actually feel beautiful tonight." She smoothed a small strand of hair back into position.

I paused. *Actually?* "Camilla, you're always beautiful. I hope you never doubt it."

Red subtly stained her cheeks as she looked at herself in the mirror. I saw a flash of unease in her eyes that made me worry.

I slipped my hand into hers. "You are beautiful, and you always have been." I smiled faintly, thinking back to our first few years as stepsisters. "Ever since we were children, you consistently turned heads. Don't you remember the boys who still worked the fields when you first arrived?"

She scoffed. "You mean the ones who were always looking at *you*."

I shook my head. "That's ridiculous. Those boys always made fun of me."

She turned to me, her eyes turbulent. "No, Evelyn. They were always looking at *you*. Everyone always looks at *you*. When you're around, it's like I'm invisible."

I frowned. "That's not even close to the truth, Camilla. You are—"

"I'm the one always being measured against *you*. Mother is constantly comparing me to *you*. Frank is always comparing me to *you*. Now, even Liam will compare me to *you*."

Shock numbed my veins, hearing Liam's name from her lips. Was she really interested in him?

"You remember when we stopped playing together when I was thirteen?" she asked, pointedly staring at me. "Do you know *why*?"

I opened my mouth, willing it to say anything other than *boys*, but she cut me off. "Mother decided it was time to train me in the art of seduction. She didn't believe I could get a man without it. It was what her mother did to her when she didn't *measure up* to her sister, and now it's what she does to me." Her mouth twisted bitterly. "My childhood was over after that."

I could only stare at her, stunned. I hadn't known. I'd thought she'd simply outgrown me.

She turned back around to face herself in the mirror. "But it's no matter. Since *you* won't be there tonight, the prince might actually notice *me* instead." Leaning forward, she dabbed a spot on her lip. "Though I suppose if not him, that handsome captain of his will do nicely." Her smug eyes cut to mine, and I stiffened, silently willing her to take it back. She didn't.

A deep heat flared low in my ribs, and I pictured the secret I had folded neatly underneath my mattress, relishing the daydream of Camilla's reddened face as she watched *me* dancing with Liam tonight. *Though hopefully they won't see me at all.*

Katerina came swooping in the door just then, wearing a sapphire gown trimmed in black lace; practically the twin of Camilla's, minus the color. "Oh, my beautiful girl! You are perfect." She kissed each of Camilla's cheeks before looking in my direction. "Make sure nothing is out of place. I want you to look from our hair to our shoes for *any* sign of imperfection."

I took in their appearances as they turned for me, carefully assessing their dresses and shoes. I smiled politely. "You both look utterly lovely. Not a flaw to be found." *On the outside, anyway.*

Katerina narrowed her eyes. "You seem in particularly good spirits this evening. Excited for us to be attending the ball without you?"

I didn't have time to respond before Father walked into the room, admiring Camilla and Katerina, ignoring me entirely. "You both look beautiful. I shall be the luckiest and most envied man there with you two beauties on my arms." He gave them each a kiss on the cheek and then offered his arm to Katerina. "Are we ready to go, then?"

We all left the room, heading down the stairs and toward the carriage outside. Father helped Katerina and Camilla get in before stepping up himself. He leaned his head out the door. "Have some food ready for us when we return, we'll likely be famished." Then he closed the door, and the carriage jolted forward.

I went back inside and closed the front door before bounding up the stairs to my room. I quickly gathered the gown I'd been hiding under my mattress and draped it across the bed so it could start to release some of the wrinkles it had collected while being folded up. Hurrying over to my washbasin, I rinsed my face, scrubbing away the dirt spots with a cloth and carefully tallying all that still needed to be done in my mind. *I'll ride one of the horses to the palace, spend about an hour at the ball, find Liam, hopefully get in a dance or two, then head back home in plenty of time so no one will ever know the difference.* I applied some of Mama's old perfume to my bare skin, the familiar aroma of vanilla and jasmine comforting me.

Using an old corset and petticoat I borrowed from Camilla's closet, I loosely tied it around me for structure. Personally, I preferred breathing, so I didn't tie it tight. Besides, I didn't have much in the way of *assets* to show off anyway. I gingerly picked up the newly-altered gown and pulled it gently over my head.

The soft fabric draped beautifully down my slim figure. Simple layers of white silk, fitted throughout the bodice, flared out naturally over my hips and petticoat. Pretty puffy sleeves sat just off my shoulders, with a straight neckline and large ruffles that decorated the bodice and skirt. I took a moment to admire myself in the mirror, hardly recognizing my own face. Even with my sunken cheeks, the bones poking through my skin, and the dark circles under my eyes, I still felt pretty. I was not nearly as rounded out and curvy as Camilla, but tonight, it didn't matter.

A few tears came to my eyes as I surveyed the gown. It had been Mama's wedding dress, set aside and saved for my wedding day. I closed my eyes, desperately wishing Mama was still here to see me in it. Of course, if she was still here, none of this would've been happening, and my life would have looked very different.

I shook my head. This wasn't the time to dwell on what could've been. It was time to enjoy what might be.

Before I was even able to start on my hair or put on my shoes, my door suddenly flew open, slamming harshly against the wall. My heart flew into my throat, and I stumbled back, nearly crashing into the mirror.

"I told you!" Katerina shrieked, pointing an angry finger at me while holding the door open for Father to enter.

He entered the room and simply stared at me, dumbfounded. Then, with tears welling in his eyes, he softly said, "Clara?"

"What are you doing? Frank! Pay attention!" Katerina's voice sounded like a dying animal. I never quite knew how she managed to make the sounds that came out of her.

I took in a shaky breath, gripping the skirt in my sweaty hands. "Father, I—"

At those words, he snapped out of his stupor. "Evelyn?" His face slowly turned a deep shade of red, and his eyes hardened to steel. "What on *earth* do you think you're doing?"

Before I could even answer, he raised his hand to stop me, and his voice lowered to a quiet threat. "You've disobeyed me, *again*."

My heart started to race, tremors wracking my arms and legs, nearly dropping me to my knees before him. Terror swirled sickening circles in my chest. My voice trembled when I tried to speak, barely above a whisper: "I just wanted to see what it was like."

I looked anxiously around the room, finding Camilla in the doorway. She looked angry with me somehow— maybe even hurt. But she wasn't the biggest threat in the room.

Father's face didn't move, and my body started to cave inward. Tears threatened to spill over at the first blink of my eyes.

The room took on an eerie silence. My gaze darted from Camilla's to Katerina's to Father's, then to my own reflection in the mirror. It was like seeing my mother looking back at me.

Something small shifted in my chest, a puzzle piece clicking into place. Mama's dress gave me courage. The last words she ever spoke to me filtered into my mind: "*I want you to stay brave and strong just like you are now. Keep finding the beauty in everything. Never lose hope. Wait for a great love, and put your whole heart into it. I'll always be with you, even if you can't see me.*"

Even if she wasn't here physically, she was still with me. I used those words to fan that inner flame I had only so recently rediscovered. *Stay brave and strong. Never lose hope.*

Without looking away from my reflection in the mirror, I flatly asked, "Why do you hate me so much?"

Father's reflected face flinched. But he didn't answer. He just stared back.

Stay brave and strong.

Anger burned in my chest as I slowly turned to look at him. Buoyed by my mother's gown and her remembered words, I realized I deserved an answer. I stared into his hardened eyes, my own hushed rebellion, and I allowed myself to *feel* that deeply buried and bitter betrayal. It tasted acrid in my mouth, but it had been tucked away long enough.

If he can still love my mother, what's stopping him from loving me?

A furious need for justice swelled inside my chest burning away all precautions. I was *his* daughter. I was *Mama's* daughter.

I am brave and strong.

I yelled.

"*Answer me!*"

With shaking hands curled into white-knuckled fists, reddened cheeks wet with tears, and a deep fury burning me from the inside out, I finally demanded my answer. Although I kept my voice strong and loud and my stance sturdy, the minute the words were out, my traitorous body trembled uncontrollably.

Father stumbled back, as if my eruption had physically pushed him. Emotions flashed through his eyes, too many to decipher what they all were.

I choked on a sob. "I'm your daughter too! Have you forgotten that?" I gestured to the mirror, my pointing finger shaking like a leaf.

"I am your daughter too!"

A blanket of silence fell over the room again, everyone stunned by my outburst.

"Don't just stand there, Frank, *do* something!" Katerina motioned wildly in my direction, but Father didn't move.

"Fine. If you won't, I will." Stepping around my father, she stalked over to me with predatory intent. "Take it off." She held out her hand, waiting.

My eyebrows shot up and I tried to jerk back but she gripped my shoulder, pulling me closer to her as she whispered in my ear: "I win." Stepping back again she held out her hand and motioned her impatience with her fingers. "Take. It. Off. Evelyn."

Shocked tears welled as I stared at my stepmother's smug, terrible face, but I refused to let them fall.

I refused to look in the mirror at my mother's beautiful wedding gown as I slowly unbuttoned and slipped it off my shoulders. The smooth silk fell to the floorboards with a soft rustle, exposing Camilla's old corset and petticoats hidden underneath.

I refused to look at my father, who stood back and did nothing, who treated me like a stranger in my own home.

I refused to do anything but stand there defiantly, staring back at Katerina with all the strength I could muster.

I am brave and strong.

Katerina's eyes narrowed at my silent challenge. "Camilla, get over here and help me."

Camilla's eyes darted back and forth between us, panic gleaming in her dark eyes. Katerina simply stared her down with a long look that I was sure could somehow freeze time itself, and Camilla stiffly moved to stand before me. I saw a flash of grief—or was it pity?— wash over her face before she knelt down and gathered my dress from the ground, forcing me to step out of it.

Katerina held out her hand again and Camilla placed the wadded up white material in her palm. Then she stormed out of the room, heels clicking harshly against the solid wooden floor.

"Camilla! Frank!" She bellowed from down the hall.

The two figures slowly trailed behind, and I followed after them.

Katerina stood in her room next to the dying embers of her

fireplace. The wicked glint in her eye had me lunging toward her a second too late.

My mother's dress was almost immediately eaten up by the famished flames and I dropped to my knees before the fire, finally closing my eyes, too angry and ashamed to move.

"There." Katerina sneered, brushing her hands together as if they'd been dirtied. "Now, be quick about this, Frank. We need to get to the palace."

Katerina and Camilla quickly slipped out of the room, their clanging heels fading down the stairs. Father still stood behind me, silent, unmoving, staring at the fire.

I didn't dare turn around, bracing myself for his punishment. But he couldn't do worse than what Katerina had already done. The beautiful white silk curled and blackened, as the flames happily danced around it.

His heavy steps brought him closer and my body tightened expecting pain. But instead of hitting me, or yelling, or snarling, or going for his switch, he knelt beside me and pulled me into an awkwardly crushing hug.

His broad frame shuddered, and I realized he was crying. Torn between wanting to push him away and wanting to pull him closer, I waited, frozen in place. My father hadn't embraced me in years, and I hadn't realized how much I'd missed it and longed for it, until this awful moment.

He slowly pulled away. Carefully, gently, he cupped my face in his hands, using his thumbs to wipe away the streaming tears. He didn't say anything. He only stared at me.

My mind went numb. I couldn't feel the tears on my face any longer. Mother's dress, *my* future wedding dress, was now gone. Burned to ashes.

I didn't know how my lips managed to form the breathy question, but somehow I asked, "Why?"

He dropped his hands, his eyes squeezing shut. "You look just like your mother did," he whispered. "I loved her so much, Evy."

Evy. He called me Evy. I hadn't heard the sound of my nickname on his lips in so long.

"Me too, Papa."

His eyes widened. I hadn't called him Papa in seven years. Not since Mama died. Katerina had demanded I call him "Father" or "Sir," for it was much more dignified. She said using the word *Papa* made me sound like a child.

A deep sorrow shadowed his eyes before he closed them again. "I'm not your Papa, Evelyn."

The matter-of-fact statement snapped me out of my musings. "What?"

He shook his head and stood back up. "I'm not your Papa. Not anymore. I haven't been for a long time."

Confusion creased my brow and I reached out to him, a strange desperation tightening in my chest. I couldn't let him walk away. Something inside me was breaking, something I would never get back again. "What are you talking about? You'll always be my Papa."

"No." That simple word sent a bolt of panic and a wave of nausea deep into my gut. "That man is gone. He died with your mother."

He was silent for a moment longer, then he wiped a hand down his face, sighing heavily. Speaking under his breath, he muttered, "I'm sure it's better this way. After this stunt, it's clear what must be done."

I stopped reaching, stopped breathing. Katerina's words echoed in my mind. *"I win."* The world slowed and tilted as I stared up at him, afraid to move even an inch for fear that I might somehow break.

"Katerina's right. It's time for you to go, Evelyn. You don't belong here anymore."

Light flashed in front of my eyes, and I sat back onto my feet, dazed. I couldn't comprehend what he was saying. My heart beat heavily, reverberating inside my chest and head. I could almost feel myself cracking open. *This isn't happening.*

His eyes hardened. "After tonight, I'm finding a new household to give you to."

No.

"I have a new family now, and it's clear you don't fit into it. I tried to make this work, but I can't."

No.

Tears dripped off my chin, landing on my lap with near audible *plops*, but I couldn't feel them running down my face anymore. I looked down at my hands; I couldn't even fidget, they were shaking too uncontrollably.

My voice was nothing more than a strangled sound. "Don't do this."

He had turned away, heading toward the door, but he stopped and snapped his gaze back at me, like he was surprised I was still there. I was just as surprised that I'd even managed to speak. I felt outside of my own body, watching everything happen from a distance.

He didn't move, and I couldn't tell what he was thinking or feeling. He looked . . . *empty.*

My chest rose and fell in quick bursts now. Desperation clouded my judgment. I wanted to be *heard*. I wanted him to *see* me. I wanted him to see what he had done to us, what he had done to *me*.

I am your flesh and blood! I am the only blood relation you even have left!

The words never came out. They were lodged deep in my throat, stuffed too far down inside of me.

He didn't speak again. He didn't take it back or admit what he'd done. He just . . . stood there.

A strange and final calm took over me. I closed my eyes and breathed in Mama's scent from the perfume I had sprayed earlier. When I opened my eyes again, I stared defiantly into his. "She would be so ashamed of you."

Anguish and shame passed through his eyes. He opened his mouth, and I waited with baited breath for the apology, for the admittance—

"Frank! Stop wasting time on that wretch, we're already late! Get back down here. Now!" Katerina's squawking pierced the silence. Father bristled as if annoyed, but numbly turned towards the door and walked out, leaving me there. Alone. Abandoned.

I heard the front door slam shut with an echoing finality. Seconds later, the carriage wheels scraped against the pebbled courtyard until the sounds faded away.

CHAPTER 14

"Stop pacing." Ryker waved his white gloved hand at me in irritation. "You're going to create ruts in the flooring."

"The floor is marble. I think it'll survive." But I stopped as soon as I saw Ryker's worried reflection in the mirror. "You okay, Ryk?"

"As okay as I'll ever be." His eyes met mine through the reflection in the mirror as he brushed his already perfectly-ironed suit down. All white, with gold trimmings; the king wanted him dripping with royalty tonight, so no one could mistake him as anyone but the future king. "I'm actually rather jealous of *you* tonight."

I raised my eyebrow in question. "How so?"

"You know exactly which girl you're looking for. Your heart and your mind are already set. All you have to do is wait for her to show up, and your night is made. No guessing, no questioning, no . . . fear." He looked down at his hands now, and I saw a slight tremor.

I ran my hand through my hair, untamed as always, though I was trying to keep it nice tonight. "Most men would kill to be in your shoes this evening. Think about it! You get your pick of women tonight." I gave him a little wink and nudge. "I mean, I *know* you've had fantasies like this before."

He smirked like he was reminiscing. "Yes, but those fantasies involved scantily-clothed women that I didn't have to *propose* to at the end of the night."

I shook my head. "You're not going to have to propose to anyone tonight, Ryk."

He chuffed out a laugh, then looked down at his trembling hands. "I cannot stop shaking. I don't recall a time I've ever been this nervous."

"Stop thinking about this in such world-ending terms. This is just like when you go out in search of some . . . more temporary female companionship." I grabbed his shoulders to steady him. "You know how to read a woman better than any of us. Trust that judgement. Tonight might not be a game, but the lessons you've learned so far will help aid you in your choice. You'll know which girls just want a crown on their head, and which ones are actually interested in *you*."

He looked at me skeptically. "I know how to pick an excellent bed partner, not a *life* partner."

I chuckled. "Hopefully she can be both."

"But what if I choose wrong?" His eyes were wild, tormented. "I have to spend the rest of my life with this woman. I don't want to have to live with and deal with someone I thought liked one night, only to find she's actually unbearable. I don't want to have countless affairs and mistresses just to get through a marriage. I want what you have. What Father had. A love. Someone you love with everything in you. How am I supposed to know that just from one—"

"Ryk. Take a breath." I pulled him into a stiff hug. "I believe you *will* feel it when it's right, and you won't have to question it. And remember, the king did say you didn't actually *have* to pick someone tonight."

He pulled away, looking down at his perfectly polished shoes. "I know that. But I also know it will disappoint him if I don't find someone. He wants to see me settled, and, let's be honest here, Liam. If it's not tonight, there's no guarantee it will happen in time."

I nodded solemnly. "Just . . . have faith, Ryker. And stop putting so much pressure on yourself." I gave his shoulder one last squeeze before the door opened, Rafe's head popping in around it.

"Your Highness." Rafe bowed his head and put his fist to his chest. "His Majesty sent me to fetch you. The doors are opening, sir. It's time to escort you to the ballroom."

Ryker nodded, his chest heaving as he pulled in a deep, stuttering breath. "Thank you, Rafe."

I pulled Rafe aside before we exited the room. "Remember, you are in charge tonight. But should there be any trouble, do not hesitate to call for me. Ryker is still my top priority, always."

Rafe raised an eyebrow, and I saw a glint in his eyes before he answered, "Of course, Captain. We'll be sure to protect him from all the fawning, doe-eyed ladies."

"Jackass." I gave him a little shove out the door. Ryker chuckled, and we all left for the ballroom.

CHAPTER 15

Evelyn

I'm not sure how long I sat there, staring at the empty doorway. I blinked furiously. My body felt frozen in place, but I couldn't stand the sight of that door, or this room, or even my own reflection. I needed to get away. I needed to leave. I needed to *run*.

Willing myself to move, I clambered up to a standing position awkwardly teetering on my sleepy legs. I focused on the creaking wooden planks beneath each step: one step, two, three, four. Finally finding a rhythm, I walked as quickly as possible to the stairs, then broke out into a desperate run down the stairs.

Jimmy stood at the bottom of the staircase, watching me carefully, concerned wrinkles etched into his worried face. I didn't want him to see me right now; if I had to face his pain, I would also have to face my own. I couldn't take it. I couldn't handle the unknowns. All our plans to stay together no matter what . . . those were being burned away, too.

I kept running, stumbling through the dining nook and down the small flight of stairs. By the time I reached the kitchen, I could hardly see for the tears clouding my vision, and it was only by muscle memory that I reached the back door. Cook startled and watched me run out into the garden, but she didn't try to stop me, and Jimmy didn't try to follow. I had no idea what they knew or what they'd heard, but I couldn't bear their sympathy right now.

The outside air hit my heated skin, wrapping around me like a cool embrace, and I ran even harder, relishing the soothing winds whipping through my hair.

Don't stop.

The tears spilled over, and my bare feet ached as they tore against the rough, uneven ground.

Keep running.

Branches snagged at petticoats and skin, ripping into me. I couldn't tell where I was going, but I didn't really care. My father, Papa . . . he was gone.

A part of me had been waiting for this moment. He'd given up so long ago, but not on me, not yet, not until tonight. I hadn't realized just how tightly I was still clinging to that fragile hope until he'd snatched it away tonight.

Papa. I heard the word, but I didn't know if I cried it out loud or if it was simply inside my own head. I was so caught up in my own mind, my own horrible thoughts, that I didn't recognize the woods I'd escaped into.

Don't stop.

Vaguely, I realized I'd never been out this far before. I looked up at the canopy of limbs and leaves just in time to miss the huge root bulging up from the ground. My foot collided with the upturned root, pitching me forward, and my hands shot out to catch myself, even though I knew it was too late. I closed my eyes, bracing my limbs for the impact, for the sound of crunching bone or the blossoming of bruises. But none of it came.

Instead, my fall slowed. My hands never touched the ground. I felt weightless, suspended in time. Carefully, I peeled my eyes open. A gasp slid through my teeth.

A soft, iridescent glow surrounded me, and I saw tiny pockets of light peeking in and out of the darkness surrounding me. I was floating just barely off the ground. The lights bobbed and weaved around me, floating me down a steep ravine and gently setting me down in a grassy meadow before disappearing into the trees.

I quickly sat up, trying to catch a final glimpse of them, but the movement made my head woozy, the grassy meadow around me tilting to the side. I lowered myself back down in the thick, soft grass. It smelled fresh here; clean, like my Mama's garden used to smell.

My eyes drifted up to an opening in the sparkling canopy of trees above me. The sky beyond was just beginning to blossom into color, the sunset painting the clouds in vivid pink and shimmering gold. There was a strange sense of calm and comfort in this little meadow. Everything gently swayed in a warm breeze. My tense muscles slowly uncoiled, and my anxious breathing gradually evened out. I stared up at the sky, watching the first few stars wink into existence.

Enthralled with the quiet beauty, I didn't even notice the light footsteps approaching until a twig snapped next to me, and I jerked my head toward the sound. Bare feet peeked out from beneath a long flowing skirt, just inches from my face.

"Hello, dearie." Before I could scramble up, she sat down beside me: a beautiful woman with long silver hair and eyes greener than the trees. Laugh lines crinkled at the corners of her eyes and mouth, and when she smiled at me, a strange feeling of familiarity washed over me. I had no fear of this woman, just a kindred sense of ease in her presence. I remembered feeling like this once before, but I couldn't remember when. She lowered herself down beside me, folding her hands over her heart as she stared at the sky.

Even my breathless whisper seemed too loud for this place. "Are you real?"

"I'm as real as you are." There was a lilting mirth to her voice, and her eyes crinkled at the corners as she turned her head to face me. "My name is Chrysanthemum, but everyone calls me Chrissy."

"I'm Evelyn, but most people call me Evy." Chrissy simply smiled, like she'd known that all along. "Do I know you from somewhere?"

Melancholy dimmed that sparkle in her eyes. "I'm afraid there's not much you know about me, but we have met before. You were a bit preoccupied at the time. You were a bit smaller back then, too, but I must say you've grown into quite the beautiful young woman. Just like your mother." Her eyes welled with unshed tears. "It's a pleasure to see you again, Evy. I've wished for this day for a very long time."

"Wait, you knew my mother?" I sat up on my elbow, turning to face her.

She mimicked my posture, propping herself up on her elbow too. An easy grin tugged on her lips as she nodded. "I knew your mother very well. But before we get into all that, I need you to tell me why you were crying and running through the woods all alone tonight."

Immediately, embarrassment flooded my cheeks with heat. For a stranger to have seen me behaving that way . . . Father would be furious. "Oh, it was noth—"

She reached out her free hand to clasp mine. She looked into my eyes, her own serious, determined. "You're safe here, Evy. You can tell me."

And somehow, I knew it was true.

I swallowed hard, rolling back down into the soft grass. As I stared up at the sky, my eyes welled with tears again. Somehow these felt like old tears; like they'd spent years waiting their turn to be shed, and only now could they find their way out.

All the emotions spilled out at once, and I told her *everything*. Not just what had happened tonight, but all that had happened since Mama died. I laid out all the hurt, the sorrow, the betrayal, the grief . . .

The shame.

"I miss him. I miss my papa, just as much as Mama." A loud sob escaped from my throat, and I raised my hand to cover my mouth in embarrassment, but Chrissy moved her hand gently down my arm. She took the hand I used to cover my mouth in hers and slowly lowered it to the soft grass.

"Let it out, dearie. Those tears don't belong to you, so there's no reason to hold on to them anymore." Interlocking our fingers together, she gave my hand a squeeze, then stayed just like that, holding me gently but firmly while I wept.

She didn't shush me, or scold me, or tell me to stop. She didn't try to make me laugh to ease the tension, or try to fix my pain. She simply held my hand and let me cry. It was the most uncomfortable freedom I'd felt in years. It felt so good to just *cry*. I didn't know how long it lasted, and she never tried to speed things along. It didn't matter. There was no rush.

My sobs slowly quieted, my tears letting up enough for me to breathe in deeply again. I finally sat up straight again, rubbing at my raw, red eyes. My body ached and trembled with the aftershocks of sobs. I had no idea how much time had passed.

Chrissy straightened with me, and I could see now through my teary lashes that her eyes were also wet. She was built thin and lithe, her long hair framing her bright green eyes like beams of moonlight. Her eyes almost seemed to glow in the twilight. Still holding my hand, she used her free one to push my now-ratted hair out of my face, then gently cupped my chin. She tilted my face until my eyes met hers. Her smile was genuine and thoughtful. "How do you feel?"

"Strangely, much better." I croaked, a shiver of astonishment raising goosebumps on my skin. This night hadn't gone at all like I'd planned.

She nodded in satisfaction, releasing my hand and rising to her feet. I wiped the last few tears from my eyes before pushing up off the ground. Something moved just behind Chrissy, and I squinted my eyes until I could clearly make out the shape. My jaw dropped.

"Are those . . . wings?"

Chrissy glanced nonchalantly over her shoulder, fluttering translucent wings behind her. They seemed to capture every ounce of light and color imaginable as they moved back and forth, purples turning to greens, greens to golds, golds to pinks, pinks to blues. "Oh, yes. Beautiful, aren't they?"

I shook my head, trying to clear it. "When did we meet before?" Surely I would have remembered meeting a woman with *wings*.

Chrissy grew solemn again. "We met when you were just a baby, and a few more times when you were a little younger. But the last time we saw each other was the day your mother died."

My mind reeled, trying to remember the details of that day. The closed drapes blocking out the sunlight. Mama's pained eyes, her soft hand holding one of mine, and the other being held by . . .

My eyebrows shot up. "It was you! You were the woman in her room. The one who held our hands when she passed on."

Her eyes saddened at the memory, but she gave me a soft smile anyway. "Yes. That was me."

"Why were you there? Why could no one else see you but me?"

"Come here, Evy." She reached out to clasp both of my hands in

hers before looking me directly in the eyes. "Your mother was my
only daughter. I'm your grandmother." She paused to let that sink in.
"No one else was able to see me that day because I made it so. A bit of
magic made me invisible to unseeing eyes."

Her wings fluttered again, drawing my attention away from her
face as I worked through this new revelation. "My *grandmother?*"

"Your fairy grandmother, to be specific." She winked. "And I've
been hoping for this day for quite some time now. I always hoped you
would venture out of that estate one day. You were such an explorer
when you were tiny. Really kept your mother on her toes . . ." Her
throat bobbed, and her voice came out hushed. "I am so sorry for
what you've had to endure." She reached up and cupped my cheek.
"So much pain . . . this isn't the life your mother imagined for you.
She . . . *we* believed he would take care of you."

I somehow managed to speak past the shock. "Why did you leave
after Mama's death? Why didn't you ever come to see me?"

She pursed her lips. "Your mother wished for you to be raised
human. She wanted you to understand the human world and live in
it with ease. You never showed any signs that you inherited any of her
fairy traits, and your father . . ." She shook her head, her lip curling in
distaste. "He never knew about me. Your mother hid her true lineage
from him."

My brow creased in confusion. "Why would she do that?"

Chrissy's eyes hardened from gentle green to chips of emerald.
"Humans have a deadly history with fairies. She loved your father, but
he had his prejudices, and he made them known. So she chose to keep
that part of herself hidden from him."

"He's never even mentioned fairies to me before," I protested,
unable to wrap my mind around this. "No one has."

"I can't imagine he would have. There's likely never been a reason
to." She shook her head slightly, a dark shadow flashing in her eyes.
"Many people don't remember that we exist. We've become folklore
to some, extinct to others."

I gave her hands a little squeeze. "What happened?"

"That's another story, for another time. But let's just say your
mother kept me and her past hidden in order to protect you." She
tucked a piece of wayward hair behind my ear. "I loved your mother

more than life. I didn't fully agree with her decision, but I respected it." She lowered her voice to a mischievous whisper. "Though, I always hoped you might find me on your own one day. I *was* surprised you never showed any signs . . ." She paused, her eyes darting back up to mine. "Dearie, you must promise me something."

"O-okay." I stammered, trying to keep up with her abrupt shifts of subject. She seemed to look past me, *through* me, as if searching for something hidden deep within.

"Promise me that if you start to feel or experience any . . . *changes* in yourself, you'll come straight to me."

My brows furrowed in confusion. "What kind of changes?"

"You'll know." She tapped my hand placatingly, and I sensed that was all I was going to get out of her.

I nodded slowly, but confusion still tied my mind in a knot. "I promise."

"Now then." Her face transformed from serious to practically glowing with impish glee. "Shall I go back with you and transform your father into a toad for the rest of his days?"

I giggled at the image, but shook my head.

"Are you sure? I think the change in perspective would be good for him." She wrinkled her nose, amused with her own thoughts. I didn't know for sure if she was joking or not, but just the fact that I had found her, tonight of all nights, made my heart feel three times larger.

Faster than a blink, her arms wrapped around me in the biggest bear hug. When she pulled back, her whole face was lit up with excitement. "I have an idea!"

My face brightened, mimicking hers. She was a wondrous ball of infectious energy. "What is it?"

"You had a marvelous plan for tonight, and I see no reason why you shouldn't get to see it through."

I pursed my lips in doubt, looking down at my borrowed petticoats. "I can't. I have . . . I have nothi—"

"You have me!"

"*How?*"

"Well, obviously we fairies have just a bit of magic." She wiggled her eyebrows, circling around me as she spoke. "Mine just so happens to specialize in transformations, and right now, it seems you are in need of exactly that."

Without waiting for a response, she started waving her hands around as I stood there, gaping like a fish out of water. The meadow sparkled and warmed as if the sun was shining directly on it, even though it was night. The little lights that had been flickering between the leaves seemed to gather momentum as a crackling charge filled the air.

The hairs stood up on my neck and arms, and the trees began to groan and creak as I was lifted up off the ground in a swirling, shimmering whirlwind. I looked up to see my hair floating above me like I was underwater as the scratches, bruises, and dirt that covered my body melted away. The corset and petticoats that I still wore began to miraculously alter. Yards of fabric appeared in the blink of an eye, and every color of the rainbow flashed across my vision.

There was so much happening that I couldn't keep up with it all. I closed my eyes and let the small trickles of magic tickle my skin. The feeling was intoxicating and wild. A deep flutter of pure joy bubbled up inside my chest, spreading so quickly that I couldn't help but let out a delighted giggle.

A soft hand touched my cheek. "Evelyn, open your eyes."

My feet kissed the ground just as she spoke, and I carefully opened my eyes, staring down at my clean hands and arms until I saw the lush, dazzling fabric move. The sleeves hung off my shoulders similar to my mother's gown. A straight neckline stretched from shoulder to shoulder with a cascading silky ruffle that floated down just beyond my bust line.

The whole dress looked like a pearlescent version of Chrissy's wings. I grabbed up the skirts to twirl, watching all the colors appear and disappear, from pinks and purples to golds and greens and blues. It was a material unlike anything I'd ever seen before. Dozens of small crystals practically floated on the gown, making the whole thing sparkle in even the barest light. It was by far the most beautiful thing I had ever seen, let alone worn.

"Oh, Chrissy! It's . . . I'm . . ." I couldn't find my words. "It's all too much. I can't."

Chrissy's eyes softened as she smiled at me. "You can and you will. This dress is made specifically for *you*. In fact, no one else will ever be able to wear this gown *but* you." She grinned appreciatively, looking rather proud of herself. "Which means you must wear it. It would be a crime to let such a thing go unworn."

It was true. The waist and bodice fit me absolutely perfectly, the material flaring out over my hips, yards of glimmering petticoats helping to give the skirt its billowing shape, though the fabric was surprisingly light and airy. Not at all heavy like a normal gown would be.

"All right, my dear. It's time to let everyone else admire you for the night." She beamed from ear to ear. "We've got to get you going! The ball's already started. But don't worry, you'll simply make a memorable entrance." As she started walking out of the meadow, the trees and bushes seemed to move for her, clearing a large path back to the estate.

She turned back for a moment, frowned, then flicked her wrist. "Oh, don't forget the shoes."

I felt myself lift off the ground a couple inches, like something had sprouted beneath my feet. I lifted my skirts to see a beautiful pair of heeled shoes made out of the same iridescent silk, complete with sparkling crystals adorning the top. They didn't hurt or pinch at all. Walking in them was how I imagined walking on clouds would feel. I couldn't help the ridiculous, unfading smile plastered on my face.

I have a fairy grandmother.

CHAPTER 16

Liam

As the palace gates opened to the public and the people started trickling in, my eyes were glued to the two gilded marble staircases that wound down into the ballroom. Somewhere in the background, the music began to play, and footsteps echoed as couples moved to the dance floor.

Anxiety nibbled at my fingers and toes. So few things made me anxious, but a tiny woman with bright green eyes like summer leaves could turn me into a puddle of panic simply by fluttering her lashes. *Evy.*

My palms started to sweat as the ballroom filled with guests. I kept glancing behind me just in case I had somehow missed her entrance. Every one of my nerves was humming with anticipation, with fear, with hope.

A young woman—not the one I was looking for—tapped me on the shoulder, and I nearly jolted out of my skin.

"I always love a man in uniform," she purred, tracing her finger down my shoulder toward my chest. She began needlessly fanning herself while fluttering her eyelashes.

This is why you must stay aware of your surroundings.

I wished Ryker was here to give her some pithy one-liner; though, if Ryker *was* here, he'd probably encourage the flirtation and take her into a back room for a quick romp. I, on the other hand, did my best not to roll my eyes.

I politely bowed before saying, "Thank you, miss, but I'm afraid I'm already spoken for tonight." I turned my head back around to watch the staircase, hoping I hadn't missed her.

The girl sauntered up closer, whispering in my ear, "I'd be happy to keep you company while you wait."

I heaved a sigh. So letting her down gently wouldn't work, then. "I'd much prefer you didn't."

The girl's eyes widened, and a furious blush crept up into her cheeks as she forgot to keep fanning herself. Clearly she was not used to rejection. I may not have been armed with pithy one-liners, but my directness still worked wonders when I needed it.

She almost dropped her fan in her haste to turn away from me. "Well, I never!"

Probably not.

I had kissed a few girls in the past, but never spent any quality time with one, and never considered any girl as more than a passing fancy if she wasn't Evelyn. Since befriending Ryker, I had discovered that most girls, if not all of them, were only interested in using me to gain favor with the Crown Prince. Though my friendship with Ryker meant the world to me, always being second-best was a tough burden to carry. That was why I understood the struggle he would face tonight. He would have to determine who was there for him, and who was there for a crown. And as much as I hated being used, I supposed he was used even more than I was.

I whipped my head back around to the double staircase, searching frantically for that familiar head of chestnut hair. There were so many faces, it was hard to sift through every one, but my heart leapt into my throat when I saw Evelyn's father, stepmother, and stepsister descending into the large ballroom.

But no sign of Evy.

Bobbing and weaving through the crowd, I searched every person near them. *Maybe she's running late, or got lost in the crowd.* Either way, no sign of her. My stomach sank into a pool of dread.

Maybe she didn't want *to come tonight.* I remembered her nervousness as I walked her home. Perhaps she was still angry with me for never coming back to visit, or maybe I'd been too forward with my intentions. Before I could think more on it, a now-familiar voice squawked nearby, calling my name.

"Oh, Captain Liam! How good it is to see you again tonight. You remember my daughter, Camilla, of course."

It took every ounce of discipline I had not to cringe. My eyes rolled to the sky like an unsaid prayer before I turned to face Evelyn's family, bowing my head slightly. "Good evening, Lord Coulter. Lady Coulter. Miss Camilla." I made a good show of looking around them. "Where is Miss Evelyn this evening?"

Camilla visibly stiffened. Katerina glowered, and Lord Coulter cleared his throat, mentioning something about refreshments under his breath before he blatantly walked away without offering an explanation, let alone offering a greeting to me in return.

Suspicion knitted my brows together. "Is she well?"

Katerina started gesturing dramatically with her hands. "Oh, you know Evelyn, flitting from one thing to the next. I never do fully know what that girl is up to most days. She had a few chores still left at the house. Besides, I do think the poor dear was feeling torn up about something." A smug smile briefly crossed her face. "Oh, well! What can you do." She nudged Camilla, who stepped toward me and popped out her fan.

I did my best to choke down the bout of laughter that tried to bubble out of my throat, coughing to disguise it. Katerina gave me a stink eye anyway. "I'm going to go check on Frank. You two catch up."

Camilla fanned herself for a moment before speaking. "The king outdid himself tonight. The ballroom is stunning."

"Yes, he's quite fond of big spectacles when the timing is right." I couldn't help but glance back at the staircase, hoping with all my heart that Evelyn might still walk down the steps.

Camilla cleared her throat, leaning in to whisper conspiratorially. "Is it true that the prince is looking for a bride tonight?"

I looked back at her, trying to keep the accusation from my face. She couldn't help the fact that she was not Evelyn, or that she wanted to be a princess. "It has been . . . on his mind as of late to begin searching for a life partner, yes."

Her eyes brightened as I confirmed it, and I inwardly grimaced. "Camilla, I wish to be frank with you." I worked to smooth the irritation from my voice, but I wasn't sure I succeeded. "Sidling up to me will not get you any closer to the prince."

The only sign of surprise she offered was a slow blink. "I appreciate your honesty. It's quite rare to receive such from a man." I nodded curtly, but she continued, glancing at me sidelong. "Allow me to be honest in return. My *mother's* eye is on the prince, but mine is already enjoying the view." She paused, and I suddenly felt phenomenally uncomfortable. "If I may be so forward."

I huffed a polite, humorless laugh. "I appreciate the compliment. But I must reiterate, my sights are set on Evelyn." I paused for a moment to study her face. "You and Evelyn aren't close, are you?"

Her body stiffened, and her eyes glazed over with memory. "We were. Once."

Finally, something genuine. I prodded further—maybe I could use this to get the truth of Evelyn's situation. "May I ask what happened?"

Red tinged her cheeks, and she fanned herself once more—for real this time. "Mother didn't like me spending time with her."

I tilted my head, confused. "And why was that? What changed?"

She paused, considering. "It's hard to put into words, but Mother didn't . . . she just didn't approve."

Her hands were quaking slightly, and my head tilted to the side. Was she nervous to talk about this? What could Katerina have against Evelyn?

I quickly scanned the room, looking for Katerina and Frank. When I saw them plucking drinks from a tray carried by a nearby steward, I leaned down, lowering my voice urgently. "You've been honest with me once tonight. Do me that favor again. Where is Evelyn, Camilla?"

Dark emotions flitted across Camilla's eyes before she stoically blinked them away. I couldn't tell what she was feeling, but a sinking suspicion festered low in my stomach.

She cleared her throat, and I watched as the sultry mask fell back into place. "Like my mother said, she was indisposed. But I can tell you, *honestly*, that she was quite sorry she couldn't make it tonight. I believe she was looking forward to seeing you." She gave her fan an extra flutter, her eyes darting to the side. I turned to follow her gaze and saw Katerina approaching.

"Tell me, Captain," said Camilla, her voice pitching an octave higher, "Will you be dancing tonight, or are you on duty?"

"I technically have the evening off to enjoy, but—"

"Wonderful! Would you care to dance with me, then?"

I raised an eyebrow. "Isn't the gentleman supposed to ask the lady?"

"I've learned that if I want something, I have to take it. I would like to dance with you, Captain, but it's obvious you're currently too distracted to ask me yourself, so I will ease your burden and do the asking instead." Her lips turned up ever so slightly as she raised her eyebrow and put her fan away, offering her hand to me.

Skeptical, but desperate to get away from Katerina, I took Camilla's hand and let her lead me to the dance floor.

CHAPTER 17

Ryker

"Are you ready, son?"

My father and I stood at the ballroom entrance, watching the crowd. Sweat coated my entire body, and I tried not to swipe at my brow—how very un-princelike *that* would be. Father looked sideways at me, a grim but determined look on his face. He clapped his hand on my shoulder, a myriad of emotions running across his face.

"Ryker?" he prompted, and I realized I hadn't yet answered him.

I grimaced. "Not in the least."

He chuckled softly under his breath, and relief warmed my heart when I noted the color in his cheeks.

"You look good, Father," I said softly.

He straightened his posture at the comment, preening a little in his suit. "Today has been a good day, although it could just be the excitement talking. After all, you might meet your future wife tonight." He gave me a little wink.

All that sweat beaded at the back of my neck, threatening to slide down my back. Was it hot in here? Someone should've opened some windows. I looked over at my father's hopeful face. I didn't want to disappoint him, but I seriously doubted it would be that easy to find love in the span of one evening.

"Father . . . what if I don't find her tonight?" My shoulders slumped, the weight of expectation threatening to bow me low.

"You may or you may not. Now that you know of my . . . condition, I trust that you'll take this seriously." He stopped, turned, and put both of his hands on my shoulders looking me in the eye. "I do not demand that you succeed tonight. I only ask that you try. Can you promise me that?"

My eyes closed briefly, and I let out a pent-up breath. "Of course, Father. I promise."

His eyes gleamed full of pride as he stared back at me. Before he could say anything else, though, Apep strode up to us, robes flapping behind him. "Your Majesty. Your Highness," he greeted us, bowing low in one sinuous movement. "I saw a great many beautiful ladies in the ballroom, all anxiously awaiting your arrival."

I narrowed my eyes at him. "Apep, you advise my father constantly on matters of the kingdom. Tonight, I would ask that you lend that wisdom to me. Answer me this: if I wish to secure a happy, enduring match, how should I measure each woman tonight?"

It wasn't a question I expected a real answer to. How could one truly measure such a thing in a matter of minutes? But still, I was curious to hear his answer.

"Your Highness asks a very astute question, one that is nearly impossible to answer. But this is my answer: how does the woman make you feel when you see her for the first time?" He paused for a moment, searching out understanding in my face, but I simply furrowed my brows at him. "Not your first thought, but your first instinctual feeling. In other words, Highness, you must submit to your deeper inner level of thought. That is the only one you can be sure of. It is only once we begin pondering, doubting and second guessing that we ultimately sabotage ourselves."

Surprised at his response, and actually feeling much better for having heard his answer, I gave him a grateful nod. "Thank you, Apep. I appreciate your insight."

Apep gave me a small smile and bowed again before slipping silently away, leaving us to make our grand entrance together.

Father looked over at me and grinned mischievously. He gave me a hearty clap on the back. "Ready to enjoy an evening full of beautiful women parading themselves before our eyes?"

I laughed and shook my head at him. "Shameless."

"Now you know where you get it from." He winked at me just as we heard the trumpets herald our arrival.

"Presenting His Royal Majesty, King Amaury of Alstonia, and His Royal Highness, Prince Ryker of Alstonia!"

A hush fell over the ballroom immediately, and I felt every eye of every person in the room fall on us. All those people, all those *women*, eagerly waiting for the real festivities to begin.

Father stepped up onto the raised dais, bowing slightly before taking his seat on the throne as I stepped forward to address the crowd from the ballroom stage. "Welcome, everyone, to the annual Summer Ball. We invite you to enjoy your evening, partake in the food of our bountiful harvest this season, and celebrate the success and peace of our beloved kingdom. We thank you for your contributions in making Alstonia the most prosperous and beautiful kingdom in the land. Enjoy the evening!" I gestured for the musicians to begin playing again, then took a step back to stand by the throne.

Father gripped my forearm and gave it a little shake. "Well done, son." He motioned to the nearest coordinator to start bringing the ladies forward. "We'll start with the foreign dignitaries first. I'm excited for you to meet Jada, the Princess of Terreno. She's a true beauty, that one—and an alliance with her kingdom would be beneficial as well." He gave me a sly wink.

"It sounds to me like you've got a crush, Father." I gave him a little poke in the arm while smiling cordially to the Terreno dignitaries being led up the stage to stand before us.

Princess Jada and I spoke briefly, and though she was indeed beautiful, there was no spark between us. We did, however, make plans to discuss a partnership and new trade opportunities in the future.

I kissed her hand once before she was led away from the dais and back down into the crowd. I took a deep breath, then gave a slight nod to our coordinator, who brought up the next princess. We continued that way until I had met all five of the visiting dignitaries, none of which were love matches. The closest connection I felt so far was with

Jada, and the friendship our kingdoms could form.

As we transitioned into meeting the ladies of our kingdom, I motioned the coordinator to give me a moment before we started again. The ladies were already forming a line in front of the dais, and my heart quickened with anxiety as I looked down the long queue of hopeful and nervous faces. Searching the crowd, I found Liam dancing with a very striking young lady, but she didn't look like his Evelyn. I motioned for him to come join me, and without hesitation he dropped his dance partner and came to me. Definitely *not* Evelyn, then.

Liam caught up to me from behind as I headed for the ballroom exit. "Have you managed love at first sight yet?" I could hear the humorous inflection in his voice as he gave me a little elbow nudge to the ribs. "That cute one in the purple seemed a perfect fit for you."

I looked at him, confused for a moment before recognition dawned in my mind. I gave him my best side-eye. "Very funny. She was indeed the very precious little *niece* of a visiting princess. And, I'll have you know, she told me my sash was pretty."

I rubbed my hand down my royal blue sash, and we both burst out laughing. The tension in my chest loosened, and I was overcome with gratitude. Liam always seemed to know exactly what I needed at any given moment.

He lifted up his hands in surrender. "Okay, okay! How's it really going? Pretty sashes aside."

"Princess Jada was engaging. It wasn't love, but she was interested in forming a better friendship to connect our kingdoms."

"Excellent news!" He gave me a proud slap on the shoulder. "Are you ready for the next set?"

I sucked in a deep breath. "I needed a quick break."

"I figured." His eyes searched the crowd, and though his smile didn't falter, some unhappy emotion darkened his gaze as he bowed his head to fiddle with his suit.

I eyed him closely, then gestured with my chin toward his previous dance partner. "Is that Evelyn, then?"

He shook his head, stark disappointment written all over his face. "Her stepsister, Camilla. She says Evelyn's not coming."

"What? What do you mean she's not coming?" Anger started to

boil in my stomach. If this girl had left him hanging, there would be words exchanged between me and her family. Didn't she know the effect she had on the man? I hated seeing him like this.

Running a hand through his hair, Liam looked up at me. "All they'll tell me is that she is *indisposed* this evening and was unable to attend." He let out a ragged sigh. "Her stepmother mentioned something about not finishing her chores in time? But I don't see how that could possibly have . . . I don't know, Ryk. The whole thing feels off to me. I can't explain it, but something's wrong."

Apep's sage advice about listening to my instincts came to mind, and I realized: that was exactly what Liam was doing. My logical brain saw nothing wrong, but he *felt* it, and that was as good as truth to him. I'd never noticed before, but this was something Liam was quite good at. It was one of the ways he always knew what I needed even before I did.

Liam's fists clenched at his sides, and his jaw ticked with tension. I glanced back to where he was dancing before. "Camilla has a very unique beauty to her. Perhaps . . ."

"No." He shook his head, then looked at me in all seriousness. "I think they . . . I think they did something so Evelyn couldn't come tonight." He released his clenched fists, stretching out his hands only to clench them tightly again. Like he was preparing for a fight.

The anguish on his face was enough to stop me from pushing further. "Well then, first thing tomorrow, you go out there and check on her. Figure out what happened."

He bowed his head in defeat, rubbing the back of his neck. "Thank you." Then he shook his head and let out a low whistle as he looked at the line of ladies growing longer by the second. "Would that I could help you, brother."

"Indeed . . . want to be king instead?"

"Absolutely not."

We both laughed, and he gave me an encouraging pat on the back. "I'm here when you need me."

I gave him a knowing nod, and we parted ways. Heading back up to center stage, I took a deep breath and motioned to the coordinator that I was ready for the next lady.

CHAPTER 18

Evelyn

Chrissy moved swiftly through the air with her wings, and I lost sight of her as I carefully made my way back to the house. When I entered the front courtyard, I immediately saw Jimmy standing there, waiting in front of the most stunning carriage I'd ever seen. It looked reminiscent of a bubble with that same shimmering translucence that seemed to be a characteristic of Chrissy's magic. I could see right into the carriage and through to the other side. It was . . . dazzling.

Jimmy's outfit had been transformed into a fine-looking suit, and he blushed slightly as I appraised him. "Jimmy! You look *wonderful*."

Flashing me his brightest smile, he gave me a slight bow. "Miss Evelyn, you are indeed breathtaking." He opened the carriage door and offered me his hand to help me up. Before releasing my hand, he gave it a quick kiss, then gazed up at me. He spoke in an earnest whisper: "This is how I've always seen you, Little Miss."

Tears threatened to make a reappearance, but I rapidly blinked them away. Tear stains wouldn't go well with this outfit, now would they? "Can you even believe all this?"

"Yes I can, and then some." He winked at me, his eyes gleaming as he added, "Tonight may have taken a turn, but I want you to go and enjoy this gift you've been given. You will be the belle of the ball tonight, and you deserve every moment of it." His grin stretched from ear to ear as he carefully helped me up into the carriage, closing the door behind me. A bright giggle bubbled up inside me. I couldn't even remember the last time I felt this giddy and excited.

Chrissy glided up to the window with gentle tears in her eyes. She reached her soft hand through, clasping mine. "Tonight is a night just for you. It's finally time you enjoyed yourself. Dance all night, eat all the food, and laugh until your sides hurt." She smiled tenderly at me. "I want you to go have a wonderful time and make memories you'll never forget. You deserve beauty and joy in your life, my sweet Evelyn. May tonight remind you of that truth."

"Thank you, Chrissy. Or should I call you Grandmother?" I paused for a moment. "How about Grandmother Chrissy?"

"I would like that very much." Grandmother Chrissy kept smiling, but one of those tears escaped, slipping gracefully down her cheek.

I grinned back, taking in her joy, but sudden fear rose up and gripped my heart, kicking it into a gallop. "Grandmother Chrissy, what if they see me tonight? I won't be able to explain . . ."

She flicked her wrist again, and the air shifted slightly around me. "Not to worry, dear. No one who knows you will be able to see your face clearly. You'll be safe. Now go and have a good—"

I interrupted her, feeling the pang of loss already. "Not even Liam?"

She paused, contemplating that thought for a moment. "Oh, dear. Not even he will recognize you, I'm afraid."

My heart sank at the thought of Liam not knowing who I was. "Oh."

She leaned in, her voice dropping to a conspiratorial whisper. "That doesn't mean you can't still dance with the boy and give him some clues as to who you are. There's no rule against telling him."

I gave her hand a light squeeze. "Thank you for this. For *all* of this. I don't know how I'll ever repay you."

"This is a gift, Evelyn. Your job is to enjoy it." She gave my hand a little tap, then released me. "Now go! Have fun!" She tapped the carriage, and Jimmy snapped the reins of the horses to get us moving. "Enjoy yourself!" Chrissy's voice faded in the background.

Before I could stick my head out the window to wave goodbye, Grandmother Chrissy flew up next to me. "I forgot to tell you! I'm not sure how long this magic will last. Best be safe. It may only last a few hours, but if you leave around midnight tonight, that should give you *plenty* of time to get back home before the magic wears off."

I nodded my head in acknowledgement, and she disappeared from view. *Until midnight tonight.* My insides were jumping all around with excitement, and I couldn't help but keep laughing out loud as we made our way to the palace.

CHAPTER 19

Liam

"Captain Liam!"

I flinched. There was just something about Katerina's voice that instantly grated on my nerves. She let out an irritated huff behind me when I didn't turn around, and I couldn't help but smile slightly to myself. Just to put her out further, I kept walking forward, acting like I hadn't heard her hollering.

"Captain! Captain Liam!"

Damn. I should have known better than to think that would be enough to discourage her. I stopped abruptly, turning around to face her. The silly woman was following me so closely she almost smacked right into me. Gathering her wits about her, she smoothed down her skirt, straightening her shoulders. "Camilla was quite vexed when you left the dance floor." She pulled Camilla forward, whom she had obviously been dragging along behind her. "Weren't you, dear?"

Gratefully, Camilla raised her brows ever so slightly, which I took to be the closest thing to an eye roll she was able to give her mother.

"All the young ladies are already starting to line up to meet the prince. Won't you escort Camilla over to him?" Katerina grabbed Camilla's arm and pulled her toward me forcefully.

It was such a blatantly undignified attempt to use me that I couldn't even hold it in. I laughed out loud right in Katerina's face. "No, madam. Lord Coulter will need to escort her over to the line. I am neither her escort this evening nor your easy ticket to the prince, and I do not appreciate being used as such." Before she could say anything in her defense, I continued, "In the future, I will ask you to refrain from taking such liberties with my position and making an embarrassment of yourself and your daughter in the process."

Katerina's face turned beet red, and her eyes went wide with shock. She was clearly not used to being called out on her abhorrent behavior, but I'd had enough of her needy antics tonight to last me a lifetime. No wonder Evelyn hadn't wanted me to meet her.

Not much seemed to faze her, though, because she immediately shook off my reprimand and acted as though nothing had happened. "Fine. But would you consider at least one more dance before she has to wait in that awfully long line to meet the prince?"

She pushed Camilla into my arms without waiting for an answer, walking away defiantly. Camilla and I both sighed heavily, staring at each other. Katerina was tenacious, I'd give her that.

"Would you care to dance again, Camilla?" I asked. It didn't seem that she cared to be around her mother either; it was sheer mercy on my part to offer her a break. She quickly accepted, and I led her to the opposite end of the dance floor, as far away from her mother as we could possibly get.

As the music started back up with a new song, Camilla sighed and hung her head. "I know she's galling, but she does mean well. She just wants the best for me, even if her methods are somewhat *questionable* at times." She offered me a small smile that didn't reach her eyes.

"Unfortunately, this kind of thing happens to me far more frequently than you might think. Though I do recognize it's not your doing." I gave her what I thought might be a sympathetic smile, but it probably looked more like a grimace.

She looked up at me then, her eyes so full of anguish that I glanced down to make sure she hadn't twisted an ankle. Then she said, almost too softly to be heard: "You're far kinder to me than I deserve."

I raised an eyebrow and studied her for a moment. "And why do you feel as though you don't deserve kindness from me?"

"I'm not a very kind person." She shook her head as if trying to erase a memory. "And I especially don't deserve *your* kindness, of all people." At this, she pulled back for a moment and looked me in the eye, studying me almost to the point of awkwardness before saying, "Evelyn deserves something good in her life. You should call on her again tomorrow, if you're able. I'll . . . I'll try to help you see her."

I eyed her carefully, the suspicion lurking in my chest beginning to feel familiar. There was something she wasn't saying, a message hidden between her words, but I somehow I understood. I nodded. "I'll be there first thing in the morning."

We started moving to the music again, and I pulled her a little closer to whisper in her ear. "Tell me honestly, Camilla. Is she truly okay? What happened to her tonight?"

Camilla opened her mouth and leaned in just as the crowd quieted down, the music crashing to a full stop. Confused, I looked up at the main staircase.

Time stopped.

The most beautiful woman I had ever seen was descending the stairs. She was practically glowing; her dress seemed to capture and reflect every speck of light the room had to offer. The crowd murmured amongst themselves, and I caught a flash of uncertainty in this new arrival's gaze.

It was like an invisible thread wrapped around my heart and pulled. I released Camilla without saying another word and made my way toward the staircase just as the stranger was making her way down.

When she reached the bottom of the staircase, she looked around, uncertainty shadowing those lovely eyes. She must've been another foreign princess who'd arrived late, but somehow there was something . . . achingly familiar about her. The way she carried herself was delicately graceful, but endearingly unsteady. Even though I didn't recognize her, I felt as though I somehow already knew her.

Her panicked face made me immediately push my way forward, determined to ease her nerves. But before I could even get close enough to hail her, the crowd suddenly split in two. That was when I saw the prince moving—no, not moving, *running*—from the dais toward the girl. I'd never seen Ryker run toward a girl before. It was usually the other way around.

My heart sank.

Ryker looked positively awestruck. He bowed before the girl, and she bowed her head in response. His lips moved as he held his hand out to her, and her eyes lit with worry and confusion, but after a moment she gave him a nod. He quickly stepped forward and took her into his arms, leading her into a dance with no music. He didn't wait for the music to begin—he made the music match their movements instead.

The circle of people widened, and they danced right past me. The smiles on their faces were so wide, so genuine, it was enough to make me believe in love at first sight. I couldn't help but feel a twinge of jealousy, though. I had only ever felt this drawn to a girl once before, and she glowed, too.

CHAPTER 20

Evelyn

The carriage pulled up in front of the palace and Jimmy ran over to open my door before the palace footman could even reach us. "I'll be right here waiting for you, Miss Evelyn. And I'll make sure we can make a quick exit if need be. Go have an amazing time and wear yourself out dancing all night." With a big smile, he handed me off to the palace footman, who helped me walk up the palace stairs.

My heart hammered in my chest, but I didn't let myself look back. *One step in front of the other.*

I distracted myself by watching a few couples milling about as we made our way through the palace foyer, looking for quiet places to be alone. It brought a slight blush to my cheeks, but it warmed my heart to watch them sneak about with their smiling faces and flirtatious looks.

The footman brought me all the way to the ballroom doors. A light sheen of sweat dusted my skin as they opened the double doors for me. My breath caught at the glorious beauty of the room. It was massive and shining with white marble, gold accents, glowing chandeliers, and mirrors on every wall. Giant, overflowing flower arrangements surrounded me as I walked up to the balcony overlooking the room, bracing myself against it and peeking out over the edge at all the people below. Couples were dancing gracefully across the dance floor; laughter and noise filled the room, but never overpowered the music. There was a line of women leading to the dais, where I saw Prince Ryker meeting with each one individually.

But my heart didn't skip a beat until I found Liam in the crowd. Adrenaline-fueled joy lit me up from the inside out, a grin spreading across my face. Tonight's ordeal had all been worth it just to see him so resplendent in his formal royal uniform. Then my eye darted to his partner, and all that glimmering joy went dark and cold.

Camilla.

The way he leaned into her, pulling her in close to whisper something in her ear . . .

My eyes instantly stung. All the tears I cried earlier weren't enough to stop this new onslaught. Betrayal plunged into my stomach like a stone dropped from high above, followed by an eerie awareness of eyes settling on me. I looked around, and everywhere I looked, I was met with stunned, suspicious gazes. Even the music had stopped. Liam and Camilla were looking around, wondering what had happened, too lost in each other to notice the shift in everyone else right away.

Before he could look up and catch me staring, I quickly made my way down the stairs, hoping that by the time I reached the ballroom floor I wouldn't be the center of attention anymore. I stood out because I was late—that was all. They'd find other places to look once I melted into the crowd.

When my shoe left the last stair and clicked on the ballroom floor, I could've sworn it echoed. The music still hadn't started back up, and I awkwardly stared back at a room full of people who seemed to have nothing better to look at. I had no idea what to do, or how ladies were supposed to behave; this was my first ball, after all. Had I missed some kind of social cue?

My eyes darted back and forth, searching for an exit or somewhere to hide. Several men in the crowd were making their way toward me, Liam included. I saw his head bobbing in between the people circled around me. My heart pitched into my throat, thrumming so loudly I doubted I'd even hear the music if it ever started back up. A cold sweat broke out on my brow and my hands began to tremble. Liam wouldn't recognize me, and I didn't have an escort—was I about to get thrown out?

Suddenly, the crowd shifted and split, creating a huge pathway that led straight to the dais. I met the eyes of Prince Ryker, who was jogging straight toward me. My eyes widened at his speed and ferocity.

Oh, I was definitely in trouble. It would be just my luck, Prince Ryker himself kicking me out of the ball for not belonging there. Could he have recognized me as the peasant girl from the market?

Grandmother Chrissy had said no one who knew me would be able to recognize me, but he didn't actually know me. How specific was this magic?

My eyes widened as I desperately searched for an exit. Sweat gathered in my bust and dripped slowly down my stomach. I prayed no one would be able to tell. My breaths were coming in fast and short.

I was going to be found out. I was going to be humiliated for the second time tonight.

And then he was there, standing before me with his cropped honey-gold hair, expressive blue eyes, and glowing white uniform trimmed in gold. A silken blue sash was draped across his torso. He was dripping in royalty, and I felt more out of place than ever.

The minute he moved, I tensed up further, expecting the worst. But instead of demanding that I leave or dragging me toward the door . . . he bowed.

The *prince* bowed. To *me*.

My face must've given away my surprise, because he flashed me a reassuring, brilliant smile before he spoke. "Hello."

I dipped my head in return. "Good evening, Your Highness." My dry throat bobbed as I tried to swallow before chancing a slight smile back at him. It probably looked more like I was choking.

He reached out his gilded hand to me, fine rings covering almost every finger. "May I have the honor of this dance?"

My head whipped up so fast I almost felt dizzy. "What?" *He wants to dance with* me?

He chuckled, his hand still reached out to me. "I said, will you dance with me?"

I pointed at my own chest, my face in complete disbelief. "Me?"

He snorted in a very *un*-prince-like manner and gently lowered his hand to mine. My palm was sweaty, and I didn't realize my hand was clenched until his fingers began to tenderly unwind my fist.

"I'm not used to having to persuade a woman to dance with me. And at the risk of being almost rejected a third time, I will ask once more: would you grant me the honor of dancing with you?"

His hand wrapped around my unclamped and clammy one. I nodded numbly, my mind trying to keep up with this turn of events. He was probably thinking I was a few bristles short of a broom at this point.

My breath caught as he gently kissed the back of my hand. He took the lead, pulling me into a dancing hold. I could only stare at him, dumbfounded. "Forgive me, Your Highness, but I should warn you . . . I've never danced before."

His eyebrows flew upward. "Never? Truly?"

"Truly."

He smirked and leaned in, whispering in my ear, "Then I'm honored, and thrilled beyond measure, to be your first."

My eyes closed of their own accord as his breath warmed the side of my neck. Before I could quite recover from that, he locked my arms back in place and led me into a dance routine. I startled for a moment, tripping over my own feet while barely avoiding stomping on his, but he held me secure to him, and no one seemed to notice my missteps.

Panicked, I looked about the room. "There's no music playing, Your Highness."

One side of his mouth turned up into a mischievous smirk as he feigned shock. "What? You don't hear it already?"

Suddenly, the music started playing exactly to our rhythm, and we both laughed at the ridiculously perfect timing. He spun me around and led me into the crowd. "I planned that." Everyone moved to the sides while we danced in a wide circle.

I laughed, a loud echoing sound in the cavernous space filled with people. We were the only couple dancing as everyone else looked on. "You did, did you?"

"Naturally." His tall frame shook with mirth, and I side-eyed him before giggling.

"Why is no one else dancing with us?"

He made a show of looking around, then shrugged his shoulders. "I'm sure they will once everyone's had a good look at you." He paused to assess me again, his stare piercing straight through me. "They must also be completely taken in by the most bewitching woman they've ever seen."

A blush bloomed on my cheeks, and I hoped it hadn't spread to my neck. Embarrassment tended to turn me into a blotchy mess. "You're quite the flatterer, Your Highness, but I'd hazard a guess that they're all staring at you."

His laugh was wonderfully carefree. "On the contrary, my lady. I never flatter without due cause." His eyes gleamed as he twirled me, pulling me back in. "Besides, you are quite literally the envy of the ball tonight. It's clear that every man here wants to dance with you, and every woman wishes she *were* you."

It was an effort not to roll my eyes. "Well, that would certainly be a first."

I didn't realize I'd spoken out loud until Prince Ryker frowned, narrowing his eyes and subtly tilting his head. He chuckled quietly, a smile coming back to his face. "How refreshing."

"What is?" I couldn't help but smile back. His amusement was infectious, radiant.

"Meeting a stunningly beautiful woman with a sarcastic sense of humor." He tilted his head again to study me. "It's strange . . . and alluring." He shook his head again, as if trying to snap himself out of a trance.

The song ended and another one began, neither of us breaking apart as other couples finally began to dance around us. Instead, he tightened his hold around my waist, pulling me even closer. My breath caught in my throat at the intensity of his nearness, and he chuckled salaciously under his breath. We adjusted easily to the new rhythm, and I was grateful for such a capable partner. It seemed like my feet barely touched the floor.

"Tell me," he said, his voice low and enticing, "how have we never met before?"

"Who says we've never met before, Your Highness?" I teased.

His eyes crinkled slyly at the corners. "I am certain I would remember making the acquaintance of such a charming woman."

"Don't be so sure," I said with a snort—then instantly regretted it when Ryker's mouth fell open.

"Did you just *snort* at me?"

My face flooded with heat. "Forgive me, Your Highness."

"There's nothing to forgive." He beamed at me, and I swallowed again, desperately wishing I'd thought to drink water before all this. "So, are you suggesting we *have* met before?"

"I'm neither suggesting nor denying it." I gave my best attempt at one of those sultry smiles he seemed so well-practiced in. "I choose to remain a mystery this evening."

He barked out another laugh, this one much less poised than the others. I'd surprised him. "Oh, is that what you choose? Am I to be kept from even knowing the name of my dance partner?"

I feigned thoughtfulness, pretending to contemplate the idea, then shook my head. "I'm afraid so, Your Highness. My goal for the evening was to remain unnoticed, and I fear you've most assuredly ruined that. This is now your punishment."

He scoffed. "Please. I did nothing of the sort. You ruined that all on your own by wearing this spectacular gown and," he surveyed me up and down, "well, looking like *you*."

I couldn't help but laugh at his excessive flirtatiousness. I'd never really been given the opportunity to flirt before, and the prince seemed to gladly accept the invisible challenge. He was charming, obviously handsome, playful, confident. The arrogance I had seen in him before was still there, but now I was getting a truer picture of his character. Clearly spoiled, used to getting his way, but he clearly didn't mind a challenge, and he obviously enjoyed a little intrigue.

His hold on me while we danced was steady and reassuring. He stood tall, about the same height as Liam, but his perfect posture made him seem even taller. His shoulders were broad but lean, not as strong and wide as Liam's, but sturdy nonetheless. His hair was on the shorter side, styled back from his face, showing off his high cheekbones and square jaw. I could tell he and Liam truly were friends, because some of the faces he made were just like Liam's. They had so many similarities even while being complete opposites. His creamy skin looked and felt utterly pampered. I wondered if he could feel the calluses on my hands, or if Grandmother Chrissy had softened those up for me too. Liam's hands had been so hard and worn by weapons—and before that, gardening tools—I doubted he'd noticed the roughness of my own.

Prince Ryker was handsome and he knew it—the devilish look in his eye made that clear. But somehow in this moment, I didn't mind it one bit. Something about that brilliant smile was utterly disarming.

My gaze slowly meandered back to the crowd surrounding us, and a small shiver ran down my spine. No sign of Father or Katerina yet, but they were out there somewhere. I knew it.

When I looked back at the prince, concern clouded his face. "Is everything alright, my lady?"

I nodded. "Of course, Your Highness. Forgive me. Sometimes my mind can run away with me."

He smirked. "And where did your mind run off to?"

I tried for a smile, but it faded as I attempted to find an answer that might satisfy his curiosity. "I'm afraid my mind can be in many places at once. Here in the ballroom with you, back at my family home, out in the wilds of the forest . . . it would be nearly impossible for me to answer that question in earnest."

He considered for a moment. "Everything you said seems true, and yet . . . I feel like you're somehow becoming a master evader of my questions."

A rather undignified laugh burst from my chest unprompted, and he smiled wide before he leaned in close to whisper, "You have the most beautiful laugh."

I dropped my chin—I was blushing again, and it seemed best to hide my neck in case of blotches. "Thank you, Your Highness."

He gasped in delight. "Ah! So she *can* take a compliment."

My instinct was to give him a playful push, but I had to remind myself once again that this wasn't Liam—if I shoved the Prince, they'd probably do worse than throw me out of the ball. "I'm curious, Your Highness. As I walked in this evening, I noticed a line of ladies waiting to meet you. Is this a normal occurrence at every ball?"

His mouth twitched downward, his jaw ticking. "I'm afraid that's a new development this year."

My brows furrowed. "And what is its purpose?"

He seemed ready to laugh again, which made no sense to me. It seemed a fair question. He tipped his head to one side, a strand of that golden hair rebelling, falling across his forehead. "You mean you truly don't know?"

I shook my head. "I'm afraid not, Your Highness. I . . . am not privy to many of the goings-on in the kingdom. I'm not often well-informed."

"I see. Well, ten minutes ago I met you, so perhaps I too shall remain a man of mystery this evening. But if the night ends the way I hope it will, I'll tell you all about the reason behind that line of women."

Well, I supposed I couldn't blame him for that retaliation. I shrugged my shoulders. "That seems fair. Tell me this, at least: with a line so long, have you been able to enjoy yourself this evening?"

His grin turned sheepish. "Honestly? Not a bit. Not until you walked in."

Oh, please.

I threw back my head and laughed. "It's official. I've decided. You are the worst flirt."

He gasped, doing his best to look affronted. "Who, me? Impossible. I've already been deemed the best by many. By *most,* in fact." I rolled my eyes, trying not to guffaw again as he studied me carefully. "You really must not be from around here."

Just then the music switched again, and a broad shape approaching from the side caught my eye. Shiny buttons flashed, polished boots shone, and eyes I'd dreamed about for so many years found mine as Liam walked over.

His confident strides made my stomach seize up, and my throat dried out all over again as his dark, compelling eyes focused fully on mine.

Does he recognize me?

He tapped the Prince lightly on the shoulder and bowed, bringing his hand up to his chest. "Your Highness." He then turned to me. "My lady."

I curtsied as best I could, and when I raised my head, our eyes met once more. I couldn't explain what it was that passed between us, but it felt powerful and unrestrained. The prince bristled under my hands as Liam asked, "May I cut in?"

The room slowly quieted again, everyone straining to hear so they could gossip later about the captain asking to cut in for a dance with the prince's nameless dance partner. It had become apparent that I was somehow off-limits so long as I held the prince's attention, as no one had tried to cut in this entire time. By the looks on the faces in the crowd, it seemed that this move was most irregular.

He must recognize me.

The prince seemed to note the attentive room. He held my gaze for an extra beat, the silence deafening. My eyes didn't know where to land, darting back and forth between the men, but after a moment, Ryker relinquished his hold. He gestured to Liam with an almost mocking bow. "Of course."

Relief washed through me. Now everyone's focus could go back to the prince—and away from me.

Liam stepped toward me, and my heart stuttered. His touch was not like Ryker's firm and near-arrogant leading; his arm softly wrapped around my middle, and his hands were oh-so-gentle despite his rough palms. I picked up my skirts as the music began to play again, and Liam immediately twisted us back into the crowd. His steps were confident and sure, but they lacked the grace and style of the prince.

"Hello."

"Good evening." My voice came out breathy, almost squeaky. Nerves were sparking in my fingertips, but even so, my heart was soaring. This was why I'd come here in the first place. To dance with my Liam.

"I'm Captain Liam of the Prince's Guard."

My heart sank, but I gathered myself up, smiling politely. "Shouldn't you be guarding the prince rather than dancing with me, then?" Immediately, I wanted to snatch the words back. I'd meant for it to come out playful, but instead it sounded more like an accusation.

He gave me a little chortle, though, and that heart-melting dimple made a quick appearance in his cheek. "Normally yes, but tonight is my night off."

"Oh! Well, of course. That's lovely." The words stunted in my mouth, trying to come out smooth and sure but failing miserably.

"You deserve a night off. Naturally. You work hard, I'm sure." Heat crawled up my neck. *Lovely. More blotches.*

"Forgive me, my lady, but have we met before? You remind me of . . ." His voice drifted off as he carefully studied me, as though trying to decipher a difficult riddle.

I couldn't come up with a good enough answer, so I decided to try and avoid it like I had been with the prince. "Define *met.*"

I almost slapped my palm to my head, swallowing a groan. That was far too much of an answer already.

Liam's arms tightened around me, and my stomach swooped low in my belly. "We have met before. I knew it."

"I-I didn't say that." *Might as well have.*

He raised one eyebrow at me. "You implied it."

I fumbled for a new excuse, or a better lie. "I mean, you should hope we haven't. It would be rather insulting if we had and you didn't remember me, now wouldn't it?"

His eyes lit up like he'd caught me. "When? Where? I know you, I know I do, I just can't seem to . . ."

I blew out an exasperated sigh. "Liam, I didn't—"

His lips parted in shock, either at my informal use of his name or because he recognized the way I said it. I wasn't sure which, and I didn't have time to find out. The music came to an abrupt stop, and the moment the last note faded, Prince Ryker was there. Not missing a beat.

My dance with Liam felt ridiculously short; we'd barely had a chance to say anything to one another. I wanted to tell him who I was, but who knew what he might think or say? I mean, he had been wrapped up in Camilla just moments before I arrived.

That bitter, nauseous feeling drifted back, lodging itself in my throat as I tried to wipe the image of the two of them from my mind.

The prince cleared his throat, and Liam visibly stiffened. A knowing look passed between the two of them, like they spoke some silent language. Then the prince asked, "May I have my dance partner back now, Captain?"

A flash of irritation rolled over Liam's eyes before he reluctantly relinquished his hold on me. "It was a pleasure, my lady." There was a gleam in his eye that made my breath hitch. "Thank you for the dance."

I nodded my head in return. "The pleasure was all mine." I tried to say it as formally as possible, but I felt my eyes almost pleading for him to recognize me now. I wanted our dance to keep going, for him to realize who I was and forget all about Camilla.

He gave me no words, but I was rewarded with an intense gaze of his own. His eyes were full of longing and confusion.

I couldn't tell if he had figured it out or not, and it seemed I would never know. The prince reached his hand back out to me, asking, "May I?"

I nodded as his arm suddenly swept me close to his firm chest, knocking a gasp from me. This was nearly indecently close. In the background, I saw Liam blanch, but then an upbeat tune reverberated throughout the room. Before another anguished thought of Liam could enter my mind, the prince was bouncing us across the ballroom, as far away from Liam as possible, in a fashion that made me laugh almost hysterically. My legs and feet had no clue what to do, but he had me pulled up so close to his body that it didn't matter. My feet mirrored his.

By the time we started to slow down, I was dizzy from all the twirls and the laughter. The music shifted again as I caught my breath, and the Prince leaned in close—I wondered if he preferred to be certain he wouldn't be overheard, or if he simply knew the kind of effect whispers of this nature could have on women. His breath on my skin made tingles run down my sides that I had never felt before. "May I show you something?"

He was flirtatious, and confident, and roguish with his mannerisms, and I found I was enjoying myself immensely. His beautiful blue eyes bore into mine, and I could sense a barely-contained desperation behind them. He seemed afraid that I might say no, and his eyes darted back toward where we had left Liam on the dance floor. That made me grin. I could hardly believe it, but I thought the prince might've been jealous.

"Lead the way, Your Highness."

CHAPTER 21

Ryker

"Lead the way, Your Highness." She was still panting for breath from our energetic dance across the room—far away from Liam, and whatever madness had come over him—and a light sheen of sweat was just starting to dust her hairline. Between her soft smile, playful eyes, and heavy breathing, she was about to do me in. I had never in my life seen a prettier girl. She positively glowed.

I took her hand and led her from the ballroom as the crowd parted for us again, envious eyes on *both* of us, wishing they could make us stop to notice them. For the first time in my life, their attention wasn't focused solely on me. This beautiful maiden was intriguing to everyone, including myself. But I was the only one who would get to know her secrets.

I led her to the hidden side door that blended in with the ballroom wall. One palace guard stood nearby to make sure no one but the royal family ever entered. The mystery girl's eyes sharpened with curiosity as we entered the quiet corridor, the door closing softly behind us. Her shoulders visibly relaxed as the cacophony of sounds faded.

Not even Liam would bother us out here. *Liam.* My blood was still boiling. The fact that he had taken such a liberty, cutting in between me and this gloriously intriguing dance partner, especially when I was so obviously staking a claim of interest—never in my life had Liam done something like that. And on tonight of all nights, knowing the stakes . . . if not for our friendship, I might've had him escorted from the ballroom.

Still holding her hand, I led her to the end of the corridor and stood in front of the finely-sculpted door that always rubbed my heart raw. Mother had worked so closely with the woodcarver to design it, decorating it with winding roses and vines intertwining, representing chaos and control. I tugged out the chain that I always wore around my neck, hidden beneath my shirt, revealing the key dangling on the end.

She narrowed her eyes thoughtfully at the key. "What sort of place is this, that it needs to be kept under lock and key?"

"A very special one." I inserted the key into the lock, pausing to look at her. "I've never shown anyone what's behind this door before." Technically, it was true. *I* had never brought anyone out here. Mother had brought Liam and I, and she'd always shown her garden off proudly to those who wished to see it, but it had been years since anyone but Liam and I had laid eyes on it.

Her eyes widened with surprise, then crinkled wryly. "Well then, I'm honored and thrilled beyond measure to be your first." She beamed at me, clearly proud of herself for cleverly tossing my earlier remark back at me.

It was that moment that truly hooked me. She was everything I'd been looking for, but I hadn't even known it until I'd found her.

Unable to hold back any longer, I flashed her a flippant grin, then twisted the key in the lock, swinging the door wide open while holding out my arm to let her walk through first.

"Welcome to the private royal garden, my lady."

She gasped with wonder, and her tempting mouth dropped into an expressive O. My heart stuttered, and I found myself wondering how that mouth would taste, how it would feel pressed against mine. Her eyes darted every which way as she gingerly walked the stone path, her hands softly brushing the creamy lily petals standing on each side of the path. She looked up to admire the pale Queen of the Night flowers in full bloom hanging from an overhead trellis. Fragrant jasmine and gardenias surrounded us, hidden in the foliage and trees. Ivory rose bushes intermingled in the background. Whites, creams, and ivories soaked up and reflected back the moon's delicate light everywhere the eye could see. The garden was made for the magic of moonlight; Mother had designed it that way.

I folded my hands behind my back to keep from fidgeting, watching the magnificent woman in front of me turn carefully so she could see everything, her own hand bracing against her chest. She looked like she belonged among this garden in her iridescent, pearl-like gown. Moving oh-so-slowly, I inched closer to her until our hands lightly touched. Somehow the brush of her skin felt more intimate here than it had on the ballroom floor. Fearing that I would somehow scare her away, or wake up from this perfect dream, I carefully led her down the small path to my favorite part of the garden. As we walked, I quickly picked one of the blooms we passed, hiding it behind my back.

We passed the tiny pond where night-blooming water lilies floated as I led her to the weeping willow tree. Its leafy branches had been pulled off to the sides and tied back so visitors could enjoy the full view of the garden. This little spot always felt secluded, private. I motioned for her to sit on the stone bench, then lowered myself down next to her. Close to her. Tentatively, I revealed the freshly-plucked moonflower I'd been hiding, tucking it behind her ear. Her cheeks reddened at the small contact my hand made with her skin, and a current of energy flushed straight through my entire body.

Staring into her eyes felt like looking into her soul. They were so expressive, so vibrantly green, so incredibly alluring. Did she even realize what she was doing to me? How is it that I could feel so strongly drawn to a stranger, especially a perfectly charming one?

Soft chestnut curls draped elegantly down her back. Her hair was partially pulled back, revealing her flawless, luminescent skin and rounded face. Her lips were delicate, not necessarily full, simply feathery and inviting. Her fine collarbones and shoulders were bare, almost fragile-looking. Touching her was all I wanted to do, but suddenly, touching her seemed the most terrifying thing in the world. I'd never felt this way before.

Liam and Apep had both said that my instincts would kick in, that I would know . . .and I *knew*. I knew this girl was different. She wasn't some passing fling, wasn't like the other nobles or even the common peasant girls. She was something entirely different, both more and less at the same time. Set apart. I didn't know *how* yet, I just knew I would never be the same again. She was going to change my life forever, and I needed her to be mine.

"I must know your name." The whispered words came out sounding far more desperate than I had intended.

Her eyes widened with alarm, and I instantly regretted it. Her face fell as she lowered her lashes, avoiding my eyes. "I'm so sorry, Your Highness. But I can't risk telling you."

My brows furrowed in confusion as I tucked my hand underneath her chin, gently tilting her head back so she would look at me again. I needed her brilliant green eyes on mine. "Please, call me Ryker."

"Prince—"

I cut her off with a shake of my head. "I insist. Just Ryker."

She gave me an amused side-eye. "Well, *Just Ryker*, it's a pleasure to meet you."

Good. The playfulness was back in her eyes. My goal was to keep it there as long as possible. Leaning back on the bench, I crossed my ankle over my knee, draping my arm up on the back of the bench as my finger came up to lightly brush my lips. I couldn't stop imagining what it would be like to kiss her.

Smirking lazily, I decided to keep my inquiry casual. "Tell me, lovely mysterious lady, why are you unable to share your name with me? I've shared one secret with you—more than one, in fact." I gestured about the garden. "It seems only fair."

She sighed and started fidgeting with her hands in her lap. "The truth is, my family doesn't know I'm here. I'd be in serious trouble if they ever found out."

I sat up a little straighter at that. "You were forbidden to attend?"

She nodded carefully. "In a manner of speaking, yes."

My eyes narrowed as I raised a brow in question. So there *was* a reason she wanted to remain a mystery tonight. "Are you with one of the visiting dignitaries, then?"

She laughed at that, and the sound of her laugh . . . it did things to me. "No. No," she said firmly. "I'm from Alstonia."

The worst thought crept through my mind. *Is she already spoken for? Betrothed?* As prince, I could probably change that in one meeting with her father, but . . .

I closed my eyes to the dark terror building in my chest, forcing my voice to stay playful as I asked, "Does this mean you are not an eligible maiden, then? Has someone else already snatched you up?" I was sitting ramrod-straight now, leaning into her, begging silently for the answer to be no.

"No, Your High . . . I mean, *Just Ryker.*" Relief swam in my veins, and I chuckled at her teasing. "I'm not betrothed or married. But there are some who do not consider me eligible, either."

My brow furrowed in confusion. How could anyone not consider her eligible? Had they *seen* her? I couldn't puzzle it out, but before I could ask her another question, she offered, "I know this must all seem rather peculiar, and I promise I'm not trying to deceive you, or mock you. It's just that I'm not what you think I am. I just wanted to attend the ball and really . . . really live for a night, you know? On my own terms, without someone dictating my life." She paused. "Tonight will . . . well, it will probably be my only opportunity to do so."

"So you're a ball crasher, then?" I flashed my signature smirk, trying to reel myself back in. *Steady, Ryker. Don't overwhelm the girl.*

She laughed outright, a real laugh, loud and explosive. The kind most women were afraid to let out around a prince. I couldn't help beaming at her.

"No, no," she said. "I'm not trying to crash the ball. My family was invited, in fact."

My eyes narrowed, and I leaned back against the stone bench again, folding my arms and stroking my chin. "So your family *did* break the rules, by not allowing an eligible lady to attend."

"It's . . . complicated." She fussed with her skirt nervously, her eyes shooting up to meet mine, worry etched all throughout her face. "I'm so sorry. I'm messing up this whole wonderful moment with you, aren't I?"

I quickly reached for both of her hands, caressing them with my thumbs. "*You* are the best thing to happen to this ball. You couldn't mess this up even if you tried. I can't tell you how glad I am that you're here." I released a quick breath and her hands at the same time, startled by my own fervor. I didn't want to appear forceful or desperate. "Forgive me. That was forward."

She blushed in earnest this time, her cheeks turning the most delicious shade of pink. "That's all right. It's . . . it's nice, for someone to say they enjoy my company."

I was more than *enjoying* it, but to say so would put me at risk of crossing more lines. I cleared my throat. "If I can't have your name, perhaps I could make one up for you?"

Her lips twitched, and it was an effort to keep those few inches of space between us. "And how would you go about that, Just Ryker?"

I stood up and paced before her, tapping my chin as if I were deep in thought. "Hmm . . . well, let's start with the obvious and work our way on from there. *My Lovely Mystery Lady* feels a tad too long."

She giggled, leaning back against the bench, crossing her arms over her chest. "That is quite the mouthful."

"What about Green Eyes?"

She pursed her lips at me, squinting her eyes in contemplation. "And what if another green-eyed girl thinks you're talking to *her* instead?"

"True, true. One can never be too careful." I winked at her and she lightly chuckled at me again, shaking her head.

"Can't choose anything too common. So Mary is out," I mused.

She scrunched her nose in mock disgust. "Absolutely not."

I laughed again, taking a step back to observe her more carefully: her silky hair loosely curled down the sides of her neck and back. Her flushed skin against her pale gown. Those glimmering green eyes. She captured all the light possible and reflected it back in a magical mixture of iridescent colors.

That was it. I dropped down on one knee before her, searching her gaze for a moment before I whispered, "Iridescent."

Her breath caught, and her eyes glossed over.

I beamed at her. "That's it. I shall call you *Iridescent.*"

I felt the smile that bloomed on her face deep in my core. That kind of smile was something you had to experience for yourself; there could be no explaining it. It both soothed my pounding heart and made it beat all the louder.

"I love it." Her choked whisper was so faint that I barely heard it.

"Then it is the perfect fit." I took her hand once more, kissing the back of her knuckles. Using the distraction to my advantage, I moved back up to the bench, scooting my body closer to hers. "Tell me, Iridescent. Did you grow up somewhere nearby?" Surely there had to be at least *one* question about herself that she would answer.

She nodded carefully, but she did seem to relax a bit at my use of her new name. "I actually grew up not too far from the palace."

"Truly?" She nodded again, chewing on her bottom lip a bit. Her hand still sat in mine, and every place our skin touched tingled with inexplicable energy. I kept pushing. "What was your childhood like?"

Her shoulders loosened a bit. This seemed to be a happier place for her mind to take her. "Well, my father owns an estate on the outskirts of town, and I used to . . ." Her eyes briefly flared wider, but she quickly schooled her features back into calm. I tried not to look too smug at getting an unintended admission from her, but I couldn't help the half-smile that twisted my lips upward.

Sighing, she shook her head in defeat. "My childhood was wonderful, actually. I loved helping around the estate, especially in the gardens with my mother and in the stables with the horses. My mother was an exceptional gardener, though she never had anything this grand." She motioned out to the garden in front of us. "She would have loved having a garden like this one."

My gaze followed hers, taking in the garden. "My mother was an exceptional gardener, as well. She never once left this place solely to the groundskeeper. She was always out here getting her hands dirty and planning out where things should go."

"Was this your mother's garden, then?" she asked. *Was.* Everyone who lived in Alstonia knew my mother passed away a few years ago; more proof that she was truly from here.

I couldn't help but sober up a bit at the mention of my mother. "Yes, this was her garden. I still come out here every day just to be with her. It's private, meant only for the royal family." The words just barely caught in my throat. I was never so open with anyone but Liam, but it felt strangely *right* sharing this with her.

She was silent, giving me a moment to compose myself once more before she spoke. "That's lovely, Ryker. I'm sure she appreciates you visiting each day." She squeezed my hand, and the oddly familiar feeling of comfort nearly undid me.

She sighed quietly, looking down at her lap. "My mother is gone, too. Seven years gone now, almost eight." When her lashes flicked back up to meet mine, they were heavy with unshed tears, knotting an uncomfortable lump in my throat. To have found someone who understood that pain . . . it was beyond what I would have thought to hope for. Beyond what I'd ever thought I needed.

I attempted to clear the blockage in my throat before speaking again. "It's rare for me to connect with someone like this. I don't often talk about my mother, except with my best friend." She gave my hand another squeeze in reply, and I prayed she wouldn't sense how close I was to shedding tears of my own. My nerves were utterly unraveled by this girl.

"I feel the same. I rarely get to talk about my mother. Father doesn't like her to even be mentioned anymore. He hasn't spoken of her since she died, actually." A dark shadow of emotion crossed over her face, but before I could decipher it, she dipped her chin, hiding her eyes from me.

"I'm sorry to hear that." I nudged her gently with my shoulder. "But I'm glad to have given you an opportunity to talk about her. I'm sure she was wonderful."

She smiled gently in return. "And I'm quite glad to be talking to you about her. You're . . . *much* different than I expected you to be."

My eyebrows raised. "Oh? And what did you expect me to be like?"

She side-eyed me, and I had to force down a groan. I could read that look well enough. "I am entirely certain you don't want me to answer that truthfully," she said tactfully.

"Let me guess." I tapped my chin. "Arrogant, womanizer, unable to feel human emotions?"

She giggled again, playfully pushing me away. A lightning-fast thrill bolted through me at the casual touch. Nobody *ever* touched me like that; this woman was surprising me just as much as I seemed to have surprised her.

Still chuckling, she said, "Yes. Something like that. I saw you once before, in town, and thought you quite arrogant. Though I confess I don't get out much, and didn't really know anything about you until this moment. I clearly judged you far too severely."

"You saw me?" My eyebrows shot up. "When?" *And how did I miss you?*

She shook her head. "I can't . . . I can't tell you."

I pouted, trying to make it look playful, but sharp disappointment still needled me. How was it that I felt I could tell her anything, and she felt she could tell me nothing?

"Well then, I must ask you a more serious question." She tensed at the statement, her eyes widening slightly as her fist clenched tighter in her lap. "Why were you not allowed to come tonight?"

"I . . ." She quickly removed her hand from mine. Looking longingly back down the path we had just walked down, I watched her fists close around her skirts, as if she was preparing to run. "I don't want anyone to get into trouble."

"Surely no one intentionally kept you away?" I urged.

Her breaths started to quicken, and her hands tremored, but she kept them tightly wound in her lap.

"Iridescent." She looked back up at me, her eyes desperate and fearful. But fearful of what? "What if I assured you that no one would get in trouble? What if I gave you my word as prince? Would you share your name with me then?"

"Your High—"

"Now, don't start that again." I held up a finger to her lips and lingered there. A deep flutter started in my stomach and spread quickly, like a swarm of butterflies taking flight inside my body, but her panicked eyes pulled me back into the moment.

"You're . . . you're truly afraid, aren't you?" I whispered. The fluttering feeling darkened, hardened, and I found myself wishing I had Liam's talent with the blade. Whoever had frightened this girl so thoroughly that she would deny a prince answers, even her name . . . I wanted to find them and have a very long and thorough discussion.

"Please, Ryker, I can't . . ." She trailed off, distressed pleading in her eyes, but I pressed on. I was so close to reaching her, I could see it. I just needed to push a little harder to break through this wall.

I cupped her cheeks in my hands, gently but firmly. "Why are you so afraid? You said you came tonight so you could experience life on your terms." I searched her panicked face. "Why can't your family know you're here? Why wouldn't they be thrilled that their daughter spent the evening with the prince?"

She pulled away from me and stood up to put space between us, but I stood with her and reached out for her hand, pulling her back towards me. "I'm the prince. I can protect you. Whatever is happening to you, whoever is frightening you like this . . ." I trailed off as I reached for her, cupping the back of her head with my other hand. The heat of her body felt different now, closer than before, the room charged with frenetic energy. I could have sworn I saw the faintest colorful glow out of the corner of my eye.

"Please, Your Highness." Her pupils dilated as she gazed into my eyes. I couldn't tell if she was still afraid, or if it was from the tension between us.

I leaned my head down, our lips almost touching as I whispered, "Just Ryker."

Her breath hitched, and a familiar feeling tightened low in my stomach. Her eyes fluttered shut, and for just a moment, I forgot myself, leaning in closer. I stopped right before our lips touched, our breath mingling together.

I didn't know what was frightening her so badly. I didn't know why she had to sneak in here tonight. But I knew that I wanted her. I wanted to convince her that I was worthy of her trust. I wanted her to choose me above all others.

All at once, the clock tower let out a booming chime. We hadn't been able to hear it inside the ballroom, and she all but jumped out of her skin at the sound of it.

Panic trilled through her voice. "Wait, what time is it?"

Surely it was irrational to find oneself murderously angry at a clock for doing its job, but then again, nothing tonight had felt entirely rational. I glowered over at it, searching out the time. "It's only just midnight."

The clock struck again, sounding loud and impatient.

"Two." She said it so quietly that I almost missed it. Her eyes darted down to her dress, her fingers clutching at the fabric like she thought it might melt away.

The clock struck a third time. I saw her mouth move to form the word with no breath behind it. *Three.*

"Your Highne—I mean Prince—I mean *Ryker*. Please forgive me,

I'm so very sorry, but I must go. I must go *now*." Wrenching herself free from my hold, she lifted her skirts and made a beeline for the door.

Four.

Something was happening, something that terrified her, but I had no clue what it was.

"Wait! Stop! Please don't go!" I cried out, sprinting after her.

Her heels clacked in haste against the path. She dove through the door just as I rushed up behind her, catching the door just as it was closing. I reached out and barely managed to snag her arm, spinning her around to face me in the corridor.

I held my hand up to my heart, silently beseeching her to stop running. "I promise you, I will protect you from whatever is happening in your world. Just please, *please* trust me. Tell me what's wrong. I won't let anyone hurt you."

Five.

She looked at me with wild, frantic eyes, the eyes of a hunted thing—a cornered thing. She turned to look behind her, and I could see her measuring the space between us and the door back out to the ballroom.

Six.

She blanched at the sound of the clock tower before looking back at me. "You don't even know me, Prince Ryker. Please, you must let me go. There's nothing you can do for me. I'm not who you think I am."

Seven.

I held tight to her, desperately afraid to lose her. There were too many questions left unanswered, too many unknowns to allow me to find her again once she left the palace. "Iridescent, wait—"

Suddenly, she stopped fighting me, and instead stretched up to kiss my cheek. Every muscle of mine froze in place, her lips soft against my skin like delicate clouds. I closed my eyes, trying to memorize the feeling. Her warm breath whispered in my ear: "If you ever find me again, please don't judge me too severely. I never meant to deceive you."

Eight.

She took advantage of my disorientation, and I felt her pull out of my hold. My eyes sprang back open just in time to see her race past the guards. I heard the sharp calls of surprise and gasps as she ran through the mess of guests just outside.

Nine.

Bewilderment spun my head into a whirlwind. *What's happening? What do I do?*

"Stop! Please!" I ran after her into the ballroom, wildly searching the crowd for her chestnut hair.

Ten.

Every guard looked stunned, both by her dramatic departure and my sudden appearance. I scanned the room helplessly until my eyes found Liam's. "Liam! We can't let her leave." I pointed at the staircase— the now-empty staircase. She'd already dashed around the corner, vanishing from sight.

Eleven.

Liam instantly began barking out orders, setting things in motion while I stood there numbly, staring at the ballroom's grand doors.

Twelve.

My Iridescent. Gone. Just like that.

CHAPTER 22

I paced next to the side door where Ryker had led the mystery girl to his mother's garden, anxiously waiting for him to return. I wanted to be happy for him, truly. But there was something about her . . .

When I held her close she felt familiar, smelled familiar. Like airy jasmine and dew. Like a combination of sunlight and moonlight. Everything about her was familiar, and she'd teased me like we'd always known each other, but it was like my mind was befuddled. The image of her face always came back foggy.

Who is she?

A sinking twinge of dread wriggled into my chest as I kept staring at the near-invisible side door in the ballroom. I was going to drive myself mad before I figured this out. Glancing around the room, I did my best to avoid catching the eyes of the Coulters or any potential dance partner. My mind was far too overwhelmed to focus, overthinking every little detail. Like the mystery girls' strangely familiar smile and her bright, expressive eyes. Her slender fingers and collarbones. The elegant curve of her neck. The way she teased me subtly, both sure and unsure of herself.

The clock tower sounded faintly in the background, almost completely drowned out by the music and voices reverberating throughout the room. Midnight. I shook my head, trying to will some clarity into it. *They've been back there a long time.* I tried not to think about all the reasons it could have been taking this long.

Suddenly, the side door swung open, revealing the mystery woman. She bolted past the guard, past the people in the crowd, and up the main staircase.

Ryker followed closely behind her, chest heaving, eyes wide. "Stop! Please!" He looked around, desperately searching until he found my eyes. "Liam! We can't let her leave."

I didn't know what he meant by that, but I sprung to action, setting the two nearest men on her heels. Rafe came flying out of the corridor next, followed by John. I pointed to where she was headed. "Looks like she's making a run for the carriages. Go after her—go on horseback, or you'll never catch up to her." They raced off to the stables.

I walked over to Ryker. He was panting, pacing, his eyes frantic. He raked a hand through his hair—I'd never seen him this unhinged, at least in such a public arena. "I can't lose her, Liam!" He grabbed onto my suit jacket. "She's it! I . . . I mean, it's *her*." An inaudible groan escaped his mouth. He looked crushed. Palming the middle of his head, his hand swept down his face, his expression bewildered beyond measure.

The king and Apep approached us, pulling us back into the private guarded corridor. Guards opened the nearest door, and the king confidently strode in, motioning for Ryker to sit down while pulling up a chair next to him.

"What in the world is going on, Ryker?" His face was stern, authoritative, but still curious.

Ryker looked up, his face stricken, like a man punched in the gut. "I found her, Father. It's *her*."

The king raised one eyebrow. "Then why was she running from you?"

Almost as if speaking to himself, Ryker started mumbling, wiping sweat from his brow. "She looked so afraid. Something about the clock chiming startled her and I . . . I lost her. She said she had to go, that she was sorry . . ." He wiped down his face with his hand again, visibly trembling. He was never this inarticulate. "She said she didn't mean to deceive me." Groaning, he leaned back in the chair, both hands covering his face now. "I don't understand what just happened."

I knelt down in front of him. "Tell me everything you can, Ryk. We'll find her. Let's start with her name."

He looked down at me, eyes dark with defeat, hopelessness already hanging heavy on his face. "She wouldn't tell me her name."

The king, Apep, and I all exchanged glances. I leaned closer to him. "Why wouldn't she tell you her name? Did she give a reason?"

He nodded. "She said she was here against her family's wishes. She didn't want to be found out."

"Did she give you any clues as to who her family is?"

He shook his head again. "At first I thought maybe she was with the visiting dignitaries, but she claimed to be from Alstonia. Then I asked her if she was crashing the ball, but she said no, her family was invited." Ryker rubbed his temples for a moment. "She mentioned that they live on the outskirts of town. They're close to the palace."

"That's something. If they were invited, then she's from a noble family, and if they live on the outskirts . . . that narrows down the choices. We could easily visit each estate until we found her." I stood up and started pacing the room, trying to think my way through the problem. "Did she tell you anything else? Anything that could give us a clue as to which family she comes from?"

"Well, she did mention her mother passed away, almost eight years ago. I told her we were in my mother's garden, and she told me her mother would have loved it, that she was a gardener herself. Seems she took a lot of pride in their estate."

Ryker's voice faded into the background as the room tilted beneath me. I stopped pacing, closing my eyes as stunned dread slithered through my stomach.

Interrupting Ryker, I asked again, just to make sure I heard him right: "She said her mother died almost eight years ago?"

Apep looked at me suspiciously, but the others seemed unaware of my rising panic. Ryker nodded confidently, "Yes. There can't be many widowers among the nobles in that area, can there? Unless of course they remarried, that would be no use to us." The blood drained from my face as he looked back up at me. "She looked so *sad*, Liam. So scared. I couldn't bear seeing her agony. And her eyes, she has the most beautiful green eyes . . ."

No. *No.*

My chest tightened, squeezing my heart painfully, and my eyes were too dizzy to focus. The floor tilted again. I felt as though I was sweating through every piece of fabric.

This couldn't be happening.

The door abruptly flew open, and Rafe, John, and the other two guards filed in. Ryker was on his feet in an instant, while the king patiently waited for an update. I was unraveling. I didn't know what I'd do if they had her with them.

They made quick bows, dipping their heads to him. "Your Majesty, Your Highness. The girl got away." My body physically deflated in *far* too obvious relief, but again, no one seemed to notice. "We were barely a few minutes behind her on our horses, I don't . . ." Rafe shook his head, looking completely bewildered. "I don't know what happened. Her carriage tracks simply stopped. Disappeared. There was no trace of her. It's like she vanished into thin air."

Ryker sank back down into his chair, burying his face in his hands, despair weighing down his shoulders.

I shook off my own emotions, forcing my spine to straighten. "Your Highness, we will find her." I turned to Rafe and John. "We know that she's from a noble family that lives on the outskirts of the nearest town."

"But that's got to be over twenty families," Rafe said.

I stared back at him. "And if we have to visit each and every one, we will." Turning back to Ryker, I asked, "Is there anything else, Your Highness? Any other clue that could help us identify her?"

Ryker grew silent for a long moment, his eyes closed and his brow furrowed in concentration. When he opened them, doubt clouded his eyes. "I don't know. She mentioned that she loves the outdoors, and horses . . ."

Rafe snorted. "Yeah, her and every other maiden in the kingdom."

"Watch your tone, boy." The king's sharp reprimand instantly quieted the room.

Ryker looked over at me with pleading eyes. "She wouldn't give me many details. I tried to wear her down, but—"

"I'm sure you did." I winced at my own irritated tone. This whole mess wasn't Ryker's fault, but still, even in this he had to come first. He was trying to take Evy from me. *My* Evy.

He frustratedly ran his hands through his hair. Everyone else in the room grew quiet, staring at me. Apep's scrutiny was the worst of it; he looked like he knew exactly what was going through my mind. But then again, he always had that smug look on his face.

I couldn't breathe. *Evy.* Why hadn't I recognized her?

I couldn't comprehend it. Evy with Ryker . . . my queen. His wife.

Nausea jolted in my stomach at the thought. The pain of it all was nearly unbearable. It felt like someone had reached inside my chest and was slowly squeezing my heart.

"Liam?" Ryker was looking at me now. "Brother, you're paler than the dead. What's wrong with you?"

I shook my head and tried to straighten my spine again, waving my hand casually. "I'm fine. It's not much to go on, but I think we can still find her, given this information. Even if we have to conduct interviews with every maiden we come across."

Ryker stood up immediately. "I'm going with you." Before I could begin to protest, he continued, "I *know* I'll recognize her the moment I see her. That will help speed things up."

There was no good reason to deny him, so I nodded, looking to the other four guards in the room. "First thing tomorrow we start searching the estates. Gather more men to accompany and protect the prince, and let's go map out a plan."

Ryker and Apep helped his father out of the room, saying a quick good evening to the guests still in attendance before they retired, each and every one murmuring curiously about the mystery girl who ran away from the prince.

My men and I mapped out a route for tomorrow before I finally allowed myself to retire to my room. I almost expected Ryker to be there waiting for me, but thankfully my room was quiet and empty. Thoughts churned heavy in my mind, just the same way my stomach was churning in dismay.

That's why she felt so familiar. But was I so unfamiliar with her now that I couldn't even recognize her when she was standing right in front of me? When I'd held her in my arms, when I'd spoken to her? Even now I could barely picture her face, how she'd looked at me during our brief dance.

A deep, soul-searing agony filled my chest until it hurt to breathe. It wasn't me she danced with all night. It was Ryker.

It wasn't me who took her to the moonlit garden. It was Ryker.

It wasn't me she came to see tonight. It was *Ryker*.

A slow, terrible shaking began to take over my body as I pictured them dancing and laughing and twirling across the grand ballroom. When I thought of how she must've looked while they were alone together, under the moonlight in his mother's garden, sitting beneath the big willow tree.

Ryker was the Crown Prince, and she was his to claim if he so chose to. And what girl in her right mind would ever turn down a prince in favor of a guard, even a captain?

Heat flooded my eyes as I pictured Ryker telling the king that she was the one. That Evy was the girl he wanted to marry. I choked back a despairing sob.

My best friend. My prince. My future king. He loved *my* Evy.

And, even worse: what if she loved him in return?

CHAPTER 23

Evelyn

We raced away from the palace. Two guards followed closely behind on horseback; it was only a matter of time before they would catch up to us. My heart beat so loudly in my head I barely heard the carriage hitting the uneven ground. Jimmy was practically flying down the path, urgency in his voice as he shouted the horses on. The magic was dwindling already.

The town square came into view as we rounded a bend directly in front of us, and relief flooded my body. We were almost there. Glancing out the carriage window, I noticed it start to fade around me. I gasped, looking down at my dress. The fabric melted away to reveal my borrowed petticoats and corset in its place. My skin was scratched and bruised and dirty again. I cried out to Jimmy, who was already slowing the horses so we could come to a full stop. He ran around and helped me out of the disappearing carriage just as it evaporated away in a burst of light.

Jimmy and I were left standing on the side of the road in our old clothes. My shoes had disappeared, leaving my feet bare. We stared at each other, mesmerized by the magic, until our two horses began prancing around anxiously and we heard the sound of rapidly approaching hooves.

"Quick, jump on the horse!" He pointed to a patch of forest off to our left. "We'll need to ride in there to hide our tracks." I nodded, and we both ran for the horses. Jimmy gave me a little boost up and I winced, my body feeling the physical toll again. He then easily swung himself up and over his own steed's bare back.

The approaching hooves grew louder and louder as we made our mad dash into the dense forest. Jimmy led us deep enough inside that we were hidden by the natural camouflage of trees and brush, but we had to slow our speed. There would be no racing the horses through this thick wood, so we carefully picked our way across the uneven terrain. It was a gamble, but one we needed to take in order to escape unseen.

I could hear the royal guards puzzling over the way our tracks had simply disappeared. They couldn't make sense of it, and good for us, because now they were too distracted to even think of looking in the forest.

I smiled at Jimmy, and he smiled back as we crept slowly through the trees and brush until we finally reached the other side of town. We jumped back on the road that led to the estate, riding home hard and fast.

CHAPTER 24

Evelyn

The sun didn't seem to know just how eventful of an evening I'd had last night, because it woke me at the usual time, forcing me to drag my tight, aching body out of bed. Even so, memories of the night before twirled dazzlingly in my mind, bringing a smile to my face.

Last night had been a completely surprising dream. Between meeting my grandmother, learning that *fairies* exist, witnessing the most spectacular magic, and dancing with Ryker and Liam—no matter how quickly it had all flown by, it was everything I could've possibly hoped for. More than that, even.

I changed quickly into my normal working dress and made my way downstairs to help Cook prepare breakfast. As I slipped into the room, Cook gave me a once-over with worried, exhausted eyes. She looked far too tired, like she'd been fretting well into the night. The concern in her eyes made the threats Father had given last night replay in my mind, but I tamped down the terror, determined to cling to the joy instead. There wasn't much I could do besides grin and bear whatever was coming next. I gave her a quick hug and a peck on the cheek, smiling reassuringly as we wordlessly busied ourselves with breakfast preparation.

As soon as I heard the usual ring of the breakfast bell, I dashed up the stairs to divvy out the breakfast plates.

They all looked rather worse for the wear themselves. All three moved slowly, particularly Camilla, like they were still sore from dancing and mingling. I guessed by the way Katerina was rubbing her head that she'd indulged in a few too many fine glasses of champagne, but she brightened when she saw me, like she'd just remembered something important. "Frank, dear," she chirped, side-eyeing me smugly, "Wasn't last night just lovely? *Captain Liam* danced with Camilla several times. He couldn't keep his hands off of her!"

Camilla scowled, giving me an uncomfortable look. "It was only twice, and both times were interrupted."

Katerina waved her hand in dismissal. "That's neither here nor there, darling. It's obvious you've grabbed his attention. Don't downplay it now."

Camilla merely sighed, starting at her breakfast.

"Frank, dear," Katerina pressed. Father shot her a look of utter irritation—because of her nagging or because the sound of her voice was so grating, I couldn't be sure. But Katerina simply stared back, unflinching. "Were you able to make that *deal* we spoke about last night?"

His shoulders slouched forward, and his eyes darted briefly over to me before he bowed his head. "Yes, of course."

It was then that I noticed the deep, dark circles under his eyes. He looked like he hadn't slept for several nights.

"And?" Katerina prompted him.

He sighed. "And it's done."

A small, cruel smile crossed her lips. "Well then, aren't you going to tell everyone the news?"

He closed his eyes and breathed deeply in through his nose. "Evelyn will no longer be working for this family."

The water I was pouring into Camilla's cup overflowed. It was all I could do not to drop the pitcher with it.

"You stupid, clumsy girl!" Katerina admonished. "Perfect proof as to why we need to find better help around here!"

Father grimaced, but it was Camilla who spoke up. Her tone

was obnoxiously haughty, much like her mother's, but her eyes were nervous when they flickered to me. "You already said that last night. What's the actual news?"

I could feel the shakes beginning to build up in my limbs, but I tried to control them, busying myself with swabbing up the mess before it could spill onto Camilla's skirt.

He turned his attention to her. "I found a new home for her last night."

Camilla gasped.

Freezing in place, my fingers still buried in the soaked rag, I looked up, facing Father straight on.

I never dared to do that. But if they were already getting rid of me, what was the point of holding my tongue any further? Why did any of this matter at all?

I let go of the rag and let the water start dribbling down the table, into Camilla's lap and onto the floor. She didn't even seem to notice.

"A new home? Or new employment?" My voice was low, simmering just on the cusp of anger.

Camilla stiffened, and Father's eyes tightened at the edges. I didn't dare look at Katerina, but I could still feel her stinging glare on my skin.

Father leaned forward in his chair and folded his hands on the table, looking me straight in the eye. "I have found a family that is willing to take you on as a maid in their home. They will be here soon."

Shock rippled through my spine. Doing my best to keep my voice from wavering, I asked, "What do you mean, they will be here soon? *How* soon?"

Somehow I knew already, even before he answered. This was it. I was getting what I had both craved and feared above all else: an escape, but not a triumphant one. I was getting out, but I was still losing.

A strange, numb warmth coated every inch of me. I looked around the table, slowly, as if in a dream. My eyes met Katerina's: the woman who had hated and degraded me every day since she'd arrived at this estate. Her eager eyes relished my anguish and shock, but I wouldn't give her the satisfaction of seeing me crumble.

I lazily moved on to Camilla, who looked as shocked as I did, but still stoic as ever. Unfeeling, unmoved, and unable to love anyone but herself. It was hard to imagine we were ever truly close. Watching her in this moment, she looked as if she didn't care at all what happened to me. Perhaps she was inwardly celebrating that she would have Liam's attention all to herself from now on. The unwanted image of them holding each other close last night filled my mind, and my heart sank even further into my chest.

Lastly, my eyes travelled to my father's. He looked . . . disappointed? Angry? Sad? Whatever it was, it didn't matter, because when I stared into his cold eyes, all I could see were my memories. Papa laughing while kissing Mama, helping me pick out wildflowers in the meadow, eyes crinkling at the corners with adoration as he looked over at Mama and me, his arms embracing me, picking me up and twirling me around high in the sky.

I realized in that moment that it was done. I had lost the only thing I had truly ever wanted.

An unbearable ache tightened inside my chest.

He doesn't want me.

"They should be here to collect you in an hour or so," Father said, as matter-of-factly as one would discuss whether it was raining outside or not.

I closed my eyes. The room was entirely silent.

He doesn't love me anymore.

"You work for the Hallefords now," he finished.

The Hallefords. I didn't know their name, nor had I ever met them or any of their staff while at the market. For all I knew, they were nobles from a distant town. Many had traveled to the ball last night from all over the kingdom.

I dropped my eyes to my hand, still clutching the wet rag I had been using to clean up the spilled water on the table. It was all dirty, torn up and stained, near-ready to be thrown away.

Camilla broke the silence next, surprising me with her boldness. "How can you give her away, Father? She's your own blood!"

He sat back in his chair, the picture of ease. "I wrote to the king this morning, asking for her to be removed from the Coulter line."

"You *disowned* her?" The incredulity, the near-*fury* in her voice startled me. Camilla never stood up to Father or Katerina, least of all on my behalf.

His eyes narrowed, clearly displeased with this admonishment from his *good* daughter. "She's no longer a part of this family, Camilla. It's what had to happen."

No longer a part of this family.

Without meeting my father's eyes, I asked, "What will my name be?"

Father took a moment to answer, and when he did, his voice was softer than before. "Whatever the king assigns to you."

It was strange to think I would no longer be Evelyn Coulter, daughter of Frank and Clara Coulter. Even stranger that a simple piece of paper could deem it so. But if I was being honest with myself, he'd stopped treating me as a Coulter a long time ago.

There was nothing left to lose. Not my home, not my family, not my name. So I steadied my face and steeled my nerves, refusing to allow any emotion to shine through. My chin lifted from the rag to meet his eyes again. "Will I actually be paid for my work in this new household?"

He blinked in disbelief, but didn't scold me. "Yes, they will be paying you a nominal fee for your work."

I nodded stiffly. "And will I be allowed to take anything with me?"

Katerina squawked, "Absolutely not! Everything in this house belongs to us girl, how dare you even ask such a—"

"Katerina, *stop*." Frank's order was loud and clear, lined with a distinct edge that instantly quieted her. I'd never seen him do that to her. "You are allowed to take any personal items you wish."

With one quick nod, I drifted out of the room and up the stairs . . . for the last time. Gently closing my bedroom door, I washed my face and hands, then rummaged around for anything I would want to take with me.

I only had time to grab a few items, the ones that mattered most to me. My threadbare baby quilt, my mother and I's favorite book of tales with a few dried flowers pressed between the pages, and a small hair clip that Mama used to wear in her hair. Everything else of my mother's was kept in Father's room, far away from me.

I used the quilt to wrap my meager items together, hoisting it over one shoulder as I took one last look around my room. My eyes snagged on my mirror, and I stepped up to it, looking at myself like I had last night. My hair was tied back by a dirty cloth that helped keep the strands out of my face while I worked and served breakfast. My face was emaciated and pale, nausea and grief robbing it of its color. *Iridescent.* I wasn't sure whether to laugh or cry at the memory of Ryker's beautiful name for me. It felt like a mockery now. Without my grandmother's magic, I was *Wretched.* I was *Hollow.*

I closed my eyes to the sight and walked out the door.

Cook and Jimmy were right there waiting for me in the hallway. I hugged them both, but held back my tears. I didn't want to cry. I refused to see this as anything less than a blessing.

Jimmy, however, let his tears flow freely as he whispered in my ear, "We love you, Little Miss. We *will* come find you." He kissed my numb cheek and hugged me one more time. "It's better this way. You don't deserve any of this, but it's better this way."

"I know," I lied, forcing a smile as I released him.

Cook clung to me next, handing me a bushel of dried leaves. "I thought you might like a little private tea stash." She gave me a small, brave smile before her sweet face crumpled and she fell into uncontrollable sobs.

"Oh, Cook, don't, please—" It was harder not to cry when I was watching her cry. I hugged them both. "I love you both so much."

It was all I could say, but it wasn't enough to encompass all that they meant to me. I just didn't have any words left to try.

Jimmy gently pulled Cook away at the sound of horse hooves crunching over the pebbled courtyard. Moving through the motions, I made my way down the stairs. Frank and Katerina greeted an old, gray-haired man with smiles and firm handshakes outside the front door.

Before I could reach the front door, Camilla swept in front of me, blocking my path. She caught my hands, gazing at me with a desperate apology in her eyes. "I didn't want this, you know. I never wanted this." Her hands trembled in mine—how strange, for her to be the one shaken. "I always wanted a sister. You were supposed to be that sister."

I stared into her eyes, a cold callous forming over my heart. The voice that came out of me didn't sound like mine. "I don't forgive you."

She was the easy victim of those words. I wanted to yell them from the top of a mountain, wanted to scream them in Frank and Katerina's faces, but Camilla was the only one who would care. She was the only one they would hurt. So she got to be the lucky recipient.

Her eyes filled with shock and shame. She dropped my hand as if I'd burned her, tears flowing freely down her cheeks.

I had never been so cruel, had never said anything like that before, but I was entirely too angry to care. The images of her ripping apart my mother's gown, taunting me about Liam in the mirror yesterday, watching while Father beat me, leaving me to struggle by myself these past few years without a friend or a sister to rely on, leaning into Liam's embrace last night . . . no matter what her reasons, it was all too fresh, and I was far too hurt to pretend as though I wasn't.

I refused to look back at her as I crossed the threshold of my home for the last time.

Frank watched me as I approached, and the briefest shadow of emotion flashed across his face before it hardened again. He motioned for me to stand next to him, but he was careful not to touch me. "Lord Halleford, this is our housemaid, Evelyn. She's quite proficient in her duties and is excellent at anticipating needs. I know you will find her a great asset to your home."

Lord Halleford beckoned me forward. "Come here, girl." He then proceeded to look me over like I was a piece of livestock. He circled me once, raising my arms up and squeezing my shoulders. He stood off to the side of me, touching a finger under my chin. "Open your mouth, girl."

I imagined a wall surrounding me, building it brick by brick in my mind. His poking and prodding faded into nothing, and my outward emotions felt sufficiently caged in. I heard him softly counting, and before long he said, "Yes, she'll do nicely. A bit on the skinny side, but *we* have plentiful food, so we should be able to remedy that." I almost grinned at the sly jab regarding the destitution of the Coulter estate. He motioned to one of the carriage footmen. "As agreed upon, here is the cow you asked for in exchange."

Katerina gave a small exclamation, clapping her hands in glee as the cow was brought over. "Oh, it's perfect, Lord Halleford."

The lord gave her an impatient nod before turning back to me. "All right, girl, away we go. Is this all you have to bring with you?"

"Yes, sir."

He nodded and turned to enter the coach. The footman shut the door soundly behind him, and I looked around helplessly for a moment, unsure of where I was supposed to go. The footman then moved to the back of the coach and motioned for me to follow him. We sat on a small bench that jutted out behind the coach, and my heart slammed into my throat as we lurched forward, pulling away from the estate. *My home.*

Frank and Katerina had already turned around, closing the front door before we had even pulled out of the gate, but Frank took one last look back at me before shaking his head and shutting the door.

And that was it.

CHAPTER 25

I knocked firmly on the door to Ryker's room. It was barely light out, but I could already hear him up and moving around. I'd known he would be more motivated than usual to start this day, but then again, so was I.

The door swung open. Ryker was already dressed and ready to go, his jaw clenched, determination lighting his eyes from within. We'd decided it would be best for him to disguise himself as a guard today; we didn't want a mad dash of women pretending to be his mystery maiden. Once we visited the first noble, we knew word would spread quickly about who we were searching for, and we had to do anything we could to avoid delays.

"We've got a lot of ground to cover today. How soon can the men be ready?" There was a frantic look about him that mirrored my internal feelings exactly.

"The men will be ready within the hour. I . . .may be a bit longer."

Ryker paused, tilting his head in question before recognition dawned on his face. "That's right. I forgot you were going to go check on Evelyn today."

Inwardly I grimaced when he said her name, but outwardly I

simply gave a curt nod. "If that's still all right with you. I'll come join you all soon after." I paused awkwardly, shuffling my feet. "I won't take long, I just—"

"No need to explain, brother," he interrupted, placing his hand on my shoulder. "Of course it's all right with me. If I get to worry about my girl, it's only fair you get to worry about yours."

He offered a small smirk, but I almost flinched. A pool of dread gathered in my stomach. I'd never lied to him before, had never held anything back from him, and I hated doing it now. But I had to talk to her first.

Rafe knocked on the chamber's main door, and Ryker rushed over to answer.

"Your Highness." Rafe gave a quick bow, crossing his fist over his heart.

"Good morning, Rafe," I called across the room, motioning for him to join me as I moved to stand by Ryker's small table. "Come in. Let's go over the plan again so you can brief the men."

He moved to stand next to me, looking over the map of the kingdom. I pointed to the first estate on their list. "You'll be heading to the western outskirts first, starting here." I turned to Ryker at the opposite end of the table. "Rafe already has the list of all the nobles you'll be visiting. Let him take the lead on inquiry until I can catch up to you." I moved around the table to put my hands on Ryker's shoulders. "Your role is to use your eyes to spot her, not to be seen yourself. Keep your identity hidden for as long as possible. I know that will be a struggle for you," I teased, giving him a small wink, "but there's no need to flaunt your royalness today."

Rafe shook his head, rolling his eyes and the map up to take with him.

"Oh, ha, ha," Ryker deadpanned. "Go see your lovely lady Evelyn, and hopefully by this afternoon you will have helped save your future queen and become a kingdom hero." I tensed, but dipped my head in acknowledgement. He gave me a sturdy shove out the door, then turned to Rafe. "When do we head out?"

Rafe gave me a knowing smile and waved me off. "Whenever you order it, Your Highness."

I ran down the hall toward the stables, where my horse was already saddled and waiting for me. I decided to forgo breakfast—my stomach was too queasy to take a bite anyway. I headed out in a rush toward the Coulter Estate.

The Coulter Estate was quieter than I'd ever heard it.

I dismounted and cautiously approached the home. The sinking feeling I'd had ever since last night sharpened itself into something more frantic, more dangerous. Deep in my gut, I knew that something had happened to Evelyn. I could only hope that I wasn't too late.

I knocked on the door, my heart pounding in my chest. *Please let her answer the door.*

But Katerina was the one who greeted me when the door swung open, looking the happiest I'd seen her yet. "Oh! Captain Liam, what a wonderfully pleasant surprise. Today is a good day indeed." She motioned for me to enter the house. Her overwhelming cheer was somehow more off-putting than her sneers and smug looks. "Come in, come in! You must be here to see Camilla. She had the most lovely evening with you last night. I'm so pleased you've stopped by for a visit so soon."

This wasn't just politeness. She was practically gushing, triumph written all over her face, looking at me like she'd won some sort of prize. It set me on edge.

I walked into the foyer, glancing around for any trace of Evy. Their small dining room was off to my right, and I had to look twice, surprised by the state it was in. There were plates of food sitting untouched, a big puddle on the floor, and a soaking rag festering on the table, as though breakfast had been hastily abandoned.

I cleared my throat loudly, masking the disgust that worsened the sick feeling in my stomach. "Forgive me, madam, but I'm here to see Evelyn. You mentioned last night that she was indisposed . . . or not feeling well. Whichever it is, I came to see how she's doing today."

Katerina's eyebrow quirked upward. After a beat too long, she said,

"I'm afraid she's still indisposed. She's unable to have visitors today."

I narrowed my eyes, searching her for hints of a lie. "Is she ill?"

She put on a bright, albeit fake, smile. "Oh, she'll be just fine, dear! She just doesn't want any visitors right now. You do worry so. Such a thoughtful friend you are."

I was just opening my mouth to retort, fed up with her games, when I saw Camilla hurrying down the stairs, her skirts gathered in one fist in her haste.

"Captain Liam! What a pleasant surprise. I had a lovely time last night, and I would adore it if you'd take a walk with me this morning. The crisp morning air is so refreshing, is it not?" Her smile remained, but her eyes were sharp, staring into my soul. She gave me an almost imperceptible nod.

Katerina seemed pleased by Camilla's suggestion. "Oh, what a splendid idea! You two go walk the grounds for a bit together." She glanced around the room, blanching slightly as she realized what I had been staring at. "We were just finishing our breakfast, so this will give Cook some time to get the mess cleaned up."

I nodded to Camilla in silent understanding, ignoring Katerina completely. Evy's stepsister casually walked over, looping her arm through mine as she led me back out the front door. Her adoring looks and smile disappeared the minute we were away from the house.

She glanced over her shoulder several times, but kept us moving until we were safely hidden behind a tree surrounded by overgrown weeds. She hadn't said a word yet, and my discomfort was starting to build, wondering what her intentions were.

"Camilla," I said, pulling her attention to me. "Tell me what's going on."

Tears pooled in her already puffy eyes, and she laughed, a bitter sound with no amusement. "More honesty, Captain?"

"If anyone in your family can manage it."

She flinched, her face crumpling. "Fine. You want honesty? It's too late now. *We* were too late, both of us. I didn't do what I could before, and now . . ." The tears began to fall down her cheeks in earnest, and dread grew deep roots into my stomach.

"What's happened, Camilla?" I stared her down with a look that usually made men wither before me. "*Tell me.*"

She choked back a sob, her voice cracking as she said, "She's gone, Liam."

Those words punched me in the gut, all my breath whooshing from my body. "What do you mean, *gone*?"

Camilla took a deep breath, anguish twisting her beautiful features into something almost grotesque. My lungs couldn't pull air in fast enough; terror pulled my chest taut, so tight it was nearly painful. If Evy was hurt, or worse . . .

"You should know the whole story, or as much of it as I can tell you quickly." She did her best to steady her gasping breaths, but she wasn't faring much better than I was. She wiped at her eyes before speaking again. "Evelyn's practically been a servant in this house since we moved in. My mother wanted her out of the way, and Frank obliged. It was free labor, after all." She avoided my gaze, which was a good thing. Flames filled my ears with searing heat, and violent fury squeezed through every muscle in my body, willing me to take action. I was seconds away from storming the house and dragging Frank Coulter out by his neck.

"I . . . I was too afraid for myself," Camilla continued. "I never came to her aid, never really helped. But I didn't lie to you before. There was a time when we were friends—sisters, even." The heat of shame stained her neck and face. "Mother hated our friendship. She said she didn't want me to be around Evelyn any longer. She warned me to stay away . . . she ordered me to stay distant." Her eyes still had a desperate edge to them as she raised her head, tears gathering in thick droplets on her lashes. "I couldn't tell her no. If I'd defied them too . . . what if they'd started doing the same things to me? What if it was *me* on the floor, whipped within an inch of my life?"

Her last words echoed inside my soul: *Whipped within an inch of my life.*

Horror and hostility twined together, heating my bones. Camilla held back another sob as I grabbed her shoulders. "Where is she, Camilla? Is she okay? Is she *hurt*?"

"Last night, we—" She cut off, stumbling over her words. "She tried to go to the ball, Liam, but we stopped her. Mother wanted to make sure she was out of the way so that I could spend time with you, maybe even the prince. We . . . we made it so she wouldn't be able to attend."

I paused, puzzled, trying to fit all the pieces together. *But she was there last night. How did she manage it?*

Camilla's voice dropped low. "Frank made arrangements last night with another noble."

"Arrangements? What kind of arrangements?"

Her teeth gritted against a sob, and she choked out, "He gave her away. Her own father traded her for a damn *cow*. Mother wanted her out of the way, and Frank . . . Frank made it happen."

A cow. They'd sold Evelyn for a *cow?*

Fury cooled the burning in my bones, freezing every emotion into ice. "How long."

"What?"

"*How long* has he been doing this to her?"

She wiped at her damp cheeks, pulling in a shaky breath. "It started just a little after we moved here."

My heart skipped a beat. I counted the years in my head. *Ten years old.* That was right after I left, right after her mother died. The world tilted dangerously, and I had to reach out to the tree for stability. Closing my eyes, I clutched my chest, unable to reach the tearing sensation in my ribcage. *I left her here. She's endured this all alone.*

Camilla sniffled, musing quietly to herself, "She never complained, really. We were closer back then. She . . . she spoke of you often."

I opened my eyes, focusing on Camilla's shrewd face. "Did you play a part in her mistreatment?"

She faltered at the question, and her face paled with guilt. But she offered no excuse, no explanation. She simply whispered, "Yes."

I trembled with a rage I had never felt before as I stared at the ground, ready to rip anything in my path to shreds. This wretched family didn't deserve her. My own labored breaths and Camilla's quiet sobs were the only sounds, until I heard a branch snap behind me. My hand immediately flew to the pommel of my sword as I turned around.

The old man approaching put his hands halfway up, eyeing the hand on my pommel. "Easy, Liam. It's Jimmy."

"Jimmy?" I asked. This haggard old man before me couldn't possibly be the same as the lively man I'd been used to seeing every day as a child. "You're . . . you're still here?"

He nodded and tried to smile, but it couldn't seem to form past the pain in his eyes. "Yes, son. I only meant to tell you what's happened here. But it seems Camilla's already started that conversation." Camilla's breath hitched behind me, but Jimmy paid her no mind. His eyes were red and swollen from crying, but he remained calm. "Evelyn needs you. Please, Liam, there's no time to lose."

I reached out my hand to his and drew him behind the tree with us. His grip was still strong as ever, but his wrinkled face and graying hair looked run-down and weary. It seemed Frank's mistreatment had stretched beyond his daughter.

"It's so good to see you. We've all missed you." He looked me over quickly, chuckling under his breath. "I'm proud of who you've become, and what you've made of yourself." He patted my cheek. "Evelyn missed you so . . . Liam, she's been given to a new household. It happened just under an hour ago, they've already taken her—"

I cut him off, confusion warring in my mind. "How is this possible? She's his daughter. How could he get away with this?"

Camilla sniffled, scornfully wiping her eyes. "If you're treated one way long enough, you become it."

Jimmy just scoffed and shook his head, tightening his jaw. "Frank sent a letter to the king first thing this morning, requesting that Evelyn be removed from the Coulter line and given a new surname." He lowered his head. "The Hallefords came this morning. They took her back to their estate."

I couldn't believe what I was hearing. I wracked my brain to try and picture Lord Halleford. I was not acquainted with him, but the name was familiar . . .

"All of us who love her want them to pay for what they've done." He chanced a hard glance over to Camilla, the closest thing to an admonishment he could give. "But that's not what Evelyn needs right now. She wasn't safe here, Liam." He paused, letting that message sink in. "She's had a very hard life since you went away. I don't know the Hallefords, but I would guess that she's far safer there than she was here." He leaned in, lowering his voice, speaking in a conspiratorial whisper. "But she'd be even safer under *your* protection."

I couldn't get a grip on all the emotions bombarding me. All I knew was that I wanted to run someone through with my sword, preferably Frank Coulter, and hold Evy so tightly in my arms that no one could ever hurt her again.

Jimmy gripped both of my arms and made me look him square in the face. "If you are somehow unable to . . . *provide* for her yourself," he said, clearing his throat awkwardly, "please, just make sure she finds a better life." His eyes filled with tears again, and I could feel the despair pouring through the grip in his hands.

I nodded firmly, clapping him on the shoulder. "I promise you, Jimmy, from today onward, she will have a far better life. I will make sure of it."

I saw the relief wash over his whole body. "Thank you."

Camilla gazed at us, somewhat calmer now. Her face still looked tortured, but her eyes met mine with quiet pleading. "Tell her I'm sorry. Tell her I did what I could now, even if I couldn't before."

I gave her a brisk nod, and she slowly moved back toward the house.

Jimmy gave me a little push toward the gates. "Go, take care of our girl." He tried to smile, but it fell short. "The Halleford Estate is somewhere on the west side. I wish I knew more."

I gave him a confident nod and raced back to my horse. I tried picturing the map that my men and I had pored over last night in my head, but my mind was foggy and unfocused, only able to focus on the horrifying image of Evy beaten, bruised, abused all these years. I mounted my horse and rode out of the gate.

The Halleford name felt fresh in my mind, like I had seen it recently. It would've been on our list to visit with the Prince this week, and I tried to remember all the lords we had planned to visit today.

My brain slammed to a halt with the realization. The first name on the list for today, the reason I recognized . . . *the Halleford Estate.*

Ryker was already there.

CHAPTER 26

Ryker

The last few days had left me utterly drained. First Father's declining health and the looming threat of the throne, then Liam's ragged emotions over reconnecting with his long lost Evelyn, and now the first girl I had ever truly fallen for had run away from me. It felt like a bad omen for how my kingship would go.

"The first estate is coming up, Your Highness."

I looked up to find Rafe at my side, eyeing me with caution. I wondered what expression I'd been wearing on my face. "Excellent. Thank you, Rafe."

I wished Liam was here with me. I knew he needed to check on his Evelyn, but with all the nerves swirling around inside me, I couldn't help but feel that I had been demoted to second place today. Liam was my best friend, practically my brother, and I relied on him constantly. Probably too much. But still, it felt wrong that he wasn't at my side for this.

"I'll take the lead so we can keep you concealed as long as possible," Rafe stated, then watched me, waiting for my confirmation. I nodded once, and he seemed satisfied by it, moving to the front of our group.

I suppose, if I thought about it, I was doing exactly what Liam was doing today, putting the search for my Iridescent in front of all other responsibilities. I chuckled softly to myself at my own hypocrisy, and our unavoidable sameness. The guardsman next to me flashed a quizzical look my way, and I just waved my hand, brushing away my strange behavior without explanation.

The Halleford Estate loomed in front of us, already bustling with activity this morning. Their carriage was parked in the front courtyard, making it look as though they were either just leaving or just returning from somewhere. As we entered the courtyard, Lord and Lady Halleford came out to greet us. They looked intrigued but concerned by our small cluster of royal guards. I didn't blame them; this certainly was *not* a normal occurrence.

Rafe hopped off his horse and approached the couple. "Lord and Lady Halleford, I presume?" They nodded in confirmation. "We are the Royal Guard of his Royal Highness, Crown Prince Ryker, and by order of His Majesty the King, we have been tasked to find a maiden who attended the ball last night. Were you both in attendance?"

Lady Halleford clapped her hands together, bouncing on her heels. "Oh! Are you looking for that stunning girl the prince danced with last night? Oooh! Darling, do you remember her? Oh, she was a dream. The two of them together . . . it was so romantic."

I couldn't help but smile, listening to Lady Halleford gush over my mystery woman. Perhaps the whole kingdom would feel the same way about her that I did.

Lord Halleford shifted on his feet, grimacing at his wife's high-pitched squeals. "Yes, dear, I remember." He patted her hand placatingly. "But what does this have to do with us?"

I surveyed their estate while Rafe explained the situation, asking if they had any children or eligible young maidens in their stead. I hadn't really expected success here—we'd known Lord and Lady Halleford were up there in years—but disappointment still echoed through me when I saw no sign of my Iridescent.

Lady Halleford hung her head low, as if disappointed that they couldn't magically produce an eligible maiden for us to inspect. "Our children are all fully grown with wives and husbands of their own, I'm afraid. No eligible maidens hiding here."

"No one is visiting you? Or has stayed at your home within the last week?" Rafe prompted.

Lord Halleford shook his head. "No. We've had no visitors."

Rafe nodded, dipping his head. "Thank you for time," he said before heading back to and swinging up on his horse.

In the background, I saw an older maid pop her head out the front door and whisper to Lady Halleford. As the group started to turn around and head out for the next estate, I heard Lord Halleford's voice boom, "Lord Coulter is a mockery to the court. He can't even clothe his own staff! What's your name again, girl?"

A small tingle went up my spine at the feathery voice that answered him. "Evelyn, sir."

The name struck home. The Coulters? Evelyn? As in *Liam's* Evelyn? No. How could that be? Why would she be at the Halleford estate?

The guardsmen around me all stopped as well, shuffling anxiously on their horses. Rafe and I made eye contact. Lord Halleford had mentioned Lord Coulter, and Evelyn wasn't a common name in our kingdom. Rafe turned his horse back around, narrowing his eyes at Lord Halleford.

This didn't make sense. Lord Halleford had just called her a servant. I turned to look at the girl now standing in front of Lord Halleford. Her long chestnut hair was pulled back and tucked underneath a square cloth. Her clothes did look worse for the wear, hanging off of her limbs like she'd been working in a poor house. Her shoes looked like the newest item on her, but even they were clearly worn from frequent use.

My voice rang out before I could stop it. "Lord Halleford, did I hear this young woman's name was Evelyn?"

Her whole body went perfectly still at the sound of my voice, which only raised my suspicions. I nodded to Rafe, who trotted back over and dismounted his steed again.

He gently approached the girl. "Evelyn?" Her shoulders were practically drawn up to her ears, her whole body trembling. "Are you Evelyn Coulter?"

"Coulter!" Lord Halleford huffed indignantly. "What is the meaning of this? Speak up, girl. Tell them who you are."

She turned her body slowly to face Rafe, keeping her face down to the ground. "I have no last name, sir. I am a servant here."

"See? There you have it." Lord Halleford raised his hands in an exasperated gesture. "Even Lord Coulter would never stoop so low as to hire out his own *daughter*. Get back in the house, girl." He pointed to the door, and she obediently moved away from the crowd.

Behind me, I could hear another set of horses hooves approaching, flying at a breakneck pace. Above them, Liam's voice rang out: "Wait! Evelyn!"

Liam's horse skidded to a halt right before hitting our group, and Liam leapt off, bounding toward her like a man let loose from a tether. The girl whipped around, her hair flying in an arc with her, tears spilling down her cheeks as she took in the sight of him. My heart nearly wrenched out of my chest at the agony on her face.

Liam reached out and pulled her into his embrace just as her legs gave out. She hid her face against him, crying quietly into his armor.

"Evelyn. I'm so sorry. I didn't know. I didn't . . ." Liam blinked furiously, forcing back the tears, but the red tint in his nose and cheeks gave him away.

"What is the meaning of this?" Lord Halleford crossed his arms over his chest. "Why are you all upsetting my servant?"

Liam wrapped a protective arm around Evelyn's shoulders, maneuvering her away from the old lord before turning to address him. "She is *not* a servant, yours or otherwise. This is Lady Evelyn Coulter."

I couldn't stand it a minute longer; this whole thing had gone on too long. Lord Halleford scoffed, motioning to Rafe. "Just moments ago she admitted she had no last name, and called herself my servant. You are mistaken, sir. Kindly let go of her and be on your way."

"I will *never* let her go again." Both a warning and a promise from my Captain of the Guard.

This was going to end badly—I could see it in the tension in Liam's shoulders, in the slowly-reddening face of Lord Halleford. It was time for me to step in.

"Liam." When he looked over at me, his grip on the girl tightened. I furrowed my brows at him, stepping out into the open. "We will get to the bottom of this. I promise you."

"Oh! Oh, Your Highness!" Lady Halleford dropped into a deep curtsy.

Lord Halleford followed, his face flushing darker than before. "Forgive us, Your Highness. W-We didn't recognize you."

"And you weren't supposed to. But now it seems we have a little debacle to untangle." I turned to face the Hallefords. "When did this girl come to be in your employ?"

Lord Halleford straightened and brushed down his jacket. "Just this morning, Your Highness. We only barely arrived, just before you."

"And Lord Coulter gave you no surname for her?"

Lord Halleford had the notion to look somewhat ashamed—a bit late for my taste. "No, Your Highness. I . . . I didn't even give it a second thought."

I motioned to Liam. "This is my Captain of the Guard, who happens to have known Lady Evelyn Coulter since their youth." I turned to face Liam, motioning to the girl. "Captain, would you say that this woman is in fact Lady Evelyn Coulter, and not a nameless servant like she claimed to be?"

Liam's eyes welled with tears as he looked back at her. He didn't try to hide them this time. He cleared his throat. "Yes. I can, without a doubt, attest to this being Lady Evelyn Coulter."

"That blackguard! That crook! I should've never trusted a deal with that pirate!" Lord Halleford's face was so red, it was a struggle for me not to laugh.

"Now then, Lady Evelyn. Please face me." I turned to Liam and the girl, folding my hands behind my back. "It's all right, Liam. Whatever's happened, we'll set it right."

Liam flinched. He hesitated for so long that the silence waxed awkward. I could understand his protectiveness toward the poor girl, but why did he feel the need to protect her from *me*?

Evelyn squeezed his hand before slowly unraveling herself from his embrace, raising her eyes to look up at me.

My knees nearly buckled.

Her eyes were glistening with tears, guilt, and shame. Her cheeks were wet and darkened with a deep blush. She looked terrified and horrified all at once. There was dirt on her face and dust in her hair. Her dress was filthy. But she was *beautiful*. Her bright green, unforgettably sincere eyes beseeched me in a way that was all too familiar. I couldn't help taking one step toward her, my knees still shaky, shock numbing my skin.

I know those eyes.

"Iridescent?" That one word was all I could manage, more of a trace of breath than a word itself. "It's . . . it's you. You're . . ." I shook my head and tried again, forcing more strength into my voice. "How?"

"Please, forgive me." Fresh tears ran down her cheek creating new rivulets through the dust on her face. "I didn't mean to deceive you."

I closed my eyes, remembering where we were and who exactly was with us. *Liam.* My heart sank. This dazzling, mysterious woman that had stolen my heart last night was *Liam's Evelyn.* I felt dizzy for a moment, like the world was spinning backwards, but I was perfectly frozen in time.

Could he have known? They danced briefly last night before I had the musicians cut off the song. Was that why he'd been so bold, stealing her away after I'd so clearly staked my claim? My attention drifted back to her face, and I reached out to wipe away those tears. I couldn't stop myself. Not even for Liam.

"There's nothing to forgive," I promised her, as gently as I could make myself speak.

Her entire body began to tremble with trepidation. I quickly wrapped my arms around her, cupping her head to my shoulder and pulling her closer. Her arms were neatly tucked between us, her body releasing sporadic tremors.

I would protect her however I could. I didn't care what people saw or what they thought. I understood now why she didn't tell me her name; she said it was complicated, and she was right. "Please. Please don't cry. We'll figure this out. You're safe now. I . . . *we* have you."

Liam's determined gaze met mine over Evelyn's head, and in that moment, an invisible line was drawn.

I released Evelyn just enough to look her in the eye. "You're coming with us. We'll talk more about all of this and what to do next." I reached up to brush away more of her tears, then leaned in to whisper in her ear. "I understand now. I do not judge you, and I am not angry at you."

Her eyes widened, and she nodded slowly, taking in my words. Overcome with a deep urge to make her feel safe, I kissed her forehead, but immediately regretted the action when I saw Liam's eyes go cold. This had become more of a mess than I'd ever thought it could be.

I gently handed her off to Rafe. "Help her onto my horse and lead her away for a moment. She doesn't need to witness any more of this nonsense. We'll head back to the palace as soon as we're done here."

Rafe nodded his head and slowly guided Evelyn away from the scene. Liam bristled slightly, but Rafe was *extremely* careful not to touch her more than necessary. I couldn't blame him. Between Liam and I, what this girl had just been through, and the fact that she looked frightened out of her mind, even boisterous, irreverent Rafe seemed sobered by it all. I appreciated the care he took in escorting her.

By the time I was able to tear my attention away from her, Lord Halleford was huffing and puffing and mumbling under his breath. "I knew this deal was too good to be true. That slimy Coulter was just trying to rid himself of a problem and give it to *me* instead."

My eyes narrowed at Lord Halleford, and I raised myself up, looking him directly in the eye. I paused to collect my thoughts while giving him my best cold stare.

Lord Halleford returned my stare with an icy one of his own, though there was fear buried beneath it. "Your Highness, this is absurd. I traded my best milking cow for her! Lord Coulter deceived me!"

I addressed Liam without turning to look at him, keeping my eyes fixed on Lord Halleford. "Liam, go grab her things from inside." He gave a curt nod and strode toward the front door. Lady Halleford went along with him, mentioning that Evelyn hadn't brought much with her, but that she knew right where it all was.

"If you take her, you owe me for the cow and help that I've now lost," Halleford demanded, his chin raised high.

I raised one eyebrow, offering him a smirk. "Oh, do you suppose so? Hmm . . . perhaps spending some time in the stocks for attempting a slave trade would change your mind." I motioned to one of the guards behind me, and he moved toward Halleford immediately, who rapidly lost all color in his face.

"No! My Prince, Your Highness, please . . . I didn't pay money for her, it was just a simple trade." The guard made his approach slowly, and I appreciated his assessment of the situation as Lord Halleford sputtered and stumbled backward, still pleading. "Lord Coulter is the one who approached me! He deceived *me*! It's not my doing . . ." His panic built up as his eyes darted back and forth between me and my guard. "I tell you truly! Please!"

Liam came back swiftly, holding very little in his arms: a quilt, wrapped around what could only be a few other items. Barely anything, certainly not enough to have brought to a new home. My heart sank, but I forced myself to not look back toward Evelyn.

"It's true, Lord Coulter did deceive you. That young woman," I motioned somewhere behind me, "is Lord Coulter's daughter by blood. She is a lady of the court, so it seems as though he deceived you in more ways than one, and will be dealt with accordingly. Considering the majority of your innocence in this deplorable situation, I will be lenient and leave you to stew over your transgressions in peace. *For now.* This will be your repayment." I did not smile or sneer, I kept my face perfectly neutral, allowing my words to sink in.

"Yes, Your Highness. Thank you, Your Highness. Very fair indeed." He bowed before me, so deeply he could've reached down and touched his toes, and I decided I would deal with him and Lord Coulter later. *After* I got all the details from Evelyn.

I nodded in dismissal, turning around and walking swiftly back to my horse. Evelyn's back was to me, and I saw Liam stuffing her things into his saddle bag. His face, though visible, was unreadable.

My mind was spinning, trying to process the madness of this, and the obvious abuse Evelyn had endured. It was unfathomable. I didn't know how to navigate it.

Liam approached me, offering his counsel in a hushed voice. "Let's return home, get Evelyn cleaned up, get her a solid meal and some sleep, then question her about what's been going on. One thing at a time."

I nodded to Liam, thankful yet again for his clear-headed wisdom. I raised my voice to give the order. "Back to the palace."

Where there had been some banter and excitement on the way here, the whole group was now grimly quiet. Everyone knew this wasn't over yet; there was no true relief from the tension. Finding Evelyn had been nothing short of a miracle, but I'd never been at odds with Liam before. We'd never truly been in competition with each other, never fought over anything, not policies or training or women. Nothing. I didn't know what to do. I had to fight for her, but how could I do that without turning it into a fight against *him*?

We all got back on our horses. I swung up behind Evelyn and wrapped one arm around her waist, keeping her steady. She tensed for a moment as we set off riding, but then slowly relaxed into my arms. I couldn't help but sigh a little, my own tension easing a bit. I'd found her. She was back with me, and she was safe.

Liam rode quickly past us to the front of the line, and Evelyn stiffened, dropping her head in silence. I leaned my head down, pressing my cheek into her hair, ready to whisper in her ear. Her body briefly shuddered, and I pulled back quickly, giving her space. Still, I kept my voice low. "I know this feels complicated right now, but I meant what I said. We'll figure this out, Evelyn. No one will ever hurt you again."

She turned her head just slightly into mine, whispering back, "Thank you, Ryker." Then it was my turn to shiver.

CHAPTER 27

When we arrived at the palace. Ryker called for a team of maids to help care for Evelyn. He put her up in the finest guest suite, usually reserved for family, and conveniently only a few doors down from his own . . . and mine. She was ushered inside to bathe, eat and rest, and the door closed behind her. I was afraid I might never get the chance to talk to her now. What if Ryker kept her from me?

I brought her things out, knocked on the door, and handed them off to the maid who answered. Heading back to my room to take off my armor, I came in to find Ryker was already there. Sitting at the foot of my bed, he looked up, his face determined and harrowed.

"You knew." His tone was cold and frustrated.

I nodded, my head turned down.

Ryker stood and started pacing with his hands clasped behind his back. "Why didn't you say anything last night?"

For a moment I paused, merely staring at him. I loved him. My best friend, practically my brother. We'd been a unit, a team for seven years, but the thought of him with *her* made my insides revolt. I swallowed, desperately trying to saturate my dry throat, but my voice still came out thick. "I just wanted a chance to talk to her first."

"To talk her out of being with me, you mean." I'd seen him stare others down in this way, but I'd never experienced it for myself. He looked down his nose at me, even though I was the slightest bit taller than him.

I shook my head. "No, Ryker. No matter what, I was going to bring her to you, and if she chose you, I would have walked away." I looked at him pleadingly. "I still will. I just wanted to talk to her, to figure out what was going on. I needed to know." I rubbed my hand on my forehead, my thoughts spinning. "I didn't know . . . I didn't know what she was enduring." My voice cracked, and Ryker softened. "I left her there, Ryker. I promised I would come back and I didn't. I abandoned her. I don't deserve her, but I still need to know. I just . . . I need to know."

He put a hand on my shoulder and led me back to the bed, where we sat side by side. "I know, Liam. I understand." He paused and leaned forward, his elbows resting on his knees, his fingers steepled in thought. "Obviously I want you two to talk. It's clear that needs to happen. And of course the choice will be hers—all hers. I don't want her love to be forced either, Liam."

Relief washed over me like a bucket of cold water in the winter. "I'm grateful to hear it."

We both sat silent a moment longer before he asked, "Why didn't you go back to see her?"

I dipped my chin to my chest. "I was afraid. In my mind I'd already lost her somehow, and I didn't want to face it. I was afraid to be too late . . ." I trailed off, realizing that all of this was my own fault. If I had gone back to see her, I could've already gotten her out of this mess. She would've never danced with Ryker at the ball last night, and neither of us would be in this predicament.

Ryker sighed into his hand, then ran it down his face. "What a mess this is."

I nodded. "At least she's safe now."

I hoped he'd hear all the unspoken things I wanted to say but couldn't. How sorry I was. How much I loved her. How heartbroken I felt. How worried I'd been.

He nodded silently in agreement. He sat next to me for another minute before standing and walking to his bedchamber door. "I told her to call for you as soon as she's ready." He brushed his hand through his hair, then turned back to look at me with a hint of a smirk. "I mean, it's only fair for you to go see her first, now that you're competing with a prince."

I gave him a half-hearted laugh, gratitude flooding me even as I felt the weight of our bond shifting, changing for the first time, making room for this new and strange conflict. "Thank you, Ryker."

CHAPTER 28

Evelyn

T he maids all washed me within an inch of my life. I hadn't been scrubbed that hard since, well, ever. Their collective gasps when they realized the bruises on my body were not spots of dirt made me cringe. I gritted my teeth and clenched my fists, trying to keep the tears from my eyes. When one of the maids saw me flinch, she stopped everyone in their tracks. From that moment on, they switched from their scrubbing brushes to soft cotton cloths. Gratitude flooded my exhausted body, and I let myself give in to their ministrations.

The maid who'd noticed my pained face was pale and slender, her wispy red hair all tied up in a semi-tight bun on the back of her head. Her pastel-green eyes were troubled. Clearly the leader of the group, she was the first among them to speak up: "I'm so sorry, miss, we didn't realize . . ."

I nodded silently, my ears heating with embarrassment as I bit back the tears building up in my throat.

The tension in the room weighed heavily on me, so I tried a joke, hoping it would help ease the pressure. "Thank you all so much for your diligence. I don't think I've ever been quite so clean." I gave them all a little smile. "Just the hot bath alone is the best luxury."

The maids kept their faces down and finished their jobs thoroughly. Once they deemed me appropriately clean, they dried me off with swathes of soft cloth and brought out a new dress for me to wear. It was a lovely shade of light blue, with a brand new corset and petticoats to match. It was too much. My eyes stung, and I blinked furiously to keep any tears from falling.

"Please, not very tight." I held my hands over the corset as they gently pulled it snug to my body. "I'll be honest with you all, I've been a servant for the past seven years. It's . . . very unnerving to have you all attending to me."

The same redhead who spoke to me earlier smiled encouragingly. "We understand, miss." She then motioned for the dress from the other maids. It slipped over my too-thin figure with ease.

I rubbed the pale blue fabric between my fingers. It was soft and fine. High-quality material. My throat swelled up, and I had to fight off tears once more. Clearing my throat awkwardly, I said, "May I ask your names?"

"Oh! Of course, miss. I'm Brigitta," the beautiful redhead said. She motioned to the maids behind me. "This is Anna and Feleen."

I nodded to them both in response. I didn't know if I'd remember their names. Everything around me was blurry and unfocused. I could barely distinguish one girl from the other, but I didn't want to be rude. "Pleased to meet you. Thank you all for your care."

"It is our pleasure, miss," said one of the other girls, Anna or Feleen. They all gave me small bows of their heads, then sat me down in front of the vanity and started brushing out my wet hair. I refused to look in the mirror—I was tired of the reflection I saw staring back at me. Too much had happened, and I was the last person I wanted to look at.

I felt the girls all watching me, and I closed my eyes to the uncomfortable scrutiny.

"Miss?"

I looked over in the direction of the voice and met the worried face of Brigitta.

"Are you all right, miss?"

I nodded slowly, "Yes, I'm alright, thank you."

"Wouldn't you like to look at yourself in the mirror, miss?" This voice came from my opposite side. Anna? Or was it Feleen? She was shorter and adorably curvy, including her rounded face and button nose. Her soft brown hair was pulled back into a low bun with wispy tendrils framing her face, and her brown eyes were kind and playful.

I shook my head and looked back down at my hands, picking and fidgeting in my lap. "No, no. I'm quite alright. I trust you ladies to do whatever you think is best."

Another awkward silence as they kept brushing out my hair.

"You are very beautiful, miss. I only mean to say, if I had your face, I would be staring at myself all day long."

Brigitta scolded the girl in a hushed voice, and I could feel a silent argument going on behind me. The other girl, the one who was brushing my hair, started to shake quietly in what I assumed was laughter, which helped. She was tall and willowy and pale. Her face, her light blonde hair, even her eyebrows were fair, but all of that just made her warm brown eyes pop out even more. She exuded kindness and patience.

I looked back over my shoulder to the brunette girl, making my best guess. "Anna, right?"

She and Brigitta immediately stopped their bickering, and she brightened. "Yes, miss."

"Thank you. You're very sweet."

She blushed, and Brigitta tsked at her. "Anna, stop fishing for compliments."

Anna scowled. "I wasn't fishing!"

Feleen finished brushing my hair, setting the brush down on the vanity and meekly raising her eyebrows at the bickering duo. I giggled softly at her quiet reaction. I was surprised I was able to smile right now, let alone laugh. What a difference an hour could make. I remembered back to the few times that Camilla and I had bickered playfully in a similar way, and a sharp pang stabbed into my chest. I had been cruel to Camilla. In all fairness, she had been cruel to me too, but I didn't want to repeat the same hurtful cycles.

Shaking off my wayward thoughts, I turned around in my seat so I wouldn't have to face the mirror any longer. "How long have you three worked here?"

Brigitta jumped in first. "I've worked at the palace for nearly eight years, miss."

"I've been here for three!" Anna chimed in.

Feleen stood quietly for a moment. "I've only been here a year, miss."

"Are you all treated well here?"

"Oh yes, miss!" Anna exclaimed. "It's wonderful to work at the palace. Not only do they pay the best, but they are also incredibly kind . . . except for Marie. She's mean."

"Hush, Anna! Remember your place." Brigitta scolded her, and Anna immediately bowed her head.

I gave her a small smile. "I promise not to tell a soul. But I'm very glad you're all treated well here."

They brought me some new slippers for my feet, trying on different sizes to find the right fit, and I ran my hands down my dress again, relishing the feel of the fibers under my fingertips. "This really is a lovely dress. Who does it belong to?"

"You, miss," Anna chuckled.

I put my hands on my hips, giving her a skeptical eye. "No one knew I would be arriving today, so I know better than that."

Brigitta looked me over. "It was one of the nobleman's daughters here at court. She's about the same height and size as you."

"She happily donated this dress to your wardrobe! She said she wants to be on the good side of the future Queen of Alstonia." Anna's face lit up as she said it.

My breath caught in my lungs. The room suddenly felt too small and dizzy. *Future Queen of Alstonia?* I swayed a little on my feet before the girls all rushed to me, easing me over toward the bed, all speaking at the same time.

"Easy there."

"I'm so sorry, I thought you knew!"

"Hush, Anna. She's clearly been through an ordeal. We need to give her time."

The girls fussed, and someone handed me a glass of water that I downed gratefully. I realized in that moment just how alone I felt. I didn't really know the prince, though we clearly had made some sort of connection. Cook and Jimmy weren't here . . .

Cook and Jimmy. A new level of terror and dread struck my already-rising nerves. Hopefully they were okay. They knew how to handle themselves with Father.

The girls all looked a little frantic, and I realized I was almost hyperventilating. I tried taking in big deep gulps of breath to ease my rising panic, thinking about Cook and Jimmy. But that barely did anything to calm the rising dread that was threatening to spill over my lungs at any given moment. And what would Becca think when I stopped showing up in town? She wouldn't even know where I was.

Waves of anxiety and panic began to crash down on me, until the only person I could think of was Liam. Hopefully he was still here; hopefully he still wanted to see me. I wasn't sure if he would, now that he knew . . . everything.

I rubbed my forehead as my thoughts swirled, making me dizzy. "Could I possibly see Liam? Is he in the palace?"

"He's just down the hall. I'll fetch him for you, miss." Brigitta took off at a brisk pace as another glass of water was placed in my hands. Feleen looked at me with worried eyes. Anna was cleaning up the tub area.

I sipped the cool liquid, sighing in relief. "Thank you, Feleen. The water is just what I needed."

"Can I get you anything else, miss?"

I shook my head, then hesitated. "Actually . . . would you sit with me?"

Feleen's eyes widened, but she sat next to me on the bed. I reached over and grabbed her hand. "I know we all don't know each other yet, but I'd be honored if you'd call me Evelyn, or Evy for short. Liam calls me Evy."

Anna gasped. "Oh goodness, we can't do that, miss! You're practically royalty now."

I looked down at my lap. "I am nothing of the sort."

Feleen's fingers curled around mine. "You are far more, Miss Evelyn."

I looked up, startled, but she held my gaze, even as my eyes burned with more tears.

There was a brisk knock on the receiving room door, and Anna rushed up and out of the room to get it. Feleen gave my hand another gentle squeeze. Her kind spirit was like a balm to my parched soul. Even so, my hands started to shake, and I carefully set the water down on the small table next to me. Anna popped her head back into the bedchamber. "Miss? The Captain is here to see you."

"Could you please let him in here?" The two girls looked a little shocked, and I realized that I had just asked for a man to be shown to my bedchamber, which was highly improper. But I didn't think I could move, and besides, it was *Liam*.

Before the maids could say another word, Liam appeared at the door. "Give us some privacy, please." His voice was commanding, but still gentle. Anna and Feleen gave quick bows and left the room, shutting the door behind them.

We sat there in silence for a moment, simply staring at each other. He looked a little worse for the wear. Dark crescents sat underneath his puffy red eyes. His hair was all mussed and messy, as if he couldn't stop running his hand through it. That one piece of hair that loved to hang over his forehead was acting up again. His usually broad, sturdy, upright posture was angled forward in a defeated hunch. He had changed out of his armor into a soft shirt and simple pants—he looked like he'd just come back from training or riding.

I broke the silence first, unable to handle the tension. "Liam, I . . ."

Before I could finish, he fell to his knees in front of me, gripping me close to him. I felt his body convulse as he let out a sob near my hip. I draped my body over his, holding him as close as I could. "I'm so sorry, Evy . . . I'm so, so sorry."

His desperate apologies just made me cry more. "Please, Liam . . . please forgive me."

He lifted his head, making me move my whole body so he could straighten up. He cupped my face in his hands, wiping away my tears even as his own slipped down his cheeks. "It is I who needs to ask your forgiveness, not the other way around."

I could only imagine what a mess we must look like: Liam, the stoic, brooding Captain of the Guard on his knees before me, both of us with blotchy red faces, crying in excess. It almost made me smile. I placed my hand on his cheek, and he leaned into it, closing his eyes. "Liam, there is nothing to forgive. I am the one who has deceived you. I didn't mean to—"

"If I had known, I would've come back, Evy. I would never have left you to endure that evil by yourself. I would've taken you away *years* ago." Removing his hands from my face, he balled them into fists at his sides, standing up to pace the room in front of me. "I'm going to kill him. He's no father to you, he doesn't even deserve to breathe the same air. I'll lock them *all* up! I swear it to you. I'll do whatever I can—"

"Liam," I interrupted him, "you're not going to kill my father." I gave him a small smile. "But I appreciate the sentiment nonetheless."

He sighed heavily and opened his mouth to say something, but I cut him off. "Last night, I . . ."

"I know, Evy. I knew last night."

I blinked at him in shock. "You did?"

"Not until you ran away. The prince gave us some details, and I pieced it together." He came back over to the bed and sat next to me, clasping his hands in his lap. "I tried to see you this morning. I went to the Coulter Estate."

I swallowed the lump in my throat. Had it really only been this morning that everything had gone so wrong? "That's how you found me?"

He nodded. "Camilla and Jimmy told me."

"*Camilla?*"

"She asked me to tell you that she's sorry. She didn't do what she should have before, but she did what she could today. She was scared to tell me, but she did. I . . . I think she's been afraid for a long time."

I bristled slightly at his defense of her. He seemed to notice the change; his eyebrows furrowed before I asked, "So are you and Camilla now . . ."

His face widened in shock, "What? No. Never."

"Well, never say never." I turned away from him, anger heating my face. "You two were awfully close at the ball last night." I hated the jealous, petty tone that came out. I cringed at my own words, but I couldn't help it.

"Evy . . ." He sounded breathless, and I couldn't tell if he was irritated by my pettiness or if he just felt sorry for me.

I groaned and fell backwards on the bed, covering my eyes with one arm while the other held my churning stomach. I felt the bed sink next to me as Liam settled himself beside me. I turned my head to look over at him, but he was staring straight upward as he slowly inched his hand toward the one resting on my stomach. Carefully pulling my arm to lay between us, he entwined our hands together finger by finger. I couldn't help but soften. This was how we used to spend our days as children together: lying back in the grass, hands clasped, staring at the sky.

He turned his head to look back at me, a crooked smile tugging at his mouth. A deep, fluttery feeling sat low in my stomach as I stared back at him. His face grew serious for a moment, and I felt the energy in the room shift. In my mind I imagined he might lean over to kiss me, and I quickly took in a breath. That small sound seemed to break the tension of the moment, and he closed his eyes before returning his attention back to the ceiling.

"Why didn't I recognize you last night, at the ball? Why didn't you tell me who you were?"

It was my turn to close my eyes. "I did see you, almost immediately. But you were holding Camilla." His body tensed beside me, his hand tightening around mine. I closed my eyes again, picturing the whole scene, and I drew in a ragged breath, remembering how betrayed I'd felt. A lone tear rolled down my face. "And when we danced, I was afraid to tell you. I thought you preferred Camilla. And it . . . it hurt. And the prince was there, and I wasn't supposed to be. And you . . ."

The bed sank a bit more. Liam had turned onto his side to face me, removing his hand from mine to prop his head up. He stared directly down at me, so close I could feel the heat from his body radiating toward mine. The tension in the room started to bubble again, and my stomach swooped uncomfortably.

"Evy . . ." The way he said my name sounded like a prayer, quiet and low. His thumb traced the line of the single tear that had slipped down the side of my face. The heat his thumb left behind nearly burned my skin. The whole gesture felt more intimate than we had ever been with each other.

"The moment you saw between Camilla and I . . . that was me trying to ask her what had really happened to *you* last night. She was about to tell me before you entered the ballroom and distracted everyone—myself included." His lips turned up at one edge, revealing his side dimple. He reached his hand over to move a wet strand of hair from my brow. That touch alone made my lashes flutter. "Even though I didn't recognize you, I felt drawn to you. I thought you were the most beautiful woman I had ever seen, and I was only a few steps away before Ryker reached you first." His eyes immediately lost their gleam as a shadow of regret passed through them.

I hadn't even noticed it, but somehow, our bodies were even closer together now then they had been before. Liam's long, broad body was towering over me, and I was leaning into him. His arm was draped across my stomach. I felt cocooned by him, and I wanted to stay in his arms for as long as humanly possible. Liam looked into my eyes, and whatever he saw there sparked a new fire in his.

His heat surrounded me as he lowered his face to mine. His arm gently swept around my stomach as he began to lower himself slowly, his body sinking steadily onto mine. His hand slid carefully up my spine, sending shivers throughout my body. Liquid warmth pooled low in my belly, waking up my senses and filling me with a longing to be closer to him. I'd never felt this before. Not with anyone. Not even with him. I had been too young back then, but he'd always been older. Even though it was only by three years, those years always seemed to make him more clever and experienced.

I started to wonder just *how* experienced, shuddering at the thought of him holding other girls like I had seen him hold Camilla last night, like he was holding me now. Suddenly, fear reared its ugly head. He was too close, this was too much, I didn't know what I was doing—

His breath brushed across my face, and I gasped at the intimate sensation. Did I want him to kiss me? *Yes. No. Maybe.* I wasn't sure. Both of our eyes began to close naturally, and I felt my body and mind surrendering.

Yes, I wanted him to kiss me. I loved Liam, I'd always loved Liam. I didn't care how many other girls he'd kissed—*well, that wasn't entirely true*—as long as I was his last kiss.

His lips parted, and he breathed, "Evy . . ."

Then my bedchamber door suddenly swung open, startling us both.

Liam and I bolted upright out of our embrace, separating quickly.

Ryker stood there, one hand on the door and the other clenched in a fist at his side. I looked down in shame, my whole body flushed. The prince had brought me to his home, given me this gorgeous room, clothed and cared for me, and here I was . . .

Liam, however, did not cower. He looked Ryker straight in the eye, with a rage like I'd never seen from him. It radiated out in a challenge of sorts. The room felt so ripe with tension I almost choked on it.

Ryker moved out of the door frame, still holding the door open. "I'd like a moment alone with the lady." When Liam didn't budge, Ryker's eyes softened, pleading with him. "Please."

I could feel Liam simmering, and I realized we hadn't even taken a moment to truly talk yet. His awkward pause at Prince Ryker's obvious plea was uncomfortable at best, and downright intolerable at worst. But Ryker never lost eye contact. It was several more moments before Liam finally gave a curt nod and stormed out the door without looking back.

CHAPTER 29

Ryker

Never before in my life had Liam looked at me the way he had today. It was obvious I had interrupted an intimate moment between the two of them, but the way he'd challenged me with that look. . . I had never seen him wear that face, not even when dealing with the criminals of the kingdom. It was downright devastating.

Evelyn looked almost as shocked as I was, but she didn't seem as unnerved. In fact, her face fell when Liam left the room without so much as a glance back at her.

Clearly, this wasn't going to be as easy as I originally planned.

"I'm so sorry, Your Highness." Evelyn's whole body slumped as she sank onto her bed, her head falling into her hands as her shoulders silently shook.

Quickly moving to her side, I gently grabbed her wrists and brought her hands down so I could see her face. Her beautiful, though currently splotchy, face.

"Please, it's all right. I know the bond you two share is strong." I clasped her hands in mine and held them to my chest, willing her to look up at me. "Evelyn, I'm not angry with you. I don't blame you. Liam and I didn't know that we were *both* searching for you, which I know . . . complicates things." I reached up to cup her face, turning her to look at me. "All I'd like to ask for is a chance."

Her eyes widened. "A chance? Why? For what?"

Had I not made myself abundantly clear at the ball? "Evelyn. You might be his Evy, but you're my Iridescent." A smile tugged at my lips as I recalled the moment I'd nicknamed her. Even without her celebratory finery, it still fit. I was pleased to see a light blush dusting her cheeks. "Last night, with you, was one of my happiest moments. I felt we found a true connection, you and I. And I know we were only given a small moment in time together, but it was enough to convince me that this is worth pursuing. That *you* are worth pursuing. If . . . if I am mistaken in thinking that we shared something last night, if Liam is the only one you care for, please tell me now. I will step aside if you ask me to."

She looked to the floor immediately, her voice was quiet and ragged. "You aren't mistaken. But I . . . oh, the moment you just walked in on, and after all you've done for me today—" She sucked in a ragged breath. "I don't mean to act ungrateful or unkind. I wasn't trying to use you in any way, I swear to you. I really am so, so sorry, Ryker."

My smile widened. "Say that again."

She shuddered with guilt, trying to shield her face again. "I am so, so sorry—"

"No, Evelyn, no. I mean the part where you called me *Ryker* instead of *Your Highness*."

She gasped in a small breath, staring at me intently, searching my face for any sign of a joke or trap. Presumably finding none, her gaze softened before she whispered, "Ryker."

She said it with such reverence. No formalities. I was no longer a prince trying to find a bride; I was just a boy, trying to woo an incredible girl, and when she said my name, it felt like magic.

I closed my eyes for a moment before looking back at her, giving her my most charming smirk. "There's no sweeter sound than my name on your lips."

She smiled at that, her cheeks pinking. She turned her head away again, and I let her this time, squeezing her hands instead.

"Evelyn—"

She interrupted me, her tone almost mischievous as she repeated my words: "Say it again."

I laughed quietly, happy to oblige. "*Evelyn.*"

She grinned so wide that her nose crinkled, and it was suddenly a bit difficult to breathe. "There. Now you know my name."

I cocked an eyebrow at her. "But what if I prefer calling you Iridescent?"

She chuckled softly. "Well, you are the prince. I suppose I can't deny you calling me anything." I shot her an amused look, and she giggled. "I don't mind it, truly. It *is* special to us now."

My heart stuttered, and I huffed out a fast breath of air. This girl did things to me that I didn't know how to handle.

"I want you to know my intentions clearly." That made her look back at me again, her bright green eyes wide with apprehension, long lashes still wet with tears. I was overwhelmed just looking at her. Sucking in a bracing breath through my nose, I continued, "I intend to woo you, to court you, and hopefully make you Queen of Alstonia one day." She gasped again, but I cut back in quickly. "I know it may seem like a lot. Especially with all you've gone through as of late. All I'm asking of you today is to be given a chance. To be told if I *have* a chance."

Her eyes dropped to our clasped hands, those glimmering eyes deeply thoughtful. She took in a deep breath before asking, "And what about Liam?"

I nodded, thinking my answer through carefully. The question was a valid one, and one that I was struggling with. I wanted her to know the choice was hers, even if it ended up breaking my heart. But I would do everything in my power to have her choose me. I was besotted, and I couldn't picture anyone else by my side, nor did I want to entertain the thought. Not when I had her: charming and witty, kind and beautiful, funny and easygoing. She was my perfect match in every way.

"Liam and I have already spoken, and we want you to know that both of us will respect your decision. I won't force you into anything, Evelyn, and neither will he. You may stay here in the palace as my special guest and as part of my court until you decide what you'd like to do. You are and should have always been treated like a Lady of the Court, so I'm making you as such. This will remain your room, and I promise you," I prayed she could see how sincere I was, "my generosity will not disappear should you choose someone other than me to spend your days with." I brought her hands up to my chest again to emphasize my next words. "You matter to me, Evelyn. Enough for me to do my best to woo you, if possible, but also to humbly back away should you choose another. Not that that's ever happened to me before." I couldn't help but give her a little wink. My wry smile felt false, like a mask plastered to my face.

I couldn't name Liam specifically. It felt too hard to be pitted against him while staring into the eyes of the girl we both wanted.

She swallowed hard, a wrinkle forming between her brows as she took that in. The afternoon sunlight was starting to stream through her window, lighting up her chestnut hair to glowing bronze. It was drying into soft waves around her face, and her pink lips were just slightly parted, making them look all the more kissable. I so desperately wanted to draw her body into mine and show her how I felt without words—which I guessed was exactly how Liam had felt. In fact, it was likely what I had interrupted not five minutes ago.

I brushed some of her rebellious hairs away from her face instead, tucking them behind her ear. "Now, I know you've had quite a lot to take in today. Is there anything you need? Ask and it shall be given."

She hesitated. "Water would be nice. And . . . and maybe a little food? If it's not too much trouble."

Selfish. That's what I was. Completely selfish. I had been so fixated on winning her heart that I had forgotten entirely to *feed* the poor girl. I jumped up immediately, snagging the pitcher of water on her small dining table and filling her cup. I handed it to her. "Here you are, my dear."

She smiled gratefully before promptly guzzling the entire glass. She sighed in relief, then looked up at me sheepishly. "Forgive me. I'm just so parched." She let out a long sigh. "Today has been . . ."

I took the cup from her, refilling it and handing it back. "You mentioned being hungry, too." I couldn't help but chuckle when her head bobbed up and down enthusiastically, almost spilling her water. "Hm. Well, I do believe I can remedy that."

I gave her a little wink, and as if on cue, her stomach growled loud and proud. She blinked up at me, startled, and then we both broke into laughter. Seeing her smile and laugh was quickly becoming one of my favorite sights. I wanted to be the one that made her laugh every day. For the rest of our lives.

"Well then," I said, clapping my hands together, "I think it's best we take a quick tour of the palace. Yes?"

She looked over at me reluctantly, a deep weariness settling into her eyes. I smiled and leaned down to take her water cup, whispering, "I was thinking we might start with the kitchens."

Her eyes lit up. "Now, *that* sounds like the exact kind of tour my stomach had in mind." Her stomach growled again as if in agreement, and we both laughed some more.

I tucked my arm around hers as we walked out of her suite and down the hall, heading toward the descending staircase that led to the main kitchen. Taking on a more serious tone, I leaned into her, speaking softly. "When you're ready, I'd like to discuss what's happened to you. Specifically in regards to your father." She tensed, but nodded silently. "I want you to know that I *will* be punishing him. I just need to know more details about what he's done."

I paused for a moment, unsure of how to bring this next topic up gently. "Your maids . . ." I swallowed back the lump forming in my throat. "I asked them to inform me of anything obvious or strange as they helped you today. They let me know that you had many bruises, a few fresh wounds, and some older scarring." Her breaths were becoming more labored, but she nodded her head anyway. I bent closer to her and whispered, "Did he hurt you, Evelyn?"

She swallowed hard, taking a long moment before answering. "He never hit my face or anything like that. He . . . he liked to use a switch." Her hand brushed down some invisible wrinkles on her dress. "But he only ever did it when I disobeyed, or if he was unsatisfied with my work."

The rage that bubbled up inside me was something new. This gracious woman was trying to defend a man who didn't deserve even one ounce of her protection. Brigitta had told me that bruises covered her arms and legs, but the scars and swollen wounds were only on her upper thighs and buttocks. I remembered Evelyn moving uncomfortably in the saddle several times on our way back to the palace; she'd probably been in significant pain bouncing around on that hard saddle. The thought of bringing her pain made me cringe. I would need to tell Liam of this discovery. Not only would he *want* to know, but he *needed* to know the crimes of this man before he arrested him.

I cleared my throat, trying to rid my mind of its murderous thoughts. "Did he do anything else to you?"

She shrugged, staring at her feet. "Not . . . not really. It would be hard to explain."

It wasn't really an answer, but it had only been a few hours since her plight had been discovered. At least she'd confirmed the harsh beatings. Plus, we had irrefutable evidence of his plot to sell her off today.

Rounding the bend after descending down a few flights of stairs, the smells from the kitchen wafted in our direction. I tapped her hand encouragingly in the crook of my arm. "You can have anything you want. Just say the word. I'll introduce you to the whole kitchen staff and our head chef."

She smiled up at me, but her eyes were guarded and alert. I knew it would take time for her to trust me, but today felt like a good start.

CHAPTER 30

I watched them walk arm and arm out of her suite. The bitterness of this reality was starting to settle in. If Ryker wasn't my best friend, not to mention the Crown Prince, this all might feel easier. But I couldn't give her a kingdom even on my best day, and even if I could, I *hated* competing with Ryker. I ran both hands through my hair, and then turned all of my anger into a hard punch at the wall.

"Easy there, Captain. What'd the wall ever do to you, eh?" I looked up to find Rafe standing off to the side, rubbing the back of his neck awkwardly. He offered me a sheepish smile. "Hey, Cap."

I rubbed my knuckles and gave him a brusque nod. "Rafe."

"I, uh . . . I know this must be tough, but if it's any consolation, I sure am glad we got her out of there." Rafe offered up a half smile, half grimace, which made me chuckle bitterly.

"Yeah, I know. All this is worth it if it gets her out of that place." I shook out my throbbing hand, my knuckles swollen and red from the punch to the wall. Even with that pain, my thoughts swirled with the memory of Evy lying beneath me, safe and flushed in my arms. I inwardly groaned.

I'd just needed to hold her. To show her how much I loved her.

To feel like I had some control over what had happened to her. If she was in my arms, then I knew she was safe. But right now, she was in Ryker's arms, and I'd never felt more out of control. I hated Ryker's timing. I clenched my fist, striking the wall again, relishing the painful sting from the unforgiving marble stone.

Rafe moved forward hesitantly. "Need to blow off some steam? We could go spar for a bit, if you wanted. No offense, but there's only going to be one winner in the fight between your fist and a giant stone wall."

I hung my head, ashamed of my behavior. My men had never seen me like this—*Ryker* hadn't even seen me like this. Rafe stood next to me, a supportive presence. He loved to tease and play, but he was one of the most non-judgemental men I had ever met, accepting just about everyone and everything. He was one of my best friends, and the best Second I could have asked for. I was especially grateful for his friendship right now, with the potential loss of both Ryker and Evy weighing so heavily on my heart.

We walked silently together toward the training yards. A few of the men looked our way as we walked by. I could see some heads shaking, pity in their eyes. I knew word traveled fast, but everyone was looking at me as if I had already lost the battle—or, in this case, the girl.

Donning our practice gear, Rafe and I began the timeless sword-fighting dance with ease. Rafe was always more graceful than I, but I was still the more dominant opponent. Duck here, swing there, block, pivot, lunge, repeat.

As was expected, a circle formed around us, but no one was placing bets like they normally would. Instead, they were simply cheering–cheering for me, specifically. In a wonderfully strange way, it made my heart feel lighter. This brotherhood of mine was rallying around me, supporting me. They knew, and they cared.

Rafe and I both knew this skirmish wasn't about winning or losing, it was simply an outlet. We both held out for longer than usual, exhausted and dripping with sweat, but there was no real winner by the time we were spent, and I was grateful for the release.

When we couldn't take it any longer, we shook each other's hands. "Thank you, my friend," I said, ruffling his shaggy dark hair and clapping him on the shoulder.

Rafe nodded, his hands on his knees, breathing heavily. "Anytime, brother." He threw me his signature cheeky smile before sucking in another deep breath.

I laughed. "We may need to do this more often. You're getting out of shape, Rafe." He just glared, attempting to stand up tall, but failing miserably. I laughed again, leaving the training yard drained but more at peace. It was time to clean up and prepare for dinner.

As I walked back to my room in the palace, I spotted Evelyn walking by herself in the side garden. She hadn't seen me yet, so I was content to sit there and watch her for a few minutes. She moved through the garden as though everything fascinated her. I saw her lips moving like she was talking to someone; it wouldn't surprise me in the least to hear her talking to the plants. She used to do that when we were younger. I moved in closer, clearing my throat.

"Oh! Liam! You're all . . ." She trailed off as her eyes traveled over me, practically swallowing me whole. The loose fabric of my shirt was clinging to my sweaty frame, and I loved how she soaked up the view, that touch of red peppering her cheeks.

"Sweaty, yes. Forgive me." I tugged at my shirt slightly, still huffing from the exertion. "I just came from the training yards and saw you out here."

She walked over to a nearby bench and sat down. I saw her briefly wince before motioning for me to join her. I reminded myself to ask her about that soon as I stepped closer, giving her a sly smile. "I'd better not get too close. And I should probably stay upwind, so you won't be offended by my . . . *manly* aroma."

She chuckled softly, looking around. "It's nice to see some of how you grew up after leaving the estate."

"Is that what you were thinking about just now?" I leaned against a statue next to her bench. I still couldn't quite get over the fact that she was *here*. My mind was still trying to catch up on all that had occurred. Had the ball truly only been last night? It felt like a lifetime ago.

"Yes, actually. That and many other things." She folded her hands in her lap, picking at her fingernails. "I've always wondered what your life was like after you left. Sometimes I would picture you training.

I would imagine what you would wear, and picture a sword in your hand fighting off all the other boys in the room. It was easy to imagine, since that's what you always used to do on the estate anyway—minus the sword, of course." She chuckled softly, but it faded fast. "And then I would imagine myself here with you. Maybe even training with you."

I laughed softly. "You in training would definitely be a sight. I think you would be the only one to make our training fatigues look good." I winked at her, but her sad smile made me realize she hadn't been joking. These were things she'd imagined to get her through the pain and loss, and I was making light of it.

I moved to sit next to her then, aroma aside, and quietly asked, "What happened, Evy? I can't understand it. Your father . . . I never imagined he could . . ." I curled my hands into fists. "I don't understand how he could treat you like that. It doesn't make any sense to me."

She looked up at me, taking a long pause before answering. "You were just a boy when I last knew you, Liam. So much has changed since then. While you were here training at the palace, I was serving my father and his new family their meals, cleaning up after them, tending to their needs and the needs of the estate." She stood up then, pacing for a moment. "I did my best. I really tried. I tried to be a good daughter, to be obedient . . . but it was never enough. I haven't known love from my father since Mama died . . . but I guess he's no longer my father now, is he? Now he's just Frank."

Her eyes looked so lost. I didn't know what to do. "I'm so sorry, Evy. I should've been there. I should've gotten you out."

She looked down at me, and for the first time, I saw anger flash in her eyes. "It wasn't your responsibility, Liam."

"But if I had come back . . ."

She cut me off. "Then you would've kept your promise, but you would have discovered a horrible reality." She sat back down, fidgeting with her hands in her lap again. "And there wouldn't have been anything you could have done. I belonged to Father . . . to Frank. He had full control over my life. I know you feel guilty about not coming back, but it wouldn't have changed my circumstances."

"I could've told the king and gotten you out, Evy. I could've marri—"

She shook her head, effectively cutting me short. "He wouldn't have let it happen."

"Why didn't you leave before? Why did you stay?"

A shadow passed briefly over her eyes. "I was trying to wait until I was eighteen and could leave legally." She shook her head again, speaking as if to herself. "But that's not the whole truth, is it? I suppose I never actually wanted to leave. I realized that today. Saying goodbye, being forced to leave . . . having the choice taken from me . . . Leaving was never what I truly wanted." She got a far-off look in her eyes, "All I wanted was for him to love me again. I kept waiting . . . kept hoping he—" Her voice cracked.

"Would that I could take away your pain, Evy." I reached out and gently took hold of her hand, rubbing my thumb over her skin.

She avoided my gaze. I could feel her pulling away from me, lost in her own thoughts. With a heavy sigh, she said, "I never want you to feel like this, Liam. Never."

I stared at her, a deeper worry weighing down my gut. "Evy . . . what exactly did he do?"

She looked over at me, her eyes so dull they almost looked through me. "I can't talk about it yet. I'm sorry."

Withdrawing her hand from mine, she started walking away. I watched her go, feeling more helpless than ever. She might be physically safe now, but this Evy knew more pain than I could ever imagine. She wasn't the same; but then again, neither was I. She was still my dream, still the future I wanted, but we had a lot of lost time between us. My heart broke at the realization that even without Ryker involved, this never would've been as easy as I'd wanted it to be. The damage had been done, and now it was time to pick up the pieces. But no matter what, I would never leave her again, I couldn't. I would prove to her that I could be there for her, that I could keep my promises. No matter what.

Chapter 31

Evelyn

It was strange, waking up without hunger pangs twisting my stomach or new wounds stinging my skin. When I opened my eyes, the instinctive panic that came with waking up somewhere unfamiliar made the spacious room around me suddenly feel cramped.

I tried focusing on the details: the gold trim accents around sky blue walls and draperies, the muraled ceiling depicted a summer sky full of clouds and cherubs, my cream-colored bedding that burgeoned like a cloud over the bed. It was hard to tell if I'd slept so soundly because of the exhaustion of yesterday, or because my body was unused to such comfort and safety. The big oriel window faced the more public palace gardens, the ones I had been walking through last night when Liam saw me.

Liam.

I had been unfair to him last night, caught up in my own hurt and anger. My heart leaped into my throat, and swirling guilt wrapped around my ribcage. I tried to breathe, but breathing became difficult.

I focused on the small table with two chairs by the window, then moved my eyes to the fireplace facing my bed. Dying embers barely smoked in the cool morning air. The room was elegant and surprisingly homey. I had expected the palace to be opulent, but not cozy.

But even so, this wasn't my room. Or my house. Or my bed. These clothes didn't belong to me. *I* didn't belong here. I didn't even know my way around enough to leave without someone guiding me.

My heartbeat picked up its pace as I tried to focus on the mural again, desperate to escape what I knew was coming next. I stared at the painted clouds and playful cherubs, but I couldn't control my erratic breaths any longer. Sweat beaded on my brow, and that dreadful, endless black pit churned deep in my chest.

I didn't know what to do in this foreign place. I somehow felt more trapped here than ever. In a matter of seconds, my body seized up, paralyzing me in place. I knew I should try moving—moving usually helped these spells—but my limbs wouldn't budge. I wanted to cry, but I couldn't get enough breath to do that either, so I just laid there, frozen under my covers, my breaths too small and too fast.

There was a soft knock on the door, so I closed my eyes and tried to look asleep still. I didn't want my maids to see me like this. They would think I was being ridiculous and ungrateful. Holding myself as still as possible, I waited as they entered the room. I heard one of them murmur sternly to the others before they began tending the fire, fresh logs barely making a sound as they added them to heat the room back up. I heard the familiar rattle of a breakfast tray being placed on a table, then the *gentle whoosh* of curtains being opened. Sunlight cut across my eyes, but I did my best not to flinch.

Without uttering another word, they quickly slipped out of the room. I laid there a moment longer, willing my heart to slow down. The scent of breakfast foods made my stomach churn with nausea. My face was hot to the touch, and I was certain I was going to be sick. Gaining movement back in my limbs, I ran to the washbasin to rinse my face. The cold water helped a little, but the spell was only just beginning.

I gripped the edges of the washbasin as my body trembled. I couldn't even hold myself up as fresh tears sprung to my eyes and my legs went limp. I collapsed onto the floor with an aching, pathetic sob, crying as silently as I could. My body shook uncontrollably as I clutched at my nightgown, my frantic mind wanting it off, wanting the familiar scratch of my tattered old dress. Even if it was worn out and embarrassing to be seen in, at least it was *mine*.

I hated my body. I hated its reactions. I hated my tears. I hated my fear. I hated myself. I was safe now, so why didn't I feel better? Why couldn't I keep it together? For seven years I was able to hold all my pieces together, so why was I falling apart now? I should feel grateful. I should feel *safe*.

It's not supposed to be like this.

In the stories when the damsel gets saved, everything ends happy. Everyone is whole and full of joy; the damsel doesn't *keep* suffering. So what was so wrong with me?

Heaving sobs wracked my body now; I stopped trying to hold them in. I was going to make myself sick if I kept this up.

I heard the door to my bedchamber open again, and dread filled me. I tried to stifle my sobs, but there was no use. I was lost in the unending dread.

Feleen was the first to burst into the bedchamber. A look of horror crossed her alabaster face as she fell to her knees before me, searching me for any physical cause to this commotion. Brigitta and Anna rushed in after her. It mortified me, being seen this way. They knelt by my side, trying to dry my tears, whispering encouraging sweet things, rubbing my back, trying to soothe me like I was a child. But my body kept trembling, the tears kept flowing. I couldn't speak; only wordless whimpers escaped me. The girls drew a warm bath and helped me in, handing me a glass of water. I felt outside of my body, looking down at the scene instead of living it.

Slipping into the warm water helped calm me. They added some dried lavender, which gave off a calming aroma. Their eyes were full of pity. I hated it. But they didn't know any better. They were doing their best.

They dried me off, gave me a clean shift, then helped me back into bed. They brought the tray of food over, and I shooed it away, gagging. I asked them for a cup of tea from the stash Cook had left me instead, and then for some privacy. They all left reluctantly.

Humiliation and shame clung to me like a second skin. I must look so fragile to everyone. But I didn't want to feel fragile, not anymore, never again.

There was a soft knock at the door before it opened slowly. I assumed it was the maids again, so I didn't bother looking over, focusing on sipping my tea until I heard Ryker's voice. "Good morning, Evelyn. May I come in?"

I quickly set my tea down, trying not to spill the heated liquid on me. I fluffed my hair and wiped at my eyes, trying desperately to appear fine, but there was nothing that could be done. "Yes, um, of course, Your Highness." I couldn't even smile; after all that crying, my face felt numb.

He came over and sat on the edge of the bed. He looked at me with all the sincerity in the world. "Evelyn, are you well?"

"Yes, of course." I wanted to be strong, to put on my normal act, to pretend that everything was fine. I was used to that, having to be strong for everyone else. But then, everyone knew I wasn't *fine* now, didn't they? I wasn't fooling anyone this time. Besides, my maids must have alerted the prince to my rough start to the day. There was no other reason why he would be here. Humiliation heated my skin. "Please don't trouble yourself worrying about me. I'm sure that you have many princely things that need your attention today."

He chuckled. "Yes, there are many *princely* things that I do each day." Then his eyes sobered. "But you are important too, Evelyn. Your maids mentioned you were ill this morning."

"I'm quite alright. It was just a bad dream, that's all. Thank you for your concern." I stated it as confidently as possible. I almost believed myself.

He nodded his head absently, lost in thought. When he looked back at me, he wore a smile like he'd just had the most splendid idea. "Would you like . . . I mean, is there anyone you'd like to have come visit you here at the palace? A friend, or someone you trust? Someone who might help you feel a little less alone in such a big new space?"

His question caught me off guard, and at first I felt slighted at the suggestion that I might need anyone. But then I thought about walking in the garden alone last night, and running into Liam, only to realize we didn't really know each other anymore. The pain of that realization had hit me hard; when I saw his face, I still saw the boy I had loved, once. But he wasn't that boy any longer, and I wasn't that girl. He didn't know what my life was like after he left, and I didn't know what his was like either. So much had changed in our separate worlds. I'd thought I wouldn't feel alone with him around, but I still did. In fact, the memories of what we had been brought me more grief than anything else. It was strange, missing someone who was right in front of you.

But I did have one friend. One who knew me now, who loved me for who I currently was, and one I would adore seeing here at the palace. She would be a breath of fresh air within these extravagant walls.

I hesitated. "I can invite a friend to come stay with me? You're sure?"

"Yes, of course. It would be my honor to meet and host any friend of yours." His smile was genuine, without a hint of pity.

"I'm afraid she's not of noble blood. She wouldn't have the proper attire for Court or anything like that." I dropped my chin, fidgeting with the covers tucked around my chest. "I'm already such a burden on you. I wouldn't want to add to that."

Ryker reached out to clasp one of my hands, rubbing his thumb over my skin. His jeweled rings that covered almost every finger felt cool and foreign, yet somehow soothing against my flushed, oversensitive skin.

"Evelyn, you could no sooner be a burden here than I could be a goose." I barked out a surprised laugh at the ridiculous comment, and he grinned in response, clearly pleased. "What's her name? Write her a note of invitation, and I'll have someone deliver it to her today."

"Truly?" I couldn't help the excitement in my voice.

"Truly." His smile was so broad, so adoring, so beautiful. His golden hair was a little messier this morning than I'd seen before; it almost looked like he had rushed getting to me and hadn't bothered to finish off his normally-polished look. The thought made me feel strangely special; maybe I was getting to see a different side of the prince, one that most others would never see.

"Her name is Becca Smith. She lives in Hoddleston; her father is the cobbler there." I smiled wider, thinking of Becca being at the palace. "Oh, she'll be a delight! You will love her. Everyone does. She's going to be so excited, she's always wanted to visit the palace!" I threw myself forward, embracing Ryker. "Thank you!"

My heart felt freer now just thinking about Becca being here with me. Ryker looked quite pleased with himself, too. I jumped up, new energy flowing into me as I threw the covers to the side and ran to the writing desk in my other room. Ryker's eyebrows flew up, and he chuckled as he followed me out to show me where the pen and paper was. I penned a fast letter to Becca and handed it to Ryker, who had moved to stand behind my shoulder. His presence was already becoming more familiar to me, more comfortable, and it made little sparks flit back and forth in my stomach. I stood to hand him the note, and he kissed my hand.

"Take your time this morning," he said. "Relax in your rooms here, or explore if you'd prefer. As you mentioned before, I have some *princely* things to do, but hopefully I'll get the chance to see you again later. Would you be willing to join my father and I for dinner this evening in his private suite?"

"Dinner? With you and your father? As in, the king?" My eyes widened and my stomach sank.

Ryker chuckled. "Yes, the king. We usually have dinner around eight o'clock." He paused for a moment. "Liam will be there as well, along with my father's advisor, Apep, and some other members of the court."

I inwardly shuddered at the idea of having a private dinner not only with the king, but with several strangers. Secretly, I still harbored ill feelings toward the King. He was the reason Liam was taken from me at so young an age. It was well-known that Liam was the youngest recruit to ever join the ranks. Taking him away at the age of thirteen . . . it had never been done before. Not that I would ever tell anyone—it was treason to speak ill of the king—but my ten-year-old self still struggled with the idea of meeting another father who had caused me such considerable pain. Even if he hadn't known it.

Ryker's eyes were wide with hope. Sometimes I was struck by how young he looked. Much more like a boy compared to Liam's more hardened, manly features. I knew they were about the same age, each one about three years older than me, but every once in a while they looked years apart.

I didn't want to disappoint him, or let on that I dreaded meeting the King. So instead, I nodded. "I'd be delighted."

"Excellent! I'll have an attendant come escort you—if I can't come myself, of course." He winked. "But the good news is, you're already settled in the Royal Wing, so my father's suite is just down the hall. It won't be hard to find the right room."

My hand flew to my mouth. I hadn't realized . . .

Ryker kissed my hand one more time. "I can't wait to see you later, and now I'm anxious to meet this dear Becca of yours."

I flashed him another smile, unsteady though it felt, hugging him one more time. This time he took advantage of my embrace, his arms wrapping tightly around me, holding me closer and for a tick longer than what would normally be considered appropriate. It wasn't until his body was pressed against mine that I realized I was in a simple cotton shift, no robe or corset or petticoats to put any extra layers between my body and his. I could feel every ridge of his hard body pressing into every soft part of mine. The heat of embarrassment rose up my neck, and I tried to pull away, but his hand reached up to cup the back of my head as he gently ran his fingers through my untamed hair. Such an intimate gesture; I'd never had a man do that to me before, and it made my body feel like melting butter as my eyes fluttered closed.

He leaned in even closer, and the hairs on my arms began to straighten. Those floating sparks became a tumultuous storm of light and heat in my stomach as he whispered against my ear: "I'll see you tonight." His lips brushed ever so lightly against my sensitive skin, making my whole body stutter.

Then he pulled back, giving me a roguish, knowing smile before he left the room.

I darted back into my bed chamber and immediately pulled on a robe, covering myself—a little too late, but it still made me feel better. When I sat down to finally eat some of my neglected breakfast, relief rushed in at the thought of Becca being here with me soon. I was amazed that Ryker was able to read me so well and sense what I needed before I could even think of it. He made me feel seen, and I hadn't felt truly seen in a very long time.

CHAPTER 32

Ryker

I took a moment to catch my breath outside of Evy's chambers. She had no idea how stunning she was, or what her enthusiasm—and that incredibly thin cotton shift—did to me. I could've held her in my arms all morning, running my fingers through her hair like that, the feeling of her slight form in my hands with her soft curves flush against me.

The appreciative embrace she gave me still lingered on my skin, and I felt like a young boy all over again, far too excited that a pretty girl hugged me. I couldn't help but chuckle at the thought. How was it that she was so different from the other girls I'd been with? And how was I so different with her?

Smiling to myself, I silently congratulated my own stroke of genius in thinking she might simply need someone familiar around her to feel more at ease here. She'd just experienced so many changes, I'd thought a familiar face might help her feel more at home.

"Your Highness?" An attendant cleared his throat uncomfortably before me.

Right. I'd forgotten that I'd called for an attendant the minute I shut her doors.

I rubbed my forehead, attempting to calm my swirling thoughts. "Forgive me. I need you to deliver this message to Miss Becca Smith in Hoddleston. Her father is the cobbler there. She'll be staying in the South Wing; have the maids get a room ready for her, and if she pens a reply, please wait for it and bring it back directly to Miss Evelyn."

I handed him the note, and he bowed deeply. "Yes, Your Highness," he said, then scurried off.

I almost felt bad placing Evelyn's friend in a different wing, but I had put Evelyn near me here, in the royal North Wing. Hopefully she would understand. I hated leaving her alone for the day after what Briggita had told me she'd walked in on: Evelyn curled up on the floor in a little ball, sobbing and shaking uncontrollably. But at least I'd left her in good spirits with the anticipation of her friend coming to visit.

Not two seconds later, Liam stood before me. He embodied the Captain of the Guard today, rigid and formal in his posture. He still had a job to do, and so did I, and getting back into a normal routine was the best thing we could do for each other. Liam always shadowed me throughout the day, but for the first time in our lives, it felt . . . awkward.

I cleared my throat uncomfortably and raked my hand up the back of my neck, but it was Liam who broke our tense silence.

"Is she all right?" His low voice was full of concern, but he wasn't demanding to see her or sidestepping me to get to her. He had asked me, and trusted me with an answer. That was a good sign.

"She had a pretty rough morning. Brigitta came and got me."

He nodded; he already knew that Brigitta was to report anything concerning Evelyn's well-being to me.

"Liam, you should know . . ." I could barely get the distasteful, ugly words out of my mouth. "Brigitta told me yesterday that Evelyn's body is covered in bruises and scars." Liam stiffened at this knowledge, but I hadn't even told him the worst part yet. "However, more importantly, she had fairly fresh wounds and welts lining the backs of her legs."

Liam's face turned the most vivid shade of red that I had ever seen. The look of rage in his eyes was enough to scare even me. I could practically feel the fury radiating off him, but he still remained silent, waiting to see if I had any more information to offer.

I cleared my throat. "Evelyn confirmed to me yesterday that her father would often beat her. She didn't mention anything else, but she suggested that there was further mistreatment as well."

"Well, that part was obvious when I visited her home," Liam finally said, but the words were like freshly-sharpened daggers. Then his face fell, and I knew immediately he was blaming himself.

I raised my hand to his shoulder. "It's not your fault, Liam. It never was. You can't take on this burden."

He just shook his head, staring at the floor.

"I wanted you to know because I'm headed to Father's room, where I'm hoping to discuss how best to handle the Coulter situation."

He bobbed his head up and down in defeat, then raised his chin and stared longingly at Evelyn's door. Taking in a deep breath through his nose, he turned to me, nodding his head brusquely. He was normally a man of few words, but today might've been a record.

I nodded back and took off down the corridor to my father's suite. The physicians were already there with him, and I was dreading their prognosis. Liam followed as my silent shadow and planted himself stoically outside my father's bedchamber door.

Without knocking, I allowed myself entry to my father's room, attendants rushed to and from with a nervous energy that put me on edge.

"Your Highness." Apep bowed low, but stood directly in front of me, blocking my path to my father.

"Apep." I nodded my head in response. "What is the latest update?"

"It's not promising, Your Highness." He stayed in front of me, eyes glued to the floor in remorse, shaking his head. "He seems in good spirits, though. And, of course, he's been asking for you."

I started to move past him, but Apep placed his hand on my shoulder, looking solemnly into my eyes. "Your Highness, you need to start preparing yourself."

My stomach dropped as I nodded again, unable to do much else with the warning. Apep released my shoulder and moved to my side, following me as I walked into Father's bedchamber. He was lying in his grand canopied bed while the physicians all gathered in a corner of the room, quietly debating some procedure or another.

"Good morning, Father." I sat on the edge of his bed and held his hand, just like I had done with Evelyn mere moments before.

"My son." He smiled brightly at me. His eyes were still so full of life, but also sorrow. "I'm afraid I haven't much time now." He gestured to the arguing physicians. "They're debating ways to prolong my life, but I know it's not possible." He shook his head. "Before there's any more talk of harsh realities, I want to hear all about Evelyn. Will I get a chance to meet her?"

I was so close to tears I could barely nod my head without them falling. "Yes, Father. I've just been to see her, and she'll be joining us for dinner this evening." I paused. "But speaking of harsh realities, I'm afraid I've discovered that she was treated quite poorly by her family."

"Yes, I did hear that." He stopped me with a wave of his hand. "Apep has been updating me on the monstrosity that is Lord Coulter." His face took on a red sheen of anger. "To think he would trade his own daughter like that. It repulses me. Scum of a man."

I couldn't help but chuckle slightly. My father, ever the protector. It was why the kingdom loved him so much, and one of the many reasons I loved him, too.

"She's struggling to adjust here at the palace, so I allowed her to invite a friend to come keep her company. I think it will do her heart good to have someone she trusts around. Plus, I'd like to talk to you about my ideas for punishing the Coulters. I've been weighing some different options in my head." I looked up to dismiss the physicians, but saw Apep was already ushering them out of the room. At least his insistent eavesdropping was helpful on occasion.

"That's a splendid idea. I'm sure she'll be far more comfortable with a trusted friend."

Apep closed the doors behind the exiting physicians and himself, giving us some much-needed privacy. I sagged in relief.

Father's hand came down gently on mine. "You can trust him, you know." Father's voice was low and tired. It was obvious he had been keeping up appearances, even for the physicians.

My brow furrowed. "Trust who?"

"Apep."

I pursed my lips, holding back my snarky retort.

"I'm serious, Ryker. Out of all the people in your life, Apep may be the one you can trust the most."

"And how is that? More than you? More than Liam?" I didn't let him truly answer before I continued, "Apep is a slithering, weak man, desperate to gain your favor. Everything about him screams *untrustworthy*. I've always wondered why you keep him around."

Father sighed long and heavy. "He does come across that way sometimes, yes." He cleared his throat, asking for some water, which I gently helped him drink. "Let's talk about more pressing things, like your lovely Miss Evelyn and her horrendous family."

We talked about how to deal with the Coulters, plans for my succession, and about my feelings for Evelyn, including the pickle we were all in because of her past relationship with Liam. He offered some good insights, but mostly just encouraged me to let things run their course.

Kissing him on the forehead, I left his bedside to some very capable attendants who entered the room. He looked all too pleased to have the women doting on him. *Small victories, I suppose.* Apep and Liam were both waiting outside. They followed me to the office, where Liam stood guard just outside the door, while Apep and I looked over a few current requests and signed some of the papers that Father and I talked about. A maid brought Apep and I lunch, and I realized it was the first time I was taking on Father's duties and working with Apep directly. Luckily, it felt quite seamless.

Apep grunted, pulling my attention to him. "Your Highness. I'd like to get to know this *Evelyn* you've brought back to the palace. I haven't had the chance to meet her yet. Perhaps I might get a . . . private introduction?"

I cringed a little at his slimy tone, but nodded politely. "I'd be happy to introduce you tonight at dinner."

"Excellent. Tell me, have you questioned her yet about her curious behavior at the ball?" He paused, raising one eyebrow. "It seems quite strange that she had to leave at a particular time, that neither Captain Liam nor her own family was able to recognize her . . . and that she managed to retrieve such a fine gown and carriage when her family is near destitute. Don't you agree, Your Highness?"

His voice always seemed to slither when he spoke, but today, there was also an underlying edge to it. Something more biting, like an accusation. I glared daggers into his eyes as I spoke. "She's not a fairy, if that's what you're insinuating."

Fairies were a topic we didn't often bring up. The peasants had their folktales and stories they passed down to each new generation, but I had learned early on that the Penvardens did *not* speak of fairies. I knew the history: my great, great grandfather had defeated the evil fairies and brought peace to our land. Fairies, if they ever even existed, no longer lived in this land, and it would be my job as king to keep it that way.

Apep pursed his lips. "How can you be so certain, Your Highness?"

His face was blank, steady with an unnatural focus. Father had *just* told me to trust him, but this conversation was making me more and more *un*trusting of the man before me.

I sighed exasperatedly. "If she was a fairy, she would've removed herself from the abusive situation she was in with her family with her magic. But instead, she served her own family like a common maid, and was beaten on a regular basis." I paused, raising my eyebrows for emphasis. "The logical answer is that there was nothing more nefarious taking place other than her fear of being found out. Do not sit there and pass judgement where it is not due, Apep."

Apep simply nodded his head. "Excellent point, Your Highness. I am truly sorry to hear she's had such a horrific experience."

Apep himself was practically timeless. Some days I thought he was ancient; other days he looked barely older than me. Tall and willowy, he rarely stood up straight, but instead always hunched his narrow shoulders like he was carrying a heavy burden on his back. And those giant black robes he always wore . . . hideous. Even though I'd never seen, I'd always assumed he was all skin and bone underneath. If anyone was going to be accused of being a fairy, someone ought to accuse *him*.

Apep stirred his tea thoughtfully, "It still doesn't answer the questions about her attire for the ball, though. It seems curious to me that someone treated so poorly could have dressed like that." He looked up at me then. "It truly was a magnificent dress."

That made me pause. "Yes, it was. And I'm sure she has a perfectly reasonable explanation for it."

Apep glanced up at me over his tea cup. "I do not doubt it." Then looked back down and quietly sipped his tea while scanning the few documents that lay before him.

The dress had been spectacular, and very . . . unique. I had never seen anything like it before, which was why I was convinced she was some sort of visiting dignitary at first. A princess from another kingdom, perhaps. I hated to admit it, but Apep had made an excellent point. I shook my head, trying to erase the questions gnawing at my mind, going back to signing and reading through the large stack of papers on the desk.

CHAPTER 33

Evelyn

When the knock on my door came that night, the butterflies woke once more in my stomach. But this time, they weren't floating around; they were scratching and clawing and beating their wings to get out.

I didn't feel ready to meet the king, and I still wasn't sure I even wanted to. The only thing that made me feel better was knowing that Becca would be here soon. She had sent word back to me, telling me she was beyond excited to hear from me—and to visit the palace—and she would be arriving tomorrow.

The girls had just finished getting me ready. I wore another new dress, this time stunning green, with a square neckline and long sleeves. They said the color helped bring attention to my green eyes. I was grateful they were considering things like style and color. I'd never had to worry about such things before, and had no idea where to even begin.

My hair was pulled up and tucked into neat little curls tonight, and they'd even used my mother's old comb to complete the look. I was thankful to carry a little piece of her with me tonight. It gave me courage.

Brigitta opened the door to my sitting room and told the attendant I'd be right out. Feleen squeezed my hand in encouragement. "The king is very kind. You will like him."

I appreciated her attempt at comfort, but the image my mind held of the king was not kind at all. My hand trembled slightly in hers, and she gave me a soft smile before leading me out the door to my escort.

We walked all the way to the end of the long hall, where the double doors to the king's suite opened without us even knocking. Nodding my thanks to the attendant, I entered the private dining room.

The sound of light chatter filled my ears and the scent of delicious savory foods wafted to my nose. I'd expected a small room and table, but was surprised to find a very spacious room with a long table that could seat at least thirty people, maybe more. I wondered what the main dining hall looked like, if this was considered an intimate dining space. All of it was intimidating, and my already-frayed nerves bristled.

The minute I walked through the door, both Liam and Ryker jumped up and started toward me. My face instantly heated at their dual approach, and I hoped it wasn't too noticeable with the additional rouge Anna had added to my face. As they both neared me, Liam conceded to Ryker, who looped my hand around his arm. He leaned down to whisper into my ear—he seemed fond of that little move. "You look absolutely stunning tonight, Evelyn."

I gave him a small smile. "Thank you."

He patted my hand soothingly—I think he could tell I was nervous. Liam followed closely behind us, and I struggled to not turn around to look back at him as Ryker led me over to the dining table. Just a moment later, the king came gliding through a door in the left corner of the room. He was an imposing figure. The moment he walked into the room, I felt the dynamic shift. It was quite obvious he held all the power here. His eyes were deep, vivid blue, unlike Ryker's sky-blue gaze, but his barely-greying sandy hair matched Ryker's perfectly. However, the King's hair was much longer than Ryker's, very regal-looking, hanging around his shoulders. His eyes were bright with excitement, but there were tired shadows wrinkled underneath, almost like something was ailing him. It was strange to see him in person. The cruel, demanding man I had always pictured in my mind looked nothing like the welcoming man standing before me now.

"Our very own mystery maiden from the ball, in the flesh. I'm honored to make your acquaintance, Lady Evelyn."

He stopped before me, and I clutched Ryker's arm, unwilling to let go. I dipped into the lowest curtsy I could manage. "The honor is mine, Your Majesty."

When I stood back up, I saw his face was even closer now, studying me intently. There was a steadiness to him that was strangely comforting, but somehow still intimidating.

A sly smile spread slowly on his lips. "My, my, but you are quite the beauty. No wonder my boys are both so taken with you."

I felt my entire neck heat with embarrassment, and I was certain my skin had turned beet-red. My body started to cave in, attempting to hide any splotches on my skin.

"*Father.*" Ryker's tone was reprimanding, but still playful.

"What? Can I not compliment a beautiful woman?" He winked at Ryker, then offered me his elbow. "Walk with me for a moment, Lady Evelyn."

I slipped my hand into the crook of the king's arm, praying he couldn't feel my tremors. He walked me out of the room through another set of doors and into a smaller, far more private room that was lined with shelves full of books around a petite fireplace. The musty, sweet scent of old paper mixed with a faint hint of smoke made the entire room perfectly cozy. If only I could stay in this room for the duration of the dinner. It felt safer. My shoulders loosened a little, and I was able to straighten my body into a more confident stance.

A large oriel window lined with soft fabrics and pillows overlooked an expansive green space that made up part of the palace gardens I had yet to explore. The king walked me over to it, releasing my arm while we both took in the calming view.

"My wife used to love this view. She would sit in here and read for hours every day." The king's voice was wistful.

I looked down at the window seat, imagining myself sitting there reading, periodically gazing out at the green space beyond. It sounded like a wonderful dream.

"I can see why," I replied. "I could quite easily curl up in here and read all day long myself."

He then turned to look at me. "Ryker told me about your history with Liam." I nearly jumped out of my skin, fear clamping down on my heart. What was he going to say? Would he demand I choose Ryker? Would he tell me to stay away from Liam? Would he—

He interrupted my cascading thoughts with a hearty chuckle. "I can see why they're both besotted. I may not know you well yet, Evelyn, but anyone who manages to catch the hearts of both my boys has to be a true treasure."

I blushed again. "Thank you, Your Majesty. You're being far too kind."

He cleared his throat and looked back out the window. "There will come a day soon where both of these boys will need each other for support. I pray they will keep their heads about them while you're around, though I doubt they have much control over it." He huffed a small laugh under his breath, then his expression sobered. "I wish it were my wife here to offer you sage advice, but alas, you get only mine."

He turned to me again, his thoughtful eyes full of sincerity. "What I will tell you is to not be afraid of your feelings. You can have strong feelings for more than one person, you know. Eventually, decisions must be made, but don't focus on what could hurt. Focus on what could heal."

I remained quiet for a moment, taking in his words. I may have always hated the man who had taken Liam away from me, but I could not hate *this* man. This man who seemed to care so genuinely for both Liam and Ryker, and now even me. His words were encouraging, and even if I didn't completely understand the context in his mind, I appreciated them nonetheless.

"Thank you, Your Majesty. I appreciate your counsel." I smiled gently up at him, and he smiled back down at me. Somehow, even though I'd feared this, I found myself entirely comfortable. There was a peace about him that made me feel safe.

He took back up my arm, looping it in his, readying us to walk back into the dining room. But before we even made it a step, I abruptly blurted out, "Why did you take Liam away when he was so young?"

He looked down at me, eyes wide and startled. Whether it was my actual question or the fact that timid little me just asked something so random and, well, forward, I couldn't tell. I hung my head, my face fuming in shame, and waited for the reprimand.

His head turned back out to look at the green space again, but he didn't drop my arm. He didn't laugh at my absurd behavior or chide me for my question. I took a peek at his face, but he didn't look angry at all. In fact, he looked . . . sad.

He swallowed before speaking. "Genuine people are hard to find these days. Liam is a genuine person." His head swiveled back down, making very direct eye contact with me. "As are you, for that matter, and Ryker—though Ryker shows it a little differently." He chuckled, shaking his head in fond memory, then he sobered. "I didn't know Liam existed until I saw him delivering produce to our kitchens one afternoon. He . . . he reminded me of someone I once knew." He patted my hand again, though it felt like he was comforting himself instead of me. "Forgive me for taking him from you. I simply wanted to give him a better life."

I didn't know what *that* meant, but again, the sincerity of his words told me they were true. His reaction was so forlorn I almost felt worse now for asking the question.

Without another word, he turned and led me back out to the dining room. Speaking so quietly that only I could hear, he confessed, "Ryker updated me on your situation. I want you to know that I am deeply sorry for all the loss you've endured, and that I was a part of it, even if unintentionally." He paused as we reached the dining room table. I saw his eyes glaze over for a moment, and it was then that I noticed the considerable lines framing his eyes. He looked tired—no. More than that. He looked the way Mama had looked when she left this world. His complexion was wan, and there was a light sheen of sweat on his brow. His overzealous personality hid what was obviously a deeper, more serious ailment.

He turned to face me, looking directly into my eyes. "I can tell that you didn't deserve a single moment of it, but you are an incredibly strong person to have persevered anyway. You're a survivor, Evelyn. A quiet warrior. And I do believe you would make a most excellent queen."

My eyes stung with tears as I looked up at him, unable to formulate a response. He winked at me, tapped my cheek lightly, then released me to greet a few new guests who had arrived. I turned away from the table, taking a moment to gather myself.

"Evy? You okay?" Liam's low timbre was like a warm blanket thrown over my shoulders. I was grateful he was here tonight, even if it made things a little awkward. I always preferred seeing his familiar face; I probably always would. Right now, I wanted to bury my face into his chest and have myself a good cry while he held me. Talking with the king about him made me somehow miss him even more, but had also given me such intense relief. I was relieved the king had never been evil or cruel; he had just been looking out for Liam. That was the best thing I could've asked for, for this boy I had loved so dearly.

I swallowed back the growing lump in my throat. "Yes, I'm fine. The king is very . . . kind." I quickly brushed my fingers under my eyes and turned around to face Liam, who was smiling at me fondly.

"I agree." He shifted his weight so that he was a bit more relaxed. "He treats me like his own son. He has ever since Ryker and I connected. After growing up without a father, it's been a blessing having him in my life."

"I was mad at him, you know. For taking you." I gave Liam a sheepish smile. "I never thought I'd meet the man that took you away from me, let alone like him."

"I felt the same way when I arrived here. But the king has a way of changing your mind." He smiled thoughtfully, clearly lost in a good memory.

A small bell rang out, and an attendant called out, "Dinner is served! Please take your seats."

A light rumble of quiet shuffling echoed in the space as we all turned toward the table. Liam pulled out my seat, which just so happened to be next to his—both Liam and Ryker sat on either side of the king, who was at the front of the table. I darted my eyes around the rest of the table. Several others were in attendance, all nobles by the looks of them, both men and women. The chair beside me pulled out, and a dark figure sat next to me. His black robes were strange, and his demeanor even stranger. When our eyes met, he held my gaze, and a dangerous chill crept up my spine. This man seemed . .

. otherworldly. I couldn't decipher his age. His eyes were both dark and light, like a swirling whirlpool of contradictions. I felt lured in by him, and it unnerved me. Unfamiliar cold tendrils crept up my spine like icy fingers caressing my skin. I shivered and looked away.

"Everyone, please allow me to introduce Lady Evelyn Coulter." The sound of my name pulled me back to the table of eager stares in front of me, and I saw Ryker gesture to me. I did my best to smile, bowing my head politely to the collective table. "Lady Evelyn, to your right is Apep, the Royal Advisor."

Apep smiled at me calculatingly. Nothing about him seemed very genuine or kind. I shivered again, trying to ease my rapidly-growing nerves.

Ryker went around the whole table, introducing everyone in attendance, but it all went in one ear and straight out the other. I probably wouldn't be able to recognize these people once they left this room today.

The first course was placed in front of us, a creamy soup that smelled divine. The servers worked efficiently, moving at a brisk pace. Everything felt so formal, I was starting to worry that I would somehow break decorum by accident.

"It's a true pleasure, Lady Evelyn." Apep's slippery voice felt unnervingly intimate in my ear.

I flinched, looking back up at Apep, pursing my lips slightly. "Pleased to meet you, ah . . ." I puzzled my brow at his lack of title. "Forgive me, sir, do you simply go by Apep?"

He smiled again, but this time it seemed more genuine, almost reaching his eyes. "I do indeed."

"Well then, pleased to meet you, Apep." I smiled politely, not wanting to insult the royal advisor the first moment I met him. The corners of his mouth tilted up again, but didn't actually form a smile on his face.

I cleared my throat, trying to force words out past the lump of nerves in my throat. "I've never heard a name such as yours before. Where does it come from?"

His eyes lit up. "Ah, the origins are very interesting indeed. Would you believe you are the first person to ask me that, Lady Evelyn?"

My eyebrows lifted in surprise, "That does surprise me. You seem quite the curiosity. I wonder as to why no one has ever inquired about it before." Even as the words left my lips, I realized their impropriety, and my eyes widened. "Forgive me, sir, I did not mean that to sound—"

He cut me off, narrowing his eyes at me. "But it is you that is the curiosity, are you not?"

I instantly felt hot all over. I hadn't touched a bite of my food yet. Those invisible cold tendrils slithered up my spine again, and I clamped down a shudder.

"Evy? Are you all right?" Liam leaned over, thankfully interrupting Apep's scrutiny.

I was already messing up—being far too improper with my words and insulting the royal advisor. Not eating my soup or remembering anyone's name. That familiar dread was beginning to weigh down my stomach, stealing my appetite. *Not now, not now . . .*

I brightened my face and mentally shook off my nerves. "Yes, of course. I was just speaking with Apep." I focused on the delicious soup in front of me, taking a spoonful, even though the smell of food made my stomach turn. "It's delicious."

I glanced toward Ryker, but his attention was elsewhere. He was speaking with several men at the table, and I couldn't quite hear what they were saying. My ears felt clogged, my head felt foggy. The all-too-familiar cloying fear started to build in my stomach, and my heart started thumping hard against my chest. I closed my eyes at the impending episode. *Not now!*

Apep leaned into my personal space, lowering his voice for my ears only. "How many secrets you must hold, Lady Evelyn."

"Excuse me?" I bristled, turning to look directly at Apep. Our faces were so close he could've kissed me. He was staring at me so intently that for one wild moment, I feared he might *actually* kiss me. *What is wrong with this man?*

A knowing smile curled on his lips, and he leaned back again, speaking louder this time. "I'm thrilled Prince Ryker discovered you at the ball. How serendipitous it must feel to be rescued from such a horrible situation and put up in a palace, being treated like a queen."

I tensed, my hand curling into a fist around my spoon. I huffed out an exasperated breath. "I'm not here to be treated like a queen.

This arrangement is temporary, as I'm sure you well know."

"Hmm." Was all he said, mostly to himself.

That was his only response? *Hmm?* Was this what everyone thought of me? Why on earth did I have to be sitting next to this man? Flustered, I looked down at my soup again, taking another spoonful.

It was decided. I officially hated this man. How dare he think I was only here to take advantage of Ryker's generosity. And yet, guilt slipped in—wasn't that exactly what I was doing, staying here this way?

"You know, I was very curious to meet you. The mystery girl from the ball. The one that instantly bewitched our *beloved* Prince." He said *beloved* like he smelled something bad. "And now that I have met you, I see why he made such a fuss. There is something quite special about you, isn't there, Lady Evelyn?" He paused, taking a slurp of his soup, the sound grating on my sore nerves. Somehow he made everything he said sound like a threat. The dread that had already pooled in my stomach began to overflow. Why was he so curious about me? He was the one that looked like the walking dead with his dark robes and his pale, ageless face. I supposed it was a good thing he couldn't hear my thoughts.

The corner of his lips turned up almost immediately after I had that thought.

"Evy?" Liam was staring at me again, his brow furrowed.

I shook my head a bit, pulling myself back to the table. "Forgive me, Liam, did you say something?"

"No, but I'm worried about you. You look flushed. Is something ailing you?"

I raised my hand to my cheeks, angry at how often they gave me away. "I'm quite all right. Just feeling a little overwhelmed." I forced a smile, afraid he would see right through it and discover I was inches away from being unable to breathe.

Out of the corner of my eye, Apep gently dabbed his mouth, studying me. "Fearful little thing, aren't you?"

Liam stiffened, his eyes darkening as he leaned forward to catch Apep's gaze. "What did you just say?"

Apep's eyes grew wide at Liam's clear admonishment, as if he'd just realized where he was, that other people could hear him. "Forgive me,

Captain. I was merely getting to know Lady Evelyn here. She seems rather on edge. I was hoping to help ease her nerves."

Liam shook his head as the servants switched out our plates for the next course. He started to say more, but the king engaged Liam just then, while Apep continued to stare at me. Did anyone else at the table notice his excessive attention?

"They're all too busy with their own mundane conversations to notice us, Evelyn." He said my name reverently, intimately. I hadn't made that comment out loud, had I? All of my senses were firing off warning flares. A sheen of sweat formed on my brow. My heart felt like it was going to burst.

His lips turned up at the corners again, and I saw a flash of glee in his gaze.

What was happening here? Who *was* this man?

"You'll learn, Evelyn. In time." His eyes were alight with mischief.

I hadn't asked one question out loud—all of them had been in my mind. I stared at him in mute horror, my mind whirling with the possibilities. Servants came and exchanged our plates for the third course. I hadn't even taken a bite of the last one. I took a deep breath to try and calm my nerves, forcing myself to study him back.

Without giving it much thought, so as to not give myself away, I decided to give him a little test. I made my thoughts loud, like I was yelling them in my head: *"What are you?"*

He blanched, dropping his utensil. It echoed above the light chatter at the table.

I gasped.

He *had* heard me.

"Lady Evelyn, are you quite all right?" I realized it was the king calling out my name, watching me with concern.

Flustered, I dipped my head. "Yes, Your Majesty. Forgive me, I was just startled."

"Was Apep asking too many questions? He has a tendency to do that." Ryker glared Apep down, like he needed to back off. Was this a common occurrence? Did they know he could hear thoughts?

"On the contrary, Your Highness. Lady Evelyn has been asking *me* the questions." He smiled slyly.

"I haven't heard her ask you much of anything, Apep," Liam

chimed in, leveling a scrutinizing look at the advisor. Thank goodness he had been paying attention. He didn't seem the least bit amused.

Apep paled slightly, but he held Liam's gaze. I wondered what thoughts were flashing through Liam's mind. That thought made me smile slightly.

Apep cleared his throat. "Ah, yes, it would be hard to hear."

I blanched at his strange display of honesty.

He scooted his chair back and addressed the King. "Forgive me, Your Majesty, but I'm afraid there's an urgent matter I need to attend to this evening that slipped my mind. Would you please excuse me?"

The King waved his hand in dismissal at Apep. "Yes, of course. Good evening, Apep."

Apep bowed. "Good evening, Your Majesty." He dipped his head to the rest of the table, letting his gaze linger on me as he smiled. This time it fully reached his eyes, but it was almost more unnerving than his halfway attempts. He looked downright giddy that I had discovered his secret. "It's been a true pleasure, Lady Evelyn."

He quickly exited the private dining room, his movements sinuous and swift. I couldn't understand what had just happened, what I'd uncovered. But the cold tendrils left my skin, leaving me far too warm.

Liam put his hand on my shoulder, his eyes trained on the door Apep had exited through. "What was that all about?"

I shook my head, looking down at my untouched plate. "I'm really not sure," I croaked. I took a few bites, hoping that the distraction of eating would help calm my frazzled nerves.

The conversation swirled around me, though everyone at the table kept stealing looks at me now. Sweat began to gather in the small of my back, but I took a deep breath, trying to block it all out. *Breathe. Just keep breathing.*

A harsh cough suddenly pulled my attention to the head of the table. The king was bent over, one hand over his chest and the other over his mouth, suffering a coughing fit. When it was over, he slumped awkwardly in his chair. Both Ryker and Liam jumped to his aid, asking anxious questions, but he waved them off. His skin was pallid, and there was a fine layer of sweat on his brow.

Ryker turned to one of the servants. "Fetch the physicians. Now!"

The servant made a mad dash out the door.

The king composed himself long enough to take a drink before rasping, "Forgive me, dear friends, but I must adjourn for the night. I have not been feeling quite myself today. Please stay and enjoy the rest of the meal."

Low murmurs and deferential head nods acknowledged the king, but there was a heavy blanket of unease that fell across the small crowd. Had they seen what I had caught earlier? Did everyone know that the king was considerably ill, or was that being kept secret?

Liam and Ryker helped the king back toward what I assumed was his bedchamber, and the servant returned with a physician in tow.

The table grew silent as everyone looked around at each other, curious and concerned. Their glances often lingered on me, which made me feel completely exposed, sitting by myself at the table. Just as one of the men across from me made eye contact and was about to speak, Liam and Ryker came back into the room.

Liam pulled out his chair to sit next to me again, easing some of my nerves, but Ryker remained standing to address the crowd. "Forgive us for not warning you." Ryker took a deep breath before continuing, "My father has been feeling a little under the weather. The physician is seeing to him now." He sat back down and raised his glass. "Let us finish our meal together, and pray for his speedy recovery." We all drank together in honor of the king.

Two more courses were served, and I was able to eat a little more with Liam's reassuring presence next to me—and Apep's disconcerting presence gone. No one really spoke to me throughout the rest of the dinner, but many curious glances flitted my direction. It wasn't a night I was eager to repeat. I was not only out of place, but on display, some kind of strange side show for people to gawk at. I hated their curious attention.

Once the evening had officially ended, I had no desire to speak with anyone, and Ryker was quickly surrounded by the nobles inquiring more about his father's health—merely out of concern, of course, certainly not for gossip's sake. I rolled my eyes at their all-too-obvious intentions.

Liam came to stand beside me, offering his arm. "Would you like me to walk you back to your suite?"

I shook my head, gently pushing his arm down. "No, thank you.

I know the way now, and I'm feeling quite tired."

"I'm sorry tonight was so tense." Liam studied me, anxiously biting his lip. "Did you get enough to eat?"

I smiled softly at him. "It was fine. I had plenty to eat, and I'm glad I got to see you, if nothing else."

"Same here." He smiled sadly and gently kissed my hand. "Goodnight, Evy."

I slipped out of the room quietly and rushed back toward my suite, relieved to be alone. The hall was eerily quiet, setting my senses on full alert. I couldn't see anyone, but I had a sneaking suspicion I was being watched. The hour was late, and the shadows felt deeper than normal. Maybe it was all just my imagination; I had already felt so unsettled by Apep at dinner, I was sure to be on edge. But the feeling lingered.

I quickened my pace, wanting the safety of my suite. I latched the door solidly shut behind me, leaning my head against the cool door, fighting to find my breath.

I was so tired of constantly feeling scared. And if I didn't feel safe here, surrounded by guards and kings and people who cared about me, would I ever feel safe again?

CHAPTER 34

Evelyn

The next morning, the moment my eyes opened, one thought crossed my mind: *Becca is coming today.*

I leapt out of bed, the thrill of that thought waking me up immediately. It would be so good to talk to her about everything that had happened—and *so much* had happened, I could hardly decide where to start. I didn't know how soon she would arrive or what to do until she did, but it didn't matter. Today was a good day.

I had already dressed and brushed out my hair by the time the girls delivered my breakfast. I was in the middle of telling them all about Becca and how much they would love her when there was a knock at the main door. Feleen went to answer it, and I heard Liam's low timbre coming from the sitting room.

I jumped up, my excitement building. "Liam! Come in!"

He quickly appeared at my bedchamber door with Feleen in tow, almost huffing at his apparent speed. He smiled at me, big and bright, and I could tell he enjoyed seeing me in such good spirits.

"Would you like to have breakfast with me?" I gestured to the tray filled with all kinds of goodies. "There's plenty."

"I do have some time this morning before I'm on duty." His easy smile lit up his whole face as he moved, swiftly crossing the room before the girls could object. Taking the seat directly in front of me at the small breakfast table, he popped a grape in his mouth, grinning cheekily.

I couldn't help but smile broadly back at him. He looked to the girls. "Could I trouble you ladies for a cup of coffee?"

Anna immediately curtsied and went to fulfill his request. Liam settled in, giving me a quick once-over. "So, tell me why you're all smiles today. Not that I'm complaining." He winked.

"Becca is coming to visit today!" I squealed. He looked a little puzzled, like he was trying to figure out who I meant. "Do you remember the girl you saw with me in town? That was Becca."

Recognition dawned on his face as Anna handed him a cup of coffee, smiling extra demurely. I bristled slightly. I knew Anna was just being Anna, but I hated that she was being it with *Liam*. All the girls had already assumed I'd matched with Ryker, constantly calling me the future queen.

"Thank you," he said to Anna without looking away from me, which appeased me a bit. "So, how is it that Becca secured an invitation to the palace?" He took a sip of his coffee, raising his eyebrows at me.

I looked down for a moment. "Well, um . . . Ryker thought I could use a friend, and asked if there was anyone I'd like to invite to visit me."

A dark shadow crossed his eyes for a moment, and I tried not to flinch—I'd worried that bringing up Ryker would upset him. But that darkness was gone as quickly as it came, and he smiled thoughtfully. "That was clever thinking of him. I can't wait to meet her again. Do you know when she's coming?"

I shrugged. "She didn't say, unfortunately. It looks like I'll be stuck staring at the wall until she arrives."

He laughed. "Well, perhaps we could all do something together tonight to celebrate her arrival. The boys and I often go to the tavern if we have the night off. Maybe you ladies would like to join us?"

There was a mischievous gleam in his eye. I pursed my lips, squinting at him speculatively. "Why do I feel like you've got an ulterior motive that comes with this offer?"

He cocked one eyebrow. "Maybe I do," he said, his mouth arching into a half-smile, giving me a glimpse of my favorite dimple.

I mirrored that smile back at him. Being around him was always so easy. Even if we didn't know each other anymore, there was still a simplicity that permeated our time together. He and Ryker both had a strange effortlessness to them; they were oddly alike while still having their own respective personalities.

"So? Does that sound like a plan?" he prodded.

I realized I hadn't answered him; I'd gotten lost in my thoughts, lost in staring at him. His dark, perpetually-mussed hair; his warm skin, tanned from the sun; that strong jaw, with extra shadow from his facial hair; and deep, soulful eyes. His self-assured expression told me that I was staring a little too pointedly at him.

I cleared my throat, blinking hard. "Yes! Yes, of course, that sounds like a lot of fun. And I'm sure Becca would love it too."

"Excellent." He took another sip of his coffee, and I loved how that bold, sharp scent mixed with the earthy musk of Liam. It smelled comforting; more like home. Looking out the window, he sobered, looking deep in thought for a moment. "I'd also like to get some time alone with you, to . . . talk."

I raised an eyebrow at him. "We're talking now."

"I mean . . ." He took a deep breath, then exhaled heavily. "Evy, I want to know what happened after I left. I want the details. *All* of them. Nothing left out."

My breath caught. "Liam, I . . . I don't know if I want to tell you all the details."

He set down his coffee cup, meeting my eyes. "Why not, Evy?"

My fingers twitched, and I started picking at them. My voice came out as barely a whisper. "I don't want you to think less of me."

"What?" He looked stricken. "How could you even think . . . I could *never* think less of you, Evy. Never."

"It's just—" I fluttered my hands in the air, trying to find the words. "I feel like it will hurt you to know. Even *I* haven't thought about all the details. Honestly, I don't *want* to think about them. And I fear it will only burden you further, since you already blame yourself so much."

He reached across the table and gripped my hand. "Evy, you could never burden me. I want to *share* your burden."

"Liam, the girl you remember is gone. I'm not her anymore. I haven't been for a long time." I looked down and tried to pull my hand away, but he still gripped it tight.

"I know that. I know these things have changed you. I'm changed, too. But you're still *you*. Nothing and no one could change that."

Tears welled in my eyes. How could he see me like that? I was only a burden, being passed around by people who didn't truly want me. If I barely recognized myself anymore, how could he?

"Evy, you will always matter to me. I know you think I left you, forgot you, moved on . . . but I didn't. I *can't*. You have always been in my heart. I missed you. I missed you *every single day*." He breathed in shakily, brushing his other hand over his face. "I was so ashamed, Evy." His voice cracked. "I didn't think I could handle my heart breaking all over again."

The confession made my breath catch.

His eyes had tears in them now, and his face was red with embarrassment, but he still held tight to my hand. "You have always been the sun to me, Evy. You are the light shining in my dark places. My favorite companion. My . . . my heart. I never wanted anything or anyone else, and I never will. It was you, Evy. Always you."

Always you. I closed my eyes, savoring those words.

He took a deep, shuddering breath, his eyes pleading for something, anything from me in return. He looked so unsure of himself.

I leapt out of the chair and embraced him. I had waited so long to hear those words. He pulled me onto his lap, and I nuzzled my face against his neck. His arms tightened around me, and he buried his face against my hair, breathing deeply like I was oxygen to him. I did the same, breathing in his loamy cedarwood scent.

We both stayed like that, silent, simply holding each other. But it wasn't uncomfortable. In his arms I felt enveloped, safe, home. His grip tightened gently around me, one hand reaching up to caress my hair. I hadn't been held in so long . . .

Overcome with emotion, I gently kissed the pulse point at his neck, and Liam took in a sharp breath, his whole body stiffening at the contact. I could feel his heart pounding against his chest—had I done something to frighten him? I tentatively raised my head to look at his face. His eyes were slightly hooded, but there was no fear there, only desire. His lips were slightly parted, and the hand that had been stroking my hair cupped the back of my head instead, slowly twisting the strands between his fingers. The intensity of his gaze liquefied my insides. He leaned in slowly, his eyes traveling lower . . .

A small knock came from the main doors, and I heard one of the girls answer it. A stranger's voice said, "Miss Becca Smith for Lady Evelyn."

Liam's grip loosened, and we each let out a breath, the tension rushing out of the room. Reluctant to pull apart, we sat there together for an extra beat of time before he brushed my cheek with his thumb, then leaned in to kiss my forehead. "It's okay," he said, sensing my unspoken apology. "I know you're excited to see her. We can talk more later."

I nodded a bit, quickly unraveling myself from his embrace. I was surprised the girls hadn't opened the door yet to announce Becca—but then again, who knew how much they'd heard of our conversation? Or how much they'd seen? Maybe they were trying to give us some privacy.

I quickly straightened my dress, praying there weren't any suspicious wrinkles left behind. When I opened the doors to the sitting room, Becca's nervous face brightened into the biggest smile. We both squealed like tea kettles, then ran into each other's arms, laughing so hard we almost toppled over.

Becca backed away, holding my hands and arms out to survey me. "I couldn't believe it when they said you were staying at the palace! Explain. Now. All of it, every detail."

I laughed. "Soon, I promise. But first, are you settled in already?"

"Oh yes, they took my things to my room already. It's . . . somewhere." She flicked her wrist dismissively, like it didn't matter where. "I asked them to bring me straight to you."

I acknowledged the waiting attendant, who was beginning to look a tad awkward. "Thank you so much for delivering her personally," I said. At that, he bowed and left quickly.

I turned back to Becca just as Liam slipped out of my bedchamber. Her eyebrows shot up to her hairline, and I grimaced inwardly. I wasn't going to hear the end of this.

I cleared my throat. "Seems like some quick introductions are in order. Becca, meet Brigitta, Anna, and Feleen. They're my maids here at the palace. They're wonderful women, and they've taken great care of me."

They all blushed at the compliment and bowed their heads to Becca, who scoffed, "Oh, no. No bowing here. I'm the daughter of a cobbler. Each of you is more of a lady than I'll ever be." They all smiled at that.

I gestured to Liam after that. "This is Captain Liam—but you already met him once, in town." I paused awkwardly, struggling to find the words to explain what else he was to me.

Thankfully, Becca didn't seem to need any further clarification. "Oh, I remember *you*." She gave him a knowing smile and a pointed once-over. "So tell me, Liam, what are your intentions with my girl here?"

Mortification made me want to curl up in a ball and hide, but I laughed it off instead, widening my eyes at Becca in warning. "You do *not* have to answer that, Liam, but we will see you later tonight. Though you'll probably need to come get us, because we won't know where we're headed."

Liam smiled big and bold, looking straight at Becca. "A pleasure seeing you again, Miss Becca." He bowed his head slightly, and his gaze intensified, holding hers with calm confidence. "My intentions with Evy are quite simple: to convince her to fall madly in love with me, then spend the rest of our days together, as it should have always been."

My face drained of all color. To hear him say that he wanted to marry me—that he'd *always* wanted to marry me—made my heart stutter and swell. I remembered when my life had been good and easy and full of love, counting down the days until I was old enough for Liam to propose so we could make it official in the eyes of the grown-ups. I wanted those days back, too, but . . . how could life ever be like that again? I hadn't believed in a happy ending for myself in a long time. Now that my future was laid out before me, a blank canvas waiting to be colored in . . . it was unnerving.

"I would be happy to escort you ladies to the tavern tonight." He gave me a wink, then turned back to Becca. "I'm so glad you're here, Becca." He headed for the door, but not before turning back around and flashing us his signature dimple smirk. "I'll see you ladies tonight."

Becca's mouth gaped as Liam left my suite. She turned back to me, her hands on her hips. "Like I said. Every detail. *Now.*"

We both laughed again, and I asked her if she'd had anything to eat yet as we sat down at the little breakfast nook in my bedchamber. I began to fill her in on everything that happened in the last few days. I left out the part about discovering my fairy grandmother—instead, I only told her I'd rediscovered my grandmother, and she was the one who'd helped me get to the ball. I also conveniently left out what I had discovered last night about Apep reading my mind. There were some things that still felt too unbelievable. Apep was one of them, and I needed to ease Becca into all of this.

The girls brought us a new pot of tea every few hours, joining in the conversation themselves on occasion. Becca had a way of including everyone, making them feel comfortable. I loved that about her.

A few hours later, Becca and I decided to get some fresh air and take a walk outside in the gardens.

"Evy . . ." My name was heavy on Becca's lips. She looked at me as if she was in pain. "I wish I'd gotten you out sooner. Convinced you to leave. I didn't know he was hurting you so badly. I couldn't have imagined . . ." Her eyes welled with tears. "I should've done something. Made you stay with me and my family. Hidden you away. Something."

Grasping her hand, I shook my head. "No, there was nothing you could've done. No matter what, I wouldn't have left. I didn't want to. I mean, I did, but . . . not really." I was silent for a moment, caught up in my thoughts and memories. "I think a small, hidden part of my father knew that leaving was the best thing for me. Maybe that's why he gave me away."

Becca scoffed. "Don't you dare give him credit where it's not due."

I looked down, my eyes burning. "I just wanted my papa back. I thought maybe if I was good, if I became the perfect daughter . . ."

"Oh, Evy." She turned and swept me into her arms. "You shouldn't have to prove yourself to anyone. Especially not to your own father."

The words stung. I knew there was truth in them, but I had held on to that hope for so long. If I could just be better, be what he wanted, then maybe he would . . .

But I was wrong. I'd always been wrong.

Becca pulled back and brushed a wayward hair from my brow. "So, what now?"

"I really don't know." I said, shrugging.

"Well, now you're free. *And* you have both a prince and a captain who want your heart." She smirked, but my face fell. "Evy, what's wrong?"

I looked at her, holding back tears. "I don't know what to do."

She tucked my arm into hers, and we resumed walking. "Personally, I think it's unfair they've put you in this position."

"But without them, I'd be stuck as a servant at the Halleford Estate. I don't want to be ungrateful."

"Evy, after what you've been through . . ." She shook her head.

"I know, Becca. But I don't really mind the distraction, you know?" I smiled slightly, and she snorted.

"I'm sure. It's certainly not the worst problem to have."

I let my smile fall away. "Honestly, it's . . . it's very overwhelming."

Becca flipped around and gripped my shoulders. "Of course it is, Evy. What they're asking of you is ridiculous. It's too much. They're both being selfish, and you need *time*. Time to heal and mourn and, frankly, time to not worry one lick about boys." She released my shoulders, winking at me. "Not like I'm one to talk. I love to worry over boys." I laughed quietly, and she smiled wider. "One day I'll snag a good one, and we'll start our own shop right next to Papa's."

"What will you do for your shop?"

She shrugged. "No idea. I just want a man who's good with his hands." Her eyebrows wiggled suggestively, and I laughed out loud again, an intense wave of relief washing over me. It was so wonderful to have her here.

"Evelyn!"

We both whipped our heads around to see Ryker jogging toward us. I turned back just in time to see Becca's eyes go wide, her mouth popping open.

"Hello, ladies! I saw you walking and I was hoping to introduce myself. Miss Becca, I presume?" His smile was so contagious, and his sandy-colored hair loved the sunshine. He looked molded from gold.

Becca dipped into a brief curtsy, "Yes, I'm Becca. Thank you for allowing me the opportunity to come visit my girl here." She smiled at him, but I could instantly tell it was fake. Protective Becca was in full bloom.

"It's my pleasure. I could tell *our* girl needed a friendly face around here." He smiled at me with a quick wink. I couldn't help but notice his use of *our girl*, and apparently neither could Becca, because she bristled at his response.

"*Our* girl?" Becca cocked a brow and rested her hand on her hip. "Staking a claim already, Your Highness? Seems a little bold, given that you've only known her for what? Five days now?"

Oh, my. She was going to get herself killed.

Luckily, Ryker just laughed. "And now I see why she chose you to come be with her. I can tell you're a very good friend, Lady Becca."

"Just Becca. I'm no lady." She was going to challenge him on everything, wasn't she? I hung my head, shaking it a little.

"All right then, *Just Becca* it is." He flashed me another wink, and I blushed, remembering our joke from the garden. His bright smile hadn't faltered; he seemed to be enjoying her challenge. I was grateful he wasn't insulted. I hadn't seen him angry yet, and I wasn't sure I ever wanted to. "When did you arrive?"

"Early this morning, actually. Came straight to Evy." She looped her arm into mine, staking her own claim. Affection welled in my chest for this brave, wonderful friend of mine. I loved Becca like the sister I'd always wished Camilla had been.

"I'm glad to hear it. Stay as long as you like," he said briskly.

He turned back to me, but before he could change the subject, Becca asked, "And how long will Evy be staying here?"

His gaze darted between the two of us. "Well, we—" He cleared his throat awkwardly. Usually he was so well-spoken and articulate, it was strange to watch him stumble over his words like this. "We haven't discussed that yet. But she knows she's welcome here for as long as she'd like to stay." His piercing blue gaze met mine. "And I hope it's for a very long time."

Becca pursed her lips. I could tell she didn't trust the prince; she'd informed me earlier of his well-known rakish reputation. Obviously, I hadn't heard much about his reputation prior to coming here, but it didn't match the man I knew at all.

He drew in a fast breath, clearly ready to switch subjects. "I was going to ask you ladies what your plans were for dinner this evening. I'd love to host you tonight and give you a proper royal welcome."

I opened my mouth, but Becca was quick with the reply. "We've already got plans with Captain Liam and some of his handsome men-at-arms this evening."

For the first time, I saw him bristle. "Ah. I see." He took a moment to compose himself, fidgeting with his coat sleeves. "Well, I'm sure it will be nice to get outside the palace walls for an evening. Forgive the intrusion, Lady Becca." I could tell he called her that on purpose just to ruffle her feathers a little. "However, I do need to borrow Evelyn for just a moment. Please excuse us."

He didn't actually wait for her permission as he led me away, and she watched us go, looking ready to pummel him. Turning around to face me, I saw his face change. A more vulnerable and pained look flitted across his eyes. "I wanted to speak with you after what happened last night, but I haven't had a moment until now."

I wasn't sure what event he was referring to. Apep's strange behavior? Or his father's one-on-one time with me?

He cleared his throat, and alarm built in my stomach when I saw tears welling up in his eyes. "I'm sure you've made your own conclusions, but I wanted to tell you personally that my . . . my father is not well."

Pity and sorrow immediately tied a knot in my chest. "Do you know what's wrong? Is it something they can cure?"

Ryker lowered his lashes and gave a sharp shake of his head. "No. He's been unwell for quite some time now, but it's been progressing far more quickly lately. The doctors don't know what he has or how much longer . . . ." He huffed out a long breath. "He's . . . he's dying, Evelyn."

"Oh, Ryker." I pulled him into an embrace, and his arms laced tightly around me, like I was the only thing keeping him upright.

"Please stay," he whispered into my hair. "At least until *after* I am King. It would mean so much to me. Having you here, it helps. I feel stronger where you're near me." His voice broke, and it broke me to hear it. I didn't want him to be in such pain. I was so sick of pain.

I pulled away just enough to slide my hand over his heart. "Of course I'll stay. Whatever you need." His relieved sigh made me feel a pang of guilt. "How long do you think you have with him?"

He placed his hand over mine, hanging his head. "No one knows, but it's feeling . . . short." His voice cracked again. "Definitely not long enough. I don't feel ready for this."

"I'm so sorry, Ryker." And I truly was. He'd already lost his mother, and I knew what that felt like. I knew how hard it was to lose that stability, that guidance.

He smiled softly at me. "Just you being here has brought me so much joy, Evelyn."

That pang of guilt struck even deeper at his words, and the rising anxiety in my chest tightened its hold on my heart. I couldn't add to his pain. I wouldn't.

I nodded and glanced back over at Becca, looking to distract him from my rising panic. "Thank you again for thinking of inviting Becca. I already feel a burden lifted just by having her here with me."

"I'm glad," he chuckled. He studied her until she looked up and scowled at him, and he quickly averted his gaze. "She doesn't think much of me, does she?"

I half-smiled. "She told me earlier about your . . ." I bobbed my head from side to side. "She told me about your *reputation* throughout the kingdom." I was so embarrassed to be saying these things out loud that I also hurried to say, "I assured her my experience with you has been the exact opposite. She just needs to see what I see."

His smile lit up his whole face. "I'm pleased to hear that last part." He brought my hand up to kiss it, then slowly walked me back over to Becca. He stopped me short just before we reached her. "I want you to know that you *are* different, Evelyn. With you *everything* is different. Please believe me."

The knots in my stomach tightened as I smiled softly at him. "I know, Ryker."

CHAPTER 35

Liam

"Please try to be on your best behavior tonight. Evelyn's friend Becca is also visiting, so we'll have two *ladies* we'll be entertaining. Emphasis on the *lady*. Do you hear me?" I tried my best to look intimidating, but instead of respectful nods, I was met with lascivious smiles.

Rafe jumped up next to me, his expression uncharacteristically solemn. "You heard 'im, gents! Not only is it our job to help the captain make a good impression on his lady love tonight, but now we have a new *lady* to distract . . . I mean, *entertain*." Rafe winked at me as howls of laughter came up from the men standing around us. I should've known it was too good to be true.

"Oh, forget it! I don't even know why I try." I waved my hand at the men, exasperated. "I'm picking up Evelyn and Becca, and we'll see you all there." They saluted, and I couldn't help but smile. These men had become my family, my brothers. After Mother and I moved to the palace, I was sent to the barracks to live and train, and she was given a housekeeping position with a lord in town. She worked there for several years, until her heart gave out. I never really talked about it. Mother and I weren't very close, and we didn't speak much after she delivered me to the palace. Mostly, I was too angry that she had pulled me away from the Coulter Estate, and she was too proud. The men of the guard were my family now, and I was grateful to have their support tonight.

"Well, let's get going!" Rafe slapped me on the back, jolting me from my internal thoughts. "I'm quite ready to officially meet the most beautiful woman in the world."

I cocked an eyebrow at him. "And what makes you think you're coming with me?"

His smile widened. "You said there were *two* ladies, which means you're in need of a second escort, my friend. And I'm more than happy to assist." He gave me a wink and a small shove out the door.

My hands shook slightly as we made our way to Evy's suite. When she'd kissed me on the neck this morning, I'd nearly jumped out of my skin. The heat that had coursed through my veins had been unlike anything I'd ever felt before.

I wanted her. For the rest of my life. I wanted to be given the chance to hold her like that whenever I felt like it. To be kissed like that, so intimately, because she was mine. To kiss her intimately in return. Just imagining my mouth on her made me have to adjust the way I was walking.

Tonight was my chance to convince her that we were still *us*. I wanted her to truly see *me*—to see who I'd become, and how much of me was the same Liam she had always known.

"Hey." Rafe moved to stand in front of me. "You're overthinking this. You've got to relax, Captain."

I shook my head and closed my eyes, expelling a sharp breath.

He nudged me with his shoulder. "Look, I know it's been a long time since you two really saw each other, and now Ryker is all mixed up in it, which complicates things. But you've loved this girl your whole life. Don't give up without fighting for what you want, yeah?"

What if she chooses Ryker? Am I kidding myself thinking I have a chance?

Rafe snapped his fingers in front of my face, bringing my attention back to him. "We're all rooting for you, Captain. The men gave you a hard time tonight, but we want you to get the girl. We feel as invested in this as you." I frowned at him, and his face reddened. "Okay, not *quite* as invested as you. But you know what I mean. We want to see you happy, Liam."

I clapped him on the shoulder. "Thanks, Rafe."

"I got your back." He gave me a solid pat on the back, then knocked on the door in front of us.

One of Evelyn's maids answered. Anna, I think. She was a pretty little brunette with soft brown eyes to match. Her eyes widened as they darted back and forth between Rafe and I. We both nodded to her, and I said, "Are Evelyn and Becca ready?"

"Nearly, sir. They should be right out." Anna curtsied, fluttering her eyelashes at Rafe. He preened at the attention, and I rolled my eyes, stifling a laugh.

Evelyn and Becca came out of the bedchamber giggling, and Rafe and I both snapped to attention. I glanced out of the corner of my eye, waiting to see Rafe's reaction to *the most beautiful girl in the world* when she wasn't wearing rags. But to my surprise, his eyes were glued to Becca, his lips slightly parted. I'd never seen him look at a girl like that before.

I gave a small bow to both ladies. "Good evening, ladies. Evelyn, Becca, may I introduce to you my second in command, Rafe."

They both nodded to Rafe, and I offered my arm out to Evelyn. She smiled, taking it gracefully.

"Hungry?" I asked her.

She smiled and nodded. "Famished, actually."

We both turned back to see Becca cross her arms and shift her weight, looking Rafe up and down, one eyebrow raised. Rafe himself looked frozen in place, his eyes not moving from Becca's face. "I think mine's broken."

Evy and I both had to cough to cover our laughter.

Becca looked him over again before squinting one eye. "I suppose you'll do. Though I usually try to make sure my dates aren't as attractive as I am." She gave him a knowing look, and Evelyn giggled next to me.

Rafe shook off his shock and reached out for her hand, giving it a long, lingering kiss. "The name's Rafe, my lady."

"Yes, I heard. Are you just going stand there sucking on my hand all night, or are we going to go eat somewhere?" Then she turned to me. "How many of your guards will be there tonight? Perhaps I could exchange this one for a different one."

I couldn't stop the boisterous laugh that came out of me as Rafe went red. He had most certainly met his match. He straightened up and pulled his shoulders back. "I'll have you know, *my lady*, that most women would fight tooth and nail to be on this arm." He flexed his bicep to emphasize his point.

I couldn't keep myself from rolling my eyes, and Evelyn laughed outright.

Becca feigned shock. "Oh my, what a terrible brute you are, making women fight over who's to be forced into taking your arm? And to think I was going to give mine over willingly. Perish the thought." Her voice took on a fake snooty timbre as she turned to Evelyn with a glint in her eye. "Evelyn, dear, tell your captain here he should pay better attention to his second's brutish ways." Rafe huffed in exasperation, and the rest of us laughed in unison.

"Oh, come here, pretty boy." She looped her arm through his. "I'm hungry, and since your arm is the only one available, I won't even make you fight me to take it."

He shook his head again. "That's not what I mea—wait. Did you say pretty?"

Becca turned to Liam. "Not the quickest one in your pack, is he? At least he finally caught on." Then she gave Rafe a sideways wink.

Rafe turned bright red. I didn't think I'd ever seen him blush before. Not many people could best him in wits.

We took off for the tavern, laughing the whole way as Rafe tried to defend himself by claiming she was far too distracting with her excessive beauty. As we walked into the tavern, the comforting smell of stale ale and dusty boards put me a little more at ease. The men were already rowdily conversing at a long table while the barmaid passed around the ale.

"Ah! Captain! You made it." John looked over Evelyn from top to bottom, and I felt her shrink away from his scrutiny. "This must be the infamous Evelyn. At your service, my lady. The name's John." He gave her a deep bow and reached out to take her hand, giving it a chaste kiss.

"Pleased to meet you, John." Evelyn dipped her head graciously, and I could've sworn I was falling more in love with her by the second. I'd missed that little glint in her eye when she was amused.

John turned back to the men and made a face as everyone cheered.

"And this must be her lady-in-waiting." John picked up Becca's hand to give it a kiss, too, but she ripped it out of his grasp.

"Excuse me, sir, but kisses must be earned, and I didn't say I was waiting for anything. Scoot over, boys!" She wedged herself right in the middle of the pack of men. They all looked stunned for a moment while she waved down the barmaid. "I'll take another one right here, please."

Evelyn's face lit up as she watched her friend make herself at home. As I led her over, the men immediately made room to let Evelyn and I sit next to Becca on the bench seat.

"All right, gents. I'm here tonight to have a good time and to grill you all about your boy Liam here. If he's fixin' his eyes on my girl, I need the dirt." My eyebrows shot up, and I looked over at her in surprise. The melody of Evy's laughter hit me like a straight shot to the heart. It was the most beautiful sound in the whole world. I loved hearing her laugh so freely.

"Careful, boys, this one's a real ball-buster." Rafe cocked his thumb to point at Becca while rolling his eyes.

At first I was nervous his crude comment would offend, but Becca gave him a sassy wink. "He's right."

The table gave a raucous laugh, and everyone started talking over one another. I could tell each man wanted attention from Becca, and she was happy to entertain. Tonight felt easy. Like old friends catching up.

Someone set an ale in front of Evy, and she gingerly took a sip, then scrunched her face up in disgust.

"Have you never had ale before, lass?" One of the men who sat across the table from us had his eyes focused on Evy's very delicate sip. I almost bristled at his attention on her lips, but decided to let it go. Everyone here knew she was off limits . . . twice over.

She shook her head. "I'm afraid I've not had the opportunity before now. But I'm unconvinced I was missing out at all." She made another disgusted face, and I chuckled, taking a long drink of my own.

"Ha! Well, let us all show you how it's done!" He looked around the table, and I saw what was coming even before he said, "Boys! This little lass here needs a proper lesson on drinking ale."

A resounding "Aye!" came from around the table, and I couldn't help but smile. We all took a second to look around at each other, and Evy's eyes widened with excited curiosity. I gave her a lazy grin.

In unison we tapped our ales three times on the table and chanted, "Here's to the guard, the bottle and friend! Here's to a good night we hope never ends!" We each guzzled down all of our ale and slammed the empty mugs back down on the table, with several whoops and hollers ringing out from the men.

I leaned in to whisper in Evy's ear. "There's a dirty version, too. But I'll make sure they spare you." I gave her a little wink, and her face brightened to a beautiful shade of pink.

I both loved getting to be a part of some of her very firsts and hated that she had been sequestered from the world for most of her life. My heart ached at the realization that her life had truly been stripped from her. This curious, playful woman was experiencing a tavern for the very first time, tasting ale for the very first time, listening to a bawdy drinking chant for the very first time. I felt a swell of protectiveness bubble up in my chest. I never wanted to let anything hurt her ever again. And I wanted to be a part of all her firsts.

"Give us ladies a chance to jump in this time! Another round of ales for the table!" Becca's voice rang out above the crowd, making the table cheer again.

Mugs all in hand, we made sure the ladies were ready before we did it all again. Evelyn wasn't able to chug her ale like the rest of us, but Becca certainly held her own. I was impressed.

After the food came out, it was time for the questions to begin. Becca asked general questions about the guard at first, and then about me specifically, while also taking a jab or two at Rafe every now and then. She was a natural with people, and not only were half the men at the table already in love with her, but I suddenly understood what a good friend she must be for Evy. That carefree, playful spirit I knew as a young girl was kept alive through her friendship with Becca.

Evelyn turned to me, looking up at me in earnest. "I can see why you're so happy here. They all love you, Liam. I'm so happy that you were so well taken care of."

A shadow flashed through her eyes, and guilt weighed heavily on my chest again. While I had been here, building friendships and a new kind of family, she'd been abused by those who were supposed to love and care for her. I silently moved to take her hand under the table, weaving our fingers together. I gave her a little squeeze, and when she squeezed back, my chest swelled. Unable to help myself, I gave her a kiss on the top of her head. She leaned into me, laying her head on my shoulder.

It was hard to fight back my obnoxiously-large smile. I could tell the ale was already going to her head—her body was becoming more and more relaxed, and her laughter came easier now. She hadn't had much yet—but then again, this was her first time, and she was a small woman. I supposed this was right on time. I rested my head on hers, breathing her in, relishing every second of it.

When the barmaid came over to hand Evy another ale, I made a motion that she was not to receive any more. The barmaid gave me a knowing wink and sauntered away. It was then that I realized just how quiet my men had become.

I looked up to find everyone's eyes on us. My eyebrows shot up as I took in all the men staring at me with their happy, dopey-drunk faces. I wanted to laugh, but I didn't want to disturb Evelyn or make her aware of the attention. I looked helplessly over at Becca, who smiled and winked reassuringly.

"Okay, gents, give us ladies all the dirt. We want to know everything about Mr. Perfect over here." She cocked her thumb at me. "Surely you've got at least *one* embarrassing tale to brighten his cheeks up a bit." She rubbed her hands together with a puckish smile.

Evelyn raised her head from my shoulder, looking around the table with curious eyes.

"What about the time we caught him with his pants around his ankles next to the Madame Bowflies?" called one. The table rang out with conspiratorial laughter.

Evelyn raised her eyebrows at me in question. I pulled my hands up in surrender. "It's not at all how it sounds, I swear."

The whole table laughed and jeered.

"Nah . . . you couldn't even pretend that good ol' Liam visits the brothels," John interjected. "The man's only ever had eyes for one lady and one lady only."

The group quieted down a bit, every man taking his peek at Evelyn's reaction. She was now beet red with embarrassment. She had to know they were all talking about her, but instead of smiling or joking, she looked down at her empty mug of ale, then back up at me. Was she trying to play coy? The tips of her mouth started to turn up, which brought about my own smirk. The table busted into laughter again, moving on to the next story.

"Is it true?" Evy's quiet voice hung in the air.

"Is what true?" I whispered back.

Evy looked at me, her eyes narrowing for a moment. "You haven't . . . courted other girls? Gone to brothels?"

I looked down at our clasped hands sheepishly. "They're right in saying that I've only ever had eyes for one girl. But I can't say I haven't done *anything* with others. I've . . . kissed a few." I swallowed, afraid of what she might think at my confession. Most of the men had guessed it, but not many ever said anything about it. I ran my hand through my hair, studying her face. That stupid little strand of hair I couldn't ever tame fell in front of my eyes again, and she smiled a bit. "I've never been serious with anyone before, though. It never felt right."

Her smile stayed in place, but she looked a little surprised. "You're too handsome to not have been with a girl or two before."

The longing in her look nearly knocked me over backwards. I realized then that we were both leaning in toward each other, our mouths angled toward each other much like they'd been this morning. But the table had gone silent again. Everyone at the table was watching us once more, including Becca. They were all rooting for me, and I couldn't help but feel the pride in that moment. However, when I looked back down at Evelyn, her entire face was burning red. I caught the panic in her eyes and immediately knew I'd messed up, putting her on the spot like that. She quickly stood up and aimed for the door, and Becca was right behind her. The boys tried to act like they weren't curious, but I would never call this group of men *subtle*.

Becca turned back to us for a moment, putting her hands out in a soothing motion. "Don't worry, we'll be right back. Just need a bit of air. We drank a lot of ale, after all." She winked and quickly followed after Evelyn.

The table chuckled at her levity, but they hung their heads a little lower as they silently watched the ladies hurry out the door.

Rafe sauntered over, his dejected expression looking about how I imagined mine did at the moment. "First of all, she's really something, Liam. Second of all, so is her friend." I almost laughed—it seemed we were both smitten, and at a loss as to what to do about it. There was no one who could help us with this condition except for the two women who had just left the table.

John chimed in, "Wowee. If those aren't some of the most beautiful women in the whole kingdom, then I don't trust your judgement of beauty. Sure you don't feel like sharing her, Liam?"

I glared at him while everyone else laughed.

"Does she have a sister?" Another man called out.

"All this time we thought she was a figment of your imagination, but here she is, in the flesh. You're a lucky man," said another of my men, winking.

The table grew quiet again as reality hit me: I might *not* be the lucky man. Ryker could end up being the lucky one just as easily.

A blanket of awkward silence draped over the table before the front door suddenly slammed open, one of the guards on duty barreling into the tavern, eyes wild with worry as he searched the crowd. When his eyes met mine, my heart dropped. I knew immediately what was wrong.

I jumped out of my seat, grabbed my cloak, and headed toward the door. I could feel Rafe, ever my right-hand man, directly behind me.

"Is it…?" I asked the guard.

The guard nodded, and motioned for us to join him outside. "The physicians don't think he'll make it much longer. He asked me to bring you to him."

I nodded, searching until I saw Evelyn and Becca walking toward us, concern written all over their faces.

"I apologize for cutting the night short, ladies, but I'm afraid I've been summoned by the king and must return to the palace." I turned to Rafe. "Rafe, please make sure they get back to the palace safely."

I reached out to kiss Evy's hand. I could tell she knew what was going on—sorrow was written all over her face. I dipped my head to

Becca, and Rafe nodded to me, placing a steady hand on my shoulder before I headed back to the palace.

CHAPTER 36

I didn't slow down, not even when I nearly skidded into the door before careening into the North Wing. When I entered the king's chambers, physicians were already surrounding the bed with worried faces. One stood to the side, taking the king's pulse, while the others spoke in hushed tones across the bed to each other. All of them were shaking their heads and grimacing. I'd known there wasn't much time left, we'd been told as much, but this still felt too sudden. Apep nodded to me as I approached the king's bedside. He was standing off to the side, like a guard in his own right. I didn't see Ryker yet, and my heart sank at the thought of this news reaching his ears. He would be devastated.

I knelt beside the king's bed with my head bowed. His face was ashen and strained, his eyes squeezed shut like he was in pain. I hated seeing him like this.

When I knelt, he jerked forward with a weak cough. He stretched his hand out toward me, crying out, "My son! My son . . ."

I stood and grasped his hand gently. "Ryker is on his way, Your Majesty. He'll be here soon."

The king looked around the room at the fussing doctors, a glimmer of his old authority shining in his eyes. "Leave us. There's nothing more you can do about it now, and we all know it."

The physicians dipped their heads and left the room. Apep and a few of the king's guards stayed.

"Come here, son." The king patted the side of the bed, but when I didn't make a move to sit, he pleaded, "Please Liam, sit next to me. There's something I need to tell you."

He looked so desperate, so vulnerable, so sick. It was hard for me to breathe or think. How had this come on so quickly? It felt far too fast—but then, he had always been a proud sort of man, keeping everything to himself, never wanting to burden others. Especially Ryker.

Honored by his request, but nervous all the same, I slowly sat on the edge of his bed, feeling like an imposter. Grabbing my hands, he looked me directly in the eyes, his own full of panic and pained beyond what physically ailed him. I'd seen that look on men's faces before: they wore it when they were about to confess to something terrible.

"I should have told you this a long time ago, but I couldn't . . . I couldn't tell Charlotte. And after she died, I didn't know how to tell Ryker." The words flowed from his mouth like a dam had broken open, spilling out words faster than he could speak them. "I swore your mother to secrecy. I threatened her. She had no choice. I wanted to be near you, to see the man you'd grow to become. I demanded you be brought here. Be raised here." He raised his hand to pat my face. "I'm so sorry, Liam."

The room constricted as he stared into my eyes. I remembered the day I was forced to leave the estate, right after I kissed Evy for the first time. I remembered riding with my mother to the palace. I remembered the hate that radiated off of me in waves. I didn't speak to her the entire journey. I remembered the tears that were streaming down her face when we arrived, and when she reached out to embrace me, I pulled away. She spoke briefly with the guards, who took me away to the barracks and set me up with new clothing. I was provided a brief tour, then brought straight to the king. Ryker had been there, too. The king looked so pleased to have me there, welcomed me, told me I was to train with Prince Ryker and that my mother had been placed with a nearby lord as a servant. I rarely saw her after that. She never visited the palace, never asked to come see me. I took that as a sign she didn't care.

A deep, painful pressure clamped down on my chest.

"Liam, it was never a mistake that I called you *son* more often than not. Your mother and I . . . we . . . it was only a few times, but we weren't cautious."

My heart was beating so loudly I could barely hear him. "What are you saying?"

He gazed at me with such gentleness, such shame. His voice cracked as he confessed: "You . . . you are my son, Liam."

The shock must have registered on my face, because the King gave me another reassuring pat on the cheek. "I should have told you sooner. But it's the reason you were recruited so young. I didn't want you growing up to be a farm hand. I wanted you here, with me, with Ryker. I wanted you to be important and well-respected." Tears began to run down his cheeks. "I missed so many years with you. I was so angry with your mother for keeping you from me. I didn't find out about you until you were thirteen, that's why you were brought so suddenly, I—" He rambled as quickly as his mouth could move, his desperation mounting. "I'm sorry about your mother. I know you two didn't have the best relationship because of me, but I've been so proud to watch you grow. My boy. My Liam."

Shock, disbelief, anger, grief, guilt, and joy all swelled inside my chest. I was so shaken I didn't even hear the footsteps running down the hall before Ryker came bursting through the door.

"Father!"

The King reached his other hand out to Ryker, but never let go of mine. I tried to move away, but he held me firmly in place. As sick as he was, his strength in this moment had not wavered. Ryker looked us over in confusion until the king cried out once more. "My sons! My sons!" More tears streamed down his face.

Ryker frowned, but when he took in the shock on my own face, his eyes narrowed like he was trying to solve a puzzle. The king brought his attention back to him. "There's something very important I need to tell you, Ryker. I am so proud of you. I am proud of the man you've become, and how you continue to grow. You are going to make a great king. Better than I."

Ryker's face now rivaled the king's, thick streams of tears falling down his cheeks. I was numb, shaken, unable to react. I had so many questions running through my mind.

"Is there nothing that can be done? Father, please, it's too soon. I'm not ready for this. I can't do this without you." Ryker choked on a sob.

"Listen. Listen to me, my boy. You *can* do this, and you won't be alone. I should have shared this with you so much earlier, but I was . . . I was afraid. I didn't want you to think less of me." He looked back over at me for a moment, squeezing my hand before turning his face back to Ryker. Ryker's eyes kept darting back and forth between us. "I have kept this secret from the both of you for too long. It's your right to know." He took a deep breath. "Liam is your brother, Ryker. Your true brother, by blood."

Ryker's eyebrows soared up his forehead as he looked at me in shock. "What do you mea—"

"I had an affair, Ryker. I never wanted your mother to find out. I never meant to hurt her like that. I am so sorry, son. I truly loved your mother, but when I met Liam's mother . . . I was besotted. I couldn't help myself. Your mother never knew. I kept it from her. The two of you were born only months apart, but I didn't know Liam existed until his thirteenth year. That's why he came to live with us." The king closed his eyes and leaned his head back, as if in a great deal of pain. Tears leaked down his cheeks, and the room held its breath.

When he opened his eyes again and tilted his head forward to look at us both, he sighed. "You two will need each other more than ever now. Rely on your bond and trust one another. There may be dark days ahead." He let out a sob. "But I believe in my boys. I love you both so much."

A heartbeat passed, and the room fell silent as the king took another gasping breath. He was fighting to stay here, to be here as long as possible with us before the darkness took him. Turning back to me, he spoke so quietly I had to lean in. "Tell her I'm sorry."

"Tell who, Father?" Ryker was leaning in too, not wanting to miss a moment with his father . . . *our* father.

He laid his head back against the pillow and closed his eyes.

"Evelyn." He squeezed my hand again. "She looked so sad last night. I contributed to her broken heart by taking you away . . . I should've told you. I should've told Charlotte. Your mother died, and I never even visited her. It wasn't her fault." He was rambling now. I had seen it before—when someone knew it was their time, they did everything they could to unburden themselves, confessing every little secret to try and absolve their souls before they left this life.

Ryker's eyes were frantic, listening to every word, hanging on to every second he had left with his father.

" . . . Find my journal. It holds everything you'll need to know."

Realizing I had tuned out the king's ramblings, lost in my own thoughts, I shot a confused look to Ryker. Which of us had he been speaking to?

The King's eyes were closed now. "Apep, you must give them the journal and keep them safe from harm."

We both swiveled our heads to look over at Apep, who seemed unmoved by what he was witnessing. His face made no recognition of what the king was saying, and he didn't bother to look either of us in the eye, either. He just stood there, waiting patiently for it to be over.

The anguished look on his face began to calm, and his tense muscles uncoiled. Holding both of our hands, his grip slowly loosened. There was a pregnant pause in the room, but the king's breaths had stopped. There was only silence.

Then Ryker jumped to his feet and shook the king, his face and body crumpling. "No! It's not your time yet. You're not allowed to leave!"

It had happened so fast. I couldn't process. I couldn't think. I couldn't understand it. All this time . . .

I stood, numbly walking around the bed to put my hand on Ryker's shoulder. He turned to look at me, tears coating his face, and I pulled him into an embrace. Nothing else mattered in that moment.

He was my brother. My true brother. Not just my brother in arms, but my blood brother. The shock of that revelation was still settling in, but somehow . . . somehow, it felt like we'd always known. We'd always called each other *brother*. Now it was just official.

When we released each other, he leaned back to truly look at me. His eyes were bloodshot with anguish. He collapsed over the king, *our father*, with wracking sobs. I surveyed the room, taking note of all who were present for this kingdom-shattering revelation.

As if he'd read my mind, Apep stepped forward. "I have seen and memorized each of your faces. Should news of what was revealed here tonight reach the public before we are ready to announce it, you will be considered a traitor to the crown and hanged for treason. Is that understood?" The guards all straightened, nodding their heads in agreement.

Apep walked around the bed and placed a hand on my shoulder. "I always knew there was something special about you." His eyes gleamed for a moment, but then his face became completely somber again. "We'll have to be careful with this knowledge. There are those who would take advantage of your brotherhood." He looked pointedly at Ryker. "I'll give you both a moment to grieve in private."

As Apep ushered everyone out of the room, Ryker and I sat side by side, my hand on his shoulder while he cried silently over the king. My eyes stung as a few tears escaped. This loss *hurt*. Even knowing it was coming, it was still too sudden.

"I can't believe he kept that secret from us for so long." Ryker ran a hand over his blotchy, swollen face. A small, tentative smile graced one side of his mouth. "Although, I do remember being the first to call you brother. I guess that officially makes me the smarter one."

I chuckled softly, placing my hand back on his shoulder. "That you did, and that you are." I paused to glance back over at the king, who looked like he could simply be sleeping, before facing Ryker again. "I'll always be here for you, Ryk. That won't ever change."

Ryker lowered his head and nodded. "Thank you, Liam."

CHAPTER 37

Evelyn

A heavy blanket of despair rested over the palace following the death of the king. The king had been beloved by the entire kingdom. Even I felt the grief settling over us all. My one brief meeting with the king had made such a lasting impact on me. He had somehow managed to go from resented to cherished. I would never forget the kindness and the care he'd shown toward me.

The night of his death had started out wonderful. Becca had been in her element entertaining and flirting with a bunch of attractive, rowdy men. I'd gotten the chance to see Liam as he was now, surrounded by his friends—maybe even family. The respect and admiration they showed him made me proud. He wasn't the boy I once knew, but the man he had become was certainly just as special.

These days, everyone was focused on preparing for Ryker's coronation. I hadn't seen Ryker or Liam for days, and the shift in the palace staff was nearly suffocating. No matter where I went or who I talked to, they all treated me like their future queen. The mounting pressure was unbearable.

"Do you want to talk about what's going on?" Becca's question snapped me out of my wandering thoughts. We were sitting at the breakfast table in my borrowed chambers, sharing a pot of tea.

I feigned innocence. "What do you mean?"

"Well, I know everyone is talking about you becoming the next queen, and I've been watching your reactions." She gave me a little wink, then sobered. "Do you need to talk about it?"

My cheeks pinked, and I hesitated, shame pinching my stomach.

"Evy, there's nothing you ever need to hide. Not with me." She paused, staring at her tea. "I know you haven't been sleeping well."

I hadn't. Instead of showing its face in the morning, the terrible dread had started attacking me at night. Every single night.

I sighed, twining my fingers around my cup. "No, I haven't been. I don't know, Becca. I feel like some kind of imposter. I don't want to let anyone down."

"Like who?"

I bowed my head. "Ryker has done so much for me."

She eyed me over her tea cup as she took a sip. "You feel like you owe him." It wasn't a question.

"Because I do."

"You don't," she countered immediately.

"How can you say that? He rescued me from the Hallefords and put me up in this suite, in the Royal Wing, no less. He made sure I had new clothes, shoes, and plenty of food every day. I want for nothing here. And besides, he has asked me to stay until after his coronation." I shook my head. "Everyone knows I'm only here because of him. They know he brought me here. They know he's picked me as his future queen. I don't want to look . . . ungrateful."

"Has he asked what *you* want?" Her eyebrow lifted in question.

No. "Becca, I know you're all for Liam, but Ryker is a good man, too."

She shook her head. "I can tell he's good with you. But does he ask you what you want, or does he tell you what *he* wants?"

I looked out the window, hating the thoughts running through my head. "I don't want to talk about this."

She let out an annoyed huff, but eased back into her seat, giving me a bit more space. "Okay, I won't push it. I'm sorry."

We sat in silence for a time before I whispered, "I'm scared."

"What are you scared of?" Her eyes were full of concern now.

"Just about everything. Leaving. Not leaving. Being left. Being hurt. Being the one who hurts someone else." My eyes welled with tears.

Becca moved immediately, wrapping me up in her arms and cradling my head to her shoulder. "You have a right to be scared, Evy. But don't leave yourself behind because of that fear."

She released me just enough to look into my eyes, cupping my face in her hands. "You may feel small and insignificant, but you are nothing of the sort. You are important, and you are loved more than you could ever know. I'll help remind you of that every day."

I tried to blink away my tears, but they fell anyway.

Then she smirked. "And so will Liam."

"Ha! See?" I couldn't help but smile. "I knew you were all in on Liam. Poor Ryker doesn't even stand a chance in your eyes."

She rolled her eyes, "*Poor Ryker* he most certainly is not, but maybe one day he'll grow on me." She smiled slightly. "Like a fungus."

I barely managed to frown at her before we both burst out laughing.

Becca held out her hand to me. "Come on. Let's get you out of this stuffy palace and go for a walk. Some fresh air will do us both good."

The warm, fragrant air nestled around us like an invisible blanket as we walked through the sculpted hedges and manicured rose bushes. Even so, I couldn't keep from shivering. The summer months in Alstonia were always warm and balmy, but for some reason I felt a chill in the air, like I was both too hot and too cold at the same time. It felt like being feverish.

My fingers carefully danced over soft petals in shades of bright red, pink, and yellow, avoiding the thorns while my mind wandered. Every now and then I thought I could see an iridescent shimmer around a delicate bloom. It made me miss Grandmother Chrissy. I wondered when I'd get to see her again . . . *if* I'd get to see her again.

"Hey, Ev? You feeling okay today? You keep shivering. Are you coming down with something?" Becca's honey-brown eyes looked me over as we walked arm in arm between the rose bushes.

I shook my head. "I don't think so. I just feel off today." And I did feel more amiss than usual. Like something inside me was changing, shifting, becoming something new. I felt a bit like a butterfly trying to crawl out of its chrysalis.

Grandmother's voice popped into my head. *"Promise me that if you start to feel or experience any . . . changes in yourself, you'll come straight to me."*

I need to talk to Grandmother.

Becca nodded like she understood. "Even with me here, I know it's still been hard on you. Are you missing home today? I mean, are you missing your estate?"

My eyes dipped to the ground, and I watched my feet as we walked. "None of this feels real, you know?"

"I get it. It feels like a dream, even to me. I mean, how else could I dream up a man as fine as Rafe, hmm?" She winked, then her face turned serious. "Of course, he can't ever know I think that."

I chortled. "Of course not. That man needs *no* help with his ego."

We fell into another companionable silence. My nerves had calmed slightly, and I was grateful for the respite from my seemingly-consistent tension.

"Becca . . . there's something I've been wanting to tell you, but I'm afraid you'll think I'm crazy." I could feel my nerves building up again. The small respite hadn't been enough; that familiar cloying feeling was starting to creep over me again.

Becca's eyes grew serious, and she stopped to look at me, reaching out to grasp my hand. "You can tell me anything, Ev."

"Do you . . . do you believe in fairies?" I earnestly searched her eyes for any indication that she thought the question was ludicrous.

"Of course I do," she scoffed. "Why would I not? They used to live in Alstonia, you know. Before we had kings."

I furrowed my brow. "How . . . how would you know that?"

"I thought everyone knew that. Oh—but your father was always part of the royal court. The Court doesn't talk about fairies. That's why it's not taught in schools. It's passed down through the generations instead." She lowered her voice to a whisper. "You see, the fairies disappeared after a few evil fairies started taking humans and forcing them into slave labor." She grimaced, not expanding on that thought. "One man, someone in the Penvarden line, rallied against the fairies and all but eradicated them. That's why the Penvardens are royalty now. The people made him king as reward for his victory over the fairies."

I stood there, stunned, staring at Becca like *she* was the crazy person. "I have never heard that tale in my life."

"No, I imagine you wouldn't have, not with Frank as your father." Becca practically spat his name. "Though, I suppose he would've been raised the same way. Sometimes I wonder if the royal court even remembers fairies exist anymore. Although, I guess you just proved that. You really had no idea?"

"Well, I . . . I always thought I'd seen them as a girl. Sometimes." I dipped my head. "Have you ever seen . . . ?"

"A fairy?" she finished for me. "No. Or at least, not that I *know* of. They look just like us, you know."

We started walking again. "My grandmother . . ." I began, but faltered.

"I *have* been curious about her." She raised an eyebrow, giving me a shrewd look. "Are you ever going to tell me about her?"

As we turned a corner around some taller hedges, familiar icy tendrils snaked up my spine again, making me shiver. I knew now that these weren't part of my usual dread—these came from somewhere else. I had my suspicions, but I couldn't be sure.

I pulled Becca to an abrupt stop, and she made a surprised sound just as a dark figure stepped into our path, blocking the way.

Apep.

Becca looked over at me, a strange fear washing over her eyes. Perhaps Apep had that effect on everyone.

"Forgive my intrusion, ladies. He gave us a slight bow, then turned his attention to Becca. "Miss Becca, is it? How pleased we are that you're able to be here for our dear Evelyn during this time. However, if you don't mind, I need to have a word with her alone. Go on ahead, and she'll catch up."

Much to my horror, Becca went eerily silent, her defensive stance easing into a more relaxed posture. Her confusion and fear faded, her eyes glazing over, empty of all emotion and thought. She bent her head in a slight nod and curtsied before she silently moved on to the next rose bush without me. I'd never seen Becca curtsy, not even to the prince.

Fear instantly shot up my spine, and my attention swiftly shifted back over to Apep. His all-knowing eyes ran up and down the length of my body, and his mouth turned up in a mocking smile. "Lady Evelyn. It truly is a pleasure to see you again."

I bristled at his blatant perusal of my form, glancing desperately over at Becca. She was swaying slightly beside the next rose bush, dreamily focused on what must have been the most interesting flower in the world to have captured her attention so thoroughly.

"Becca," I choked out. She didn't even blink.

What did he do to her?

Apep simply stood there, appraising me as I met his dark, calculating eyes. A silent challenge thickened the air between us. I knew he could read my mind, but I wanted him to know that I would not be cowed by him, even though a terrible panic was screaming inside my head. As he stood before me, I realized he was a tall figure, but he seemed to be all skin and bone. His large black robes completely covered his slim frame, hiding his figure from view. His body looked almost frail, but if you looked closer, you could tell he was nothing of the sort. He was all sharp angles and weedy muscles that made him look like a walking weapon.

He smiled, but it certainly did not reach his eyes. "You have no idea, do you?" he whispered, almost to himself. "My dear, beautiful girl, what a treasure you are."

I eyed him carefully, deciding to throw niceties out the window. "What do you want, Apep?"

"Did you ever discover the origin of my name?" he asked, throwing my mind off-balance. A sardonic smile bloomed on his face. "It would surprise you, I think, but perhaps not as much as it might surprise others. I think you've already met my kind before, or something close."

My brows furrowed in irritation. "I don't know what you're talking about."

He raised an eyebrow at me, "Are you still pretending? You've seen the magic, Evelyn. You know it exists. Weren't you just discussing it with your dear Becca?"

In the span of a blink, Apep suddenly stood directly in front of me, his body mere inches from mine, his face even closer. His scent washed over me with his quick movements, something ancient-smelling that was bitter and astringent mixed with a sweet smokiness that felt contradictory. He was so close I could feel his breath on my face as he whispered, "Who was it? Who helped you come to the ball?"

I stumbled a step backward. "What are you talking about?"

"Are they on your mother's side or your father's?" He audibly sniffed at me. "It must be your mother's. The magic is too strong to have it be from your father."

I shook my head as the invisible icy fingers snaked their way around my skull. "What are you talking about? I—"

"Our kind must stick together, Lady Evelyn. Now that I have found you, I could no sooner let you go." His eyes softened, but only slightly.

My blood sizzled under my skin, and my stomach churned. That black terror was sweeping through my body at an alarming rate. My lungs would barely bring in any air. I jumped when he suddenly pressed up behind me, his cold hands on my waist.

"I know what was done to you," he purred into my ear. "I know the hurt you've endured. But tell me this: was it because of what you are? Many others have endured your same fate, or worse yet. You're not alone, my Evelyn."

Disgust ached in my stomach as his hold tightened around me. My chest constricted, and I tried to clear my fuzzy thoughts while maneuvering out of his hold. "I don't know what you're talking about. My father and stepmother hurt me, not because of *what* I am, but *who* I am. She hated me, and he followed suit. It's as simple as that. Now let me *go*."

"Hmm." Quick as lightning, he grasped my wrist, then sucked in a sharp breath. A thrilling zap of power crossed between us. I tried to wrench my arm away, but his hold was inhumanly strong. Fear spiked through me, making my entire body thrum with pent-up energy. Just as fast as he'd grabbed me, his grip loosened, and I was able to break his hold.

"Astounding." His voice held a cold wonder that made my nerves plunge deeper into my stomach.

An animalistic fury swelled up in my body as he approached me again, this time more slowly. I took several steps back, clutching my wrist to my chest. "Stay back, Apep. I don't know what game you're playing, but I don't want you near me."

My heart was beating too fast, my chest rising and falling at an absurd rate. I felt like a trapped animal. I hadn't felt this way since Father's punishments, and the sudden onslaught of memories flooded my brain with panic. Darkness gathered in the corners of my eyes.

Apep paused, tilting his head to the side unnaturally. "Forgive me. My intention was not to remind you of your father, but to get a certain reaction from you." His eyes softened again. "Please know I won't hurt you, my Evelyn. You're too special."

Tears stung the backs of my eyes. All I wanted was to run away, but I could never leave Becca alone with a monster like this.

He flinched again. My gaze narrowed. "Get out of my head."

"You projected those images so strongly, I would have seen them even if I wasn't trying to get inside your mind." The slow steps he had been taking toward me stopped. "Truth be told, you're doing a very satisfactory job of keeping me *out* of your head, even though you have no clue how. Your instincts are quite good. You make me work for it."

I gritted my teeth. "You know I don't understand anything you're talking about. Are you incapable of speaking plainly, or is all the mystery for your own entertainment?"

He smiled, a real smile, one that reached his eyes. Somehow, it made him look even more sinister. "Can't reveal too much too soon." He tilted his head again. "You really are a stunning creature. Do you know that your eyes glow even greener when you're angry? It's . . . breathtaking."

My heart dropped to my toes. This suddenly felt like a very different kind of predator. One that I didn't know how to navigate.

Becca suddenly jerked in place, a sharp groan escaping her lips. I turned toward her, Instantly concerned. "Tell me what you did to her! And stop doing it," I demanded.

He turned to look back at her. "Oh, she's all right. Just a simple suggestion spell, that's all. It must be running out. It can leave a bit of a headache." Turning back to look at me, he smirked, like something deliciously delightful had just happened. "You suck away my energy faster than I'm used to."

And that pleases him?

"It does please me. Very much so."

He was suddenly in front of me again, cupping my cheek. He sighed again as if in relief, pulling me closer before I could step away.

I swallowed down the nausea that rose in my throat. "You just admitted to me that you have magic."

He lowered his face closer to mine, but I couldn't move. I felt frozen in place as frigid vines coiled around my head. His eyes were a brilliant, swirling mixture of light and dark colliding as he nodded. "Yes, I did." He glanced over at Becca, whose face was now contorted with pain. "Charming girl. Very open mind."

"Don't threaten her."

"It's not a threat. More of a . . . *persuasion*. You'd do well to remember that though you drain my energy, others do not."

I tried to break his hold, only to realize he'd snaked an arm around my middle. My eyes widened in panic. "Please let us go."

His eyes narrowed, and small beads of sweat gathered on his forehead. He slowly released me, and I stumbled to Becca, reaching out for her.

"She's not hurt," Apep said. The minute my skin connected with hers, she jumped out of her trance, and her knees gave out. I caught her as best I could, but we both ended up in a heap of fabric on the pebbled ground.

"Evy? What just . . .?" She gazed blearily up at me, her brow contorted in bewilderment.

"Marvelous, Evelyn." Apep's eyes practically glowed as he stared at us. "It seems you fainted, Miss Becca. How are you feeling now?"

"What? I fainted? But we were just walking . . ." Becca looked over at Apep, her eyes narrowing. "Creepy old coot," she mumbled under her breath, just loud enough for me to hear.

I was too relieved to even laugh as I helped Becca up. Apep's mouth opened, but before he said anything more, his eyes darted over my shoulder. A flash of disdain rolled across his gaze before a new voice reached my ears.

"Evelyn!"

Ryker strode down the path toward us. Grief weighed heavy on his features, and he looked like he hadn't slept in days. I wanted to pull him into a hug and bury my face into his safe and sound chest. Just having him near helped put me at ease. Especially after seeing Apep's rigid body language when he sensed the prince.

Ryker greeted Becca and Apep politely, a tight smile pulling at his lips when he met the gaze of his father's advisor. "Apep. I never took you for a man to gossip with the ladies in the flower garden."

"I'm full of surprises, Your Majesty." Ryker's whole body flinched at the title that was usually reserved for his father, and I couldn't help but feel as though Apep had done it on purpose, not just because protocol now dictated he must.

Ryker cleared his throat. "Well, would you mind terribly if I took over the stroll for a while? I could use some fresh air and pleasant company."

Apep bowed his head low. "Certainly, Your Majesty." He nodded to both Becca and I. "Ladies, it's been a pleasure." He held my gaze for a moment too long, then walked back down the path. The tension in my body slowly started to uncoil the further he went.

Ryker seemed completely oblivious to our clear state of disarray; the moment Apep was out of sight, he said, "Forgive me, Becca, but may I have a brief moment alone with Evelyn?"

Poor Becca, still looking bewildered, merely nodded before finding her way to a bench. She sat down, absently rubbing her head. I wondered if I should insist I stay with her, but Ryker offered me his hand and led me behind a taller hedge for some privacy before I could think the words through.

"That man has always disturbed me." Ryker's body shivered a bit.

"If that's true, then why do you keep him around?"

He shrugged. "Father told me I could trust him implicitly. That I needed to trust him when I became king."

My heart dropped. The words of accusation I'd been ready to share died immediately on my tongue. Apep was the late king's trusted advisor, and I . . . I was barely more than a stranger, a guest in this place. A guest that could be cast out all too easily.

Unaware of my racing thoughts, Ryker looked down at our hands, then back into my eyes. His handsome features were already overwhelming, but it was the sincerity in his eyes that caught my attention. The corner of his lips turned up slightly. "I could get used to this, you know."

That smile was one of his greatest weapons, and he wielded it far too freely. Blood rushed to my face in response, and my body started to tremble. I was still coming down from the terror Apep had inspired in me, and my emotions were chaotic and confused. The other corner of his mouth rose as he moved carefully toward me, slowly wrapping his arms around me as if afraid I'd dart away. "I've been looking everywhere for you."

My heart lurched at his proximity. Apep had been holding me similarly to this, just minutes before. Ryker had no idea. But Becca was still rubbing her head on the bench, and my heart was still racing frantically. My eyes darted to his lips by accident, and I hastily looked back up at his eyes, but it was too late. A huge smile bloomed on his face.

He didn't realize the thing making me breathe so hard was fear. He couldn't sense the tension from Becca and I. And even if he didn't trust Apep fully, I couldn't tell him what had happened. Apep had made sure of that with his threat against Becca. Besides, Becca had mentioned that the royal family didn't believe in or talk about fairies anymore. I was trapped on all sides.

My breath burst out in a broken gasp as I found my voice, which was far more breathy than I wanted it to sound. "I'm sorry, did—did you need something from me?"

His brow wrinkled a bit, like he was concerned, but he didn't let go. "Mostly, I just needed you. I needed to see you."

I needed *space*. I couldn't breathe. My chest was rising and falling too fast. Unfortunately, he took that as an indication of something else. He leaned in close, murmuring, "I've dreamt of holding you like this every night since we met."

His hand gently caressed my back as he moved it to cup the back of my head. His fingers buried in my hair, and I took in a sharp breath. Even amidst my panic, a liquid heat slowly pooled at my center. I felt the world tilt on its axis, overwhelmed by all the sensations and emotions. It was all too much.

I gently but firmly pushed Ryker away. I didn't want to hurt his feelings, but I felt like I might lose my lunch at any moment, and vomiting on a prince—soon to be king—would probably land me in worse trouble than rejecting him. His eyes widened in shock, but he didn't stop me. "Is something wrong?" he asked.

"Ahem."

Ryker and I jumped apart. Becca was standing there, Rafe beside her, her arms crossed and her foot tapping reproachfully. Rafe looked uncomfortable, avoiding looking directly at us. For all his brazen behavior at the bar, he seemed far more awkward now, shifting from side to side like he wanted to run.

"Right." Ryker cleared his throat, giving me a quick, shallow bow. "Forgive me, Evelyn." He stood a little straighter and reached out for my hand again. "I did truly come seeking you out for a reason—" he sent a pointed look back at Becca, then leaned in close to my ear: "—and it wasn't just to try and steal a kiss." He winked at me as he pulled back, smirking a bit at my shocked expression. "I wanted to see if you'd be my guest at my coronation tomorrow."

Becca and Rafe exchanged quick looks. I utterly froze.

He paused, looking off to the distance as though he was searching for words. He cleared his throat. "You would be there as my *personal* guest."

Rafe shifted his weight again, and I suddenly understood why. I couldn't help picturing Liam dressed in his formal uniform, watching me walk in with Ryker as his personal guest. The idea made my stomach tighten.

Ryker looked suddenly anxious. "I apologize if this all feels too fast. It's just that . . . I feel better when you're near me. More confident. And after my father . . ."

My heart broke for him. I knew the pain of losing a beloved parent. All I'd wanted back then was someone I could trust to lean on, to care about me and support me afterward. I hadn't really seen or spoken to him since his father died, but I could tell he was suffering. I couldn't let him down.

Smiling gently at him, I squeezed his hand. "Ryker, I would be honored."

Becca and Rafe exchanged a knowing look that made me want to sink into the ground, but Ryker looked only at me, beaming like the sun, and I couldn't help but feel lifted back up.

CHAPTER 38

Ryker

"Glad you're in good spirits, brother." Liam clapped me on the back, hard. On purpose, I guessed—we both knew I was thinking about Evelyn. "Today's a big day."

My stomach tightened, and I locked my knees, refusing to let them shake. "Yes, I know."

He came to stand in front of me, both of his hands settling on my shoulders. "You ready for this?"

"No."

Liam laughed. "I think that's precisely the right answer."

I took in a deep breath. He was right. Father always told me there was never a time one should feel ready to be king. A king is a servant to his people, not the other way around.

For the last few days, I kept myself buried in my room. Liam stayed with me. We talked when I could, but otherwise didn't say much. I still couldn't process everything that was happening. I couldn't yet admit that Father was gone. But I could accept Liam as my brother. My blood brother. The thing that had changed absolutely everything and nothing all at once.

Apep solemnly walked into the room, holding the royal scepter and sash. He and Liam carefully draped the sash over my head and around my ornate coronation outfit. I looked beyond royal; white and blue and gold all over. Even the sash was gold, adorned with Alstonia's blue lion emblem on it.

Apep turned me around to face the mirror. "You look like a king. And today, you shall become one."

His face in the mirror was sincere and thoughtful. Liam, on the other hand, looked stern and rigid, but his face softened when our eyes met. I took a deep breath.

"It's time, Your Majesty." Apep moved around to my back and attached a long, deep blue coronation mantle around my shoulders. The heaviness of it instantly weighed me down, and I wondered if Father had felt this way on his coronation day. There was so much I needed to know, but I had yet to go through his things and find the journal he mentioned. It still irked me that his last words were about some journal I'd never seen, and even more so that those words were addressed to Apep.

I shook that thought away as Apep handed me the royal scepter, and I took in a ragged breath. I moved into the hall that led to the throne room; the doors were currently closed, so no one could see me yet. Liam came to stand by my side. His royal armor was all gold, with a blue sash draped across his armor and a short blue cape billowing out behind him. His dark hair fell across his forehead, swept to the right. He looked every bit the prince we now knew he was. A king, even, in his own right. There was a presence to him that had always made me feel slightly inferior, just like Father. Now I knew why. But today I needed that presence to steady me, not outshine me. It was my time.

Liam turned and met my gaze. "I'm proud of you, Ryk. You are going to be a great king."

I nodded, not trusting my voice, and lifted my chin as we marched steadily forward through the opening double doors and directly into the throne room. From the moment I stepped inside, everything was a blur. I felt the weight of the crown placed on my head, the heavy gaze of the crowd, and the burden of the mantle on my back—reminders of the great responsibility I was taking on. I heard the vows they asked me to swear, and I swore them gladly, somehow keeping my voice from shaking.

The crowd cheered my name, and my guards came forward to swear their fealty. Liam spoke for all as they knelt before me and presented their swords symbolically. Then the courtiers all bowed their heads, knelt as well, and swore allegiance to me. I was then led out to the balcony to face the people, who all took a knee when they saw me to represent their allegiance. As was tradition.

I took a breath and raised my hands high, forcing my voice to come out strong and commanding. "People of Alstonia! I am honored to be your king, and I will do my best to rule fairly, justly, and compassionately, like my father before me."

I dropped to a knee to represent my service to them, and they rose from the ground and cheered, "Long live the king!"

The evening saw a great feast in the dining hall, while a festival was held outside, the entire kingdom celebrating my ascension. Sitting to my right was Liam, and to my left was Evelyn. My heart finally felt whole when I saw her enter the room and make her way to my side. She was resplendent, wearing an off-the-shoulder gown made of silk that matched the blue mantle around my shoulders. Her chestnut hair was up and off her shoulders with loose tendrils curling down. Her long, elegant neck was far too tempting, and her jewel-like green eyes gleamed in the candlelight. She looked like a queen—or better yet, some mythical beauty we mortals were barely worthy to look at. The crowd that was gathered to eat fell quieter at her entrance, and Liam sat up straighter in his chair when he saw her. I watched him follow her with his eyes, never once looking away. Watching her with protectiveness. With loyalty.

He was so dedicated to her. I hated the jealousy that popped up. I didn't like sharing, not even with Liam. I wanted her for myself.

When she sat down next to me, Liam cleared his throat, but didn't say a word. He knew tonight was my night, and he respected that. I leaned over and whispered in her ear, "You just took the whole room's breath away . . . *Iridescent*."

Her cheeks pinked. "Thank you, Ryker," she said, whispering like it was a secret. Then she smiled mischievously. "Or should I say *Your Majesty*?"

I chuckled softly. "Well, when you say it like that, I'd happily have you call me that any time."

She timidly rolled her eyes, looking back out toward the crowd. The moment she did, she went rigid with tension.

The whole room had fallen silent, everyone straining to hear what I had to say to the lady on my left. It was a place of honor, and it was unprecedented to have a lady there that I wasn't formally courting. It was a statement. I was staking a claim.

Standing to address the crowd properly, I spoke with an authority that hopefully mimicked my father's. "Please, take your seats." I waited while everyone obeyed. "Tonight we celebrate not only my ascension to the throne, but also the just and worthy ruler that came before me, who was taken from us far too soon."

A resounding "Here, here!" came from many in the crowd.

I raised my glass, "To the late King Amaury, beloved father and just King of Alstonia!"

We all drank in silence and reverence, then Liam stood from his seat. "And to the new ruler of Alstonia, King Ryker! Long live the king!" He took a drink, then turned to me, smiling and proud.

Chants of *Long live the king* echoed throughout the dining hall, and were taken up and carried outside by the festival-goers as well.

We all drank and ate our way through the night, enjoying the feast. It was both a time of mourning and celebration. It didn't feel right without Father there, but it helped to have Liam and Evelyn with me.

The next day, I prepared for my very first order of business as king: dealing with Evelyn's father, Lord Coulter, along with his family.

When I knocked on Evelyn's door, Brigitta answered with a quick bow. "Your Majesty. Lady Evelyn will be ready in just a moment. Would you like to share some breakfast with her?"

"I hadn't thought of breakfast yet today, but that sounds lovely, Brigitta. Thank you." She directed me to the breakfast nook in Evelyn's sitting room. She set a place for me, then went off to fetch Evelyn.

Shortly afterward, Evelyn appeared through the bedchamber door in a rich green gown. It suited her eyes perfectly. I could have sworn she grew more beautiful with each passing day. I stood as she entered the room, and she dipped her head in greeting.

"Good morning, Your Ma—" I held up a hand to stop her, and she pointedly cleared her throat. "Good morning, Ryker."

She said it with such a defeated tone that it made me chuckle. "Good morning, my dear." I kissed her hand and gave her a little wink. Brigitta brought us breakfast and filled our cups with tea.

"Thank you so much, Brigitta. Everything looks delicious," Evelyn praised her. She looked up at me then and winked back, and my heart stopped beating for a moment. Was she *flirting* with me?

There was a slight sparkle in her eye, so I gave her a small smile in return, then stared straight into Evelyn's eyes. "Yes, Brigitta, it's magnificent."

Brigitta cleared her throat, stifling a low giggle as she made her way back to the bedchamber to give us some privacy. Evelyn's throaty chuckle made my pants feel uncomfortably tight.

She grabbed a boiled egg and began to peel it open. "So. You're officially King Ryker now."

I grabbed some cornbread and fresh fruit from the tray. "It seems so."

"Do you feel any different?" She dipped her spoon into her boiled egg, looking up at me expectantly.

Everything about this moment felt playful, comfortable, effortless. I wanted every morning to be like this, eating breakfast with Evelyn across from me.

I shook my head to clear my thoughts. "Not really, no. Honestly, I feel a bit like an imposter. Like a very young boy trying to wear my father's oversized clothes." I took a bite of cornbread. "Yesterday felt like a heavy weight was placed on my shoulders, but unfortunately it wasn't just the mantle." I looked up at her then, smirking. "Which was *quite* heavy, by the way. But, alas, the weight was still there when I awoke, like an invisible mantle I can't remove."

She simply nodded before looking up at me again, her eyes soft with understanding. "I believe I can understand that, at least to an extent. I have been feeling something similar myself." She paused, searching my eyes before she continued. "Being taken from my life of servitude with my father and stepmother and being placed in the middle of a palace instead, wanting for nothing . . . I feel like a fraud in another woman's clothing. Like any day now I'll wake up and realize this was all a dream. Or you'll wake up and realize I'm not worth any of this." Her shoulders slumped ever so slightly, but before I could refute her worry, she narrowed her eyes at me and turned very serious. "Regardless of how you feel, you are going to make a wonderful king. I have no doubts about that."

I couldn't stop staring into her eyes. My breakfast was being neglected more and more by the minute. "Thank you, Evelyn. Though I hate that you feel like a fraud yourself, I am grateful for your understanding. It . . . it helps me feel less alone in all of this. But you should know your gowns are all being custom-made by the seamstresses here in the palace now. They're not borrowed from another woman, they're designed specifically for you."

She paled, her eyes bewildered as she looked down at her gown. "How did they know my size?"

I couldn't help laughing. "Your maids have taken your measurements, of course."

"But who's . . ."

"I am." I stared into her eyes, willing her to see how much I cared. "I wanted the best for you."

She sucked in a deep breath and went back to eating her breakfast. "Thank you, Ryker. They've all been truly lovely." She paused. "You've been so . . ." She huffed another breath out, as if struggling to find the words. "You've taken such good care of me."

"And I won't tire of it, either." I looked at her pointedly, her face flushed just enough to satisfy me.

Everything felt so lovely and easy this morning, I hated to ruin it with my news. Originally I had thought this would be good news, but suddenly I wasn't sure. I didn't want to disturb this moment with her. I looked down, feeling a little sheepish for setting this up without informing her in advance.

Clearing my throat, I mustered up my courage. "As much as I am simply enjoying your company this morning—which I could quickly get used to, by the way," I said with a wink. She blushed. It seemed that was our little routine now. I leaned back in my chair again. "I did come here for a reason this morning."

"Oh! Forgive me. I should've assumed as much." Finishing off her egg, she piled a little fresh fruit on her plate next, looking up at me expectantly.

Dread instantly dropped into my stomach. I didn't know how to approach this topic, and I didn't want to be the reason that look in her eyes disappeared.

I brushed invisible crumbs from my pants just to buy myself a little more time. "This morning, I'll be headed to the throne room for some . . . deliberations." I cleared my throat again, my anxiety coming closer to the surface. "I'd like for you to be there with me."

She beamed back at me. "I'd be happy to be there for you. How long will you need me for?"

I rubbed the back of my neck. "Only for one family. I . . . Evelyn, I'm so sorry that I didn't tell you this sooner. What with all the preparations for the coronation, I didn't realize . . ." Looking into her eyes again, I saw the immediate apprehension. "Evelyn, today is your family's scheduled court appearance. I'd like you to be present as I dictate their punishments."

Her lips parted, and she stared back at me in shock, her spoon full of fruit hanging in the balance. Carefully setting her spoon back down on the plate, she swallowed reflexively, her face draining of color. "It's *this* morning?"

"Yes. I realize now that I shouldn't have sprung this on you. I-I thought maybe it would be easier this way, but I see now that was foolish. Please . . ." I reached across the table to clutch her hand. She trembled in my grasp. "I promise you'll be perfectly safe. I'd like you standing next to me on the dais, that's all. It's as much your punishment to give as it is mine to declare."

She nodded abruptly, then her hand flew to her mouth. "Forgive me." She leapt up from her chair, almost tipping it over in her haste to race back into her bedchamber.

I hung my head, ashamed. *That went poorly.*

I heard another knock on the door, followed by Liam's voice talking to Brigitta. She showed him to the table where I now sat alone, our half-finished breakfast covering the table.

Liam's eyes narrowed, and I sensed his rising irritation at the scene set before him.

He walked over and slapped me on the back, "Good morning, Your Majesty." He looked around expectantly. "Where's our princess?"

I couldn't help but smile slightly. *Our princess.* Clever.

It was becoming clear that we wouldn't be able to control our competitive instincts for much longer. But for now, we were still behaving civilly to each other. I wondered how soon that would change.

"I'm afraid I sprang some uncomfortable news on her." Liam simply crossed his arms and lifted a brow at me in question. I sighed. "It's her family's judgment day, Liam. I just told her, and asked her to be there."

His face twisted into a deep scowl. He grunted in acknowledgment, but didn't say anything else.

All of a sudden the doors to Evelyn's bed chamber flew open, and a very angry Becca came storming out.

"What the *fairy blazes* were you thinking?"

My eyebrows shot up into my hairline. *Did Becca just swear at me?*

Liam let out a low chuckle, stepping to the side to make way for Becca's clear and present admonishment. I glared after him. *Coward.* Wasn't it still his job to protect me?

"You arrogant bastard! You think now that you're king you can just go around springing huge life events on people *minutes* before they happen?" She crossed her arms, standing in front of me, tapping her foot on the floor and glaring a hole into my head. She gestured to the bedchamber door behind her. "Did you even think to ask her what she *wanted* before you made this decision *for* her?"

I cleared my throat and stood up from the table. "Miss Becca, you will do well to remember that I am your king, and you will treat me as such. I will forgive this transgression for now, but do not let it happen again."

"If you want to marry my best friend, you'd better get used to it." Her eyes narrowed in challenge.

I raised an eyebrow at her. "You do realize I could have you arrested right now. My Captain of the Guard is standing directly next to you."

She looked between us and smiled. "He won't arrest me. *He* happens to agree with me." Then she untangled her arms and pointed her finger at my chest. "You screwed up today, *Your Majesty*, and you don't get to throw around your royalty card as an excuse, either. Evelyn is currently hurling up her breakfast and crying her eyes out because of you! You couldn't even prepare her in the least? Let her wrap her mind around this? Give her a choice?" Becca threw her hands up in the air and turned away from me in exasperation. She took a moment to breathe before turning back around, a little more calm. Her eyes met mine with a sincerity I had rarely seen from her. "She just found out she has to face her abusers this morning. These people deeply hurt her. Witnessing their punishment may bring some peace, but it may not, too." She paused to take a breath. "You need to understand that."

Becca's voice cracked with those last words, and I saw her anger for what it truly was: deep sorrow over Evelyn's pain. Pain that *I'd* caused. I realized then that even though Evelyn appeared more at ease these days, she was still greatly impacted by what her family had done to her.

We all heard Brigitta fussing before Evelyn appeared at the bedchamber door, looking wan. Brigitta handed Evelyn a glass of water that she sipped quickly before handing it back, making her way back to the sitting room. She blinked in surprise when she saw Liam had joined us.

Liam swiftly went over to her, cupping her face in his hands. He didn't ask permission, nor was he hesitant when he touched her. I envied their ease with each other. "Evy. . .you okay?"

She pushed his hand away and walked over to me. "I'm so sorry, Ryker. I'm afraid my nerves got the best of me." She dipped her chin in embarrassment. "I didn't mean to rush out like that. Forgive me. I'm . . . I'm ready to go with you now."

I reached out to grip her hand. "Please don't apologize. I am sorry for springing this on you. I clearly have done it all horribly wrong." Becca snorted in the background, but I ignored her, offering Evelyn an apologetic smile. She attempted to smile back, but I could still feel the tremors surging through her body. I wanted to hold her close, to stop her from being afraid, but there wasn't time.

A guard knocked, then poked his head in and spoke quietly with

Liam. Liam shut the door afterward and walked back to us. "The throne room is assembled. Everyone is waiting."

He held out his arm to have me lead the way. I reluctantly let go of Evelyn's hand and started to walk out of her suite. Just before I rounded the corner into the hallway, I saw Becca embrace Evelyn in a fierce hug and whisper something in her ear that made her smile and nod. Then I saw Liam tuck Evelyn under his arm for a moment, murmuring to her under his breath. Whatever he said made her tear up a little before he kissed the top of her head. A hot spike of jealousy ran its way up my spine, and I shivered at the sensation. These were the times I didn't want to be king; instead, I wanted to be the man supporting his woman when she was grieved. But because I had caused her turmoil today, I had to live with the consequences.

CHAPTER 39

Evelyn

L iam secretly held my hand the whole way to the throne room, rubbing his thumb over my skin. The gesture was so small, but still so intimate. He gave me a little reassuring squeeze before releasing me as we walked through the double doors.

When Ryker entered, the standing crowd quieted, bowing their heads in respect. That was when I saw them: my father, Katerina, and Camilla. Emotions warred within me; their familiar faces brought forth a longing I hadn't expected, and a terror that I had. They looked at ease talking with the other nobles. They hadn't seen me yet. It looked as if they were enjoying their morning, like they were thrilled to have received a personal invitation from the king.

The moment Father's eyes locked on mine, all the air whooshed out of my lungs. I wanted to break down sobbing right then and there. His handsome, familiar face paled before he straightened his spine in trepidation. I thought that when I saw him again, all I would feel was anger, but instead the deepest sadness hit me.

I missed him. I missed him so much it *hurt*. I longed to run into his embrace and just be held. A daughter with her loving father. But that wouldn't be what happened today. I would never get that again.

I closed my eyes, breaking contact with him.

When I opened my eyes again, I opened them to meet Katerina's stricken gaze. Her face contorted into a scowl within seconds. The *hate* that poured out of her was palpable. It was so easy for her to hate me, and I didn't think I would ever understand it.

Camilla looked terrified. She wouldn't meet my gaze. She seemed to be the only one who knew what was coming; she ducked her chin in disgrace, avoiding everyone's eyes. It broke my heart to remember the last words I had spoken to her. Maybe today I could make up for that.

Liam made his way to stand off to the right side of Ryker, while I moved to Ryker's left. Apep stood directly next to and a bit behind the throne. A shocked gasp rang out from the crowd when I sat in what would be the queen's throne—that alone felt awkward enough. I assumed the gasp came from my Katerina, considering that the rest of the courtiers had seen me sit next to Ryker just last night at his coronation feast.

Ryker sat down on the edge of the throne, head held high as he looked over the crowd, allowing the silence to thicken. He looked over at me, his eyebrows raised, requesting permission to begin. I nodded, drawing in a deep breath through my nose, preparing myself for what I was about to witness.

"Lord, Lady, and Miss Coulter, please step forward." Ryker's voice echoed off the rounded walls of the gilded throne room.

Darting their eyes back and forth between me and the king, they all stepped forward and kneeled before him—before *us.* A heady mixture of vengeance and panic swirled in my mind.

Icy tendrils meandered their way up my neck, and I struggled to not look over at Apep. I could only fight one battle at a time, and fighting off his intrusion was not the battle I wanted to take on today.

I closed my eyes and opened my mind with one simple, desperate plea: *Apep, please, not today.*

Apep's robe shifted ever so slightly behind Ryker. No one else would probably even notice. But much to my surprise and relief, the icy tendrils receded, and my whole body relaxed forward. Just barely. Just enough that Apep would know I was grateful for the reprieve.

Ryker began the proceedings, his voice reverberating with

authority. "Lord Coulter, you have been charged with assault, neglect, slave trade, and piracy. How do you plead?"

My eyes widened. Some I had known, but others I hadn't. It seemed my father had secrets even from me.

Father looked up at the King of Alstonia, shock softening his eyes before they hardened again. "Not guilty. Your Majesty, I am no pirate, nor have I dealt in the slave trade. And I haven't the faintest idea about any assault charges." His face looked confident, but his hands started to shake, giving away his fear. I clenched my own fists in my lap. He turned to glower my way, pointing at me accusingly. "Is *she* the one calling for these charges?" His voice went up in pitch, and his eyes held a wild anger.

My heart sank. The last shred of hope I had unknowingly *still* been clinging to tore away. Maybe I would secretly never give up hope, but I had to believe that one day, I'd be able to fully let go and move on. I was tired of him breaking my heart again and again.

Liam put his hand on the pommel of his sword and stepped forward slightly—a warning. If my father were to make any sudden move toward me or the king, he'd certainly lose *something* in the process.

"She's disobedient and unmanageable, Your Majesty," my father insisted. "You can check your own records. I disowned her. She was not fit to be a part of our family. She's now a servant for the Hallefords."

Ryker's voice rang out above the muttering crowd in a seemingly bored tone. "Please add perjury to Frank Coulter's list of charges."

Katerina raised her head to look at me now, then back at the king. "I beseech you, Your Majesty, my husband has done nothing wrong. We are but your humble citizens, loyal to King and Country." She brazenly looked me up and down, a sneer of revulsion appearing on her face.

I tried not to look back at her. I hated this moment more than I thought I would. Nausea churned low in my stomach, picking up speed every time I felt her eyes on me. I levelled out my shallow breaths as best as I could, trying desperately to look unaffected. All I wanted now was to block it all out, to numb myself from this pain.

Staring straight ahead, I focused on one of the gilded columns

lining the back wall. *Keep your back straight, breath steady, don't look.*
Katerina continued her verbal assault. "I know she looks beautiful,
Your Majesty, but do not let her beauty deceive you as it did our family.
She is a rotten apple. A product of her late mother. We should've
thrown her out after Lord Coulter and I married, but we kept her, we
cared for her, we raised her. She's not worth a—"
Ryker held up a hand. "Enough." His voice was menacing enough
to silence her immediately. "You will silence yourself before your king.
And *never* speak ill of Lady Evelyn again." He paused for effect. "*Your*
charges have yet to be read." He gave her a pointed look that finally
seemed to instill a good amount of fear on her face. She dipped her
head back down, still kneeling.

After waiting an extra beat for the room to quiet back down, Ryker
continued, "Is there anyone here who would speak in defense of
Lord Coulter?" My eyes scanned the room as the courtiers anxiously
looked around, shifting their weight from side to side. No one saw
this coming, and no one came forward. I knew he had no friends left
at court. I knew this moment would tarnish him for the rest of his life.
And I knew that I had to do something I never imagined I'd ever do.

Ryker had just opened his mouth to speak again when I stood.
"I would like to speak in defense of him, Your Majesty." I bowed my
head in deference to Ryker, who looked as shocked as Liam, Apep,
and my father. Ryker nodded reluctantly, and my father looked like
he feared *me* for the first time.

I came to stand next to him. He was still kneeling on the floor
facing the throne. But before I could say a word, my father looked
up at me, seething, "I gave you everything. It should be *you* kneeling
before the king. You defied and disobeyed me constantly. I'm your
father. But you were always only your *mother's* daughter."

I let him talk, chanting silently in my head: *Have courage, keep
breathing, stay steady.* He may have been a cruel father, and he deserved
everything that was coming to him, but Mama had loved him. *I* had
loved him. And whether or not he deserved this, I would feel better
knowing he was wrong in every way about me. I steeled myself for
what I was about to say as his defiant, enraged eyes burned into mine.

Hardening my own gaze, I stood my ground and refused to break
eye contact. "We both know I am none of the things you have accused

me of being. I *loved* you." The courtiers present all shook their heads at him, and his raging eyes turned to the ground while his shoulders slumped. I could no longer see his expression, but I still spoke directly to him. "I don't know why you changed, or if you even changed at all. Maybe you've always been this man. I don't know what happened to the loving father I knew in my youth, but I deserved none of what came after Mother's death, and I think you know it." My voice was not harsh, but it wasn't soft either. I held my voice steady. I tried to speak quietly, but the rounded throne room carried my voice throughout as everyone in attendance strained to listen.

He kept his eyes on the ground, and his voice was a gnarled whisper as he said, "I did *nothing* wrong."

"No. *I* did nothing wrong." Those last words finally had a biting edge to them, but I couldn't find myself to regret them in the slightest. I took a deep breath and closed my eyes, waiting a heartbeat before turning to face Ryker. "Your Majesty, I can only speak for his offenses against me. In defense of my father's actions, I simply state that for the first ten years of my life, he was a loving, devoted, and generous father." I choked back the tears. I refused to cry in front of them, or in front of this crowd. "I loved him very much. And on the grounds of that love and the love my mother had for him, I ask that you consider his circumstances. He was newly widowed, carrying the burden of a young daughter and deep grief. I do not know the punishment you had in mind, but perhaps allowing him to experience some of the same treatment he imposed upon me over these last seven years would be enough. No more, no less."

Ryker nodded at me, and I dipped into a small curtsy before moving back to my seat at his side. He remained silent, and I felt his eyes on me, but I couldn't look back at him. My brave facade was quickly crumbling. The tar-like dread was bubbling up from my stomach, and my body started to cave in. No longer able to get in a full breath, let alone sit up straight, I focused on that column at the back of the room again. Liam and Apep both shifted on their feet at the intense stillness of the moment.

Turning back to my father, Ryker raised his voice. "Lord Coulter, please stand for your sentencing." My father shakily got up from his knees and stared straight at me while Ryker announced his sentence.

"Frank Coulter, you are hereby stripped of your noble title and lordship. Your estate will be given back to Lady Coulter, and you will be sentenced to work the royal fields for the next ten years. Your ships will be sold, and the money from those sales will pay back the debt you owe to your many creditors." Ryker leaned forward on the throne, and my father's attention adjusted to his. "Let me make this perfectly clear, Mr. Coulter. Until Lady Evelyn spoke for you, I was going to have you whipped monthly and imprisoned for ten years. You owe your lenient sentence to your gracious daughter, who, in spite of your best attempts to break her, is still the most kind and gracious person I have ever met."

Ryker lowered his voice then, staring at my father with an intense ferocity that I had never seen from him before. "You should be ashamed of your actions against your kin. Perhaps the time in the fields will give you some much-needed perspective."

My father finally bowed his head in defeat, and Ryker leaned back once more before asking, "Mr. Coulter, do you accept this sentence?"

He nodded, wordlessly accepting his fate. Guards came up behind him; I recognized them from our night at the tavern. Their faces were dark with barely-veiled anger. They placed manacles on his wrists and walked him from the room. He looked back at me again, this time catching my eye. The fleeting shadow that rolled across them was indecipherable. I would never be privy to the thoughts he had at that moment, and in that moment, I realized I would likely never see him again.

"Oh, one more thing." Father's eyes reluctantly darted back up to the King as the guards turned him back around. Ryker addressed the guards leading him out of the room, but his eyes were fixed on my father, cold and merciless. "Have him flogged with a switch today *before* he begins his work, and every month after that." Father cringed; the guards both nodded before leading my Father solemnly out the double doors.

Ryker's attention immediately shifted to Katerina and Camilla. "Lady Coulter and Miss Camilla, please stand." They both stood quickly. Katerina's eyes were darting every which way like she was searching for a place to run, horror creeping over her expression as she realized what was happening to her.

"Katerina, you have been charged with perjury, neglect, and assistance in the slave trade. How do you plead?"

Katerina straightened her spine, staring Ryker haughtily in the face. "Not guilty, of course, Your Majesty."

Ryker actually rolled his eyes, shaking his head before looking out to the courtiers present. "Is there anyone here who wishes to speak in defense of Lady Coulter?"

No one even darted their eyes this time. They all looked upon Katerina with the same condescending disgust that she so often wore on her own face. It seemed that she had *not* made friends among the nobles since marrying my father.

Her shoulders slowly slumped forward as Ryker scanned the audience, then finally turned to me, one eyebrow raised in question. I nodded slowly and stood on shaky feet again. Ryker's face wasn't as surprised this time, but my decision to defend them still seemed to vex him.

I made my way forward—not to Katerina, but to Camilla. I reached out and took her hand in mine. When she finally looked up at me, her face red with tears as she accepted my hand, my tears finally fell. This was how I would make it up to her.

"Your Majesty, I will not speak for Katerina. She is deserving of whatever punishment you give her. But if I may speak for my sister . . ." Camilla squeezed my hand then, and didn't let go. "She is innocent in all this, Your Majesty. Please . . ." My voice faded, strangled by the lump in my throat. Everything had become too much all at once.

Ryker seemed to understand. He softened a bit, nodding to me. "Thank you, Lady Evelyn. Please take your seat again."

I looked back at Camilla with worried eyes, and we both reluctantly let go. For the first time I'd ever seen, she looked relieved. Her hard shell was crumbling right here in front of all these people, but she didn't look like she minded. She looked like she was being rescued . . . just like me.

Walking back to my seat, I didn't cower before Katerina's seething glare, even though I desperately wanted to. I kept my chin held high, staring directly in front of me until I was seated to Ryker's left again.

Ryker took a long moment before he spoke again, and we both watched Katerina's entitled ego finally deflate.

"Katerina Coulter, I find you guilty on all counts. You are hereby stripped of your noble title, and this includes the noble title for your offspring as well. The Coulter Estate officially belongs to the only remaining Coulter noble, Lady Evelyn Coulter." Katerina's eyes flashed to mine, and the disdain on her face distorted her features so severely she looked deranged. "You will be given seven days to vacate the property and find new lodging and employment. My guards will be accompanying you back to the estate today. Should you feel the urge to destroy any part of the property, I would strongly advise against it. If any destruction is found, you will be thrown into the stocks as punishment."

Camilla's face was stoic, staring at the ground, but Katerina looked like she might truly become unhinged. Her entire body shook with rage.

"Do you accept your sentence, Katerina Coulter?"

Katerina's face was bright red with indignation. She straightened her shoulders, still somehow managing to look proud as she gave a blunt nod.

Camilla's face remained downcast as Ryker turned to address her. "Camilla Coulter, as your stepsister has so graciously requested leniency for you, I would like to offer you employment at the palace. Should you choose to accept it, arrangements will be made accordingly."

Camilla accepted her sentence with more grace and humility than I expected. "Thank you, Your Majesty. I accept with humble gratitude," she said, bowing her head low.

Guards quickly surrounded the two women and escorted them from the throne room. I wanted to follow after them so I could pull Camilla into a hug and apologize more earnestly, but I knew they would be gone by the time we exited the room.

A murmuring buzz filled the air. Everyone was speculating on what had just happened. It was rare to see a noble family stripped of their title, and even more rare to see that title go to a female relative. Ryker had just broken several traditions in one fell swoop. I wondered what the ramifications would be for him after the gossip had calmed down.

Ryker stood up from the throne, looked over at me, and reached out his hand. It was a very public and pointed gesture which could not be misinterpreted by the court. He had already seated me in the queen's throne today, and next to him last night for the ascension feast. It was obvious he wanted everyone to know who I was to him, and I knew taking his hand would solidify my position as his future queen in the eyes of the court. But I also knew it would deeply hurt Liam, and I most certainly did not feel ready for this step. I hesitated, not wanting to hurt anyone. My eyes begged him not to make me take this step, but he didn't seem to understand the plea. He didn't retract his hand.

Without another option, I took his hand and let him escort me out of the throne room. He didn't say another word to the nobles, but I saw him briefly nod to Lord Halleford, who I hadn't noticed in the crowd before. He seemed content to let the actions that had just taken place speak for themselves. Lord Halleford must have been offered leniency for turning on my father.

He kept hold of my hand and kissed it as we walked back down the hall to my suite. "You handled yourself like a queen in there, Evelyn. I don't think anyone could have shown nearly as much grace and humility as you displayed today." His eyes were boring into mine with all kinds of adoration and esteem.

I looked away, shaking my head. I didn't feel gracious. I felt shaken. My body was trembling uncontrollably, and my heart was racing. "Thank you for what you did for me, Your Majesty." I paused and looked up at him. "Does this mean I can move back to the Coulter Estate now?"

His brows furrowed in confusion, and he cleared his throat quietly. "Personally, I'd prefer it if you stayed here in the palace, but I . . . is something wrong?"

I shook my head, but didn't give an answer. As we approached my suite, I released his hand. "I need a little time to myself. Please excuse me?"

It was obvious he wanted to say more, but he simply nodded his head before I walked inside and shut the door behind me. Not another minute later, Liam opened the door without knocking. His worried face latched onto mine. "Evy, are you all right?"

I pursed my lips and nodded, but didn't really respond. My entire body was quaking like a leaf in a windstorm.

He stopped right before me and grabbed my shoulders. "I'm here if you need me." He kissed my forehead, then stepped back out into the hallway.

The minute the doors closed behind him, the tears spilled over. I didn't even make it two steps inside before I collapsed into broken and gasping sobs on the floor.

CHAPTER 40

Evelyn

"Well, you know I fully support your decision to return to the estate, but I'm definitely going to miss all this boy drama." Becca smirked at my reflection in the mirror, teasingly tugging at a strand of my hair.

The girls all laughed as they helped pin my hair up for dinner. I'd asked that they use my mother's old hair comb again, looking for a little extra courage; tonight, I would be telling the men about my decision to return to my estate.

Ryker and Liam had both requested to have dinner with me this evening. Considering it had been a few days since my family's court appearance, after which I had holed up in my bedchamber refusing to see anyone except Becca, I'd suspected the formal dinner invitation would arrive at some point.

"It's true, Lady Evelyn. Never before have we answered the door to so many attractive men. Especially so frequently." Anna's pretty, round face was giddy with excitement. She loved the boy drama just as much Becca did—maybe even more.

"We're going to miss you, though," Feleen said quietly, slipping my mother's comb slowly into my hair.

"I'll miss all you girls, too. It's been so comforting having you here with me. I suspect I'll be quite sad when I wake the first morning and realize that you aren't there with me." They had quietly become a steadfast presence in my life, and I was already beginning to feel the aching loss of them. "Would you all come visit me? At my estate? I mean, if you have days off and nothing better to do, of course . . . but please, consider it an open invitation."

The girls all gushed and squealed. "That would be so lovely, Lady Evelyn!" Anna cried, ever the excitable sweetheart.

"Of course, I suspect you'll be back here in the palace in no time." Brigitta gave me a quick wink. "In the queen's suite, no doubt?" Her auburn eyebrows were raised high as she gave me a knowing look, and all the girls tittered again.

Becca and I made eye contact through the mirror, and I could tell she saw the truth in my eyes. I didn't know if that was what I wanted, or . . . *who* I wanted. Right now, all I wanted was to go home to Jimmy and Cook and Grandmother Chrissy. I wanted to clean up the garden and bring life back into my home. I didn't feel ready to marry, let alone be Queen of Alstonia.

"Enough of this sad talk, or you girls will make her change her mind about leaving. Let's talk about my day with Rafe instead," Becca insisted.

The girls all sighed dramatically and flopped onto the bed with her. Trapped in my ornate dress and corset, it was easier for me to stay seated at the vanity. But I laughed at the sweet picture of all the girls piled up on my bed, waiting to hear all about the highly-sought-after, roguish Rafe.

"Yesterday Rafe got the afternoon off and surprised me by offering to take me to lunch at the tavern. Just the two of us." The girls all sighed again, including Becca herself. "Naturally, he drank too much, and we talked for hours before he dropped me back off here. Oh, but that man is handsome! I swear that big dumb smile of his makes my womb heat up."

"Becca!" I feigned admonishment.

"What?" Her face looked the complete opposite of innocence. "We would make really pretty babies together, that's just a fact."

We all laughed so hard, our sides hurt.

"When he dropped me off here, he didn't make a move or try to kiss me or anything. He just bowed and asked if he could see me again." She fake-swooned on the bed. "It was *the* most romantic thing ever."

I snorted. "*That's* the most romantic thing ever?"

"Yes!" Becca declared. "Usually the man is just counting down the minutes until he can stick his tongue down my throat. Which can be nice, sure, but this felt so . . ."

"Charming?" Anna breathed, fanning her face.

"That's it! Definitely charming. I mean, this man clearly has his pick of women, and he's standing at the door, keeping his hands to himself and politely asking to see me again?"

Now we *all* sighed in unison.

"That's what I'm trying to say!" Becca gestured wildly with her hands.

I loved this moment, with these women, enjoying something normal girls got to do. It was silly and fun to talk and joke like this, and I realized I had never had this before. Even Camilla and I never got to play around like this, not really. Some stolen moments here and there, but never anything so free and full of life.

I felt a pang in my chest. She would be packing her things up right now. I didn't know what would happen to her when she came to work here at the palace, or what Katerina would try to do to leverage this opportunity from her.

A brief knock at the door brought us all out of our revelry, and I knew it was time to face the men again over dinner. I stood and smoothed away the invisible wrinkles on the lovely lavender gown I'd been provided for this evening. It felt decadent with its little cap sleeves and bits of lace around all the edges.

Becca came over to hug me and gave me a peck on the cheek. "I see you lost in your thoughts again." She smiled at me. "You look absolutely lovely, Ev. Now, go make those boys behave, and don't give 'em an inch. Stand your ground. This is *your* decision."

I took in a deep breath through my nose and nodded once.

The girls all ushered me out the door, and the guard walked me down the hall to the king's chambers again. I don't know why I was surprised to be led back to the king's chambers instead of Ryker's rooms, because of course, *these* were Ryker's rooms now. Guilt threatened to overwhelm me; I hadn't been there for him during this time of grieving, and now I was asking to leave.

No. I heard Becca admonishing me in my head. *I'm not asking. I'm telling* them *I am leaving.*

Ryker and Liam both stood when I entered the room, and a servant held out a chair for me. We were all situated at the top of the table: Ryker at the front, and Liam and I facing each other across the table.

"Good evening, gentlemen." I gave them both a timid smile, my nerves already starting to get the best of me. I didn't want them to know how anxious I was feeling, so I decided to play it coy.

"You look beautiful, Evelyn." Ryker beamed.

"Yes, you do." Liam smoldered a little at being beaten to the compliment, but he had a small gleam in his eyes as he looked at me.

"I'm sure you're wondering why we both requested a private dinner with you." Ryker motioned for the servant to start filling our glasses while he spoke.

I nodded wordlessly, trying not to fidget with my hands in my lap.

Ryker continued, "We realize that we've put you in a rather uncomfortable position. We know we both care for you, and you for both of us, so we'd like to address that all together. Plus, I mentioned to Liam that you had mentioned moving back to the Coulter Estate, which is something else we'd like to discuss with you."

My eyes shot up to Ryker's. "Okay," I said tentatively.

My hands were already fidgeting, my fingers picking and plucking at one another under the table. I'd never realized how uncomfortable this conversation might make me, and I was sure I was sweating far more than normal. Thank goodness for the short cap sleeves this evening.

The first course was served, and I scooped up a spoonful of the creamy green soup, savoring the delicious flavors while Ryker kept talking. "First things first. When were you thinking you might like to move back to the estate, and for how long do you plan to stay there?"

No sooner had the words left Ryker's mouth than his body jolted a little, a pained expression contorting his face. Liam was staring him down, and I noticed his foot move under the table.

I stifled a chuckle before answering, "I'd like to move back at the end of this week. Just a day after Katerina and Camilla leave."

The men both blinked, staring at me as if stunned. Apparently this was far sooner than they were anticipating.

Ryker cleared his throat. "Well then. That's . . . soon."

I tried to channel my inner Becca; instead of backing down, I simply nodded in response.

Liam spoke up next. "Whatever you need, Evy, we'll make it happen."

Ryker shot him a look before turning back to me. "I'd like for you to take all of the dresses you've been given. They were gifts, so they are entirely yours now." Ryker paused, his face turning very serious. "And should you run into any problems, or have any needs, you must let us know immediately. We have both agreed to help you bring back the former splendor of the estate in our own ways." He smiled a little at that thought, like he had a secret but didn't elaborate further.

I nodded, quietly thanking them before we moved on to talking about how Ryker's first week as king was going. He was overwhelmed and anxious, of course, and I could already tell he was dreading me moving back to the estate. Every time he looked at me, my guilt got heavier. Leaving him during this transition didn't seem fair, but I had to think of my own needs, too.

After the last course was taken away and our wine glasses were refreshed, Ryker sent all the servants away so that it was just the three of us. Clearing his throat nervously, he said, "Evelyn, we have a couple more things we'd like to discuss with you this evening. Liam and I have already talked them out, and have agreed to our own terms." He paused and looked over at Liam, who nodded in agreement. "Of course, you can refuse our offer if you don't agree."

I frowned. "I'm listening."

They both shifted anxiously in their chairs before Ryker continued, "We both care very deeply for you, Evelyn, so we'd both like to request your permission to court you. Publicly."

My eyes popped wide open. "Wha—I'm sorry, what do you mean *both*?"

Liam spoke up now. His arms twitched like he wanted to reach out to me, but instead he leaned forward slightly. "You may refuse us, of course, but we are both asking to court you—separately, of course,

but at the same time. This means you would have two official suitors."
He paused, making sure his words reached me. "That is, *if* you accept
us, of course."

Ryker jumped back in, fiddling with his fork. "It's not uncommon
for a lady to have two suitors at once, sometimes even more depending
on her status, as well as other factors."

I felt struck stupid. Could I handle two suitors? Even if I could,
could I manage one of them being the *king*? Did I even want to?

They were both staring at me, so sincere and hopeful. I had wanted
less pressure, and instead, this felt like a lot more.

Closing my eyes, I took in a deep breath. "That feels complicated.
I don't know if I . . ."

I looked up to find Ryker staring at me intensely, like his entire life
depended on my answer. I held his gaze for an extra tick, then looked
up at the ceiling. I wished the sky was there. It was the best place to
look when I was processing or in need of answers. When I let my eyes
fall, my gaze went straight to Liam, who had a knowing smile lighting
his face. He knew my habit of looking to the sky for answers.

"What are you afraid of, Evy?" Liam's soft voice broke through the
panic building in my chest.

I swallowed timidly. "I'm so afraid I'll hurt one of you, or ruin
your relationship, or do something else to mess this all up. I don't feel
worth—"

"Don't even finish that thought," Ryker said, cutting me off,
pulling my gaze back to him. "Evelyn, we know what could happen,
but we are willing to risk it for the chance to win your heart."

I looked down at my lap, shaking my head. "What if I can't . . ."

"Does that mean you accept our offers?" Ryker asked me, his face
full of hope.

"I . . . I suppose." My voice was breathy and quiet, and both sucked
in a quick breath in response. "But I have conditions."

They both looked at me with surprised faces.

"Both of you have to promise to stay away from me for three full
months once I return to my estate."

"What?" Ryker's brows furrowed in clear apprehension.

"Why?" Liam's eyes widened in surprise.

I held my ground, just like Becca told me to, and I started to wonder if I should've asked for even more time. "Because I need time. I need time away from worrying constantly about how my actions affect one or both of you. I need time to process everything that has happened. I need time to myself without the added pressure of worrying about the two of you." I tried to smile at that part, but I feared it came out more like a grimace.

They exchanged another look, then turned back to me, both nodding tersely. "We agree."

"And I need you both to promise that no matter what happens, you will remain in each other's lives. You will continue to support each other, and you will not give up your relationship because of . . . because of me."

They both stiffened slightly at that, and I pushed, desperation tightening my voice. "I couldn't bear it. I can't be the one who ruins this beautiful friendship you have. It's too important." My throat choked on a sob, and my eyes became watery of their own accord.

"Evelyn, please don't cry," Ryker pleaded with me. "It won't be like that. We're grown men, we can figure this out for ourselves. We'll be all right."

I just shook my head, tears falling faster and faster.

"Evy." Liam stood, rounding the table and kneeling in front of me, wiping away my tears. "We may not act like it all the time, but we can handle this. We've both decided that whoever you choose to be with, we will support the other."

I huffed out a doubtful laugh. "This is . . . very strange."

We all looked around the table at each other, and they both joined me in laughing outright. Liam hugged me, and Ryker came around the table to do the same. They took their seats again as I blotted my eyes with a handkerchief.

"Definitely worth it." Ryker's broad smile was contagious as always, and I couldn't help but smile shyly in return.

CHAPTER 41

Evelyn

After dinner, I asked Ryker if I might be able to visit the moonlit garden again. Naturally, he obliged my request, but only if he could escort me there himself. Liam offered to escort us, and we all walked to the hidden ballroom corridor that led to his mother's secret garden.

Ryker politely asked for him and I to have a moment alone, and though Liam looked reluctant, he promptly posted himself outside the door to keep guard.

The garden was just as magical the second time around. I quietly walked the path next to Ryker, the fabric of my skirt swishing back and forth with every step. My mind swam with excitement and trepidation at the idea of being courted by both Liam and Ryker publicly. Up until now it had just been hearsay and speculation, but a formal courting would mean a public declaration and clear intention to wed at the end of the courtship. What would everyone think? How would I be able to handle two different suitors at the same time? How would all this end without someone getting hurt?

I already knew the answer. It wouldn't. No matter what happened, someone was going to get hurt, and I didn't know if I could live with that.

The scents of lilies and jasmine drifted up around us while the white blooms clung to the moonlight. Ryker and I walked in companionable silence while my hands softly drifted over the silky petals.

"I hate that you won't be here anymore," he whispered softly.

My heart constricted at his tone. "I know, Ryker."

"Is it my fault?" He looked so crestfallen. "Was it because of your family's court appearance? Did I ruin everything that day?"

I stopped and gripped his arm, turning him to me. "No, Ryker. That's not it at all, I promise. I'm so sorry about that day. It . . . it just was harder than I expected. I didn't want you to see me struggle so."

He slowly raised his hand to intertwine with mine. The cool metal rings on his fingers had started to feel familiar and surprisingly pleasant. "You don't have to apologize for anything. I . . . I do understand why you feel the need to go."

I tried not to sigh too loudly in relief. "Thank you."

His eyes were downcast, and I could feel the disappointment rolling off of him. My heart sank; I was already disappointing him, and we hadn't even officially started courting yet.

His voice was so quiet. "Why do I feel like I'm losing you somehow?"

My stomach tied up in tight knots as I stared down at the regal white flowers. Instead of answering, I replied with my own fears: "I'm afraid you'll discover I'm not worth all this."

I couldn't stop the tear that escaped. It was the truth. I felt this way about both of them. The desperate fear that one or both would abandon me told me that I had to be the one to leave first. I was so afraid of hurting them, but I was even more afraid of getting hurt myself.

Ryker sighed, gently rubbing his thumb over my knuckles as we walked toward the giant weeping willow. He stayed silent for a minute longer before he replied, "Evelyn, you are worth more than you realize. I have never felt this way about any girl before. It's true that I've never . . . competed with Liam before, and it's a hard thing, but that doesn't make you not worth it. *You're* the reason I'm even willing to. That either of us are." He gestured to the bench nestled between the willow fronds. "Please, sit."

As I lowered myself onto the bench, he knelt before me, grasping both of my hands and looking me directly in the eye. "The king does not kneel before anyone, but I will for you. Hear me when I say that I do not plan on losing you. I will fight for you, and if I have my way, I will win your heart. You are more than your past, and I believe you are Alstonia's future. Take all the time you need. No matter how long it takes, I will not give up on that dream. I love you, Evelyn."

His words stole the breath from my lungs, and my eyes went wide with shock. Fear reared its head as I tried to decide how to respond, but he didn't give me a chance. Instead, he reached up to clasp the back of my head and neck, twined his fingers through my hair, and closed his mouth over mine in an all-consuming and heady kiss that made my limbs go slack.

His scent surrounded me, filling my nose with musky mint. Fresh and sweet and sharp, just like him. My eyelids fluttered closed as my lips began to move with his. I had never been kissed like this before, and though I was entirely unsure of myself, I could feel his ardor pouring out through every soft caress.

I gasped as Ryker's other hand came up to rest on the sensitive area where my neck met my shoulder. His rings gently pressed into my skin. Taking advantage of my open lips, he deepened his kiss even further, leaning me back with only his hands on my head and neck for support. His tongue invaded my mouth, and that new sensation alone made my insides liquify. I melted into his embrace, releasing a soft moan, which only made him kiss me more fiercely.

A deep pressure built inside of me, begging to be released. I had never felt like this before. Powerful. Protective. I slid my arms up his sides, gripping his firm shoulders. I wanted this moment to last. I wanted Ryker to keep holding me like this, and to show him how I felt in return. Overwhelmed with sensation, I carefully, hesitantly allowed the tip of my tongue to stroke his. Ryker groaned long and low into my mouth. The sound reverberated through me, and something inside me burst to life. I felt a rushing, heady power flow out from me in a sudden burst of light.

Ryker hastily pulled away, still clasping my face. His breath danced across my skin as I opened my eyes, slightly dazed. He was breathing fast and hard, staring back at me with a look that said quite plainly that in that moment, I was his whole world.

"Ryker," I breathed, but the intense look in his eyes made me lose all train of coherent thought.

His hand skimmed slowly up my neck until his thumb gently stroked my jaw bone, then he moved higher up to lightly brush my bottom lip. "You don't have to say anything. I just needed you to know." He sat back and grasped my hands again, holding them against his chest. "I want you to be my queen, so don't think for even a second that I'll let you get away from me again . . . Iridescent." He winked before his eyes drifted back down to my lips.

The kiss had been so sudden, I hadn't known what to do, and I both feared and craved doing it again. A delicious smirk pulled at his lips.

"What? Why are you looking at me like that?" I asked, my chest still strained greedily for air.

"I love seeing your lips swollen because of me." The heated look in his hooded eyes made me suspect that he was going to kiss me again any moment, though I wasn't sure I'd be able to handle it a second time. "I've never seen you more beautiful than you are right now, in this moment." He kissed my knuckles. "And I'm anxious to see this look on you again and again, many times over."

A deep blush darkened my cheeks and crawled up my neck. I'd never had a boy tell me something like that before, let alone kiss me like that before. If only I could see myself the way he saw me.

"Come, let us get you back."

"May I . . . may I take a moment to myself before I have to go? I . . . I need a moment." I brushed invisible hairs from my face, briefly resting my fingers on my mouth. The sight made Ryker smirk wantonly, making him even more devastating to look at.

"Of course. Take all the time you'd like. Consider this garden yours." He kissed my cheek. "Liam will be waiting outside to walk you back when you're ready."

As he walked away, I stared after him, touching my lips. I was feeling so many things at once I couldn't even pinpoint them. Even the light had changed—everything around me looked brighter, more alive. I stood to walk the gardens again, the air felt thick and heavy against my skin, smelling faintly of dewy grass, earthy and sweet.

Out of the corner of my eye, I caught sight of a faint glimmer. I couldn't tell what it was or where it came from, but I recognized the almost-invisible swirling colors. As I walked further down a new path, the air settled and thinned, revealing the fragrant floral scents again. Staring out at the illuminated whites and greens, I wondered if this garden truly *was* magical.

As my heart rate settled and my lightened, I turned to look back at the bench where Ryker and I had just shared our first kiss. A gasp jumped from my mouth before I could stop it.

Surrounding the bench and encircling the giant willow was a near-translucent shimmering hemisphere. My eyes widened, scanning the area as I reached my hand out to touch the strange, beautiful wall. I felt the density of the air once again, only now I could see it. It was tangible to my touch and thick, like trying to wave your hand through water.

The flash I'd seen. Had that been this thing forming? Had it . . . had it come from *me*?

Cold claws crept up my neck, a sensation that was slowly becoming familiar. *No.* My head jerked around, looking for the source, but I saw nothing, no one. I steeled my mind, but panic began to set in. I was too open, too vulnerable, too alone.

A dark shadow towered across the path from behind me, and my stomach plummeted. Apep's presence was terrifying at worst, unnerving at best. "Good evening, Lady Evelyn." His slippery voice held a malevolent edge to it.

I turned to face him, putting on my best imitation of the scowl Katerina used when she was in her foulest mood. "Good evening, Apep. To what do I owe your unwanted and unannounced arrival in this *private* garden?"

For some reason, it was so much easier to show him what I really felt and thought. It was a strange sort of relief; I didn't have to walk on eggshells around him, because I didn't care if I hurt his feelings or not. He threw his head back and laughed in a way that seemed more real than any other reaction I'd seen from him. I tilted my head at him, confused.

"You are a true treasure, my Evelyn. It's fortuitous that you should be here alone. I was hoping to have a word with you privately."

Every muscle in my body tightened, and my instincts insisted that I say no and run in the opposite direction. But my curiosity won out. There was a strange magnetism to him; not a physical attraction. More like a moth to a flame. He exuded a raw power I had never felt before.

He smiled at my far-too-obvious study of him.

"What do you want, Apep?" My own voice surprised me with its strong, defiant tone.

His eyes glinted in the way that made my skin crawl and my blood thicken. My heart started to beat faster.

"My dear Evelyn, that is a very big question indeed." He paused as a slow, sardonic smile started to spread across his face. "I want *many* things, Evelyn, and I've been waiting a very long time for an opportunity like this one."

We were in front of a tall birch tree, the white bark glowing softly in the moonlight. The serene setting was so at odds with the tension between us.

"Shall we walk to the bench?" He offered me his arm, and I felt the pull to do as he requested. Looping my arm through his, we slowly made our way back to the bench beneath the weeping willow. The pearly shimmer that had encircled the bench was already gone, but the air still felt a little thicker, tasted a little sweeter.

I could feel something cold slinking slowly through my mind, like a slug burrowing its way inside, leaving behind a trail of slimy residue, an unwanted invasion into my brain. Raw, feral anger flared beneath my skin, and without thinking I steeled my mind, imagining walls being thrown up around it. This was something I did from time to time when the pain from Father's switch became too much, or the memories of Mama or Liam overwhelmed me at night. Whenever I felt my brain working beyond its capacity, I shored it up, blocking out everything I could.

Apep blanched like he'd just been slapped in the face, and I stared at him intently, removing my arm from his. "I can feel it, you know."

He raised an eyebrow at me, but didn't say a word.

I wiggled my hand over my head. "I can feel you rifling around in my brain."

"Hm." He turned his body toward mine as his long, elegant fingers stroked his sharp chin. "And why do you think you can feel that, young Evelyn?"

Surprised that he even believed me, I was taken aback at the question. It almost seemed as though he was trying to teach me something. Something about fairy magic, maybe? "Are you telling me others *can't* feel it?" Was that why no one else seemed to know what he could do?

One side of his mouth lifted upward. "I think you already know the answer to that."

I walked toward the bench, but didn't sit down. He looked at me so curiously, almost like he admired or revered me, but I couldn't shake how uneasy I felt around him. I had this strange sense that he wanted me to learn things, that he enjoyed my small revelations. This was the most open and honest he had been with me yet, and I wanted to take advantage of it.

"Apep, why did you stop that day in the throne room? During my family's judgement?" I asked.

He looked surprised by my question, but his eyes and face dropped away from mine, staring at something behind me instead. He looked lost in his own thoughts for a moment. "I heard you ask me not to."

Searching his face, I saw a new tension there, one I hadn't seen before. "But it was more than that, wasn't it?" I prompted.

Taking a long, deep breath through his nose, he didn't respond right away. When he looked back at me, his eyes looked . . . tortured. It surprised me to see such an expression on his usually callous and stoic face. He reached out and gripped my hand. His touch was so gentle it startled me, especially after his rough treatment the other day in the garden.

"I didn't know how badly they treated you." His voice was quiet . . . careful, even.

Now it was my turn to look away, my chin dropping to my chest.

Apep's voice sounded almost angry when he asked, "Did they know?"

My brows furrowed in confusion, and I met his gaze again. "Know what?"

"That you were different?"

"*I* don't even know that I'm different," I hedged. "My mother was, though I never saw it. I was told Father never knew."

He studied my face for a long time, his hand still holding mine. After a moment, he closed his eyes. "When I touch you, I feel a relief I've not experienced in centuries."

Did he just say centuries?

He opened his eyes again to stare at me intently. "You may not think you're special, Evelyn, but you hold something remarkable inside of you. Something powerful." He brushed a strand of hair from my face. "Aren't you tired of feeling trapped? Having your choices taken away?"

I shook my head, not understanding what he was trying to imply, but Liam and Ryker's conversation flashed before my eyes. Father and Katerina's abuse and control. The Hallefords, Mother's death, Liam's leaving . . . all the times I'd felt helpless, left without a choice.

"You *do* have a choice, Evelyn." Apep's voice was soft and slithery, accenting all the important words. "You have a choice that could free you from any restraints." He placed his hand on my chest, and I stiffened at the intimate contact with my skin. Not even Liam or Ryker had ever touched me there. "You just need to tap into it."

"You're talking in riddles again, Apep." I shoved his hand away from my chest. "This conversation is over."

He chuckled as I turned and started walking back toward the ornate door. Before I could make it inside, I heard his soft voice off to the side of my ear: "I know what you are."

Stopping abruptly, I turned back to face him, my anger rising again. "What do you mean *what* I am—"

I broke off, startled to find him standing within inches of my face. His eyes swirled wildly with that mixture of light and darkness again. His sweet and smoky scent wafted over me with the fast movement.

"I promise to explain, but you need to come with me." His voice was hushed and urgent, almost desperate as his cold hand tugged on my elbow, leading me toward a dark corner in the back of the garden.

No. "No!"

I tried to wrench out of his grasp, but his fingers dug in. A dizzy feeling began to spread through my brain as I fought against him. I needed to find Liam and Ryker. This had gone too far, they couldn't trust this man, and I needed to warn them. Anxiety sizzled in my veins as false sensations of calm tried to block my rising panic. *No, no, no.*

"I won't hurt you, Evelyn. I've waited far too long for someone like you to show themselves. It's been so long since I felt this kind of relief from my curse. You lift my anguish, Evelyn. *You* free me."

His words wound in smoky circles around me as my mind struggled to fight the false placidity pumping through my head. It didn't calm me; it was an invasion, an intrusion, somehow shutting down my rising fear. My dulled but still growing panic combined with my escalating anger was a potent mixture. In a sudden burst of energy, his hands were flung off my body, and he let out a snarl of frustration.

Without hesitation, I turned to run. My silk slippers slipped on the loose ground, but before I could even fall, Apep's cold hand wrapped around the nape of my neck, pulling me back toward his body. His other arm snaked around my middle, keeping me pulled tight against him. I tried to scream, but his hand moved from my neck to my mouth, smothering the sound. I felt his breathing increase as he went still, listening.

He whispered harshly in my ear, "You can't run from this, Evelyn. Soon you will know your importance. I have plans for you, and they'll never know. They won't believe you until it's too late."

Confusion and panic warred within me, and I gasped as Apep released me. The false sensations of calm swiftly disappeared, just as Apep did. The hidden shadows of the garden didn't betray where he went.

Footsteps thudded along the stone path, moving toward where I stood in stunned silence. "Evy? Are you okay? I was starting to worry . . . Evy, what's wrong? What happened?"

Liam appeared in front of me, and I flinched, nearly jumping out of my skin. His hands rubbed up and down my arms to help ease my trembling. "You look like you've seen the dead. Are you all right?" He pulled back just enough to cup my face. "Tell me what's wrong."

His eyes darted every which way, searching for any sign of a threat. My expression must have been something to see, because Liam looked downright frantic.

Instantly, Apep's words came flooding back into my mind: *They won't believe you.* I closed my eyes, trying to steel myself again, but I was shaken. My body trembled, and I struggled to take in a deep breath.

"Look at me." Liam blew out a frustrated breath, gripping my arms. "Breathe." As he took a deep breath in, I followed his lead, exhaling when he did.

Finding my voice, I rasped, "Apep was here. It was Apep."

"Apep?" Liam looked puzzled. "He was here? In the garden?"

"Yes. Please, Liam, we need to get away from here, away from him."

Liam stilled immediately, and his tone took on an intense edge. "Evelyn." He so very rarely ever called me by my full name. "Did Apep do something to you?"

"Please, I need . . . I need to get out of here." My chest was tightening again, my breaths coming in short and stiff as my body shook fitfully. I hated when these episodes took over me, always at the worst times. They were so debilitating. So humiliating.

Liam grabbed my hand and helped lead me out of the garden. I'd always felt safe in Liam's presence, and I didn't want to let him go, not even when we reached my suite. Brigitta, Anna, and Feleen all came out to greet me, but when they saw my face and the way Liam was holding me up, they all excused themselves to give us some privacy.

Liam sat us down on the nearest settee in the sitting room and rubbed my arms up and down, trying to help my uncontrollable shaking.

"You've got to tell me what happened, Evy. You're scaring me."

I took a deep breath. "Apep. He was there. In the garden. He—he grabbed my neck—" A sob slipped out of me. I didn't realize until then that I was crying. Out of anger, out of fear. Apep had made me feel helpless. I *hated* feeling helpless. "He told me you'd never believe me."

I could feel the fury radiating from Liam's body, but his voice was gentle when he said, "Believe you about what?"

"He can read minds, Liam. Manipulate them. Tonight he tried to get me alone somewhere, and I-I refused. He tried to take over my mind." My hands shot up to grip my head, suddenly afraid that those icy fingers would tickle at my mind again, and Liam's eyes widened a fraction. "I don't trust him. There's something sinister about him. He said I was important to him, that I was part of some plan, I . . . he speaks in riddles I don't understand." I violently shook my head, still reeling. Liam's hands reached up to hold my head steady. My eyes flicked up, silently beseeching him to believe me, to understand what I was struggling to say.

His face was full of fury and confusion as he pulled me into a tight hug. I buried my face against him, soaking in his comforting, earthy scent. He always smelled like home to me. "If you feel uncomfortable around him, if he tried to *grab* you against your will, then I don't want you around him." He sighed and buried his head into my hair. "I'm almost glad you're leaving now. You'll be safe at your estate. I . . . I never want to see that look on your face again."

I pulled back from his gripping hug and peered sheepishly into his eyes. "I'm sorry. I didn't mean to frighten you."

"You don't need to apologize for feeling scared, Evy. Never apologize for that. That's not at all what I meant." He rubbed his hand through his hair and down his face, making that little piece of hair fall over his forehead again. I loved that strand. A small piece of comfort and familiarity to cling to when the rest of my mind felt overwhelmed. I could latch on to that. "I just can't stand to see you like that. I lov—I—I *care* for you. And when you look terrified, it terrifies me. If anything ever happened to you . . ."

I nodded, hope swelling in my chest. "So you believe me then? About Apep? I saw him do it to Becca, but she seemed to snap out of it when I touched her."

His eyes softened as he looked into mine. "I believe that Apep frightened you and took advantage of you in a vulnerable state. Rest assured that will *never* happen again. I'll talk to Ryker and we'll get this whole thing squared away."

Exasperation took the place of hope. I closed my eyes and exhaled shakily. "Liam, you're not hearing me. I really think he's up to something dangerous. I think he's far more cunning than either of you realize."

"I've never liked him much, either. But Ryker's father trusted him, and Ryker . . ." Liam hesitated, then sighed. "Apep should never have cornered you, or *touched* you, especially not while you were unaccompanied." He ran his hands up and down my arms, almost as though he was reassuring himself that I was still there. His tone turned somber. "This will *not* happen again."

My body slowly began to relax under Liam's ministrations, but my heart sank at his words. He didn't believe me about Apep's magic. He thought me hysterical, or perhaps too traumatized to know what was really going on. It gutted me. Apep had been right.

Not meeting his eyes, I whispered, "Thank you, Liam."

He kissed the top of my head. "I think it's best we get you to bed and let you sleep this off. Do you feel safe now? I'll stand guard at the door if you need."

I shook my head numbly. My body always felt drained after one of my dreaded episodes, but somehow Liam not believing me made it even worse. "I'll be fine."

He helped me up and led me to my bedchamber like I was made of fragile porcelain, ready to break at any moment. All he saw in me was the little girl he couldn't save, helpless, still in need of his protection. And maybe that's what I still was, but I never wanted to be helpless like that again.

CHAPTER 42

Liam

After leaving Evy's suite, I quickly made my way back to Ryker's bedchamber. Anger was pumping through my limbs, urging me forward, and I barely managed to knock before storming inside.

"Liam? What on earth—" Ryker's eyes met mine, and the rage must've shown in my gaze, because he stopped his attendants from changing him into his night clothes and marched directly over to me. "What's wrong?"

I sucked in a breath through my nose. "Apep cornered Evelyn after you left her in the garden tonight." My tone came out far more accusing than I had anticipated, but there was no taking it back now.

"What do you mean, Apep cornered Evelyn? No one is allowed in the garden except for the royal . . ." A dark wash of grief swam through his eyes. As much as he was trying to be a strong king right now, it was obvious he was still inwardly reeling at his father's death. Everything had happened so quickly, I feared he hadn't been given the time he needed to grieve. "No one is allowed out there without my permission."

Giving his shoulder a squeeze, I recounted to him what Evy had told me about her encounter, leaving out the bits about mind-reading magic. Evy had been through so much lately, it wasn't a surprise that she was struggling to see things as they truly were. Even as a child she'd had such a ripe imagination, always talking about fairies and magic.

My chin dropped to my chest in defeat. I had failed her again. "She looked terrified, Ryk."

Ryker let out a rough huff of air. "He's taken it too far this time." He turned back to his attendants. "Find Apep and bring him here to my suite. Tell him it's urgent."

"Yes, Your Majesty." The attendant bowed and immediately left. Ryker flinched at the use of his new title. It was so subtle, most would miss it. But I understood. That title was still his father's . . . *our* father's.

Our. That was something to wrestle with later. I raised an eyebrow at him, gesturing to his nightclothes. "You're sure now is the best time for this?"

He waved his jeweled hand at me. "Best to get the matter dealt with and settled right away. No sense in waiting. Plus, this gives you and I some time to talk about your new status."

I guess it's later.

"I think we need to announce it publicly, Liam. Have a proper coronation. Allow you to become the next in line without question." Ryker paced in front of me, his hand on his chin. "It seems like the best way to deal with this matter. We'll need to—"

I stopped him there. "Ryker, you know I don't want this. I *like* being Captain of the Guard. Only a handful of people know, and they're all sworn to secrecy. What's the point of pursuing this further when we don't have to?"

"What if something happens to me, Liam? I have no other family. No wife. No children. No other kin. The title would be fought over. People would kill each other to become king . . . and how would you handle *that*? How would you protect the people from themselves?" He shook his head, gazing at me sternly. "It may not be what you want, but it's what's best for the kingdom. You wouldn't have to stop training or being a warrior. Instead, you could become a fearsome prince of the realm. The *second* most fearsome prince in Alstonia." He laid his smirk on thick for *that* comment.

A prince? Technically, by blood, that was what I was—or at least, what I should be—but why did anything have to change? Things were fine the way they were.

A solid knock on Ryker's door interrupted my thoughts before I could respond. Apep was shown into the room, looking apathetic as usual, albeit a little confused to have been summoned so late at night to the king's bedchamber. Remembering Evy's tears and terror made my blood boil, and my hand immediately went to the pommel of my sword. Apep's eyes darted over to mine before returning to Ryker. I wanted to rip him up one side and down the other just to make sure he never scared her like that again.

"Apep." Ryker greeted him with the cold, stern tone I was hoping for. He nodded to the attendant, who closed the door, leaving the three of us alone in the room. Ryker levelled his gaze once more at Apep.

"Good Evening, Your Majesty. Captain." Apep bowed to each of us in turn. "How may I serve you?"

"It has come to my attention that you confronted Lady Evelyn this evening while she was walking the private royal garden alone. Is that true?" Ryker's eyebrow raised a hair, daring Apep to say no.

"Yes, Your Majesty, I did."

I blinked, surprised by his honesty, but Ryker didn't flinch.

"As I'm sure you're aware, no one is allowed in the royal gardens besides me, people I allow inside, and the gardener who maintains it. And I don't recall giving you permission. So why were you out there tonight, Apep? Were you spying on us?"

The accusation drained the color from my face, but Apep remained stoic, calm, nearly disinterested. "I cornered Lady Evelyn to inquire after her intentions, Your Majesty. It is my duty to protect and advise you in all things, especially now that you are king. I needed to make certain that Lady Evelyn has the right intentions when it comes to you. There are many women who would try to take advantage of your position. It is my responsibility to make sure that does not happen."

This account did not match Evelyn's at all. Apep's eyes darted over to me, narrowing thoughtfully as I weighed her accounting of their meeting against his. I tried not to shiver.

"And what was your conclusion, Apep?" I asked, crossing my arms in front of my chest, inexplicably feeling the need to shield myself.

Apep returned his attention to Ryker, a sneer-like smile appearing on his face. "She is genuine, Your Majesty. The girl truly cares for you, and the kiss was entirely sincere."

The floor tilted beneath my feet, and I had to lock my joints in place to keep from falling.

He kissed her? She kissed him back? But we just talked about . . . we had just decided to...

My eyes darted to Ryker's, meeting his pleading gaze with a rigid glare of my own. I knew how Ryker kissed women, and the image of him kissing her like that made my stomach churn. If I were alone, I might've vomited.

Ryker dropped his gaze from mine and cleared his throat before looking back at Apep, who seemed to be enjoying himself a little too much. But his smile faded just before Ryker stated, "You are never to approach her again without one of us present. And you are not allowed to enter my mother's garden without explicit permission from myself or Liam. Do I make myself clear?"

Apep's eyes widened a fraction before he said, "Yes, of course, Your Majesty. I do apologize if I scared the poor girl. Knowing her circumstances, I should've been more careful in my dealings with her. Quite the fearful little thing."

I stepped forward, fists clenching. "She has good reason to be."

"That I do not doubt." Apep bowed his head slightly, but his eyes remained focused on mine, almost like a challenge.

"Fine. As long as that's settled," Ryker interrupted, cutting into our glare-off. "The next thing you should know, Apep, is that we've decided that Liam should take his rightful place as my brother and be crowned Prince of Alstonia."

Both Apep and I jerked to look at Ryker. My eyes pleaded with him, but he paid no mind. Apep, however, looked ready to burn that idea down *fast*. Perhaps he was on my side when it came to this matter.

"Your Majesty, I must insist you think about this before—"

Ryker raised his gilded hand, cutting Apep off mid-sentence. "I have considered what is best for Alstonia, and the kingdom needs a failsafe. We need structure." His eyes met mine. "There is no better failsafe than Liam. Rafe will be promoted to Captain. Liam's princehood will be announced to the kingdom, and his coronation will be set for three months from now."

That was Evy's timeline. I huffed out a long, defeated breath. At least he was thoughtful enough to know I'd want her there for support.

Apep's reedy voice slithered in. "Your father always wished to keep this a private matter, Your Majesty."

"And that was to save my mother and himself from embarrassment and shame. Now neither parent lives. This is my decision, Apep. I wish for Liam to be crowned Prince of Alstonia. Do I make myself clear?"

Apep folded inward, bowing to Ryker, though it seemed to me he still seethed. "Yes, of course, Your Majesty."

"We'll meet later this week to discuss the particulars and plans for the announcement. But for now, you are dismissed." Ryker waved his hand in dismissal, and the doors to his bedchamber opened, signaling for Apep to leave. He bid us both a good night, but I could feel the indignation rolling off of him as he left.

When the doors closed again, Ryker turned to me, the authority melting away into sheepishness. "I meant to tell you about . . . I was going to tell you about Evelyn and the—"

"The kiss?"

He nodded.

I sucked a ragged breath. "I suppose it doesn't really matter now that she'll be gone for three months." I made sure to stare him straight in the eye. "Don't think I won't fight for her, Ryker. She's all I've ever wanted. I *know* her. I've *waited* for her. And I know you *think* you have strong feelings for her, but who's to say they'll truly last? You've never kept a woman with you for longer than a night. When you break her heart, *I* will be the one there for her, and you will regret that you jumped in so quickly."

"I won't break her heart."

I shook my head, feeling all the frustration and fear and guilt that had bombarded me over these last seven years. My voice dropped low and menacing. "You are in the wrong here. Choosing her, after you knew who she was . . . who she was to *me*. You should've backed off. She's not some passing fancy for me, Ryker!"

Ryker didn't falter. "Obviously I know that, Liam. I love her just the same as you."

"Love?" I threw my hands up at him. "You don't even know what love is yet! Do you really think you fell in love with her after *one night*?"

"Yes." The look he gave me was steady, unwavering. He believed every word he said.

Brushing a hand down my face in exasperation, I struggled to find a response. We'd never really had the talk about how much this had affected me, or how much it hurt to have him try and take the one thing in the world that meant more to me than anything else. I wasn't sure we ever would. We both knew.

And he didn't care.

Keeping my chin to my chest, I didn't look up as I walked back to our adjoined door that led to my bedchamber. "Goodnight, Ryker."

There was a long pause before Ryker quietly replied, "Goodnight, Liam." And I shut the door.

CHAPTER 43

Ryker

I couldn't regret kissing her. Not tonight, not for Liam, not ever. I had seen the doubt in her eyes tonight, and I'd needed her to know how much she meant to me. Plus, I couldn't help myself. The emotions in that moment had completely overwhelmed me. I'd felt like I was losing her. And after losing Father, I couldn't deal with even one more loss. Not even a temporary one. Every bone and muscle in my body had been screaming to kiss her. It was a call I hadn't been able to deny.

Learning that Apep was in the garden during our time together certainly unnerved me. He wasn't given permission to be in there, and the fact that he took such a liberty made me think my father had given him far too loose of a leash. Not only had he been witness to our intimate exchange, but he had told Liam. Beyond that, to think that he had cornered her, interrogated her, and intimidated her, all while she thought she had been alone and safe . . . it was unacceptable. Apep would pay for this behavior.

My attendants entered the room again and silently began dressing me for bed. It had been a long week, and my mind swam with sorrow and guilt and longing. There was a new weight of responsibility on my shoulders that hadn't been there when Mother died.

One of the attendants leaned forward a bit, waving to catch my attention. "Can we get you anything else, Your Majesty?"

"No, but thank you both. I'll just retire for the evening." My attendants both bowed and left quickly through my bedchamber doors.

Before Father died, he'd warned me to be careful with Liam. He told me that if we both chose to pursue Evelyn, we would have to take greater consideration for each other . . . but I didn't know how that could work. I knew he was struggling with the idea of being a prince, but I also knew it would be the best thing for Alstonia. Of course, I had to wonder *why* Father chose to keep it a secret, even after Mother's death. *Why didn't he just tell us? Why couldn't Liam have been a prince and brother by my side for the past three years?*

It didn't matter now. Father was gone, and the decision fell to me. *Why did you keep so much from me? Why couldn't we have had more time?*

I paused, almost anticipating a response that I knew would never come.

I wish you were still here.

Father's dying voice echoed in my head: *"Find my journal. It holds everything you'll need to know."*

In the madness of my ascension following Father's death, I had forgotten about Father's mention of his journal. Apep had never given it to me, and I had no idea where to begin looking.

Every piece of me felt heavy. I crawled under the thick gold and blue covers and pulled the deep blue velvet bed curtains closed. I was still in my old room; I couldn't bear to sleep in the king's suite yet. I wasn't sure I would ever move myself there. The thought of Father's empty bedchamber made a harsh pressure clamp down on my chest.

Though Liam was only a door away, he felt miles from me. The divide between us had grown tonight. Kissing Evelyn had driven a deeper wedge in our relationship, and I feared he wouldn't be able to let her go. But I knew Evelyn would be mine. I'd felt it deep inside of me tonight. Even before I'd kissed her, an overpowering sense that she belonged with me had flooded my senses. I had pictured her as queen by my side, radiant and powerful. Flowers in her hair . . .

Kissing her had tasted like sunshine and mist, utterly intoxicating. Her scent still lingered in my memory: dewy jasmine, floral and sweet. I closed my eyes and remembered the feeling of her soft skin, like the most delicate silk under my fingertips. I pictured Evelyn after I kissed her, all swollen lips, flushed cheeks, and glassy eyes. Imagining her beside me in this bed, looking back at me the way she had looked at me tonight . . . it was almost too much for me.

Three months suddenly felt like a very, very long time.

CHAPTER 44

Evelyn

My mind was swimming and I was barely keeping afloat. The past few days had flown by quickly, but I was constantly on edge. Much to my relief, I had not even seen Apep, let alone sensed his icy presence. But I still felt wary.

I was ready to be away from here. I was ready to go home.

It was strange how much I desired to go back to the place that had housed some of my worst moments, but I needed the familiarity and stability of Jimmy and Cook. I needed to be around people who didn't want or expect anything from me. I needed to do work instead of walking palace hallways and gardens aimlessly all day. I needed . . . *something*. I couldn't describe it, but I could feel it building up inside of me, almost to the point of bursting.

My mind instantly pictured that strange, shimmering circle that had appeared in the moonlit garden. It could have been created by Apep, but I had the sneaking suspicion that it wasn't him at all. It felt . . . safe. Apep's magic never felt that way. But I didn't feel ready to face the alternative yet. Grandmother Chrissy would help me. She would understand.

My thoughts wandered as I helped the girls pack my trunks. Today, I would be back at the Coulter Estate. I actually felt excited; I wouldn't have the constant threat of Frank and Katerina hanging over my head any longer. Now it would simply be Jimmy, Cook, and me, not to mention visits from both Becca and Grandmother Chrissy.

I needed to get away. Just like Becca said. I needed *time,* not *boys.*

I chuckled to myself, and the girls all shot me curious looks. I just grinned mischievously and continued packing.

Becca left the palace yesterday so she could spend some time with her family before coming to stay with me once I was settled back at my estate. It still felt surreal to think of it as entirely my own, and I was anxious to see how it would feel being back there again.

Ryker and Liam had wanted to see me back, but I told them I preferred to do this on my own. So they compromised by sending a team of guards back with me instead. It was overkill—I'd told them as much—but this was one thing they seemed to agree on, and I let it be.

A knock sounded at the door, and I quickly answered it, since the girls were busy packing for me already. They giggled and tittered back and forth while they merrily folded all my new dresses away. I really would miss them. Hopefully they would come to visit soon.

"Evy."

Who knew one simple word could make my heart flip instantly. His voice was hushed, intimate, easy.

"Liam."

He mirrored my smile, and his devilish dimple made its appearance. I realized he still stood outside the door, looking almost afraid to come in. I pulled him inside the sitting room, and he reached back to rub the back of his neck nervously. It was such an odd thing to see this strapping man look suddenly sheepish.

"I . . . I miss you already." His face fell a bit, and I realized that he was truly struggling with my leaving today. His eyes were full of longing and something else that I couldn't quite decipher, some sort of sadness he was trying to hide.

I closed my eyes, relishing his words. For some reason, they felt like a balm to my tattered soul. He stepped closer to me, looking like he wanted to touch me, but hesitated.

"Liam?"

"Hmm?" His eyes focused on my lips before darting back up to my gaze.

"Promise you won't give up on me." It was more of a demand than a request. I didn't know where it came from, but I knew that if I lost him a second time, I might not survive it.

He pulled me into a tight embrace, whispering in my ear, "Never."

Kissing the top of my head, he pulled away an inch, his loamy cedarwood scent surrounding me as he leaned back in to kiss the corner of my mouth. My breath hitched as his soft lips faintly touched mine. I waited for him to truly kiss me, my lips aching to feel his, but he simply smirked and pulled away. Taunting me. My lashes flew up, only to meet his playful gaze. *He did that on purpose, the rogue.*

Before we could say anything more, the girls came out carrying my first trunk, grunting with each step.

Liam reluctantly turned away to scold the girls. "Don't you dare lift another one of those trunks! I'll send my men to carry them out for you." He winked to soften his sharp tone, and they all sighed with relief. He offered up his arm to escort me to the carriage.

I hugged each girl goodbye one more time, thanking them for taking such good care of me and reminding them they promised to come visit soon. They hugged me back, not one of us managing to keep our tears restrained. Even calm and collected Brigitta's eyes were a little raw around the edges.

Liam offered his arm again and we walked silently toward the carriage, his hand covering mine, comforting both himself and me. I didn't need to tell him how I was feeling; I knew he could sense it. I was both nervous and excited, overjoyed and overwhelmed. I didn't know what to expect or how it would feel returning, but I knew I was ready for it. I knew this was right.

Ryker was already waiting in front of the carriage when we walked up. Dark half-circles stained the skin just beneath his eyes. It looked like he hadn't slept much the last few nights, and my heart ached for his hidden grief.

Liam hugged me again before sending his men to fetch my travel trunks from my room. Ryker hugged me next, lingering just a moment longer than decorum permitted. I took a deep breath, soaking up his crisp, minty scent.

"Having second thoughts?" Ryker whispered in my ear.

I shook my head, rolling my eyes. "No, I'm not. Though I'm still sad to leave you all."

"I wish you would. Three months without seeing you feels *far* too long." Ryker gave me his signature smirk and kissed my cheek before releasing me.

Liam swept me up into a huge bear hug the moment I was free, spinning me around. I thought that he just wanted to get the last hug, but maybe he was trying to relieve some of my tension, too. Either way, it worked. I laughed outright, and out of the corner of my eye I saw Ryker give him a stink eye.

Before setting me down, Liam whispered in my ear, "If you need me for any reason, I'll be there. But I respect your boundaries, too." He kissed my cheek, sincerity gleaming brightly in his eyes. He reluctantly released me and moved to stand next to Ryker.

"If you ever feel like you want to shorten that three month time frame, don't hesitate to let us know." Ryker winked, and I shook my head in exasperation.

Rafe stepped up next to us with a quick bow. "You're all packed, Lady Evelyn. Ready to get going?"

I smiled. "Yes."

The footmen held the carriage door open for me as I loaded myself inside and waved to the boys out my window. "I'll see you both again soon!"

Someone—probably Rafe—tapped the side of the carriage, and we took a jolting start back home to my estate. My heart skipped a few beats, my breathing coming in gasps and sputters. I was nervous to see what state my home would be in, but also incredibly excited to see Jimmy and Cook again. And hopefully, someday, Grandmother Chrissy. Ryker had written ahead to let Jimmy and Cook know about the transfer of ownership. I knew they would be completely overjoyed to see me, which made everything feel a little easier.

We arrived at my estate just as the sun was at its highest point in the sky. Jimmy and Cook stood out front, excitedly waving. We hugged and cried before they hurried me inside to get settled as quickly as possible. Rafe stepped inside with us as the rest of the guards brought in the trunks and unloaded them in the entryway of the home.

He whistled long and low. "Oh, no."

Everything had been stripped away. The draperies, the china, the paintings, the furniture. *Everything*. All that had been left behind were paintings of my mother and I. It was shocking to see everything so bare. One last parting gift from Katerina, I assumed.

"I'll admit, I didn't expect it to be quite this bad." Rafe looked flabbergasted at the barren state of the house.

"Katerina claimed everything was hers now," Jimmy explained, his lip curling. "She sold it all."

I stood there stunned. I couldn't quite tell what I felt. Anger that she had taken everything from me yet again? Relief that she had stripped away awful memories with the things she'd pillaged? Sadness that she was such a petty person?

How was I going to refurnish this home? And care for Cook and Jimmy? It was already going to be an uphill battle to rebuild the Coulter Estate back to its former glory. And what about . . .

"Jimmy! The horses?" I turned to look at him, fear tightening my voice.

He came over and wrapped his arm gently around me. "The guards wouldn't let her take them."

I sighed in relief, my shoulders collapsing forward.

Cook rubbed my arm up and down in a soothing motion. "I saved quite a few things in the kitchen, too." She winked. "Katerina never even knew where to look for them all."

"Mr. Ducksworth?" Naturally, she had named her favorite frying pan. It *was* an essential part of her, after all.

She snickered. "Safe and sound in the oven."

Rafe raised an eyebrow, looking completely lost.

"We're having duck for dinner, dear." She winked at Rafe, who then flashed his most charming smile.

"Sounds delicious." He waggled his eyebrows.

Jimmy just rolled his eyes, and I snorted. "Such a shameless flirt."

"You love it," he boasted.

I shook my head and closed my eyes, taking a much-needed moment to process these new surprises. Jimmy ran his hand up and down my back in a reassuring way. I leaned into his side, grateful for his comfort.

We were finally free.

That evening, after the guards all headed back to the palace, we ate our first dinner together on a blanket stretched out on the floor. It was silly how much joy that simple picnic dinner gave me. I updated them on everything that happened, minus some of the more *intimate* details, but we mostly just celebrated being together without fear.

Cook was now cleaning up the kitchen, and Jimmy was checking on the horses, so I took my opportunity to visit the forest edge at the back of the house. A wide smile spread across my face as a soft glow radiated from the forest's interior. A slim, dainty shape appeared, and the giddy excitement of a little girl bubbled up in me again.

"Grandmother Chrissy!"

Her arms reached out wide as I ran into them, and she hugged me in tightly. "Hello, dearie," she whispered into my hair. "Stand back and let me get a good look at you."

Pulling away, she kept her hands on my arms, smiling her beautiful smile. I couldn't help but mirror it back at her. "You look lovely, Evy. Absolutely radiant." She raised an inquisitive eyebrow. "I was keeping an eye out, and it seems a lot has changed since we last saw each other."

I shook my head and looked up at the sky. "You have no idea."

She floated away to sit on an overturned log and patted her hand on the spot next to her. "Tell me all about it."

I laughed and moved to sit next to her. I told her about Ryker and Liam, the Hallefords, staying at the palace, the king's death, and Frank and Katerina's punishment. I stopped short of telling her about Apep, or the strange hemisphere that appeared after Ryker kissed me, even though I knew I should.

"Oh my. That is quite the change of pace."

I nodded again, looking down at my hands, contemplating how to tell her the rest. Was it just nerves? I wasn't sure. A part of me felt silly for bringing it up. What if it was nothing? Just wishful thinking or waking dreams?

"Grandmother?"

"Yes?" Her eyes were full of anticipation and love. It gave me more courage, and I took a deep breath.

"I . . . well, some strange things have been—" I pinched my eyes closed, struggling to get the words out. "Ryker kissed me."

"Oh!" She clapped her hands together excitedly. "The *king* kissed you?

You left the best part out! Now, tell me all about your first kiss."

"Well, that wasn't *technically* my first kiss." I mumbled, side-eyeing her sheepishly. She opened her mouth, but I cut her off. "It's not really the kiss so much as the . . ."

I stopped mid-sentence again. I didn't know how to describe what I'd seen. Chrissy watched me carefully, her brow furrowed in confusion.

"It's just . . . after our kiss, I saw this strange light out of the corner of my eye. It reminded me of your magic the night of the ball. It felt thick and heavy . . . like a wall, a bit."

Chrissy nodded thoughtfully. "Hmm, yes. That sounds like magic, all right. Did it have a shape?"

"Yes!" Excitement and relief broke through my voice. I wasn't going mad. "It was a large dome-like shape right over the area where Ryker and I . . . well, you know." I blushed furiously, moving on quickly. "But then Apep showed up, and he was talking in all these platitudes and I got too nervous and I—"

Grandmother Chrissy's eyes took on an edge that made me uneasy. Her voice went quiet and tense, almost too quiet for me to hear. "What did you say?"

I furrowed my brow as a faint warning pealed inside my head. "It was a dome-like shape—"

"Not that. What *name* did you just say?"

"Oh, Apep? I'm sorry, I didn't mention him before, but he's the—"

"No." Chrissy covered her mouth in shock, her hand trembling slightly. "I didn't think . . ."

She trailed off, and a tense silence grew between us. I could tell her mind was racing, but her reaction was making me even more nervous than I had been.

"Grandmother, do you . . . do you know him?"

She started, looking at me like she'd forgotten I was there. Her eyes softened, but remained serious as they rolled over me. Her hand reached up to cup my cheek. "Did he hurt you?"

Fear shot through my body. "I . . . no. Not really."

"You must stay away from him, Evelyn. You're not a royal, there's no telling what he might do to you . . ." She trailed off again, her eyes wandering away to stare out into the forest.

I gripped her hand. "Grandmother? You're scaring me. How do you know Apep?"

She sighed heavily, her head sinking.

"Do you think that magic in the garden was his?" My voice shook with desperation. This was the answer I had been both dreading and hoping to hear.

Her bright green eyes locked on mine again, and her lips turned up very gently at the edges. "No, dearie. That magic was all *you*."

Thank you for reading!

Please, take a moment to leave a review.

Indie authors (like me), make their living based on reviews. If you liked this book, and even if you didn't, please take a moment to let people know your thoughts. Reviews don't need to be long, a simple star rating and an, "I loved it!" or "Not really my thing…" is perfect.

(Amazon, Goodreads, and/or Bookbub + Social Media shoutouts are also welcomed with open arms).

READY FOR THE NEXT BOOK IN THE SERIES?

Sign-up to get email alerts about the next books in The Iridescent Series.

Stay up to date on new releases, bonus chapters, giveaways and more.

Join my newsletter:
http://bit.ly/briannenewsletter

JOIN BRIANNE'S READER GROUP

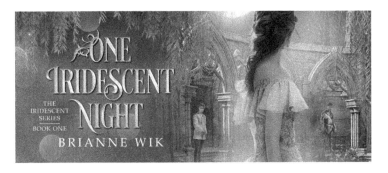

Want to come chat about the book, rant, rave and party in general?

Come join my Facebook readers group!
(Get exclusive LIVE interviews + connect with fellow readers)

Join my Facebook Readers Group
https://www.facebook.com/groups/briannewikreadergroup

ACKNOWLEDGMENTS

A dream is a wish your heart makes...
and then a bunch of hard work, amazing people
and lots of learning make it a reality.

Having struggled with anxiety/panic and C-PTSD for most of my life, it's no coincidence that I chose to write a protagonist struggling with similar symptoms. In many scenes, I often felt as though Evy and I were wading through everything together. We wouldn't have made it to the final scene of this book without a lot of really wonderful people helping us along the way.

Now I have a long list of beautiful people to thank for helping me make this dream of becoming an author, a reality. First and foremost, thank you to my Mom. You read nearly every draft of this book from it's very first rough draft to the very final version. Thank you for always believing in me, even when you think I'm crazy and have too many thoughts in my head at once. You've always kept the door open for me to explore, experience and excel wherever I can and that is the greatest gift in the entire world. To my husband Bradley for believing in my crazy whims and supporting me through them. Even if this kind of story is, "just not your thing," you're always my biggest encourager and the voice in my head telling me to, "trust the process." A HUGE thank you to Cassidy for making me look like a good writer. <wink> Your insights, feedback and edits have already helped me grow and learn faster than I could've ever hoped for. Thank you for believing in me, supporting me and encouraging me when my insecurities tried to weigh me down. To my amazing beta readers: Christine, Morgaine, Shea, Vickey. Thank you for not only taking the time to read an unfinished draft, but also for giving me fantastic feedback and sharing your excitement with me. Thank you Karri for creating amazing cover art and thank you Sarah for creating beautiful custom art of my characters and vision. To Cami for being an excellent proofreader and supporter. A big shout out to author Kathryn Marie, for giving me the extra encouragement I needed right before launching this book and saying yes to being my critique partner. Thank you to every single bookstagrammer, booktoker, blogger and author who's shared this book.

My biggest thanks of all goes to you. Thank you for reading this story. For leaving a review, for sharing, supporting and encouraging me online. Your eagerness to read more from me and your love for my characters is both humbling and rejuvenating. You help keep me going! I have so much love for you and I am beyond grateful to have you on this journey with me.

ABOUT THE AUTHOR

Discovered outside of a wardrobe when she was young, Brianne Wik was born in Narnia and raised by the Princesses in Disneyland before her house fell on a witch in North Carolina, where she got some awesome shoes and then settled down with her Rebel Prince Charming.

… you know the rest.

When not writing, Brianne can be found curled up on the couch reading all things fantasy and/or romance, watching Disney+ or Hallmark Movies, or snuggling her cat and husband.

You can connect with her personally on Instagram @BrianneWik or at www.BrianneWik.com.

Printed in the USA
CPSIA information can be obtained
at www.ICGtesting.com
LVHW091329261223
767453LV00005B/171